EIGHT HUNDRED YEARS AGO, A MAN TALKED TO THE DEVIL.

Oh damned star, oh fiendish light!
Where yesternight was but a well,
A blackish hole where hope could dwell—
Now the heavens blanch with fright,
And hope and faith are lost to hell.

AND THE DEVIL SPOKE TO HIM.

First thy flesh shall taste the flame;
Then thy soul shall know the same.
Much evil will thy own words do,
A poet's feast and devil's brew.
The stars shall never free thee, man—
But look to them, for fire can.
When thy first love has turned to smoke
'Twill mark the end of Satan's joke.

TODAY, THEY BOTH REACH OUT TO TALK TO US.

The whole affair persuaded me that what I'd stumbled onto—of all the preposterous perils of scholarship—was a *haunted manuscript*. Burned at the stake for his reputed dealings with the devil and practice of the dark arts, Geoffrey Gervaise had somehow survived for centuries, unknown and unsought—and now here he was at last, an incredible anachronism in this age of atomic bombs and space satellites, showing himself to me!

CELESTIAL CHESS

A novel

Thomas Bontly

BALLANTINE BOOKS • NEW YORK

For Marilyn, a celestial mate

Library of Congress Catalog Card Number: 78-2058

ISBN 0-345-28678-2

This edition published by arrangement with Harper & Row,
Publishers, Inc.

Manufactured in the United States of America

First Ballantine Books Edition: May 1980

ACKNOWLEDGMENT

The author wishes to thank the University of Wisconsin and the University of Wisconsin–Milwaukee Graduate School for their generous support while this book was in the making.

Why wert thou not a creature wanting soul?
Or why is this immortal that thou hast?

Marlowe, *Doctor Faustus*

These fragments I have shored against my
ruins . . .

Eliot, *The Waste Land*

1

The Librarian

A March Sunday in Cambridge, 1962. As was our custom on Sundays, we took our luncheon not at High Table but down among the undergraduates on the long benches, where we encountered Professor Haverhill gloomily devouring his cold roast beef.

"It was a shocking accident," he said, reverting to the topic which had dominated College conversation for several days now. "Simply shocking. I don't know where we'll ever find another librarian to match old Greggs." A bit of mustard clung to his shaggy mustache and I glimpsed his bad teeth as he chewed.

Archie Cavendish leaned across the table toward me, a glint of mockery in his bright blue eyes. "A horrid way to go, though, wasn't it? Crushed beneath a giant concordance to the whole works of Shakespeare! My God, do you suppose the book had it in for Greggs? Some imagined affront, perhaps, or years of ill will? The academic life seems to have its hazards after all."

Professor Haverhill gave Archie a stare that would have withered a lesser man—or a wiser. "I should hardly consider the incident cause for mirth, Cavendish. Dr. Greggs was a fine man, a good scholar, and a credit to the College." He bit ferociously into a green onion and the table was perfumed by his breath.

Colin Douglas remarked that it was uncommonly fine weather for March and hoped that the clemency would extend into the week, for the upcoming "bumps." Colin took a great interest in the College rowing club and none at all in Archie Cavendish.

"I certainly meant no disrespect to Greggs'

1

memory," Archie persisted. "Nevertheless, there's a curious irony in the whole business—the great gray scholar, murdered by his books! Marvelously suggestive, I must say!"

"Suggestive," I asked, "of what?"

"Oh, I leave that to you," Archie said. "I simply wish to observe that the scholar's life"—a quick glance at Haverhill—"is not as secure and settled as some of us have thought."

Now I understood. Archie's graduate work at Duke's had been followed by a junior fellowship—a kind of probationary appointment in the College. Neither his research nor his wit had impressed the senior fellows, and Archie would be leaving Cambridge soon to take a chemistry master's position in Yorkshire—a fate, I gathered from our late-night conversations, only slightly superior to Dr. Greggs'.

We ate in silence for several minutes. The sunlight, coming through the great stained-glass windows behind us, threw pastel dabs on the long tables, on the darkly paneled walls and on the portraits of the stern-visaged patriarchs who watched over us. A blossom of pink light rested on Professor Haverhill's knobby forehead like a friendly sprite. It skipped away when he turned to me.

"I suppose, Fairchild, that this dreadful occurrence rather upsets your plans, as well."

"There's nothing I can do," I said, "until the Special Collections are reopened."

"Yes; that's devilish awkward," Haverhill said. "I'm afraid we're in a bit of bind there. You see, the original bequest which set up the Collections specifically states that none of the materials may be used save under the personal supervision of the librarian—and Dr. Greggs is sure to prove a hard man to replace. Our holdings are immensely valuable."

"Perhaps," Colin Douglas said, "an exception could be made so that David can get on with his research. It is rather important to him, you know."

"And Fairchild's work is of considerable interest to the College as well," Professor Haverhill said. "Here we've had these manuscripts gathering dust all these years, simply because we haven't had a man who could work with them—and now that we have such a man, we can't let him get on with it. Were you making any progress?"

"I think so," I said. "I have some ideas I'm going to try out on Dr. Dilbey, who's been kind enough to take an interest in the project."

"Good man, Dilbey," said Haverhill. "He'll keep your feet on the ground."

"But don't you think something could be worked out vis-à-vis the Special Collections?" Colin asked. "David is only here for the year, and he's already put a huge amount of work into those manuscripts."

I could see that Colin's appeal carried considerable weight with Haverhill. Though an American himself, Colin had gained a permanent place at Duke's and was highly regarded by all the senior fellows.

"We'll have to look into it," Haverhill said. "There are possibilities, I expect, though I shouldn't get my hopes up, Fairchild."

Having done his bit to aid a compatriot, Colin rose to his six feet and several inches. "I must be off, chaps. Want to catch the rowing practice this afternoon, and there's a lady coming up from London I've promised to show around."

"Goodbye, Colin," Haverhill said with that sweetness he reserved for young men of whom he approved. "You'll be at our little concern this evening?"

"I wouldn't miss it," Colin said. "See you all there." And he was off, a latter-day Doug Fairbanks sweeping down the aisle, his black gown billowing behind him. I half expected that, upon reaching the stairway to the court, he would vault over the balustrade, brandishing a breadstick and singing out for the glory of Duke's.

Professor Haverhill began extricating his arthritic legs from the cunning trap of bench and table. "Well, Fairchild, I'll look into it and see if there's anything to be done. Goodbye now. Goodbye, Cavendish."

There was a note of finality in his farewell to Archie, who was needed in Yorkshire the very next term, the previous master having been injured in a laboratory prank.

"What a couple of sticks," Archie said, when Haverhill had hobbled off. "Old stick and young stick, but cut from the same bloody tree. Sometimes I wonder why I mind leaving this place at all. Perhaps where I'm going I shall encounter a few genuine human beings, anyway."

"I like that," I said. "I'm not a genuine human being?"

"Oh, you," he said with a smile. "You don't belong to this pompous lot any more than I do. That's why we get along, I suppose; but I wouldn't trust you alone with those manuscripts, either. You have the look of a born thief."

I liked Archie because of his wit, his futility, his disavowal of donnish sham, and because he alone, in his patronizing way, had been brave enough to befriend me when I first arrived in Cambridge. "Tell me—was Dr. Greggs *really* killed by a concordance to Shakespeare?"

Archie's full, florid face was ignited by a grin. "You mean you hadn't heard? I thought that story had got all over the College by now. Yes, Greggs was up on a ladder when one of the shelves collapsed. The books tumbled down on him, the concordance chief among them, and knocked him right off the ladder. Drop of some eight feet. The fall broke his neck, but the concordance, so the porter told me, landed plump on his noggin, and there they found it, the old boy's head literally buried in a book! Extraordinary, hey?"

I knew the accident had happened early in the morning, while the rest of the College was at breakfast. The library was still locked and Greggs, who had the bibliophile's devotion to order, must have been straightening a row of books here and there, going up the ladder, down the ladder, from bookcase to bookcase, a harmless moth fluttering fussily among the lights he adored.

"The library's open again," I said. "Let's walk over. I'd like to take a look at the scene of the—"

4

"Crime?" Archie asked impishly.

"Accident," I said.

Archie rose from the table, round and roguish, an overgrown leprechaun. "Are you thinking of bringing an action against the concordance, Fairchild? Perhaps you should, you know. These damned books must be kept in their places."

We left the hall, still in our gowns, and went down to the New Court. A timid March sun shone down from a colorless sky and brought a faint blush to the high stone walls that surrounded us. A few undergraduates strolled the walks. Near the porter's lodge, a party of tourists gazed up at the great Gothic spires of the chapel. I heard the insidious click of a camera as we passed and wondered into how many family photograph albums I'd been smuggled since I came to Cambridge. One gets used to that sort of thing, living, as it were, in a national shrine.

We entered the library, which more than one tourist had mistaken for another chapel. There were stained-glass windows, Gothic masonry, rows and rows of ancient books, and at the back of its long nave, an iron gate with spiked tips, which sealed off that holy of holies, the Special Collections.

Archie led me to a large, free-standing case of books not far from this gate and pointed to the top shelf, well above the ladder and a good fifteen feet above the floor, where I saw the famous concordance. The massive book looked down on us rather smugly—as if to say that whatever it had done before it could do again.

A few scholars roamed the aisles or sat hunched over open volumes. The assistant librarians seemed even more wary and furtive than usual, as if they too detected some nebulous menace in the chilly, church-like silence. I walked around behind the case and saw there was a ladder on this side as well, leading to a complementary set of shelves. There was a space of something less than three feet between the case and the wall. A single narrow window lighted the corridor, which was confronted on either end by bookshelves set flush against the wall.

5

Archie poked around the corner. "What are you up to?"

"A cozy spot, isn't it?" I asked him. "I suppose a man could hide back here, or up on that ladder . . ."

Archie glanced up. "I suppose he could, but surely you're not suggesting . . ."

"These shelves have remained stable for centuries, haven't they?"

"Oh, scarcely centuries. The library was renovated, I believe, about 1880. Greggs must have lost his balance and grabbed for a shelf. . . ."

I took a closer look at one of the lower shelves. "Screws and brackets. It would take a giant to rip out one of these shelves—unless the screws had already been loosened."

"I'm sure the police took all that into account," Archie said as we left the library. "The investigation's been closed. At worst it could have been some wretched practical joke, but why on earth should anyone want to kill a harmless old drudge like Greggs?"

"I don't know," I said. "But his death has had one certain consequence—closing the Special Collections."

"With all due respect to your work, I must say that smacks of paranoia. Those manuscripts have been lying about the library for centuries. Do you think the College would have let an American at them if there'd been a single soul in the British Isles seriously interested in the job?"

Archie had a point. I had chosen to work on the Westchurch manuscripts largely because no one else seemed interested in them, and I'd never expected my research to lead to anything more substantial than a pleasant year abroad—until lately.

"Duke's has made it abundantly clear that I'm here as a migrant worker," I said. "As soon as I've harvested the crop, I'll be shipped back to the States; but those manuscripts may turn out to be more important than anyone could have imagined."

Archie pulled up. "Fairchild, you were becoming damned mysterious about your work even before

6

Greggs was killed. Have you actually discovered something important in those papers?"

A pair of undergraduates gazed curiously at us and I waited until they had passed. "There's still a ton of work to be done. Those texts haven't had any serious scrutiny since old Throcknagle of Yale dismissed them as 'addle-pated allegorizing' some thirty years ago. Throcknagle's reputation is immense, but I've discovered some rather crucial errors in his monograph. And shortly before I left the States I talked to a former student of his, who said the old boy absolutely refused to discuss the Westchurch manuscripts—as if he found the whole subject repugnant."

"Our manuscripts—repugnant?"

Archie's loyalty was tragic, but endearing.

"They deal with some pretty grim subjects," I said. "Mostly treatises on the occult arts—astrology, alchemy, sorcery, demonology. Even an ancient Islamic text on chess. Once you get into those texts, they begin to exert a nearly hypnotic influence on your whole outlook. Some people might find it distressing—though I don't, particularly."

Archie smiled and said, "Just your cup of tea, I'll wager. But what's so important about a lot of mystical speculation?"

"I'm convinced that Throcknagle bungled the dating on these manuscripts, when he put them all in the mid-thirteenth century. There's at least one—a long and excellent poem—which is much earlier. On the basis of syntax alone, it had to have been written in the twelfth century."

"And that could be important?"

"Extremely important. The literary histories all say that the English language went underground after the Norman Conquest—that it was spoken only by illiterate peasants for nearly two hundred years. To come up with such a neglected masterpiece—in a period where there isn't supposed to be any English literature of significance—well, that would oblige us to rewrite the literary history of the entire Middle Ages."

7

"Quite a coup for one so young. And who is this giant of English verse? Anyone I ever heard of?"

"The poem is anonymous. Also maddeningly obscure. I can see why Throcknagle lost patience with it, but I'm going to make sense of that poem, and then the Throcknaglians of scholarship will sit up and take notice."

"More power to you, old boy. But I still don't understand—if someone was determined to interrupt your work, why didn't they kill you instead of poor Greggs—who was really, you know, an excellent librarian?"

We had paused outside Archie's staircase, and I looked up at the hazy sky, the Gothic spires and slate rooftops. I had always felt myself a man misplaced in time, and here, in this splendidly anachronistic environment, I seemed to see everything more clearly. Perhaps I had begun to see things that no one would ever believe.

"I suppose it was just an accident, Archie, but I can't help wondering at the way that one manuscript has been neglected and ignored over all these centuries. I'd like to learn more about who first collected these papers, and why, and who besides Throcknagle has been into them over the years."

"Dean Singer would be delighted to tell you," Archie said, "if you can stand to listen to him go on. But right now you should stop mystifying the whole affair. This is the bloody awful twentieth century. All our gods are dead, and all our fairy tales forgotten."

"There must be something," I mused, "to account for this feeling I have . . . this feeling that Dr. Greggs' death was no accident."

"Ah, now we've come down to it, lad," Archie said. "You've been working too hard, and all this medieval nonsense is starting to get to you. I should be careful, if I were you, not to spread these suspicions about. Duke's has already had more than its share of the mysterious. We were nearly haunted right out of existence back in the nineteenth century, when every undergraduate was finding a spook under his bed. Quite an epidemic it turned into. The Master finally had to pass an ordinance that the next member of the College to see a ghost would be automatically expelled. That quelled the psychic disturbances somewhat, but you bring up these 'feelings' of yours and we'll have pandemonium all over again. This lot of guilt-ridden masturbatory neurotics will go crackers at the drop of a hat."

We watched a swallow knife through the hazy sky and seek its nest near one of the gargoyles that peeped out from beneath the chapel eaves.

"I thought you didn't care about the College any more, Archie."

"I don't, but I wouldn't like to see you make a fool of yourself."

"I shall use the utmost discretion, I assure you."

Archie grinned at me. "Good enough! What you need now is a bit of relaxation, a change of pace. What do you say we take in the cinema tonight? There's a French flick at the Victoria—*la Brigitte de la Bardot* in all her glorious immodesty."

"Sorry. I promised Colin I'd go along to that musicale or whatever it is—the one Haverhill mentioned."

"God, those evenings at Bromley House are insufferable. Stop by beforehand and I'll give you something to anesthetize you."

"Thanks, Archie, I will. See you later."

I walked back around the court and left my gown at the porter's lodge for my return. Then I went out through the great thirteenth-century gate. As I emerged from its shadow, the busy Cambridge street leapt at me, clamorous and harsh, bright and glassy. The sunlight seemed brighter, glaring off windshields and grilles. The air was filled with bleating horns and noxious fumes. I paused to put on a pair of dark glasses and to pull my nerves back into shape, then set off in search of the quiet gardens and still waters of the Cam, where, stretched upon a spongy bank, I could mull over the droll contradictions of my life and work.

9

2

The Novice

Except for a shift of some ten degrees in the earth's axis of rotation, and a corresponding eastward migration of the stars, the night sky of December, 1146, must have looked to the naked eye much as it does now. Of course, the universe has been expanding these past eight hundred years; certain heavenly bodies were light-years closer to us then, others much farther away, yet in the infinity of space and to the poor instrument of vision which is the human eye, these differences would have been indiscernible. What a transplanted stargazer of the twentieth century would have noticed was the striking brilliance and fullness of the heavens. In that cleaner atmosphere and deeper darkness, the stars shone down with commanding splendor on the upturned face of the fourteen-year-old boy who sat shivering in the courtyard of a monastery on the barren vastness of the Yorkshire moors.

The boy was bound by coarse ropes to one of the ribs of a small cart, but he could move his legs a bit to keep them warm, twist his head around to gawk at his murky surroundings. His father's servant held the horse's reins, and the boy could smell the acid stench of horseflesh and piss in the frigid darkness. He could catch other smells in the courtyard, some of which he could recognize and some he could not. The lingering aroma of boiled vegetables and yeasty bread from the monk's supper—that was familiar to him; the spicier aroma of the abbot's meal was not. He sniffed the musty dampness of the massive structure which blocked a portion of his sky, detected the reek of the stables, the odor of tallow from scores of burning candles, the bitter scent of sweat, sewage and garbage from a community of ascetics. The most mysterious element in this deluge of smells was the faint hint of parchment and ink which emanated from the monastery's library. The boy knew nothing of libraries, had seen only a few books in his life and had been taught to read and write only a little French by the manor priest; yet he recognized the smell and it intrigued and gratified him.

There was no light in the courtyard, only a faint glow of candles from the chapel, where the monks were chanting their nocturnal devotions, and the eerie drone of two hundred male voices, rhythmical but atonal, halting phrase by phrase, accentuated the boy's dread. Were the monks going to punish him for his sins? The boy looked to the stars and saw a bewildering display of heavenly riches, a celestial blizzard of blazing jewels and icy diamonds. He sensed the profound depths of the night sky and measured it intuitively. A night without sunrise, offering no home, no hope, no refuge for one as wicked as he.

Had he always been wicked? The boy remembered his innocence like a fairy tale he had learned to love but was now too old to believe in. The Evil One had been there always, waiting and watchful, patient and inescapable. Perhaps he had not been baptized. Or perhaps the priest had said the wrong words or used water which had not been blessed. Perhaps, then, he could be baptized again. Was that why his father had brought him here?

It was very cold in the courtyard, and his father was long in returning to him. Megin said the stars were angels, that each point of brightness in the sky belonged to an angel of God. But the Evil One had his angels as well, and they were called devils. Megin said all the devils lived in hell, except for those who prowled the earth in search of human souls. She showed the boy and his sister how certain stars seemed to form pictures in the sky—a hunter, an archer, a king, a dragon. "There," she said. "That proves they're angels, or where did such pictures come from?"

11

The boy didn't know, couldn't guess; the sky seemed full of coded messages which he was too ignorant to understand. Just as he could not understand the peasants when they babbled in that strange tongue his father never used, and which he forbade the boy's mother to use, though the peasants were her people. Megin had a language of her own. Sometimes at night she would whisper words from her secret language, as cold and mysterious as the stars.

A door opened and a lantern spilled shadows across the courtyard. The boy's father came out with a monk in brown robe and cowl, a crucifix glimmering on his breast. The boy's father wore the fur cloak of a Norman nobleman, a knight's iron helmet and great sword, leather boots and leggings. At his command the servant quickly cut the ropes which held the boy captive in the wagon.

Climbing unsteadily from the cart, the boy felt himself taken roughly by the arm and propelled toward the open door, then along a dark gallery, nearly as cold as the courtyard and filled with the cavelike dampness of his father's castle. They climbed a stone stairway which coiled around itself like a dragon's tail. A door stood open at the head of the stairs, radiating light and warmth. His legs still numb and his arm aching from his father's grip, the boy stumbled into a room blazing with candles and warmed by a roaring fire. Colorful tapestries hung from the stone walls, bright cushions softened oak benches and chairs, and a long table held the remains of a considerable feast. At the table sat a very large man, a mountain of fat in a white robe embroidered with threads of purple and gold. Had the boy known of the civilizations of the past, he might have thought the man resembled a Roman emperor of the age of Constantine. As it was, he recognized only the authority and grandeur of the man and stood humbly before him.

"Here he is, then," his father said. "Take him and do what you like with him. I wash my hands of the devil's spawn."

The boy's gaze fell upon the bones and crumbs of

pastry that littered the table. His father had left him bound and shivering in the courtyard while he shared a feast with the enormous man in white, yet he was not resentful. He was afraid of those dark and penetrating eyes set close together beneath grizzled brows, as if pushed against the bulbous nose by the burgeoning fat of two fiery cheeks. The eyes regarded the boy with interest, with mild distaste, perhaps even with amusement. The boy had seen his father look at a peasant with that same expression before drawing his sword and striking off an ear or a finger.

"Geoffrey," the mountain said in a voice that was like an avalanche. "Is that your name?"

He nodded, withering beneath the shrewd gaze.

"And you are the young devil who befouled his own sister and murdered his cousin? God preserve me and all who dwell here from your evil." The mountain made the sign of the cross between himself and the boy with a hand gleaming with rings.

"If you think the risk is too great—" the boy's father began.

"You have paid for our risk. We know how to deal with Satan here. Stand still, boy! Has the devil taken possession of your legs along with your black heart?"

Geoffrey set his heels together and locked his knees, trying to overcome the fear and hunger gnawing at his stomach.

"Now, boy," the huge man continued, "I am Eadmer, abbot of this monastery—lord and master, protector and pastor for all who live here. You shall address me as 'Your Grace' or 'My Lord.' You shall never address me unless bid to speak. Do you understand?"

"Yes, Your Grace."

The abbot seemed pleased. A smile creased his fat face like a meandering stream. He turned to the boy's father. "He doesn't look like a murderer of his own kin, does he? Perhaps—"

"You have my word of honor, the boy's possessed," the knight said.

"Save your word for those to whom it means something," Eadmer said with a contempt that startled the boy. This abbot was truly a powerful man, for the knight stifled his anger.

"Geoffrey," the abbot said, "your father has accused you of foul and heinous crimes. He believes your soul has been enslaved by the Prince of Darkness. If this be true, and unless you receive the grace of Almighty God, you shall certainly be damned to hell for all eternity. You *do* understand the torments of hell, do you not?"

"Yes, Your Grace."

"Good. The gentry in this benighted part of the realm are most remiss, I've found, in the education of their children." Turning to the boy's father, he added, "He seems a reasonable enough lad, Sir William."

"Aye, he can be most ingratiatingly sweet and meek," the knight said. "But it's all a pose. Cross him and he's a demon."

"Ah." The abbot chuckled. "Rather like a Norman war lord, hey?" Turning to the boy again, he asked, "Do you know the story of Adam and Eve, wretched boy?"

"Yes . . . Your Grace."

"By their sin, death came into the world. By their sin of prideful disobedience came lust, wantonness, greed, gluttony, disease, envy, sloth, treachery, witchcraft and all the demons which torment and defile this fallen world. Yet their sin was also, through God's mercy, the beginning of mortal wisdom. This is what, in philosophy, we call a paradox. Cast out of paradise, wretched man consoles himself with philosophy. Such study is permitted, provided that we do not turn away from Christ, our Savior. Had it not been for your sins, you would have become an ignorant, brutal war lord—like your father here—a petty tyrant and scoundrel whose peasants no doubt pray devoutly each night for his speedy demise in one of our king's endless wars. Perhaps you would have been happier that way; perhaps all knowledge is a curse upon mankind for its original sin. But be that as it may, you have sinned, and your father has cast you out, and now your life,

14

your mind, your heart and soul, are all in our charge. Do you understand me, boy?"

Geoffrey wasn't sure. In his confusion, his eyes fell upon a square slab of wood, marked off in smaller squares, which rested on the table. On the board there were carved white and black pieces of varying shapes and sizes. The boy guessed these were the properties of a game, and he gazed upon the board as if it might prefigure the riddle of salvation.

"Ah," the abbot said. "I see you've noticed the game. Do you know what it's called?"

Geoffrey shook his head; then, remembering his instructions, replied, "No, Your Grace."

"It's called chess—an amusement of the heathens recently taken up by the nobility in the more civilized parts of Christendom and roundly condemned by certain pious frauds who have no aptitude for it. It is a game for scholars—a game of logic, strategy, cunning and will. We shall see how well you do in your studies, and how humble and obedient you are able to make yourself. If you prove a scholar, we may try you out at the board. So few of the monks here have the brains to muster a creditable game."

"Is he not to be punished, then?" the boy's father asked.

"Punished?" Eadmer said. "I thought that his banishment to this monastery *was* his punishment. Was that not your intention?"

"I brought him here," the knight said, "so that you might save his wretched soul."

"Yes, and you expected us to use the whipping post as the instrument of his salvation. Well, if he violates our order he shall be promptly punished, but I have no interest in punishing him for the crimes he may have committed under your charge. We shall save his immortal soul, if we can—with prayer, fasting and hard work; with books, with knowledge, with the peaceful, ordered existence all men live within these walls; perhaps even"—he tapped the chessboard with a fat finger—"with this game. If you have objections to our methods, you may take your son away with you now.

15

Otherwise, you relinquish all claim to this lad and he is ours to do with as we will."

The boy's father shook his head. "I don't want him back."

The abbot turned to the monk with the lantern. "Show the novice to his cell, Brother Thomas, and instruct him in the duties of his station and the regulations of our order. As for you, Sir William, if you are not afraid to spend one more night under the same roof with this fearsome creature you once called your son, you may sleep here before returning to your home."

Geoffrey could tell that his father resented Eadmer's mockery, and wondered why he held his temper. "I've already wasted too much time on this devil brat. He's yours—do what you like with him. But if you want my advice, you'll keep him in chains for the rest of his miserable life."

"I don't want your advice," Eadmer said. "I want only the money you've promised us, and—now that I've seen him for myself—the boy you're so glad to be rid of. Good night, Sir William, and a pleasant journey."

Geoffrey's father turned and strode from the room, giving his abandoned son not even a nod of farewell. Tears started from the boy's eyes. He stifled a sob of protest.

"Peace, Geoffrey," the abbot said, his deep voice expressing an unexpected tenderness. "Your father has disowned you. You'll never outlive that brute's ill will. But this is not your father's house. This is a house of God, and God is more forgiving than man. Go now. Tomorrow you shall begin your new life."

The monk who had brought him to the abbot's room now led Geoffrey back across the courtyard. The boy glanced up at the sprawling stars. Pictures, yes; the familiar constellations, ever mysterious and meaningless. Perhaps the stars were but pieces of a gaming board like the one in the abbot's room.

Alone in his cell, huddled beneath a coarse blanket on a pallet of straw, the boy saw a small fragment of that sky in the narrow slit that was his only window. He watched the stars and fought against the memories that bridled hope. Might not Satan find him even here?

It was Megin, in whose withered crone's body pulsed the blood of an ancient race, and whose eyes held the fanatical fire of a Christianity scorched by a memory of pagan rituals, who first told the boy of Satan. Huddled near the kitchen fire, Geoffrey and his sister, Margarette, listened as the hoarse voice cast its spell, reciting a horrid litany of things which prowled the darkness outside the castle.

"Aye, Master Geoffrey, Satan himself wanders the moors on a night like this. Hear that wind blow? Hear it whistle round the turrets? That's Satan's song—Satan's dreadful song calling for his sinners."

"And who is Satan, Megin?"

"He is the Evil One, the one who turned against Almighty God and led a rebellion of the angels—and all for the vicious wicked pride of boys like you, when you refuse to study your lessons or eat what's put before you. Satan knows that pride, you can be sure of that. He loves to see that pride in you as he waits for a chance to make you his own. Even now, out there on the moors"—the wind howled again in the castle tower—"he's waiting."

Margarette's eyes glistened in the firelight. "But what will he do to Geoffrey if he catches him?"

"You must pray to the Lord, my children, pray that you'll never find out. There is a fiery pit prepared for them the devil makes his own—a place of agony where sinners burn forever, though their flesh turns as black as ashes. There's no escaping that fire once Satan takes your soul."

And on windy, howling nights slender Margarette would leave her bed and creep across the big room where all the children slept together, trying not to wake her cousins but crouching at Geoffrey's side and whispering, "Brother—brother, I am frightened. Do you think Satan's up in our tower now?"

And holding her cold small body, caressing her back

17

and arms, Geoffrey would feel strong and brave, and he would hold her close until her shivers stopped and call her "little sister," and his pallet would become a snug warm nest for the two of them. Until one night . . .

"Geoffrey, what's this? Oh, my brother, what's happened to you?"

Geoffrey knew but feared to tell Margarette, for he had seen Carn, the gamekeeper's son, extract from his britches the stiff awful thing with its pink, raw-looking bulb, which at first Geoffrey mistook for a serpent or some other creature not a part of Carn himself, then recognized for what it was only when he saw the boy caress and stroke the staff until it burst with milky venom. Carn offered to take Geoffrey's own thing in his filthy hands, but Geoffrey ran away, back through the woods to the castle gate and through the gate to his hiding place behind the stable. And a few days later, riding with his father across the fields and coming upon a peasant girl cutting hay, Geoffrey looked back after his father had sent him on ahead, and saw his father push the girl down into the hay and poke beneath her hoisted skirt with the thing like Carn's, only larger and more awful still. . . .

And Satan was everywhere then—in the boy's dreams, in his waking thoughts, stalking the drafty corridors of the castle and crying his melancholy song from out on the moors; and still there was Margarette, now twelve, with breasts he cupped in his hands as she lay trusting and innocent in his arms, and she said, "Geoffrey—no, that hurts! Geoffrey, what are you doing to me? Geoffrey!"

And though he fought against the Evil One, temptation was unceasing. Megin watched him with her witch's squint, sure he was already Satan's own, and Satan himself glared at Geoffrey from out of his father's drunken eyes. Margarette came to his bed again, and again, and now their cousins knew, and Richard, the eldest of the cousins, demanded that Margarette come to him as well or he would tell their terrible sin to the manor priest. Geoffrey found them in the stable, Margarette stretched out upon the straw like the peasant girl his father had taken in the field, and his cousin: "Me first, Geoffrey, and then you." And he leapt at Richard in jealous rage and, beaten back, found a pitchfork in the hay and leapt again.

The boy tossed on his pallet, twisting away from tormenting visions. The blood gushing from the triple wound in Richard's chest . . . his father's wrath and the endless beatings . . . furious shouting in the great hall as the clan demanded Geoffrey's death . . . Megin's croaking prayers and pagan spells . . . the serpent spitting its venom . . . Satan's laughter. . . .

"Oh, Lord," the boy prayed, "O dear sweet Jesus, Christ most merciful, have pity on me!"

And in the chapel, where the monks were completing their evening ritual, a supplication was presented to the Lord in a language the boy did not yet understand, but in a desperation and anguish he already knew too well. "Defend us, Lord," the monks were praying, "from evil dreams, from nighttime fears and fantasies. Spare us, O Lord, from pollution by our ghostly foe."

3

Bromley Nocturne

"The history of the Special Collections is a most interesting story," said Dean Singer that evening, after the string quartet had performed its obligatory encore. We were sitting in the drawing room at Bromley House, a College hostel on the outskirts of town and a favorite setting for College social life. Even ladies were allowed to attend its functions on occasion. I had my eye on one in particular and meant to have a word with her before the night was over, but at the moment I was in the grip of the dean's desultory conversation.

"Yes, yes, a most fascinating story," the dean said.

He was an old man with a cadaverous face and long, lipless mouth. There was an odor of musty churchiness about his person, and the port he was sipping seemed to have gathered into two bright purple patches on his lean cheeks. One wondered if he was consistently capable of making perfect sense. "I suppose you've heard that story, Fairchild. . . ."

I made an effort to prevent my gaze from pursuing the small dark-haired girl I was anxious to talk to. I knew her, in fact; she was Viennese, a charming creature of no more than twenty, with the Blue Danube waltzing in her eyes and Tales from the Vienna Woods hidden in her coquette's heart. One of Colin Douglas's many conquests, she had attached herself to him when we were skiing in Austria over Christmas and had recently turned up in Cambridge, only to find there was more competition for Colin's attention than she had reckoned on. Colin Douglas couldn't help attracting and seducing women, just as most Cambridge bachelors couldn't help frightening them away.

The dean was looking at me with wistful irony. One sensed that people had not been paying much attention to him for years.

"I've never heard the story of the Special Collections," I said. "Not the whole story, at any rate."

"Oh, well, you won't want to hear it *all*," the dean said. "I've given my entire life to the College, and I must confess that the affairs of Duke's have come to interest me more than my own."

I wondered if the dean could ever have had any affairs of his own, but merely smiled and waited for his account. I was glad Archie Cavendish wasn't here, for he wouldn't have approved of my good behavior.

The dean settled back into his armchair and crossed his skinny legs. "The Special Collections were established late in the eighteenth century as the result of a bequest from a man named Gerald Brice. He was a fellow commoner at Duke's. Are you familiar with the term? A fellow commoner was a man of no real standing in the University, perhaps not even a degree, but one who paid for certain privileges. He could dine at

High Table, order wine from the College cellar and keep a room for his visits. All the Colleges had fellow commoners, and they helped to pay the bills through some difficult times."

I was sure that Colin had decided to give his Austrian sweetheart the slip for that elegant blonde from London I'd seen him with earlier. He had worked his way near the door and I recognized the look in his eyes—that desperately ecstatic look of the aroused Don Juan which always made me think of a dog about to piss on a post. Poor Yvetta; her only mistake was in having given Colin too much too soon.

The dean sipped at his port with rapid, nibbling little sips. "This Brice was a most peculiar chap, much interested in antiquarian manuscripts. No one knows where he got his money, though there was a nasty rumor at the time"—the dean looked as scandalized as if he'd been there to hear it in person—"that he made his fortune in the West Indian slave trade. Shocking, to think the College might owe a portion of its prosperity to that sort of business. . . ."

Colin had made a break for his freedom. He was out the door and Yvetta was left accepting a glass of port and a cracker from old Dr. Grimshaw's dotty wife. I took note of the frustration with which Yvetta surveyed the Colinless room.

"Do you know," I asked Dean Singer, "where Brice obtained the Westchurch manuscripts?"

"Most likely from a dealer who had picked over the remains of someone else's library. That was a great age of collecting, you know, and there is a tradition—not very well substantiated—that the manuscripts were once part of the Earl of Westchurch's extensive collection of medieval relics . . . but that whole library was lost during the Commonwealth period. A good many national treasures were lost during Cromwell's reign."

"Wasn't the Earl of Westchurch beheaded?"

"Oh, dear, yes. Many noble heads rolled in those days."

"He was convicted of . . . ?"

"Treason, I expect. And popery, and witchcraft, and heaven knows what."

"But why did the Puritans destroy his library?"

"Trying to root out the last traces of popery in the land, I suppose. Then too, the superstitious mind has a curious fear of the written word. Those must have been dreadful times!"

The dean shook his head sadly, and I watched Yvetta nod without comprehension in response to Mrs. Grimshaw's inane chatter.

"The odd part of the whole business, you know, was that this Brice chap just simply up and disappeared."

"Disappeared?"

"He called in the College solicitor one evening and made out his will. Said he was off to France. It was the eve of the Revolution and the will proved a prudent measure, for Brice was never seen nor heard from again. Finally the College went to court to have the will executed. All Brice's wealth and holdings went to Duke's, and the Special Collections were established according to the terms he had prescribed. Isn't that an interesting story?"

Yvetta had escaped Dr. Grimshaw's wife and was moving across the room. Anxious to intercept her, I was about to rise from my chair with a polite excuse when the dean said:

"Stranger still, Fairchild, is that an heir showed up to contest the will. Claimed his uncle, as I believe it was, was mentally unbalanced. It caused quite a scandal—most distressing! The young rogue accused his uncle of all sorts of horrid practices—orgies and Satanic rituals and all that sort of thing."

"Witchcraft? Was Brice a devotee of the black arts?"

"Stuff and nonsense!" the dean said. "Certainly he was a bit of an eccentric, but the nephew was eventually exposed as a fraud—not even a blood relative. He hanged himself a year or so after losing the suit."

This was all immensely interesting, and since Yvetta had disappeared I tried the dean on a related subject. "Someone was just telling me earlier today that Duke's experienced an epidemic of ghosts some time later. In the 1880's or '90s, was it?"

At this the dean was forced to laugh—a painful process emanating from the tomblike cavity of his chest. "Oh, my dear fellow—ho! ho!—you really must allow—ho! ho!—that any self-respecting college had to have a few ghosts on the premises in those days!"

"Then you don't think that those hauntings could have had anything to do with this mysterious benefactor, Gerald Brice, or perhaps with the manuscripts he left behind?"

The dean was driven to the extremes of mirth, and one of his bony white hands sought my arm with surprising familiarity. "You young Americans are really too amusing," he said. "Why, such a proposition never crossed my mind—but since you're so interested in the subject of ghosts, do you know to whom *this* house belonged as late as —hmm—I should say, 1920?"

"To whom?"

"Sir Percy Wickham George," the dean said grandly. "Surely you've heard of Sir Percy Wickham George."

I confessed that I had not.

The dean's pale eyes twinkled. "Sir Percy was one of the founding members of the Society for Psychical Research. It's said that séances, black masses and Druidic rituals were once performed on these very premises—all in the interests of science, of course. Sir Percy was famous for his investigations into the occult, but ghosts are rather a hobby with us in England. We don't take them too seriously. Our lives would be quite ghastly if ever we did."

I acknowledged the dean's rebuke with a smile. "Where can I find out more about the Earl of Westchurch and his collection?"

"The British Museum is very good—but the man you should really talk to about the Westchurch library has, unfortunately, just died. He was a friend of our late Dr. Greggs, a retired clergyman who lived on Hampstead Lane in London. The Reverend Samuel Stemp, for many years the curator of the Westchurch Museum. Stemp knew more about the earl and his collection than any man now alive—though, as I say, poor Stemp was himself recently killed in a freak accident."

"What kind of accident?"

"I saw only the newspaper accounts, but apparently Stemp was out for a walk along Hampstead Lane, when a lorry swerved to avoid a cat. The driver lost control, the lorry jumped the curb and drove poor Stemp through a brick wall. The driver was exonerated—several witnesses saw the cat, though it was never apprehended."

"Was it," I asked the dean, "a black cat?"

This occasioned another outburst of laughter from the dean, which quite exhausted him. I had worn the old fossil to a frazzle, so I asked if he would like me to call a cab for his return to the College.

"That would be uncommonly decent of you, Fairchild. These late evenings are not for me any more, I'm afraid."

I went out into the hall. The Bromley House butler was sneaking a cigarette before bringing in another cart laden with fancy tidbits. He was about to snuff the butt with his fingertips when he saw it was only me.

"Would you call Dean Singer a cab, please?"

"Sure, guv. Watch the cart, would you?"

He went off and I helped myself to one of the savories—a cracker spread with cheese and topped with a black olive. The click of heels on the parquet floor announced the return of a lady from the powder room. It was Yvetta.

"David—I'm so glad to see that *you're* still here, at least!"

As far back as our nights of carousal in that Austrian ski lodge, Yvetta had singled me out as the "nicest"—that is to say, the most manageable—of Colin's cronies. "Have you been abandoned?" I asked sympathetically.

"Bah!" Her tiny pink-nailed fingers plucked one of the savories from the tray. "That swine! That—that—"

Yvetta's English was not entirely adequate to her needs, and finding no term which could express her

24

feelings, she bit savagely into the cracker, as if into her betrayer's neck. I watched her fine jaw working vigorously and, as she swallowed, our relationship subtly turned. Her eyes regarded me with new interest.

"You do like me, don't you, David?"

"I'm bonkers for you, Yvetta," I said.

"You find me . . . attractive?"

I took note of the evasive glance, the coy tone which made clear her availability. Yvetta had always flirted with me; it was in her nature to do so; her upbringing required it. But it had never meant anything until tonight.

"I find you very attractive," I said, "and I've been hoping for a chance to see more of you ever since you came to Cambridge. May I see you home?"

Her smile was like a pact. "Just a minute. I'll get my coat."

I helped myself to another savory while she was gone. Yvetta had found work in Cambridge as an *au pair* girl. I didn't know if I could gain access to her room, and trying to smuggle her into the College at this hour would be difficult. I lacked Colin's resource of private digs. I lacked a good many things gentlemen like Colin took for granted.

The butler returned. His quick, shrewd eyes counted the crackers on the plate. "You've been snitching," he said. "Now I'll have to get some more ready before I can take this plate in."

"Sorry," I said. English servants always think they can scold Americans. This fellow was a dapper little man with straight gray hair and sporty mustache. I got out my wallet. "Tell me—is there an unoccupied room in Bromley House this evening?"

He glared at my wallet. "What did you have in mind, guv?"

"Oh, just a quiet conversation with a lady. Say a quid?"

"I'd be taking a risk. Me and the missus, this is the best situation we've had in years."

"Say two quid." I took them out.

He glanced at the door to the drawing room, then

made my money disappear so quickly he might have been a magician. "There's a bedroom on the third floor. Number 17. Chap who has it's in London for the week. Mind you're out by midnight. The rule says no ladies after midnight."

I knew I could have purchased a longer tenancy, but midnight would be sufficient. He provided me with a key and shuffled off with his cart. Yvetta came back, her coat over her shoulder.

I took the hand she held out to me. "How would you like to do something very daring?" I asked her. "Are you willing to break the rules?"

"The rules! I despite all these British rules! I am beginning to despise the British. . . ."

"What I have in mind is very wicked. If we're caught, it could mean my head on the block."

It took her a minute to see that I was joking. "Oh, David, you're terrible. Don't make fun of me. What is it you wish to do?"

"Come along, and I'll show you."

I led her to the back of the house, where there was a servants' stairway to the third floor. Professor Trevor-Finch, the warden of Bromley House, was a notorious misogynist and prig, and I was indeed risking my place in the College by smuggling a lady upstairs in the house where he terrorized two dozen graduate students and several servants. A man is sometimes compelled to take such risks. I had left the States the survivor of one bad marriage and several torturous affairs, and for months now I had lived a life of monkish purity. Moreover, I was thirty: old enough to realize that the day when I could seduce a girl of Yvetta's tender age was nearly past.

I unlocked the door of number 17. Yvetta drew back.

"Are you sure we should?" she asked.

I knew she simply wanted a bit more persuasion, so I put my arms around her slender waist and drew her to me. "Darling Yvetta, I may not be as tall and handsome as my friend Colin. I don't have his money or his excellent connections. But I *am* madly in love with

26

you, and Colin, as you should know by now, is not. I don't ask much, but if you'd favor a poor student with a few hours of bliss, I promise to be gentle, grateful and anxious to please."

I don't know how much of this courtly speech Yvetta understood, but she caught the gist. She put a hand on my cheek and looked up at me with eyes like dark but luminous stars.

"Liebchen, I really shouldn't—but let's!"

I ushered her into the room, where we spent a pleasant hour or so in the bed of the unknown scholar. Yvetta was indeed exquisite, a marvelous mixture of plump and slender, tender and tough, innocent and depraved. I was hard pressed to believe in my luck and found the episode curiously dreamlike, as if the young man who went to England to work on certain esoteric manuscripts never really existed, save in the potent fantasies of the anonymous lad whose bed we usurped.

As midnight approached we heard cars starting up, doors slamming, people calling out their good nights. Then there were footsteps and voices in the hall, a chorus of running taps and flushing toilets, and finally the heavy silence in which old houses rehearse their repertoire of creaks, clunks and sighs. Yvetta and I were just embarking upon a final round of restrained merriment when I became acutely conscious of a third person in the room.

I froze on the threshold of recaptured bliss. Had that rascally butler crept upstairs for a peek at what I'd purchased with my two quid? I could hear no breathing but Yvetta's and mine, could see absolutely nothing in the darkness that surrounded us, but I was sure there was something in the room with us. Caught between the lady's legs and propped up on aching elbows, I listened to the clamor of some sixth sense I hadn't known I had; and the longer I listened, the more convinced I became that the presence was something other than human. It was old, it was cold, it was unnatural and grotesque, yet infinitely sad, and it seemed to hover near us in the darkness, as if diverted from its pilgrimage across a frozen universe and drawn irresistibly toward the warmth of our coupling.

This visitation lasted only the several seconds it took my flesh to grow cold away from Yvetta's, yet its effect was devastating. My heart was pounding, a cold sweat had started from my pores, and I gasped for breath like a man suddenly plunged into an alien atmosphere.

"David," Yvetta whispered, "what's wrong?"

Reassured by the sound of her voice, I lowered myself to her pliant little body and tried to capture a sense of purpose to suit my posture. But it wasn't, as they say in those novels of sexual pathology, "any good." The abrupt departure of our visitor had left me feeling oddly bereft, even defrauded, as if I'd been on the brink of revelations which could have changed my life.

Yvetta was decent about my collapse. Of course I'd been wonderful—everything a lusty *Fräulein* could ask for. Not to worry, darling; there's always another time. We gathered up our clothes, sorted them out as best we could in the dark, and prepared to make our escape from the domain of that dragon moralist Professor Trevor-Finch.

It was a quarter past twelve as we began our stealthy descent of the Bromley House stairs. We had reached the landing of the second floor when, from a door just down the hall, there came a ghastly scream—hoarse, high-pitched, and totally abandoned. I hustled Yvetta into a closet just off the stairway and we stood in darkness, amid the smell of dust rags and furniture polish, while voices began to sound throughout the house.

"Good Lord, did you hear that?"

"Came from Finchie's room, I think. We'd better see if he's all right."

We heard the rescue party, now composed of several voices, knocking at Professor Trevor-Finch's door. There was talk of breaking the door down, or of going after the butler for a key, when the door was apparently opened.

"I'm sorry, Professor," someone said. "We heard a scream. Is anything wrong?"

"A scream? Good heavens, I *was* having a nightmare, but did I really . . . ? It must have been that Bach fugue we played this evening—always agitates my nerves. Such intricate fingering. Damn, what a nuisance! Here I've gotten you all out of bed. Terribly sorry. Won't you come in for a drink?"

There were polite refusals, apologies all around, and a general dispersal. "He was in the war, you know," I heard one voice whisper as the footsteps passed our broom closet. "The Germans had him for a year or two. It must have been beastly."

In a little while, the house grew quiet again. The reek of the broom closet had us fairly groggy by the time I dared to peek out into the hall. The door to the professor's room was still open, but all was silent within. We had to pass that door to get to the stairs to the first floor.

I led Yvetta out of the closet and down the hall. Looking into the professor's room, I saw him lying face down on the sofa, one arm dangling to the floor, his body very still. On the table nearby there was a chessboard. A white knight lay on the floor beneath the table.

"Yvetta," I said, as I walked her back to her lodgings, "I have to go down to London for a few days next week. Would you like to come along? I have a check from America I haven't cashed yet. We could do the town."

She slipped her arm through mine, her body swaying against me as we navigated the cobblestones. "I'll lose my job if I do, but what does that matter? I never should have come to Cambridge. I miss *Wien*—I must go home soon. England, phooey!"

"Then you'll come with me? A last fling, say, before you return to Vienna?"

She gave my arm a squeeze. "Why not? You are a very naughty boy, *Liebchen*. You will teach me how to break all these stupid British rules."

"I'll try," I promised, and thanked Colin for at least a hand-me-down romance.

It was after one by the time I climbed the staircase to my room, mulling over the uncanny coordinates of the evening. England had obviously been working on my imagination during the months I'd spent at Duke's. I was as much in love with Cambridge as Archie Cavendish, who pretended to hate it only because he couldn't stand to leave it, and I knew I was becoming susceptible to all sorts of things I'd never been susceptible to before.

The door to my room was ajar, although I was sure I'd locked it when I left for Bromley House. I reached in to turn on the light and entered cautiously. The room was empty, but I saw at once that someone had been into my desk. I sorted through my notes on the Westchurch manuscripts and, counting over my index cards, I noticed one conspicuous absence. It was the card on which I had attempted to reconstruct a game of chess obscurely alluded to in the long major poem. I searched the room for it without success. Finally I poured myself a stiff shot of whisky, propped a chair against my locked door and went to bed. It took me a long time to fall asleep.

4

The Widow

"Oh, yes; Mr. Stemp was devoted to chess. Poor man, he had so many innocent little hobbies."

We had paused, in the extinct clergyman's study, over a chessboard and a game *in medias res*. I noticed that black held the commanding position. White was badly down, soon to lose either his queen or his rook. Mate wasn't more than a few moves away.

"Did you play chess with your husband?" I asked Mrs. Stemp. She was a large, angular, sagging creature

30

who seemed born to her widow's black dress. I couldn't imagine her as a girl or a bride, but as a widow she was perfection.

"Heavens, no. Mr. Stemp had no patience with women at chess. Said we hadn't the intellect for it. He usually played alone."

"You mean he reconstructed famous matches from the chess books?"

"I guess that's what he did. But sometimes he just played against himself. That is possible, isn't it?"

"I suppose so," I said, without adding that it seemed rather pointless.

Outside the small house, buses and lorries rolled along Hampstead Lane with ominous insistence, their passage afflicting all the small, fragile objects that filled the darkened rooms with intermittent shudders. British homes are frequently darker than an American would find consistent with a cheerful outlook on life, and I was finding the dead man's house exceedingly oppressive.

Mrs. Stemp looked around her husband's study with a somewhat guilty air. "And what was it you wanted to discuss with my husband, Mr. Fairchild?"

I mentally advanced one of white's pawns, then saw it was a disastrous mistake. "I understand your husband was for many years the curator of the Westchurch Museum in Paxton-Brindley."

"Yes indeed; until he retired in 1957. Poor man—he had so few years left!"

"I'm told that he was an authority on the sixteenth Earl of Westchurch, Lord Peter Brindley—the one who lost his head during Cromwell's reign."

"Ah, my husband wrote a book about the earl, you know. Mr. Stemp received many compliments on his 'little book,' as he always called it."

"And was he working on anything at the time of his death?"

"Mr. Stemp always intended to revise and enlarge his book—to bring out what he called the 'definitive study' of the earl. But I'm afraid he didn't get very far

31

with it these last few years. He tired easily, and travel wasn't good for him."

"Did he have to travel a great deal in order to research his book?"

"He was always going off somewhere and coming back quite, quite exhausted. 'You'll do yourself in,' I used to tell him, 'if you don't stay home for a change and get a bit of rest.' And to think he was only a few steps from his very own door when—"

There was little one could do, when these genteel sniffles came upon the widow, but preserve a moment's respectful silence. "Do you have any idea where your husband went on these trips, Mrs. Stemp?"

"All over the British Isles, I'm sure. Often back to Paxton-Brindley; sometimes way up north. He took me along on holiday once when he visited Wimsett-by-Sea. Have you been there? Charming little town on the Norfolk coast, and not too far from Cambridge."

"Mrs. Stemp, did your husband have any papers— any notes or first drafts toward the revision of his book? It could be that Duke's College would be interested in purchasing his literary remains."

"Oh, I'm afraid I've sold those already."

"And to whom did you sell them, might I ask?"

"To a friend of Mr. Stemp's—at least, he said he was a friend. He came here the day after the funeral and offered to take all Mr. Stemp's papers off my hands, so of course . . ."

"I hope you got a good price for them."

"I believe I was quite well paid," she said, with the complacency of a woman who had never been bothered by money matters. "Mr. Regis was most generous."

"Mr. Regis?"

"I have his card somewhere about; I'll see if I can find it. As you can see for yourself, Mr. Fairchild, everything's been taken. There used to be stacks and stacks of papers everywhere in this study. I hadn't the heart to go through it all myself—quite dreaded the thought of throwing anything away—and yet what use was it all, once—once—"

"I'd appreciate it very much if you'd find me that card," I said quickly, "and in the meantime, if you don't mind, perhaps I'll just take a look around."

She glanced at me with a renewal of that skepticism I had talked my way past in order to enter her house. "I can't see that it matters very much now, or that Mr. Stemp would object, since you are, in a way—well, whatever you are. I'll hunt up that card."

As soon as she was gone, I went over the room like a burglar, checking every nook and cranny that might harbor a stray scrap of Mr. Stemp's writing. There was nothing. I was looking behind the individual volumes of several standard sets of the poets in the glass-enclosed bookcase when Mrs. Stemp returned.

She gave me the card. *Simon Regis. Bookseller, Dealer in Rare Volumes, First Editions, Literary Curiosities. 83 Blackfriars Road, London.* I slipped the card into a shirt pocket.

"There's one more thing you might find interesting," Mrs. Stemp said. "That is, if you've never seen my husband's book. There's one in that bookcase, I believe."

After a bit of looking, I found the reverend's pamphlet lodged between a volume of Byron and another of Milton—rather magnificent company for such a slender contribution to scholarship.

"That's the one," Mrs. Stemp said. "That was Mr. Stemp's study copy, but you can have it, Mr. Fairchild. There's dozens more boxed somewhere in the house."

The book had a paper cover, on which was displayed the Westchurch coat of arms, and beneath it, the title:

THE NOBLE EARL

An Informal Account of the Life and Times of Lord Peter Brindley, Sixteenth Earl of Westchurch; together with a Description of His Library. Based on records in the parish of Paxton-Brindley and on the Westchurch family papers. By the Reverend Samuel Stemp, B.A.,

M.A. Printed for the Dorset Bibliographic Society by M. J. Steadly and Sons, Ltd. London, 1953.

Mrs. Stemp watched as I thumbed through the slim volume. "Will it be of any help to you, do you think?"

"I'm sure it will," I said. I noticed that there were several loose sheets of paper inserted among the leaves, but I did not take these out in Mrs. Stemp's presence.

As we were leaving the study, my gaze fell once more on the chessboard. I was hardly an avid student or frequent player of the game, yet there was something tantalizing familiar about the situation on the board. I had encountered a similar problem not long ago, and I thought I knew where. Had the Reverend Stemp visited Cambridge before he died?

Mrs. Stemp led me down the long dark hall to her front door. Yes, Mr. Stemp often went up to Cambridge, she said. A pity we hadn't met. She held the door open and I caught a glimpse of ponderous vehicles along the street. I had one last question for her.

"Your husband was killed near here, I believe?"

"Just up the street," she said, pointing the direction. "He wasn't gone more than a few minutes when they came for me. I rushed to his side, but the body was covered by a tarpaulin and they wouldn't let me—I never got to—" Tears had begun to trickle down her powdered cheeks once more and her parched lower lip was quivering.

"I know this must be hard for you," I said, "but did the police—well, did they explain the accident to you? I mean, to your satisfaction?"

"Satisfaction?" she asked, blinking uncertainly.

"I mean, are you satisfied that it *was* an accident?"

"Oh, Mr. Fairchild, I never thought . . .! What else could it have been? Besides, there was a cat—a cat in the road. . . ."

"I'm sorry," I said. "It was just a thought. Thank you very much for your help, Mrs. Stemp, and—and—"

I was still trying to think of what sort of condolence to offer the widow of a retired clergyman recently run

34

over by a truck, when Mrs. Stemp shut the door in my face.

I walked up Hampstead Lane past the brick wall, weather-stained and mossy, which more than likely had formed one slice of bread in the fatal sandwich. A patch of bright new bricks and white mortar marked the spot. It was near the corner, and just across the side street from a pub whose front windows provided a good view of the street. I crossed over and tried the door. British pubs keep hours according to a schedule I'd not yet fathomed, but this one was open. Its interior was dark and quiet, warm with polished wood and cracked leather. A trio of old men were at a table by the window, squinting over their pints at the endless parade of vehicles.

The pubkeeper stood waiting for me at the bar, his beer-keg belly pressed against the gleaming wood. "A pint of bitter, please," I told him.

"Yank, is it?" he asked pleasantly as he drew my glass.

I'd long since given up trying to pass as a native and had learned to trade, in such situations, upon my exotic interest. Yes, I was an American; no, not a tourist; a professor of English literature, in fact, doing some research at Duke's College, Cambridge. Had the pubkeeper by any chance known the distinguished old gentleman who had lived just down the street, one Samuel Stemp?

"He didn't come in here much," the pubkeeper said, dropping his haitches. "Not a drinking man, I'd have to say. We used to see him passing by on his daily walks, howsomever—like as not, same time every day. A gentleman of very regular habits, he were."

"Did you happen to witness the accident?" I asked.

"No, I can't say as how I witnessed anything myself. I was down in the cellar bringing up a keg. But those lads over there might've seen something. You'll have to ask them."

I sent three pints over to the three old men and presently followed my offering to their table.

"Cheers," said one, lifting his glass. "Sit yourself down, if you've a mind to."

"Thanks. I was wondering if you fellas could tell me anything about the accident last week. The Reverend Stemp was a good friend of mine, and I've just been to see his widow."

"Terrible thing that was, Yank—just terrible. The rev got it right over there where you see that brick wall—and a proper bloody mess it was, too."

"I suppose the police came around to ask you all about it."

"Aye; they was here. Not much they got out of us, though. There's none of us here as got much time for the bloomin' bobbies. Not since old Arf's youngest got sent up for pinchin' a few tools he happened to find layin' about some bloody construction site—ain't that right, Arf?"

Arf agreed that was bleeding right, and gorblimey if he'd ever give another bloomin' bobby the correct time of day, by gor.

Was there something, then, which the police should have known about the accident? Something peculiar, let's say?

The three old men became cagey and evasive. I had to order another round. We compared soccer and football, baseball and cricket. I agreed the American games were sorry imitations of sports already perfected by the British. Humbly, I confessed that America had not done right by Britain since the war, that John F. Kennedy (being Irish and Catholic) was not to be trusted, but that honest workingmen the world over were united in a common cause. Finally, on our third round, I got them back to the Reverend Mr. Stemp.

"Go on, Arfie," the leader of the trio said. "You can tell him what you saw. He's straight enough, I guess."

Arfie yanked his checkered cap a bit lower over his bleary eyes and leaned close to me across the table. "I were comin' up Hampstead Lane, you see, just about to pop round here for a pint, when I notice the old chap comin' toward me from down his way. Across from him, pulled up alongside the heath, there was this little gray Anglia with two men in it—right in front of a 'No Standing' sign an' causing a bit of a jam-up. Battered old wreck of a car it was, too—well rusted at the gills and dents all over it. Well now, the reverend, he'd just about reached the corner, and there was this bloomin' big lorry comin' uphill behind him, when what should these blighters do but open up their car door and let out a cat. That's right, a bloody cat! They dumps him right out in traffic and takes off and leaves him. Now the rev, he sees the cat an' makes to run out an' save its mangy hide, an' the lorry driver, he sees the cat an' takes a quick turn to slip by it, an' that's just how it happened. The lorry and the old chap goes bashin' into that brick wall, and the bloody cat gets off scot-free, scamperin' across the heath about as lucky as a cat ever were."

"Some folk will go to any lengths to kill a cat," observed one of the old men, sadly shaking his head.

"Or a retired clergyman," I said. "You didn't get the Anglia's license plate, did you, Arfie?"

Arfie hadn't. There was no more they could tell me about the incident, so we had another pint all around and then I set out for my hotel.

I found Yvetta seething with resentment upon my return.

"I don't like being cooped up in this dreary hotel all day while you go off to those libraries or museums or wherever you go. I thought we came to London to have fun!"

"But, Yvetta, haven't we been having fun?"

She caught the direction of my glance and was somewhat mollified. "Yes, *Liebchen*, in bed it is all quite pleasant. But I thought you were going to take me places, spend money—talk to me, at least. Soon I must return to *Wien*. Aren't there things we should talk about?"

I couldn't think of any, but I did have to admit that Yvetta had a legitimate complaint. My resources were far more limited than Colin Douglas's, my interest in London's standard attractions slight. "Tell you what," I said. "Put on that sexy little frock you bought on Car-

37

_y_ Street the other day and I'll take you out for a tour of West End night life. How's that?"

She considered it no better than a token acknowledgment of her existence, but went down the hall to take her bath. While she was gone I went through the Reverend Stemp's "little book," turning first of all to the loose sheets inserted among the leaves. They were notes concerning Stemp's later researches, but they made no sense to me. I was obliged to begin at the beginning, submitting myself to the reverend gentleman's leisurely pace and inestimable sense of style.

The sixteenth Earl of Westchurch, so Stemp tells us, converted to Roman Catholicism during a period of residence in Italy as an envoy of the Crown. He married a beautiful Italian princess, whom he brought back to England in 1635. Perhaps because of his conversion, the earl became interested in those vestiges of medieval Catholicism which had survived a century of Protestant vandalism. He purchased and attempted to restore the old monastery at Blackstone, not far from Westchurch Hall. The monastery had fallen to ruins, its treasures plundered by pious nationalists, but the earl, it seems, discovered a secret chamber which still harbored a marvelous collection of medieval manuscripts. Much intrigued by these ancient books, the earl built a library for them at Westchurch Hall. He imported scholars from Oxford and learned to read the primitive version of his mother tongue for himself. By 1645 he had assembled one of the largest libraries of medieval literature in England, rivaling the great Cotton Collection in London and those at Oxford and Cambridge. Just what the earl was searching for in these ancient manuscripts is unknown, yet it did seem to his biographer that the earl had a purpose beyond mere reverence for his adopted religion. He even smuggled a Spanish Jesuit into the realm to have a look at his treasures. Of course, such activities were viewed with alarm by the religious zealots who were just then seizing power in the realm.

In the first year of Cromwell's government, the earl

was accused of treason, blasphemy and various other offenses against the Protestant sensibility. The earl's own vicar testified that the nobleman commonly practiced "certaine ungodlie and vicious actes unbefitting a Christian gentleman," and several peasants gave evidence that his wife was a "known sorceress, necromancer and familiar of diverse wicked spirits"—most of them no doubt Italian. On this evidence and that of the tortured Jesuit (captured in his attempt to escape England and subjected to engines which, as a child of the Spanish Inquisition, he should have admired), the earl was convicted and beheaded in 1649. Westchurch Hall burned to the ground shortly thereafter, and there was a curious legend (doubted by Stemp) that the earl himself had ordered the fire from his prison cell.

With this background, I returned to the notes Stemp had stuffed into the volume. Between pages 19 and 20 (recounting the earl's years in Italy): "Galileo, first telescope, 1609"; and between pages 35 and 36 (the earl's quest for manuscripts to augment his collection): "Creypool Abbey, March 12, June 6, August 21, 1639"; and the most curious of all, a sheet inserted among the final pages bearing the following: "Nova, 134 B.C., 1054 A.D., 1572 A.D., 1604, ????" Finally, there was a name written lightly in pencil and blurred to near illegibility on the back flyleaf: "G. Gervaise, d. 1175."

I was still pondering these cryptic entries when Yvetta returned from her bath, matter-of-factly tossed her robe on the bed and broke open a new package of black net stockings. Her skin was pink and glowing, redolent of bath oil and, despite her diminutive frame, as richly contoured as a Botticelli nymph.

"You live with your nose in a book," she told me, affectionately scolding, as women will once they've captured your attention.

"Hmm. I think I've had my nose in some interesting places lately," I said.

She giggled and stood up to attach her stockings to dangling black garters. "For you it is so hard to be

39

serious. Do I frighten you so much, David, that you can only make jokes with me?"

"I didn't realize I was frightened of you."

"Bah! All the English are frightened of their women. It is one reason why I can stay in this country no longer."

"But I'm not English," I reminded her, glad for once that I was not.

"It makes no difference. You and Colin—you are both very English in that respect. You have your little world and you will not allow women to intrude—is it not so? You refuse to take us seriously."

"I promise I shall be very serious this evening," I told her. "We shall discuss love and art, truth and beauty—whatever you like. But now I'd better wash up and shave, before you lose your big night on the town by standing around in that fetching state of undress."

"You see?" she called after me as I made for the bathroom. "You are never serious!"

G. Gervaise, I thought, scraping away at my whiskers. Hadn't there been a twelfth-century priest by that name, author of several obscure Latin treatises on free will? Not to be confused, I recalled, with Gervase of Canterbury, though this Gervaise was also a disciple of the great Thomas à Becket. I remembered a nasty young assistant professor who had tried to trick me on that very point during my orals for the doctorate. If it hadn't been for that prick of scholarship, I might not have remembered Gervaise, whose work was seldom if ever read. Perhaps it's time, I thought, that someone take a look at those treatises.

Before we left the hotel room, I took the precaution of hiding Stemp's pamphlet and its notes in the hollow basin of the overhead light fixture.

"Are scholars always so frightened someone will steal their books?" Yvetta asked with amusement.

"Only when one's room has been broken into once before," I said, "and when one's fellow scholars start having mysterious accidents which may not be accidents at all."

"Liebe Gott, has that happened?"

40

"I'll tell you about it at dinner," I said.

We found a pleasant little restaurant in Soho, vaguely Italian, redundantly romantic, and by conspiratorial candlelight I made good on my promise to talk seriously, telling Yvetta a good deal more about my research than she wanted to hear.

"But, David, these manuscripts—why are they so important to you? If this poet person was—how you say—off his rocker, then what good is his poem?"

"It may still be a great poem," I said. "A poet's madness may give us God's own heavenly nonsense in disguise. Besides, if I'm right about the dating and the quality of the poem, it will make my reputation as a scholar."

"And is that so important to you?"

"Of course it is. In every discipline there are always just one or two big names—men whose discoveries have transformed their entire field. It's only those men who make scholarship pay, who get the grants and prizes, the plush jobs—"

"So—it's all just a matter of money?"

I was reminded, by her womanly skepticism, of why I'd been reluctant to discuss these things with her at all. "It's more than just money, Yvetta, though God knows that's important too. But one wants to make a contribution—to do something meaningful with one's life. . . ."

Still I could see she was not satisfied, and we went around and around with it all through dinner and afterward, as we strolled arm in arm through the fog-sinister streets of London. I spent more money than I could afford, and wasted a lot of rhetoric trying to persuade Yvetta that I knew what I was doing with my life. Finally, at two in the morning, as we emerged from a "private" club where we had seen large sums of money lost at the roulette tables and large amounts of female flesh exposed for the edification of a blasé audience, Yvetta turned suddenly amorous.

"*Liebchen,* we should not spend any more of your money. Let's go back to the hotel. I want to make love to you so that you will never forget me!"

41

She was as good as her word, poor unappreciated *Fräulein*, and before the night was over I smoked several cigarettes at the bedside, gazing upon her sleeping childlike face as if seeing a loved one through the crisis of some dread disease.

At breakfast, Yvetta produced a ticket for the Dover boat-train and informed me that today she was going home to Vienna. I could have argued with her, but I didn't.

With a lump in my throat and all sorts of words held firmly behind clenched teeth, I saw her to the station. We had nearly an hour to wait in a dismal tearoom surrounded by strangers and lonely vagabonds, and we did not use it to any good purpose. Finally, on the platform itself, the great train hissing up at us from its concrete channel, Yvetta seized my hand, looked earnestly at me and said:

"*Auf Wiedersehen*. I wish you well with your studies. When you become rich and famous, and learn that it does not matter after all, look me up in *Wien*. It will be too late for us, of course. I will be old and fat, a poor man's wife and the mother of his babies, but perhaps we can have a glass of wine together and remember the old times, eh? Then we shall both feel a little sad about how stupid and stubborn we have been. . . ."

"Yvetta," I said, quite against my will, for I knew how corny her speech was, "don't leave me—not yet. Give it a chance to turn into something better."

"It will not get better for us, only worse. In some ways you are very sweet and I feel sorry for you, but I won't let you hurt me the way Colin did. You are not quite a whole man, David. There is something missing in your heart, and you will always hurt people until you find out what it is."

That afternoon I went around to the address on the card Mrs. Stemp had given me, but 83 Blackfriars Road, when I finally found it, turned out to be an empty warehouse.

5

Young Gervaise

The Abbot Eadmer:

Geoffrey Gervaise—yes, I remember the lad. Took quite an interest in him while he was here at Wellesford. Of course, we were rather in the same boat, the two of us. We had both been exiled to that sanctified sheep farm on the moors. The difference was that I had seen something of the world in my time, had studied at Paris and Salerno, had spent several glorious years in Rome, where I'd had a first-rate position in the Church, an adviser to bishops and cardinals—yea, even a familiar of the Pope. I missed Rome, you can be sure of that. The climate, the cuisine, the company of learned men, the pomp and ceremony of the papal palace—of course I missed all that. And spent many bitter hours alone in my quarters or in the chapel regretting those rash commitments of my youth which led to this exile.

No, I shan't bore you with that tedious tale. . . . I backed the wrong man; it's as simple as that. They could have vented on my ample person the wrath Abelard escaped; they could have cut off my cullions and put me to copying hymns and singing soprano in some boy's choir in the Alps. But I'd been gracious with my favors while I still had them to dispense, and a few of those favors had gone to the right people. They arranged this place of exile for me, where I might retain a certain status among men inferior to me in every conceivable way, and I was glad to get out of Italy with all my parts, believe me.

Ah, but that Bernard of Clairvaux was a firebrand!

43

There was no arguing logic with him. He simply swept it all aside with his fiery sermons and pulpit-thumping rhetoric—and all his pious tripe about the Virgin. Good Lord, the man could've persuaded the devil himself to set out on a crusade! Abelard didn't have a chance. I should have abandoned the cause as soon as the bishops dragged the eunuch before the Council of Sens. But no; I remained loyal to my old teacher (and besides, he was right!), so after the verdict was handed down it was I who arranged for the defeated scholar to present his case in person to the Pope. When he died on the way to Rome—and who could have predicted that?—I made my own peace; what choice did I have? Abelard was an arrogant son of a bitch, but if you had any sense of *largesse* in such matters, you had to admire his style.

So—it was years later, and I'd been tending the flock at Wellesford long enough to know how little it offered a man of my talents, when this perfect barbarian of a Norman knight arrives at our gate one evening with a fourteen-year-old boy in tow. Said the boy had befouled his own sister, then run a pitchfork through his cousin. He said the boy was possessed— kept screaming about Satan and some serpent that was going to carry him off to hell. There's a lot of hysteria bred into these noble families, I'm afraid, and they only make it worse by turning their children over to the peasants. No wonder the boy was half mad when he joined us!

Still, he made an admirable novice. Meek, mild, anxious to please—you couldn't have asked for a more malleable subject. True, there was something a bit strange in those piercing eyes of his, and that strangeness clouded his gaze on occasion, as if some evil memory was passing like a thunderhead across the light of his reason. Yet monastic life seemed to agree with him. He took to his lessons so quickly I was hard pressed to find a monk learned enough to teach him and finally had to take over the task myself. We read the ancients together—Cicero, Virgil, Horace, Juvenal. It was good to have someone to talk to about those favorites of my youth. The boy was interested in the vernacular too—those treasures in the mother tongue which so few of the learned can read any more. Wellesford had rather a fine collection of the old Saxon scripts, and the boy developed a great feeling for the language, though he knew but a few words when he first came here.

It was a pleasure, I tell you, to see his young mind take possession of the riches I set before him. He was a brilliant lad, and he'd had a most pitiful upbringing. That father of his! A prime example of the petty tyrants we had to put up with in England during the reign of King Stephen. I don't know if the boy ever heard about it or not, but one of the first things Henry did upon assuming the throne was to tear down the castles of Stephen's vassals. The elder Gervaise—Sir William —fought to save his little kingdom, but Henry's men put an arrow through his throat. I heard about it from the manor priest, who came running to the monastery for refuge. I asked him not to tell the boy. Geoffrey seemed by then to have forgotten all about his wretched family, and I didn't want to stir up troublesome memories.

There were reports about Geoffrey, of course—some rather disturbing ones. The monk in charge of the sheepfold would complain that Geoffrey neglected his duties, letting some lamb wander off into the heather as he sat staring up at the sky, as if trying to make out the stars in broad daylight. I took the boy off shepherd's duty. Any simpleton could tend the flock. Then there were his nightmares. The novices in his wing complained of his frequent screams at night, and I finally had to order a dram or two of wine before bed to make sure he would sleep soundly. But I suppose the most disturbing report of all came from his confessor. He came to me quite shaken, the poor old innocent. He didn't want to break the seal of the confessional, yet thought I should know—for the good of the flock, et cetera—that Geoffrey had been "seeing visions" of a most licentious sort. A young woman—his sister, perhaps—sometimes appeared to him in his cell. Sometimes she disrobed and displayed herself to tempt him. I knew well enough what ailed the lad, and I concluded that his visions would cease when he left to study at Paris, where naked females are as plentiful as lice. If more of the monks had been as honest as Geoffrey, I'm sure as good many naked females would have come to light in the confessional.

I had intended all along to send the boy to the university at Paris. I was grooming him for it. I took him through the *trivium* and *quadrivium* myself, not trusting any of the monks to handle the job properly. When he arrived in Paris, where I still had friends, the masters there would know he was old Eadmer's pupil, and they'd remember the teacher in the brilliance of the protégé. Who knows? With that fool Bernard off hunting heretics in another part of Christendom, the bishop might even think it safe to send for me. . . . Old men are fools indeed, are they not?

But I'm forgetting the most wonderful of all the boy's attributes. He was a wizard at chess—an absolute wizard! I remember our first few games, which I granted as a reward for his diligence at his studies. Like any beginner, he failed to keep track of his pieces, to look ahead, to grasp the complexity of the game. But unlike most beginners, he never lost heart. Beaten, he always studied the board and went back over the game until he understood why he had been beaten. I could see he meant to master the game and could hardly contain my glee, good chess players being so hard to find in an English monastery. Soon I was as anxious to get out the board as he was, and I suppose we more than once hurried through our daily lesson in order to get to our game.

It wasn't without moral and educational value, you know. Men win at chess not only through logic—through superior cunning and experience—but also through the exercise of those attributes of character we call "virtue": courage, self-discipline, steadiness of mind and heart, and an unwavering dedication to the task at hand. With each succeeding game I was privileged to observe the unfolding of a character which was really quite remarkable.

I remember the evening on which Geoffrey first gave proof of the power and mastery of his game. A fiendish blizzard howled across the moors. The monastery was like a tiny island in a sea of turbulent snow; we'd been sealed within the inner walls for days. Blasts beat against the roof and drafts guttered the candles, sent our fires roaring up the chimneys. The supper hour came, but I ordered food delivered to my chamber so that we could proceed with the game. The young rascal had me by the throat. He'd anticipated my every move, countered all my stratagems. I could but fight on for a draw, out of a teacher's pride, and out of respect for the strength of my pupil. As the game neared its close, I chanced to raise my eyes from the board to see Geoffrey's intense young face just across from me. He was by this time—what? sixteen?—with a face already taking to itself the hard lean contours of his line. Hair dark, brows and eyes darker, a long straight nose and prominent jaw, a mouth which when his teeth showed suggested the ferocity of his father. I saw this face by candlelight, deeply shadowed as it bent in concentration over the board, and I suddenly felt—what? My own helplessness, surely, but also a kind of awe at the composure and majesty of my pupil. It was nearly a transfiguration. And it dawned on me that I was not the boy's true opponent. The game he was playing existed only in his own mind, and his effort was nothing less than to grasp the harmony, the design, the fate which governs the cruel microcosm of the chessboard. I've never taken my chess as seriously as all that, and no doubt I have my shallowness to thank for my sanity. But I had a moment—a truly distressing moment, believe me—when I wondered if by teaching Geoffrey the game I had brought upon him that salvation he so earnestly sought—or his everlasting damnation.

For several weeks thereafter our games commonly ended in a draw. I did try to beat the boy. It occurred to me that I should stifle his growing obsession with the game and the illusion of power that it gave him.

47

But I was unequal to the task. My reign as champion of the monastery was at an end. I refused to play with him. I forbade him to play under the pretext of a Lenten penance. It was all to no avail. The seed I'd planted *would* grow—would take possession of his soul. Yet I hoped and prayed (the most earnest prayers which had come from these old lips in many a year!) that eventually he would tire of the game and, having proved whatever it was he was so determined to prove, turn his extraordinary mind to all those other matters which ought to occupy a reasonable man.

To that end, I sent him off to Paris a year earlier than I'd planned. In a way, I was glad to get rid of him; yet I missed him a good deal. I still do. It's a shame what they've done to Gervaise. God may be merciful, but man is a pitiless wolf. Look what they did to Abelard. Look what they did to Becket. Yes—I will say it—look what they've done to Eadmer. I confess I don't understand Christianity any more. Perhaps I never did. The world made sense to the pagans because they knew their gods were not to be trusted—petty tyrants and frauds who despised human courage and loved to punish man for aspiring beyond his station. That was a tragic vision some of us can understand. Christianity blames it all on the devil, I suppose. I've never met the old gentleman myself. You'd think Satan would take an interest in the soul of a fat, bored, lonely, gluttonous, intellectually arrogant old man. I could use the company. I wonder if the devil plays chess.

Master Victor of Bordeaux:

We had a bad winter in Paris the year young Geoffrey Gervaise came over from England. Let's see—that would have been the winter of '53. A man had to carry a staff when he went out, to fend off the beggars. Came in handy for wolves, too; the devils were aprowl all over the city. I saw a pack of them attack a small child near the Seine, not more than a quarter mile from my lodgings. Her father came running from the woodpile and laid into them with his ax. A few of us tried to help. I struck one of the demons across the skull and it turned on me with a horrid display of fangs, the child's blood matting the fur around its mouth. Filthy beasts; devils incarnate! One wolf down, its guts oozing from the gash in its belly, the others still managed to carry off the child's severed arm. They dragged it downriver and we could hear them snarling at one another over the prize. The father was beside himself with rage and grief. We bound up the stump as best we could, and the poor man carried his mutilated babe off to his hovel.

Gervaise came to my lodgings during this unprecedented siege of cold weather when the stars blazed and glistened at dusk like the eyes of demons. I was huddled before my small fire, my fingers too cold to hold the quill, my brain too cold to think of anything but its misery. Gervaise brought a letter of introduction from Eadmer, that fat abbot up in Yorkshire who thinks he's such a brilliant scholar because Peter Abelard once patted his behind. Eadmer may have been good enough once, but his learning was suspect by now. Abelard had been dead for years and dialectic was no longer the celebrated cause it had been when he and his theories were the talk of Paris. No, we'd been studying our Greek texts and our Arabic (I don't think Eadmer could even read Arabic or that he'd ever heard of trigonometry). Of course, we were wiser than we'd been in Abelard's day. We knew better than to antagonize the bishops or the rabble-rousers like Bernard of Clairvaux. That was the first thing I tried to impress upon Gervaise. I told him that his mind was indeed free: he could think whatever he wanted to think, and conclude whatever he liked, so long as he kept it to himself. No doubt Gervaise thought I was a dreadful hypocrite. But I've been a master here at Paris for twenty years and they're not going to send *me* off to graze sheep in the provinces, I can tell you that.

As soon as it was warm enough for the two of us to converse without our teeth chattering, I made an effort to find out what the boy really knew. His preparation was adequate—better than one might expect from a provincial education. Eadmer had given him his Latin and his Greek, his grammar, rhetoric, logic, arithmetic, geometry, astronomy and music. I saw that we didn't have to worry about basics, and Gervaise was immensely eager to learn something new. Old Eadmer had played the university up in his mind until the boy saw it as a kind of heaven where the angels themselves dispensed truths. Well, we did have things we could teach a young fellow like Gervaise. The question was: what would he go in for now that he had one of the great libraries and some of the greatest teachers in Europe at his disposal?

I suggested law; you can't go far in the Church these days without a thorough grounding in law, and of course that just happened to be my own field. But Gervaise hankered after poetry, theology, natural philosophy; it wasn't enough for him to know how the world worked; he wanted to know why it worked that way, as well. I've seen minds like his before. They can learn law, but they don't have the patience to make a career of it. They usually wind up as alchemists, astrologers, occult philosophers of one sort or another. I warned him against those fields. There's no future in magic, I told him. An uneasy alliance with the Church at best, and it wouldn't be long before all those pursuits were outlawed. If a scholar wants to amuse himself in his spare time by dissecting frogs or counting up the stars, that's his privilege, but you can't make a career of such twiddle. And don't tell me anybody's ever going to turn straw into gold or get silver out of mud, because I just don't believe it.

"Now, look at Becket," I said to Gervaise. "Look at John of Salisbury. Your countrymen. At last you've got a decent king over there in England (and don't forget Henry is more of a Frenchman than an Englishman), and it's in a fair way to become a country fit for scholars once more. I know Thomas à Becket, as it happens. Studied law with him at Bologna. If you're as bright as Eadmer says you are, I might be able to get

50

you a place in Becket's chancellory. But first you've got to learn your law."

"But where does the law come from?" Gervaise asked me. "Does it govern our actions, or does it proceed from them? Can the king legislate the lives of his subjects, or do the subjects determine the fate of kings? If laws are made by man, does he create them out of nothing or does he discover them in the world around him? Can a soul deny its own law? If the soul is immortal and the will is free . . ."

And so forth and so on. The boy seemed absolutely driven to ask the most dangerous questions. A boy like that is going to wind up either a saint or a heretic; there's no middle ground for his sort.

Perhaps I should have washed my hands of Geoffrey Gervaise and let some other master worry about him. But there was something about those hungry, questioning eyes of his. I thought perhaps I could help him learn restraint in his studies, at least. Besides, I did owe Eadmer a favor or two from the old days. Ultimately it was settled; Gervaise studied law with me.

He was diligent at his studies; I'd have had no patience with him otherwise. Oh, he might go for weeks without showing up for my lectures, and I would all but give up on him, assuming he'd found some other master to bedevil with his endless questions, or that he'd gone completely mad in the alehouse down by the river—but then he'd be back again, his brain reeling with everything he'd been reading in the interim, his tongue poisonous with questions.

Of course, he had to be feeling his freedom after all those years in the monastery. He had to drink himself sick, to mount his whores, to write his verses—the students were all writing poetry then. I heard he was quite a chess player too, though I take no interest in the game myself. Apparently he made a bit of money by it. By the time he'd been here a year or two, he had quite a reputation in this town—as a poet, scholar, talker and reveler and wastrel and gambler. God knows what he'd been saying in the alehouses! A secretary of the bishop came to see me. Wanted the boy expelled as a "contamination" to the university. I stuck up for him. I risked my career in so doing. Much thanks I ever got for it from Gervaise.

I remember one evening—this was in the spring of '55 or '56. I was coming back from a stroll along the Seine through that hell of taverns and bawdyhouses where the students live, when I chanced to pass an open doorway. I looked in and who should I see, standing up on a table to recite his latest poem, surrounded by drunkards and whores, dwarves and hunchbacks and crones, pimps and gamblers and vagabonds of every description, but my prize pupil (at the end of a week-long spree by the looks of him), Geoffrey Gervaise.

I paused in the doorway, curious to hear one of those verses which had scandalized the bishop. Gervaise was very drunk. And the whore who was curled at his feet, gazing lovingly up at him, had probably been tutoring him in the ways of vice for several days. Still, I think it scarcely justified the lurid nature of the verse, or the brazen mocking manner in which Gervaise read it out to his audience of fools. I remember but a few lines. They were in Latin, of course. I won't profane the language of law and theology by repeating them, but I'll risk a translation in the vulgar tongue. The poem, after recounting the adventures of a roguish monk set loose in the city, ended thus:

> Beware the man who fears not hell,
> For in his words foul demons dwell,
> And 'neath the glare of that one's wit,
> All withers, dies—and turns to shit!

Gervaise was so humble and repentant when, a few days later, I upbraided him for his misconduct that it was impossible to remain angry with him. "It's true," he said mournfully, shedding real tears. "God must loathe me for my sins. I am not worthy of the priesthood and should not take orders. My life has been marked for evil and I am Satan's pawn."

I quickly reminded the lad of Christ's saving mercy,

52

the love of God our Father, the constant intervention of the Virgin. No man is ever damned for his sins, I told him, but only for the denial of grace.

Gervaise remained disconsolate and further questioning soon revealed to me the heretical origins of his despair. The Albigensians had come up to Paris not long before and their heathen doctrines had clouded many an unstable mind. The prelates were in an angry mood, and I was anxious to get Gervaise out of Paris before his scurrilous verses and wagging tongue got us both in trouble. Consequently, I arranged for him to present his Master's disputation a good deal ahead of schedule. Send him back to England, that was my thought. Get him into Becket's chancellory and let King Henry worry about him—he's had plenty of practice at quarreling with Popes. Nobody is surprised at what those wild English do, anyway.

I took a special interest in Gervaise's preparations for the disputation. I thought that, with a carefully chosen set of propositions, we might just survive the exercise without disaster. We settled on an innocuous thesis concerning the applicability of Aristotelian ethics to civil and religious law. It had been done before. "Remember," I told him, "you're a lawyer now, not a metaphysician. The clerks who come to hear you dispute won't give two farts for your passionate quest for truth. Just present the issues, define the alternatives, and support your conclusions. It's as simple as that."

But nothing was ever simple for Gervaise. Give him an idea and he'd worry it limp—tear it open and paw over its innards like one of those damned wolves. He began his lecture by quoting Honorius of Autun (a safe enough starting point): "Man's exile is ignorance; his home is knowledge." In exile, Gervaise observed, men are often captured and enslaved, while in their homeland they may be free men, and beneath their own roofs may reign supreme. Yet in what does human freedom consist? He then launched into an extended and preposterous analogy in which he compared the voyage of the soul to a game of chess. The object of the game, Gervaise informed his baffled audience, was to entrap the opponent's king by limiting progressively the opponent's freedom to move his pieces about the board. At the beginning of the game, each player enjoyed an infinite number of choices. But with each freely chosen move, each player decreased by one an option of his own and perhaps as many as several options for his opponent. Gervaise had worked out a mathematical formula to demonstrate the rapid diminution of free choice for both sides, so that as the end of the game drew near the players realized that their fates had been determined by the sum total of those choices already made.

So it is, Gervaise contended, for all men. Only by foreseeing the ultimate consequence of all his decisions, and by foretelling the decisions of his opponent (what opponent? I wondered uneasily), can a man choose wisely and freely. Yet freedom adheres only to the act itself and not to one's life as a whole. Gervaise even went so far as to portray Our Lord as a chess player, obliged by the logic of His glorious ministry to accept crucifixion as the inevitable consequence of all His previous decisions. "The law," he concluded—and God help me if I knew what any of this had to do with Aristotle!—"is thus not the creation of kings or magistrates; it is not made by prelates or Popes, nor is it handed down to us from the stars. Each man is a lawgiver unto himself, his own magistrate and, ultimately, his own executioner."

It was a most incredible performance. The audience was outraged at such nonsense. Gervaise was laughed from the hall and he—the madman!—fled amid the roar of derision with a sly smile on his lips, as if in thus sacrificing his ambitions he had somehow proven his points. So it is with truth-seekers. They are ready enough to burn at the stake, so long as they are allowed to carry the wood, build the fire and light it themselves.

After this debacle, there was no hope of a degree. But as long as he was leaving France and would henceforth be the English prelates' problem, the bishop was willing enough to confer holy orders upon Gervaise. He had already passed through minor orders at Welles-ford, but was still reluctant to enter the priest-hood—as well he might have been. I prevailed upon him, since I knew only benefit of clergy could save such a head as his from the block. Besides, I hoped the office would effect a change in him. I've seen many a rake and rebel settle down to embrace their duties once the consecrating hands have been laid on them.

Within a month of the disputation, Gervaise was or-dained. I escorted him to Calais and saw him safely put on board the boat, my letter to Becket tucked inside his garments. Well, Eadmer, I thought, as the boat set sail under a brisk east wind, what England has given us we are glad to pay back with interest. I noticed that the evening sky was full of small white and gold clouds, fleeing westward across the channel, as if a host of angels (or demons) meant to accompany Gervaise to his homeland.

Things were frightfully dull in Paris for a year or two without the boy's questions to provoke me. But eventually I learned once again not to expect too much of my students. Life is kind to a teacher, by and large, when he has only dullards to contend with.

6

A Theory

Dr. Dilbey sat up abruptly. He had thought of some-thing—a brilliant alternative, a lucid refutation, an ulti-mate consequence. But no; he had simply remembered the tea which his wife had brought to the study some time ago. He poured a cup for me and a cup for him-self, then sagged back into his deep armchair, relit his pipe and resumed his contemplation of the glowing coals.

The March afternoon lay white and wet and silent outside the doctor's study. Water dripped from eaves to brick walkway, lay in bright pools around the thorny stumps of the doctor's rose garden. Half moons of steam coated each pane of glass in the French doors. Though it was getting dark, Dr. Dilbey had not yet thought to turn on the lights. I took a sip of cold tea and waited for my eminent colleague to conclude his ruminations. The only man in the College who could take a genuine and informed interest in my work, Dr. Dilbey was much given to metaphysical speculation. Together we spun fine webs of reason across the universe, dangled suns and stars by the fragile thread of logic, harnessed whole galaxies to the service of our first principles—and then held our breath lest the whole delicate structure should come crashing down about our ears.

Now, every proposition in religion and philosophy seemed equally frivolous to me, but these were afternoons to be cherished in their own way. We did not have such afternoons in America; we would not have known what to do with them, would have grown impatient, bored, anxious. We would have skipped altogether the most exquisite part of such discussions—the long silences, the profound pauses, the deep dreamy quietude of mute reflection, during which I gazed upon the silver teapot glinting firelight beside Dr. Dilbey's chair. By half closing my eyes, I could enlarge that kernel of silver fire until it seemed a gigantic star burning in the utter darkness and emptiness of space—a God-star feeding the All, a gem blazing in the navel of the infinite. The good doctor and I stoked that blaze and kept it alive. We fed it words, concepts, theories—anything to nourish its flame—for what else was there, really, in the darkness outside this ring of enchanted brightness?

"Geoffrey Gervaise," Dr. Dilbey said, startling me from my reverie. He repeated the name solemnly, as if it were an incantation. "So you think, Fairchild, that you have identified the author of the Westchurch poem as Geoffrey Gervaise?"

I was sure of it, but I said only, "The evidence *is* persuasive, wouldn't you say?"

Dr. Dilbey held back his judgment of the evidence. "And this Gervaise, you say, was burned at the stake?"

"In 1175. I found an ancient letter in the British Museum. It's addressed to Henry II and written by a deputy who was sent to Creypool Abbey to investigate a rumored execution for witchcraft. Apparently the local people took matters into their own hands before the king's justice could be invoked. I'm sure that would ordinarily have angered Henry, but in this case the deputy writes as if he believes his lord will be relieved to learn that the matter is over and done with. One possible reason for Henry's willingness to overlook that violation of due process was that Gervaise had been a protégé of the recently murdered Becket."

"And were there other reasons, do you suppose?"

"Gervaise had been a fugitive for nearly ten years. We know he left the court in 1165, after Becket was exiled to France. I think I have him spotted as a village priest in Wendlebury—which is fairly near Westchurch Hall, as it turns out—for a short time. Then he drops out of sight—no reference to him at all in any of the records I've searched. However, about 1168 we find reports of a 'mad priest' roaming England, from monastery to monastery, stirring the monks to religious fervor, reviling the nobles, sowing seeds of rebellion among the serfs. . . . He is said to be a sorcerer in league with Satan, yet is also said to be a good and holy man who champions the oppressed and converts sinners. If this is our man, you can see why Henry was willing to overlook certain irregularities in his prosecution for witchcraft."

"Hmm. Yes. Henry always had his troubles with the Church. But I've always thought there were no witchcraft trials in England until the reign of King John."

"No doubt there were a good many impromptu executions which were never recorded," I said. "This one is embedded in a sheaf of legal correspondence where it could easily be missed, and it's a very guarded reference. Nonetheless, we do know there was considerable interest in sorcery in twelfth-century England. It's frequently difficult to tell the necromancers from the men of science and their primitive experiments."

"Yes," Dr. Dilbey said, "and of course it must be assumed that certain Druidic customs and rituals survived, especially among the country folk. . . . But tell me, Fairchild, isn't the twelfth century too early for this manuscript?"

I briefly explained to Dr. Dilbey the basis on which I was prepared to challenge Throcknagle's dating of the manuscript. I mentioned certain phonetic and syntactical survivals of Old English, the evidence of an early northern dialect, the many obscure references in the poem to twelfth-century personages and events. I could tell that Dr. Dilbey was impressed by the thoroughness of my research.

"So far as I can see," he said, "it's the early dating of the poem which constitutes your major discovery, Fairchild. And it is an astounding one. Of course, you'll have to convince the skeptics who swear by their Throcknagle that this really is a significant and substantial work of art. Throcknagle was rather hard on your poet, you know."

Throcknagle, I thought, was an ass. But what I said was: "I think I can do that, once I get back to the manuscript. I'm anxious to read it again in the light of the possibility"—I had nearly said "the fact," but caught myself in time—"that Gervaise is the poet. I think it's going to make a lot more sense than anyone ever suspected it could. His execution for witchcraft is a case in point. Then there are the other things we know about him, or can reasonably surmise: his Saxon-Norman parentage—noble on his father's side, peasantry on his mother's—his early education in a Yorkshire monastery, his years in Paris and at the court of Henry II, his association with Becket, his crusade or whatever it was across England, his presumed knowledge of law, philosophy, the classical and Islamic philosophers, his probable influence by the Albigensians and the cult of courtly love, his interest in science, astrology, chess—"

"Chess?" Dr. Dilbey said. "I say, you really ought to

have a look at my monograph on the *Quaedam Moralitas de Scaccario.*"

"I have. It was most helpful, especially your notes on the rules of medieval chess. Chess is a controlling metaphor throughout the poem, and Gervaise was reputed to be a master at the game; his skill is mentioned by Peter of Blois, among others. It may well have endeared him to Becket, who is also said to have been an excellent player. In the poem, several games of chess seem to be progressing simultaneously and are used on a variety of allegorical levels: the chess game between two rival knights, the game between a master and his pupil, the game between the king and his minister (possibly Henry and Becket), the game between the courtly lover and his mistress (an elaborate seduction ritual which one finds often enough in the literature of the period)—and finally, what seems to be a game between good and evil, or possibly Christ and Satan. It's at this point that the poem becomes exceedingly obscure, and there are all sorts of references to the stars and the signs of the zodiac which I haven't begun to sort out."

"Fascinating," Dr. Dilbey said. "And amazing that no one's gotten into all this before. Tell me—you've read Gervaise's Latin treatise?"

"It's intolerably dull. The work of a young scholar trying to impress his mentors at court—chiefly Becket and John of Salisbury. Something extraordinary must have happened to Gervaise once he gave up his ambitions of rising in the Church. He became a mystic, a dreamer, a student of the occult. Celtic mythology enters into it somehow, and various Gnostic and Manichean doctrines. The effort to reconcile such stuff with his Christian perspective may have cost Gervaise his sanity, but it made a poet of him—a poet, if not of Shakespeare's stature, well then, say, of Christopher Marlowe's."

"Interesting that you chose another doomed poet, Fairchild. Perhaps we should have a special category for those poets whose personal misfortunes render their work all the more poignant to us. The list would be a long one. But really, it is too soon to claim any special niche for this particular poet. Your work, I should say, has just begun."

"Indeed, and now it's come screeching to a halt, thanks to the closing of the Special Collections."

Dr. Dilbey mused briefly. "I know how hard it must be for you, and yet I think you can afford to have a little patience with us. To have discovered, this early in your career, material which could keep you well occupied, oh, for a lifetime, if you really go into it as you should—it's a fantastic stroke of luck. It makes me sorry I didn't pay more attention to the Westchurch manuscripts myself."

"You know, Doctor, that brings to mind a question—if it isn't too presumptuous. . . . I've often wondered why you never took an interest in those manuscripts. As a fellow of the College, you've had them at your disposal for many years."

"I did set out to do something with them shortly after I came to Duke's. I expected to make quite a good thing of them, but—I don't know how to explain it—as soon as I got into them I experienced a strange oppression and sense of dread. It was quite disturbing. I'd had a sort of nervous breakdown after the war, and it was weak and irrational of me, I'm sure, but finally I just couldn't bring myself to work on the Westchurch manuscripts. There they sat, waiting for someone of your energy and imagination to tie into them. . . . But tell me, have you never experienced anything similar to my distress while working on those manuscripts?"

"No," I said with a smile. "On the contrary, the manuscripts have fascinated me from the start. But old Throcknagle may have had some of your feelings. He certainly did an uncharacteristically sloppy job on his monograph, and I did hear, from one of his former students, that in his later years he couldn't bear to discuss the Westchurch manuscripts at all."

Dr. Dilbey put another match to his pipe. "Actually, there was another chap. I was hesitant to mention him earlier, but now that you've fully committed yourself to this project, I think I should tell you about poor young Jameson."

"Poor young Jameson?"

"He was a research student at Queen's back about 1950. Brilliant young chap; most promising. He received permission from the fellows to pursue a dissertation topic involving the Westchurch collection. For months he virtually lived in the library. The strain of those long hours finally broke him, I'm afraid. He was apprehended while attempting to set the library on fire. Some of the petrol he'd splashed about got on his clothes, and the only casualty was poor Jameson himself, whose burns proved fatal."

"And his dissertation?"

"It was never written—though a quantity of ashes found in his room at Queen's may have been a first draft. You see, Fairchild, it would be wise to proceed with caution. A madman wrote that poem, and madness may sometimes prove a communicable disease."

I gave Dr. Dilbey's words considerable thought, then said: "Tell me, Doctor—has it ever struck you that the Westchurch manuscripts have had a particularly bloody history?"

"I'm sure there's blood on everything in England—everything older than a couple of centuries, at any rate. But whose blood were you thinking of, in particular?"

"Gervaise himself, for openers—if I can prove he was both the author of the poem and the mad priest whom the people of Creypool put to the stake in 1175. Then there's Lord Peter Brindley, sixteenth Earl of Westchurch and reputed discoverer of the manuscripts, who was beheaded for treason and blasphemy in 1649. Next we have Gerald Brice, the fellow commoner who donated the manuscripts to the College, and who was said to have been a former slave trader with an interest in witchcraft. He disappeared in France on the eve of the Revolution. After which those manuscripts gathered dust in the College library for nearly two hundred years. We can dismiss the various reports of ghostly occurrences in the College during that period, but the fact remains that the only scholars to take an interest in those manuscripts—Throcknagle, yourself, and this young Jameson you've just told me about—all found them, as we might say, too hot to handle. And now that I've come along, and have for some reason proven immune to the spell these papers seem to cast, two deaths have occurred within days of each other and my work has been brought to an abrupt halt just as I've reached the threshold of discovery."

Dr. Dilbey sat up. "Two deaths, Fairchild? I assume you're referring to Dr. Greggs' unfortunate accident as one, but who is the other victim?"

"You've heard of the Reverend Samuel Stemp?"

"Once the curator of the Westchurch Museum and a west-country antiquarian of some standing, I believe."

"Also, a friend of our late Dr. Greggs. And recently killed in another freak accident. I talked to Stemp's widow in London last week. She gave me his pamphlet on the Earl of Westchurch, in which I found a few of Stemp's notes toward a future revision. Everything else—all of Stemp's papers, so far as I could tell—was purchased from his widow by a person named Simon Regis. He claimed to be a dealer in rare books, but his shop turned out to be an empty warehouse, and the London Booksellers' Association says they've never heard of him."

"And these papers—they could prove important?"

"Extremely. Stemp had been all over England gathering new information on the earl. He may have had some clue as to what the earl himself was searching for when he collected those manuscripts. On the notes I have, Stemp alludes to Creypool Abbey and lists several dates on which the earl may have been there—apparently armed with a telescope he purchased in Italy. On top of all that, I found the name 'G. Gervaise' and the date of his death lightly penciled on the back flyleaf of Stemp's book. It was after that discovery that I began my search for Gervaise through the records of the British Museum."

Dr. Dilbey pondered the glowing coals in his hearth, the room now in almost total darkness. "And what does it all add up to, do you suppose?"

"My best guess at the moment, Doctor, is that both Stemp and the Earl of Westchurch knew that Gervaise was the author of the poem. They knew other things about him, apparently, which I don't, and which enabled them to interpret the poem in ways which are still beyond me. For some reason, that information proved dangerous to Stemp. I'm half persuaded, you see, that neither Dr. Greggs nor the Reverend Stemp died an accidental death. Someone—or possibly some group of people—seems determined to make sure that the secrets of the Westchurch manuscripts remain secret."

Dr. Dilbey relit his pipe, his match revealing for a moment a demonic caricature of his gentle scholar's face. "Really, Fairchild, this is all terribly speculative. If you do have evidence of murder, you should certainly inform the police."

"At this point I'm still just groping—trying to account for what is certainly an intriguing chain of events, wouldn't you say?"

"Intriguing, yes. Conclusive, no. I should be especially careful in this matter to avoid any imaginative theories or hasty conclusions. Things often have a way of looking more coherent than they are, especially if we are overly eager to posit the intervention of—hmm—supernatural agencies—as an explanation. That, I daresay, is the classic error of the superstitious mind. You're not a superstitious man, are you, Fairchild?"

"I never thought I was. I've never been interested in the occult, or in what are commonly called 'mystical experiences.' But this whole business has got me wondering, Dr. Dilbey, and my imagination has been tremendously stirred by this magnificent poem."

"I expect it has. Which is all to the good, provided you are able to keep your feet on the ground. I'd be the last man in the College to question the integrity of your work. If you have reason to believe you may be in some personal danger, you should certainly go to the police, but I think you yourself have quite enough detective work to do, simply in regard to the authorship and meaning of the poem, without taking on the investigation of what may well turn out to be imaginary mysteries."

"I quite agree, Doctor. And I do hope the College will let me return to work on the manuscripts as soon as possible."

"Yes; well, I have talked to the Master, Fairchild. It's a terribly difficult matter. Still, I should think by next term—"

"But that will leave only two months before I exhaust my grant!"

"The College might be able to provide you with a small stipend for the summer," Dr. Dilbey said. "We may even be able to arrange something to keep you here next year—that is, if your research turns out as well as it now seems it will. I've been thinking, Fairchild: this may be a bit premature, but—provided things could be worked out, and all the fellows approve—would you be interested in staying on in Cambridge . . . permanently? As a fellow of the College, I mean?"

I sat back in my chair, glad the room was too dark for Dr. Dilbey to see the grin which had spread across my face. I had never dared to hope, all these months that I'd been learning and aping the ways of the Cambridge scholar and gentleman, that I could qualify for inclusion in such an exclusive club.

"Why, yes," I said cautiously. "I think I could be persuaded to stay on—if I was really wanted, that is."

"I've been much impressed with your work," Dr. Dilbey said, "and it's time we got some new blood in the College. Especially in the arts. These damned scientists have made a virtual laboratory of the place! I intend to see what I can do."

And at that moment—as if it had only been waiting for Dr. Dilbey's modest proposal—a clock somewhere in the house struck the first of five melodious chimes.

"Goodness me—we seem to have quite used up our afternoon," Dr. Dilbey said. "I'll see what can be done, Fairchild . . . on all counts, you know—on all counts."

"Thank you, Doctor," I said, rising from my chair. "And thanks for your time. I really appreciate the interest you've taken in my work."

We groped our way across the dark room and stepped into an even darker and draftier hallway. "By the bye," Dr. Dilbey said. "Do you have any plans for the vac?"

"If there's no hope of getting back to the manuscripts before next term—"

"None whatsoever, I'm afraid. Still, there are a few possibilities you might look into. Do you know Professor Trevor-Finch?"

I had not forgotten the warden of Bromley House, nor his inexplicable scream on the night when I myself seemed to have brushed against something beyond comprehension. "Isn't he a physicist?" I asked Dr. Dilbey.

"Theoretical physics. They say he's done extraordinary things with the quantum theory—not that I understand any of that. His family home is somewhere on the Norfolk coast, not far from Creypool Abbey. He's quite a good sort, and might be willing to show you around. I need scarcely add that he's an important man in the College—our next Master, some people say. It wouldn't hurt at all to make a friend of Trevor-Finch."

"Then I'll certainly try," I said. "But I understand he dislikes Americans."

"Not at all. He is frightfully keen on politics, and no doubt he disapproves of your country's foreign policy—we nearly all do, you know. But he often befriends American scholars—in order to argue politics with them. You do have political convictions you could argue for, don't you?"

"Only very ordinary ones, I'm afraid, but perhaps they'll interest the professor."

"Give it a try," Dr. Dilbey said. "He's one of those we'll have to win over—and it will do you good to take a bit of a holiday, in any case."

He held the door open for me as I got into my raincoat. By the streetlight at the corner, I saw sheets of rain streaming across the early winter darkness.

"Thanks again, Doctor—and please thank your wife for the tea."

"Think nothing of it, Fairchild. Give me a ring next

term and we'll set up another conference. I'm fascinated by your discoveries."

As I stepped out, and just before Dr. Dilbey shut the door, I heard a sudden outburst of children's voices somewhere in the house. I had nearly forgotten that Dr. Dilbey was a family man. His large brood was always out of sight and soundless whenever we had our consultations. Apparently his wife had taken the lid off a moment too soon, and it struck me as a poignant revelation: children kept from play while scholars deliberated their esoteric theories. Bicycling back to the College, I tried to imagine the family life of my colleague. Would the great gray scholar suffer his little children to come to him, to sit on his knee and play with his nose and glasses? Would he let them scatter stars and planets at his feet? The incongruity of the vision sustained me on the long, wet trek across town.

7

A Man of Science

I had seen him strolling in the fellows' garden from time to time and dining at high table; we had even nodded to one another on occasion and exchanged a few tentative smiles; but my first conversation with Professor Kenneth Trevor-Finch took place at a College sherry party a few days prior to the close of the winter term.

"So you're the young American who's come to work on the Westchurch manuscripts," he said, as we found ourselves facing one another over the sherry decanter. "David Fairchild, isn't it?"

I confirmed that it was.

Trevor-Finch poured sherry for us both, handed me mine and led the way, with some vague indication that

I might follow, to a quiet corner of the room. We were in the Master's lodge, with its charming view of the Old Court, chapel spires bathed in the mellow light of a setting sun. A few students were heading toward the archway that led to the dining hall. Doves banked in the amber rectangle of sky and settled on the chapel eaves. Trevor-Finch scowled at the placid scene as if calculating the number of atomic particles employed in its manufacture.

"How are you liking Cambridge, Fairchild? Bit of change from all that 'rah-rah sis-boom-bah' business you have over in America, I expect."

I told the professor that I found the life and style of Cambridge very much to my liking.

"Hmm. Everyone does, you know. Yanks especially. Yet it doesn't seem to have done much good, does it?"

"I'm not sure I understand you," I said, in that careful voice that always made me feel as if I were wagging my mongrel American tail.

The professor chuckled. He was a tall, round-shouldered, pipe-puffing don of middle age whose quick, nervous eyes (I am almost inclined to call them "shifty") inspired a particular uneasiness. "What I mean to say is, for all our missionary efforts and all our hospitality to your countrymen—which I heartily approve, by the way—we haven't had much success in civilizing you Americans, now, have we?"

I looked closely at the professor's long face, his pale eyes and extended upper lip. I couldn't tell if he was quite serious; perhaps I was being tested.

"I'm sure you find much to disapprove of in my country," I said, "and no doubt I would agree with most of your criticisms. But we have been civilized for several centuries."

Professor Trevor-Finch laughed in my face. "America—the great barbarian bully of the world—civilized? Tell me, has there been any remorse or second thoughts in your country about Hiroshima, let us say?"

"Hiroshima?"

"Surely you recall what your government did to Japan in the Second World War—incidentally establishing the potential for a world-wide nuclear holocaust."

"I believe most Americans felt at the time that we had to drop the bomb in order to shorten the war," I said, naïvely supposing that most Englishmen remembered whose side we'd been on.

"Had to!" Trevor-Finch blustered. "The poor Nips were trying to arrange a treaty at the very moment the bomb went off. They were down, they were beaten, they simply wanted to get out of the whole affair with their national pride intact—which was precisely what your government refused to allow them. Have you ever heard what Rome did to Carthage? They not only sacked the city, slaughtered the inhabitants and burned all its buildings; they also poured salt on the ground so that nothing would ever grow there again. That's the kind of barbarism I'm talking about, Fairchild. Savagery!"

"I think all the Allies, including England, had agreed to accept only unconditional surrender from the Axis," I said.

"Tommyrot," Trevor-Finch replied. "No one but an American President could've ordered that bomb dropped on those innocent civilians. Besides, Churchill was a barbarian too. More of a Yank than a proper Englishman. His mother was an American."

I was beginning to see why the professor was such a feared debater in Cambridge political circles. Accepting defeat in one arena, I tried to engage him in another. "My field is medieval literature, Professor, not contemporary affairs. There was plenty of barbarism in this country, too, in ages past."

"Of course, but at least we had no atomic bombs to throw at one another in those days, or I'm sure there'd be very little England left for you to putter about in. I'm a physicist, mind, but I've often thought it a pity that America developed a technology before it had taken the time or trouble to produce a civilization capable of handling the fruits of modern science."

He chuckled again and I sensed that I had just been

treated to one of his favorite aphorisms. "Have you ever been to America, Professor?" I asked him.

"Briefly, a couple of times. Couldn't wait to get back to England. Same thing happens whenever I go on the Continent. The French are a decent people, by and large, but those Germans . . . ! The majority of your countrymen are of German extraction, I believe."

"So, I believe," I said quickly, "are the majority of yours."

"Oh, if you go back *that* far," Trevor-Finch said, with a look of surprise in his pale eyes. "But we've had so much longer, you see, to mitigate the Teutonic strain, which has moreover been diluted by various infusions—"

"The Normans," I said, "were originally Vikings—another Germanic tribe. As were the Danes, the Picts, the Franks, the Saxons, the Scots. In fact, if you go back far enough, all the peoples of Europe have a common ancestry. They were all barbarians at one time, Professor. They collected heads as trophies of war. They believed in demons, goblins, fairies, werewolves, vampires, witches. . . . They tortured innocent people and sometimes even burned them alive."

Trevor-Finch pulled back as if I'd accused him personally of such atrocities. "I'm quite aware that man has only recently crawled out of the swamp, as it were. My point is simply that we in England, thank heavens, have gone beyond all that."

"I hope so," I said, angrier than I quite realized at the time. "And yet I wouldn't call those silly prejudices of yours a particularly enlightened response to the problems of the world."

Professor Trevor-Finch turned so red in the face that I was afraid I'd never get an invitation to Creypool now. But in the next moment he laughed and said, "Good show, Fairchild! You put up a spirited defense, for a political ingénue! I'm not quite the chauvinist that I seem—though I must admit I have very little love for the Germans. Few of us in England who remember the last war do. But we shall have to go into all this at greater length some other time. Tell me, how are you getting on with your research? Have you managed to make any sense out of all that medieval gibberish?"

I decided that the professor was one of those individuals who couldn't help being offensive. "I was beginning to catch hold of a few things," I told him, "when I was denied access to the Special Collections. I'm anxious to get back to work, since I'm very close, I think, to some important discoveries."

"Really! But I understood that most of that material is impossible nonsense, even for a specialist."

"It has always seemed that way, but I'm in possession now of certain facts which may enable me to crack the code."

Trevor-Finch raised his eyebrows. "So it's written in code, is it?" He chuckled as he refilled his pipe. "A bloody code, hey?"

"Are you at all interested in that sort of thing?" I asked, the American tail wagging furiously now.

The professor watched a bit of pipe smoke curl away from the window. "As a matter of fact, codes *are* my special line. The codes of nature, Fairchild—the secret messages of the universe, which we are only now beginning to decipher. As for those manuscripts the College is so bloody proud of—no, I can't say I care about what they have to tell us, except for a certain geographical coincidence. My family is a very old one, you see, and has lived for centuries on the Norfolk coast. There are the ruins of an old monastery nearby, which you may have heard of."

"Creypool Abbey," I said. "I've been wanting to visit it for some time now."

Trevor-Finch's gray irises swiveled beneath droopy lids to focus sharply on me. "You have! Then I suspect you've heard of the insane monk who's supposed to have taken refuge there—back in the twelfth century, I believe it was."

"Geoffrey Gervaise," I said, and wondered if the professor had actually flinched at the mention of the name. "I'm particularly interested in him. I've been toying with the possibility that he may be one of the authors of the Westchurch manuscripts."

Trevor-Finch seemed at first not to react. He stared so fixedly at my collar that I began to wonder what he saw there. Finally, he drew himself up, sipped his sherry and made a face highly critical of the Master's cellar. "In that case, Fairchild, you certainly should visit the abbey. There's not much left to see, I'm afraid, but the village parson is something of an authority on our local legends. I suppose you know this Gervaise—was that his name?—was executed for witchcraft?"

"Burned at the stake," I said. "The first instance on record in the Christian era—but I'm surprised you've heard about that, Professor."

Trevor-Finch smiled to himself as he recalled our earlier exchange. "I take a passing interest in such matters, when they're close to home. We may have inaugurated the practice of burning witches, but I assure you we gave it up a long time ago. The abbey is supposed to be haunted, though."

"By Gervaise?"

"I don't know if he's ever told anyone just who he is," the professor said. "A tall, gaunt figure in a monk's robe and cowl is how he's usually been described. The common folk are dreadfully superstitious, and that goose of a parson doesn't help matters. Nevertheless, you ought to have a look at the place while you're in England. I'm sure it can be arranged—perhaps during the upcoming vac, if you've no other plans."

"I'd like that very much," I said. "I've no plans at all."

"Let's get you down for several days, then, shall we? I'll be there next week to visit Mama"—he pronounced the word in the Victorian fashion, with the stress on the second syllable—"and we should be happy to entertain you. There's a good deal to see in the area, and of course we shall want to continue our debate on the existence of an American civilization. I do enjoy getting the other chap's point of view, even when it's incredibly naïve."

71

"I can be very stubborn," I promised him.

"So much the better. Your visit has the makings of an interesting experiment."

"Experiment?"

The professor's nervous eyes nipped at my neck, my shoulder, and leapt across the room. "Merely a scientific turn of phrase, Fairchild. I shan't subject you to anything too drastic. Perhaps a mere"—he chuckled almost fiendishly—"a mere vivisection of your American ideals."

"Oh, well, in that case," I said, and laughed the matter away, for it seemed that when it came to ideals, I really had nothing to lose.

That night Colin Douglas and I played squash at the College courts on the outskirts of town. No mention was made of Yvetta throughout three vigorous games, though I thought that Colin (always an athletic sadist) pushed me even more unmercifully than usual. He had youth, strength, talent and clean living on his side, where I had only guile and spite to keep me in the game. I was dripping sweat, my breath still a series of gasps, as we had our lemon squeeze in the gallery above the courts.

"You've not been playing, David," Colin said. "You really shouldn't let yourself get out of condition. You're reaching an age where you can't afford to remain sedentary."

"Or to go up against a fanatic like you," I gasped. "I was never much of a physical sort at all, until you took me in hand."

"That's the trouble with the academic life in America," Colin said. "It has no balance, no vigor, no physical dimension whatsoever. No wonder American scholars are such a sorry lot."

Colin had a right to criticize America; he'd been born there, but his parents had had the money, and the good sense, to get him into an English public school when he was still relatively unspoiled by an American education. His "firsts" at "dear old Tunbridge," as he called it, had opened the doors of Oxford, and his undergraduate triumphs there had got him into the London School of Economics. His London Ph.D. had led to his fellowship at Cambridge, and it was only a matter of time until he made senior fellow, or left academic life for an excellent career in government or business.

I appreciated Colin's patronage (so much more useful, if less appealing, than poor Archie's) and enjoyed studying such an exemplar at close range, but it was difficult to like a man whose advantages in life so exceeded mine in every way. Sometimes I couldn't help wondering on the court how that aristocratic sneer of his would look forming itself around a mouthful of broken teeth.

"I've been meaning to ask you," Colin said, as we gathered up our gear for the bike ride back to the College. "Whatever became of that little creature you carried off to London—that Austrian bird?"

"Yvetta and I had several pleasant days together," I said, "and then she decided to return to Vienna. I think she was rather disappointed in England—and in you, Colin."

"So that's how it was, was it? I'm not sorry you took her off my hands, David. She was becoming rather an embarrassment over here. Continental girls seldom get on well in England. They expect entirely too much of us."

"All Yvetta expected," I said, "was for one or the other of us to deal honestly with her. We just weren't capable of that, Colin."

"Deal honestly with her? Good heavens, I never promised her anything, I'm sure of that. What did she tell you about me, anyway?"

"That you're afraid of women. That you can't take them seriously. That you're not quite complete as a man, and that you'll always wind up hurting people until you are." I didn't add that Yvetta had applied those criticisms to me, as well.

"Hmm. That was rather hard, wasn't it? Still, I suppose it's fair enough. One doesn't want to get too serious about a girl like that. Poor little twit!"

I decided to cap the conversation with a line from

Henry James I'd always admired. "She would have appreciated," I said, "our esteem." But the reference rang no bells for Colin Douglas.

Back in my room by eleven, I got into a bathrobe, gathered up my soap, deodorant, shaving supplies and shampoo, and went across the courtyard for that Spartan exercise which was still an ordeal for me—the College shower.

These showers had been added to the College in recent times and, to spare the ancient walls and preserve architectural authenticity, had been built underground, just off the lane that connected the Old Court to a narrow side street of the town. You passed through a gloomy archway, followed the lane beside a churchyard full of crumbling tombstones, descended a flight of unlighted stairs, and came out into the large, cold, damp, frequently filthy and vile-smelling dungeon that served the sanitary needs of the entire College.

None of the showers were in use at this late hour. I turned on a spigot and slipped into the rush of hot water. Enveloped in steam and dripping suds, I recalled what a pleasant time Yvetta and I had had one afternoon in our hotel bathtub. How sweetly her soapy breasts had filled my palm, how lovely her white tummy was as it broke the water! I resisted the urge to procure prompt relief from the past week of celibacy and left the dungeon some little time later, clean of body but not yet entirely pure of mind, totally unprepared for the sudden sensation of dread that swept over me as I stepped out into the lane.

I stood quite still, my skin giving off steam in the night air, and in the dim light of the lane I probed the shadows of the little churchyard across the way. There was nothing there to account for my tingling scalp and sprinting pulse, yet my sense of alarm did not lessen. If anything, it became more intense as I watched and listened, feeling once again my helplessness and vulnerability in a world suddenly bristling with invisible menace.

Then, turning toward the archway that led to the

74

Old Court, I saw that this time there might indeed be something to validate my fright—for within the heavy shadows of the archway another shadow, of more or less human shape, awaited my approach. Whether it meant to speak, to attack or simply to reveal itself, I recognized its presence as a threat. It was not human, I knew that at once. But what on earth was it? The air reeked of spiritual contamination, of some screaming infamy from ages past, of which the thing in the shadows had been either witness, victim or agent. Ancient, ugly, pitiful and perverse, yet not without a sort of quaint dignity, the thing stood there waiting for me as if it knew who I was—as if we had unfinished business between us.

Oh, God, I prayed, or perhaps protested; there must be some mistake! I'm not the sort of man who sees visions. Could I be misreading some harmless inanimate object propped against the wall? Was someone trying to play a trick on me? Dressed only in robe and slippers, I couldn't retreat down the lane and around the corner to the busy street that passed the main gate. Nor could I return to the showers, for the thing could easily corner me there. The graveyard was bordered by an iron fence which, even if I could clear it, would leave me trapped between fence and church, the back door of which was surely locked. No, there was nowhere to go but straight ahead, and nothing to do but meet the phantom head on.

Still, I hesitated, drawing back from what gradually defined itself to me as a spiritual sodomizing. Had the shadow actually taken on the shape of a monk's robe and cowl, or was I interpreting too freely its fluid ambiguity? I saw how easy it was to lose faith in one's senses, one's reason, and to suffer a sudden paralysis of the will. I might have stood there forever—or throughout the night, at least—quite stymied by so unexpected and unwonted a salutation from the void, if the presence had not suddenly disintegrated. At first I couldn't guess what good angel had provided my deliverance; and then I heard footsteps coming up the lane behind me—brisk, purposeful, yet unhurried footsteps, accompanied by the sound of a man trying without much success to whistle a strain from a Bach concerto. I recognized Professor Trevor-Finch.

"What—Fairchild, is that you? You'll catch your death of cold haunting this alleyway. Is something the matter?"

"Good evening, Professor. I was just coming from the showers when I"—my glance rose above the steep, dormered rooftops of the College—"when I noticed how bright the stars are tonight."

Trevor-Finch looked up. "My word, yes—an uncommonly fine display for this time of year. Are you interested in the stars? If so, I have something down at my place you should find quite fascinating."

We were proceeding together through the shadowed archway, where I saw nothing which could explain my vision of a few moments previous. "And what's that, Professor?" I asked.

"I'll save it for a surprise," Trevor-Finch said. "I may have several little surprises worked up for your visit. This your staircase, then? Better run along up. It's no sort of night to be out stargazing in a robe."

As I entered the stairway, I heard him mutter—surely he meant for me to hear—"An odd lot, these Yanks!"

8

Rogue's Night Out

"So you're off to Norfolk to visit Trevor-Finch," Archie Cavendish said over his last spoonful of soup. "When do you leave?"

"Tomorrow morning," I said, "on the nine forty-five train."

"Hmm. Then I expect I won't be seeing you again.

Unless you can manage to make a short stay of it. I'll be leaving myself before the vac is over."

"I'm sorry to hear it," I said. "I'll miss you."

Archie glanced down the table, then said in a low voice, "You'll be the only one. I've had the distinct feeling for several weeks now that I'm the only mourner at my own wake."

The atmosphere in Hall that night did rather resemble a wake. Most of the undergraduates had already "gone down," as leaving the University is so aptly termed, and we were a lonely little group at High Table. Silent waiters attended to our needs like spirits in bondage to our dark arts, and chandeliers blossomed faintly above our heads. The entire College seemed to sigh over visions of its vanished glory.

"Quite an exciting time you'll have of it, I'm sure," Archie said. "If you're a good boy, Finchie may show you his tower laboratory. He listens to the stars, you know. Radio astronomy is one of his many hobbies. Your archetypal Renaissance man, old Finchie, with a dabbler's interest in just about everything—including young Americans."

Old Professor Haverhill roused himself from some glum colloquy with his soup, glared at Archie and tore several layers of mucus from around his vocal cords. "Professor Trevor-Finch," he said, "is a fine man, a brilliant mathematician and a credit to the College. You should consider yourself honored, Fairchild, to have received an invitation to his ancestral manor."

"He is rather an eccentric, though," said young Brian McMann, who was some sort of engineer. "I heard he had a difficult time of it during the war. The government had him doing weapons research and they sent him behind enemy lines to look at some German missile plans. He was taken prisoner and the Krauts quite put it to him."

"The war," intoned decrepit Professor Grimshaw, who was known to sport a glass eye and a permanent steel plate in his skull, "ruined all our lives."

Archie pulled a long face, but his blue eyes retained their leprechaun's twinkle. "I daresay you'll get your fill of quaint Anglo-Saxon attitudes at Abbotswold, as Finchie's 'ancestral manor' is called. But what are you doing tonight? I'm sure to be beastly company, with my own exile staring me in the face, but we might be able to get up a bit of fun."

"What did you have in mind?" I asked.

"Let's see. . . . No licentious foreign movies on this weekend, so the cinema's out. No parties to crash, either. The town's a bit of a bore during the vac. Oh, I say! Have you ever been to the dance hall?"

McMann dropped his fork. A bit of Yorkshire pudding sprang from his mouth as he released a burst of laughter. "Cavendish! Good Lord, you don't still go there, do you?"

Arche shrugged and grinned, redness rising to his temples. "Come, McMann—you were glad enough to tag along with me a few years ago, before we started dining at High Table. I don't see that it's so demeaning to fraternize with the townies. Besides, when a man's as depressed as I am, he'll stoop to anything."

"What," I asked, "is the dance hall, and what's so dreadful about it?"

"It's where you'll find all the working birds and their teddy bears," McMann said, "the farmers from the fens with manure on their shoes, all the wretched shopkeepers and their dreary, dismal 'intendeds.' You two will get your heads bashed in before the evening's over."

"Nonsense," Archie said. "It's a perfectly respectable establishment. A bit working class, I grant you, but one never knows what one might run into. What do you say, Fairchild—shall we give it a try?"

We set out for the dance hall as soon as Hall broke up. It turned out to be quite a walk, which took us far beyond the cluster of colleges to grim streets of row houses, factories, fish-and-chips shops and shabby pubs with motorcycles parked out in front. I had never seen this part of Cambridge before.

"Archie," I said as we walked along the narrow sidewalk, "what do you know about Sir Percy Wickham George?"

"A former owner of Bromley House, I believe."

"Yes, and one of the founders of the Society for Physical Research. Was he a Duke's man?"

"I don't think so. He may have taken some interest in the College, since we rather had the corner on uneasy spirits in those days."

"That's what I was wondering. Dean Singer told me that Sir Percy conducted a number of experiments. Were there any in the College proper, do you recall?"

"There may have been. Do you think some *ghost* bumped off Dr. Greggs and buggered your plan to become the world's leading medievalist?"

"Not exactly. But what would you say if I told you—"

"Hold up, lad. We mustn't let scholarship interfere with lechery, and there's the dance hall dead ahead. You be a good chap now and forget about your medieval poems, hum? Later on we can stop by my room for a nightcap. I have a book which might interest you."

We paid our shilling, entered the barnlike building and climbed a flight of broad carpeted stairs. I could hear music; there was an immense quantity of potted foliage in the outer lobby and a columned archway which gave upon a large, dark, high-ceilinged room where a revolving globe cast splotches of color upon the crowded dance floor and upon the rows of chairs along either wall, where maidens sat waiting for an invitation to dance. The bar was at the back, and on a stage hung with glistening curtains a dozen tuxedoed musicians produced a wistful imitation of American jazz.

I was amused and touched by the small-town hokum of it all: pale young ladies with empty eyes; nervous swains uncertain whether to approach or to gather in groups of their own sex to talk about football; balding, pudgy Don Giovannis slyly nuzzling their buxom, stout-legged Donna Annas. . . . I found the dance hall's desperate parody of gentility so crushingly reminiscent of the proms and sock hops of my youth that I couldn't help wondering if I had stumbled upon the common denominator of the Anglo-American soul. What snares of self-knowledge had Archie led me into?

"First things first," Archie said. "We must catch hold of the festive mood. To the bar, Fairchild!"

We each got a gin and tonic and took our place on the rim of the dance floor, where I observed that Englishmen seem to feel dancing ought to have some purpose beyond the public embracing of women who might not accept an embrace in private. His partner held at arms' length, the British male moves steadfastly around the dance floor's outer boundaries, as if determined to accomplish a certain number of laps before the music stops.

Archie stood very stiff and straight, a frightened light in his eyes as he surveyed the prospects. "Looks like rather slim pickings this evening. You can never tell about this place—sometimes a feast and sometimes a famine. Now, there's a rather nice . . . oh, she's with her steady, I see. What about . . . no; much too old, now that I get a good look at her. They ought to make some of these women show their birth certificates at the door. Is there anything here worth our while? Or should we shove off?"

"Archie," I said, "you didn't drag me here just to look at the girls and run away. They're not all repulsive. I'll ask one of them to dance if you're afraid. Pick one you like. I'll dance her around the race track a few times and turn her over to you."

Archie put a hand on my shoulder. "Would you, really? That would be damned decent of you. I always have a bit of trouble getting started at these things. Let's see—suppose you take a crack at that smashing little redhead over there for starters. I'd like to know if she's game."

"Archie, for God's sake, they're all game! That's why they're here."

"Yes, but they don't all like College men. They rather shy away from us. You'd better do what you can to disguise your American accent, too. There's been a good deal of anti-American feeling in Cambridge since that new air base went in."

"Just relax, Archie. I'll deliver the redhead to you in time for the next number."

I dodged fox-trotting couples as I crossed the dance floor, then presented myself to the little girl with red hair, pert nose and sharply defined breasts within a clinging satin blouse.

"Good evening, miss. May I have the pleasure?"

The redhead glanced around and, seeing nothing better, gave me an apprehensive smile and got to her feet. Soon we were making tracks around the dance floor with the best of them, for it was either move along or get run over.

"You're a Yank, aren't you?" she asked.

"Oh, no—Canadian," I told her. "We don't like the bloody Yanks any more than you do."

"At one of the Colleges, maybe?"

"No, I'm with an accounting firm down in London. Just up for the weekend because I heard what a swell place this was. You dance very nicely."

"Thank you," she said, and let me hold her a bit closer. Our thighs touched ever so lightly as we negotiated the turn before the bandstand. On the sidelines, Archie watched us with envious eyes. Was this what a first-class British education did to a man? But then, how did one explain Colin Douglas?

"I brought a chum up with me," I told the girl. "Do you have a friend here, by any chance?"

"Just my boyfriend," she said, and looked over my shoulder as if he might be sneaking up on us. "Well, he's sort of a boyfriend. I see him here a lot. He works in a garage and he thinks he's stuck on me."

"Can't say I blame him. My friend's sort of stuck on you too."

"Oh, yeah? Well, I can dance with whoever I like," she assured me. "Is that your friend over there, gawking at us?"

The band had entered its final chorus and we were nearing Archie's station. "Let me introduce you," I said. "He's very shy, but I know he's dying to dance with you. Then maybe you and I can have another dance later."

"All right," the girl said. "My name's Brenda."

The music stopped; I gave Brenda to Archie with a few words of introduction, and said I'd be at the bar. Archie gave me a desperate look over Brenda's amber locks, but I took no pity on him and quickly made my way to the bar. There had to be another girl or two like Brenda in the crowd. I was a little sorry I hadn't heard about this dance hall earlier.

The bartender still hadn't taken my order when a row broke out on the dance floor. Somehow I knew Archie was in trouble and made my way toward a congested knot of dancers. There I found a giggling Brenda, a florid, flustered Archie and a hulking young brute in a silver-studded black leather jacket.

"Now see here," Archie was stammering. "There's obviously been some sort of misunderstanding—"

"You said it, mate," the brute replied, "and I'll misunderstand you into next week if you don't take your hands off me bird."

"I'm not your bird, Charlie Marrow," Brenda said, and looked at me to save her from Charlie's clutches.

"What's the problem, Archie?" I said, calmly coming between him and his antagonist.

"Your friend doesn't know how to dance," Brenda said. "He keeps stepping on my toes!"

"Yeah; well, I'll flatten his nose," Charlie Marrow said.

"Easy, Junior," I said, hoping the boy had seen enough American gangster movies to recognize my menacing tone. It had worked with quarrelsome young Britons in the past, since the English believe all Americans are gangsters, anyway. Not this boy, however. He gave my shoulder a vicious shove.

"Don't 'junior' me, you fucking Yank bastard!"

I was stuck riding my bluff. "All right, punk—back off! Any more lip out of you and we can meet outside."

"You're fucking right we will," Charlie said, and swung away from us, dragging Brenda along by the arm and apparently off to seek support from his mates—of whom I suddenly noticed several, gazing stolidly at us from the sidelines. All in black leather jackets and motorcycle boots.

"Gorblimey, Fairchild—now you've done it," Archie said. "I was managing quite adequately before you tried to bully him."

I found it hard to believe that anything too unpleasant could happen to us in Cambridge, but Archie insisted it was time to be off. "You don't know how they hate us on this side of town. It's been going on for years. Come along; I'll do my best to save our hides."

"All right, but it's been a damned disappointment, this dance hall of yours."

"It nearly always is," Archie said sadly, and led me down the stairs.

There was no Charlie waiting for us outside, and Archie set a quick pace back toward town center and the protective embrace of the College walls. We were nearly out of the neighborhood when a squadron of motorcycles rounded the corner and came snarling down on us.

"Run for it!" Archie said.

I didn't see how we could outrun a company of motorcycles, but perhaps Archie had been through this before. He set off up a narrow lane between two factories and I pounded along at his heels. Back on the street, the motorcycles squealed to a stop, sputtered angrily, then came up the lane after us.

Archie went over a fence, across some railroad tracks, through a coalyard. The motorcycles couldn't follow, but we heard them growling somewhere in the darkness, seeking a way to outmaneuver us. I might have been frightened, had I not found the whole adventure so incredible. Motorcycle gangs in Cambridge?

We were still a long way from home and crossing an open marketplace, its booths boarded up for the winter, when the cycles—four of them—caught up with us. Archie and I ducked in among the booths and darted from lane to lane, but the cyclists outflanked us, skidding to a stop both fore and aft so that we were trapped in a narrow passageway.

"This is it," Archie said. "We might as well make

the best of it. You take the big bloke and I'll handle the other three. If they have knives or chains, you'd better use your jacket as a shield."

Knives? Chains? I suppose the sight of refined, genteel Archie suddenly puffing himself up for combat helped me keep my nerve. A warrior's glint had entered his eyes. His head lowered itself into his large chest and shoulders, and his doubled fists were huge. I should have known that all those years on the playing fields of Eton and Cambridge had given Archie a taste for blood.

They came at us from both directions. I had trouble singling out my man in the onslaught of bodies. We grappled *en masse* in the narrow passageway. Leather was in my face, studs scraped my cheek. I took a blow behind the ear and fell to my knees. A good deal of grunting, punching and groaning was going on over my head and I was sure that Archie was taking a terrible beating. When a boot came down on my hand I grabbed a denim calf, heaved and twisted, came off the cobblestones to put my head into a leather gut, then into somebody's chin. Something brief and ugly happened just to my left. I turned around and discovered that Archie and I were standing alone over a crumpled mass of leather jackets, one of which emitted a groan.

"Now then," Archie said, and gave one of the jackets a knee as it tried to rise. "That wasn't so bad, was it?"

He was bleeding from a cut lip and his cheeks were flaming red, but I could see he'd been enjoying himself. We left the marketplace and were soon in a part of town where, Archie assured me, we had nothing to fear from battered teddy boys. "I expect we taught that lot a lesson, anyway," Archie said proudly. "I should have told them we were from Duke's. They keep score, you know. Each College has to hold its own, or the townies won't let a University man walk the streets."

We stopped at a pub near the College, where Archie quickly consumed three pints of bitter, for it was near closing time. With his cut lip, bruised cheek and fired-up eyes, he looked like Oscar Wilde just emerged from a free-for-all of demented poets.

"I say, I'm glad now we went to the dance. Did you enjoy it?"

"You were marvelous, Archie. I never dreamed you were such a killer."

"I've been repressing that part of my character far too long, it seems. Scarcely proper for us older chaps to mix it up with the young ones, though perhaps I shall find some use for my hidden talents when I become a schoolmaster in Yorkshire. God, how I dread it! I've been at Cambridge for ten years. Do you think I can function in a place like Yorkshire?"

"Surely it won't be that bad," I said.

"You don't know Yorkshire. Though I daresay that after Cambridge, anyplace would seem like purgatory. No one leaves this town willingly."

I understood that, and could have given Archie some lines from Wordsworth or Tennyson to put a pedigree on his plight.

When the pub closed, we adjourned to Archie's room. He lit the gas fire, gave me a glass of Scotch and a small book he'd found in his cluttered bookcase. "You asked about Sir Percy Wickham George. This is a pamphlet the College put out when it purchased Bromley House from his heirs. Take it as a memento of our friendship. I intend to get rid of everything that reminds me of this place before I go. Amnesia, they say, is the only analgesic for exile."

"Before you forget everything," I said, "I wanted to ask you about Professor Trevor-Finch."

"I don't have any literature on him. Our fields are rather far apart, and Finchie was never much impressed with my work. Never even gave me one of his offprints, the bloody snob. Theoretical physicists are like that."

"Why does everyone—or at least all the younger dons—snicker at the mention of his name?"

"He's an odd duck," Archie said. "Him and his musicales and his political clubs and his ancient Norfolk family! To hear him go on about it, you'd think he was the last of the Norman conquerors, the silly faggot."

"Faggot? Is Trevor-Finch queer?"

"I shouldn't be telling you these things. After all, you'll be his houseguest soon. It's all just bloody gossip, anyway. They say he had a wife once, and that she ran off on him while he was in that German prison camp. Made quite a misogynist of him, though I understand he's devoted to his mother—and to his daughter too."

"I didn't know he had a daughter."

"Oh, yes. About our age; still single. Has a career of sorts in London. I've never met her, since I haven't been honored by an invitation to the 'ancestral manor.' But Trevor-Finch makes a practice of inviting young men down to Abbotswold. Usually has no use for them afterward, as if they've disappointed him somehow. Some people say he's trying to line up a husband for his daughter, or a lover for himself. Tossup which would be the more abominable, I daresay!"

"How long has Trevor-Finch been at Duke's?"

"Let's see. He would've come about 1953, just after he won an international prize for his work on the quantum theory. All the Colleges were after him, and we thought ourselves damned lucky to get him."

"Why do you suppose he chose Duke's over the others?"

"We *are* rather an elegant bunch of swells. You'd be surprised, seeing the old fuddy-duddies at High Table, how many of them have enormous reputations in their fields. And they're likely to make Finchie the new Master when Sir Henry retires; that's been in the cards all along."

"Is there anything else I should know about him?"

"That about covers it. He'll either subvert your politics, marry you off to his daughter, bore you to death with his cant, or bugger your backside." Archie laughed. "There's still time to call it off. I could use the company during the last days of my vigil."

"I think I'd better go to Abbotswold. But I'd like to

come up to Yorkshire to see you, once you're settled. I hope to be here through the summer, at least."

"That would be splendid. I'm sure we'd have all sorts of lurid adventures in those factory towns."

"There's an old monastery I want to visit—a place called Wellesford."

Archie put the back of his hand to his brow. "You and your monasteries! Perhaps you don't realize it, embedded in the twelfth century as you are, but we've been industrialized in England, oh, for centuries now."

"So you keep telling me. But aside from your lab work, and those nasty explosives you make, you don't seem very keen on that side of English life either, Archie."

"Why should I be? And my explosives are not nasty. We've recently developed a formula which the munitions people are dying to get their hands on. But don't you see? That's just the point! We're all immune to commerce behind these protective walls. You don't know what it does to one, morally, to come of age in a place like this. It's a pretty little fairy-tale land, but it's all too bloody safe. It blinds a man to what life is really like out there, in the howling wastes of poverty and greed. Don't you wonder what's out there?"

"You forget," I said, "that I hail from those howling wastes. We have plenty of poverty and greed where I come from—plenty of reality, if that's what you want to call it."

"Yes, I know," Archie sighed. "I've seen plenty of your kind—refugees from that brave new world you have over there. Pilgrims in search of your Mecca— only you have no Mecca. You've rejected one world and can't quite smuggle your way into another, so you wander like lost souls amongst all the libraries, museums, palaces and cathedrals of Europe, never quite seeing or catching hold of anything that lies outside those musty though God knows elegant interiors. It's called, 'Finding oneself,' I believe—as if a self can exist at the end of some tourist's itinerary like a pot of gold. Yet it's a kind of fear, isn't it? A fear of life."

"Well—aren't you afraid?"

"Of course I am! I thought you understood. I hate to give all this up. It's beautiful—but it's also false as hell, and I do believe that in a way I'm actually lucky to have been one of those called but not chosen. Oh, there will be weeping and gnashing of teeth, and I shall scratch pitifully at the door and beg to be readmitted, but eventually I'll go off to meet my fate in Yorkshire."

I finished my drink and stood up. "Good luck, pal. May you find yourself a beautiful, loving, red-haired female Yorkshirite, and fornicate your way to reality."

"Ah," Archie said, beaming. "I shall go in that hope!"

I left Archie's room and made my way along corridors I'd learned to fear after dark. Safely back in my own room, I threw a few things in a suitcase for tomorrow's departure, then sat by the window for a while with the lights off, looking down on the Old Court. It was true enough, everything Archie had said, and it reminded me again of Yvetta's parting words in the London station. So I was afraid. So I was incomplete as a man. So my infatuation with a batch of medieval manuscripts was simply a neurotic's attempt to avoid all those aspects of life at which he'd proven wretchedly inadequate. So be it! It was my life, and I'd waste it as I chose!

I was surprised to see a light appear behind one of the windows directly across the court, and I idly wondered if, with so few of the College still in residence, the shade of some long-dead scholar hadn't returned to cram for a long outdated examination. "Don't worry about it," I wanted to tell the ghost. "It doesn't matter. Nothing matters any more—except to fools like you and me."

9

At Court

King Henry II was a traveling man with a sprawling domain to oversee, and everywhere that Henry went off across the British Isles or beyond the Channel to Aquitaine and Anjou—his court was sure to follow. And wherever Henry laid the royal head and fed the royal person, be it the castle of a vanquished earl or the hut of a swineherd, his court was, as it were, in session.

In April of 1158 the royal caravan was nearing London after an Easter Court at Worcester. At the fore of this lengthy train of mounted knights and marching minions rode the king himself and his noblest nobles—the Lord High Steward, the Lord High Chancellor, the Lord High Treasurer and diverse other Lord Highs. Behind them came the petty nobles, advisers and parasitic kinsmen, followed closely by the king's guard of horsemen, archers and foot soldiers. Behind the soldiers came the young bureaucrats of the court—the clerks, limners, scriveners, lawyers and officials of small account. This sizable contingent was followed in turn by the royal servants—chaplains, heralds, watchmen, huntsmen and houndkeepers, falconers, tentkeepers, washerwomen and water carriers, cooks, servers, stewards of the larder and workmen of the buttery. Finally, bringing up the rear of this great parade, came the itinerant scholars and poets who clung to the royal train—the actors, singers, dancers, dicers, gamesters, jugglers, prostitutes, pimps, buffoons and barbers. The king's possessions (including the voluminous legal paper his chancellory produced at every stop along the way) were hauled along in carts. A few mounted guards hung back to protect the carts and the carriages of the ladies, but Henry had little to fear from thieves or marauders, England having become under his vigorous rule a most peaceful and well-ordered kingdom.

For four years the king's justice and passion for administrative efficiency had been at work in the land, and the wounds of a long period of tyranny, anarchy and civil strife were nearly healed. London, into which this troop of regal gypsies now rode, had become one of the most prosperous cities of Europe. Had the bankers, artisans and merchants had ticker tape and confetti ready to hand, they would surely have sent it blizzarding down across the path of the burly, bug-eyed, flushed and laughing king.

Back up the road, the party of chancellory clerks had come in sight of the city's gate.

"Well, Gervaise," said a red-bearded young man in a gray woolen tunic, "I expect I know where you'll be off to as soon as we're settled at Westminster. Which bawdyhouse will you tear apart this evening?"

Geoffrey Gervaise, a tall, thin man with a black beard and long black hair, his lean face distinguished by a pair of fiery dark eyes, looked straight ahead at the rooftops and spires of the city. "No, Bartholomew, there'll be no whores for me tonight. I gave them up for Lent, and now that Lent is over and Our Lord has risen once again, I see no reason to fall back into my old ways. I like feeling worthy, for a change, of this cross which hangs around my neck."

The redbeard laughed and slapped the ass's hindquarters to keep pace with Gervaise. "You've entirely too much conscience for your vocation! If you meant to practice celibacy, you should've stayed in the monastery. I give you two nights; a week at most. After all, who knows where we'll go from London, or when again we'll encounter such a plenitude of fat, sassy tarts? Unless, of course, it's back to Aquitaine, where even noblewomen will spread their legs for a clerk."

"I hope not Aquitaine," Gervaise said, eyes fixed on

one of the distant steeples. They might have been the eyes of a prophet, burning with desert brilliance—or the eyes of a madman.

"If you're determined to be good," Bartholomew said, "I suppose I can be good with you—for tonight, at least. How about a game of chess? You promised me a chance to avenge myself."

Gervaise's smile deepened slightly beneath his beard. "If you like. But I warn you, Bartholomew, I can't be beaten."

"Not even by our chancellor?"

"I've played Becket twice. We drew both matches. But once I understand his game, I'll beat him as well."

"Ha! No one will ever understand Thomas à Becket's game! He's a deep one, Gervaise. I just hope he's smart enough to keep on Henry's good side."

"The king loves Becket."

"Aye, but the more he loves them, the more vicious he becomes if he ever turns against them. Our fortunes depend upon Becket's, and frankly, I wish he were a shade less brilliant and a good deal less familiar with our king. That's my opinion, for what it's worth."

"No doubt it would be worth a year in the dungeon if the wrong people heard you voice it," Gervaise said. "We are clerks, and the inner machinations of the king's court have nothing to do with us."

"Gervaise, your ingenuousness astounds me. The rumor is that Henry's just waiting for old Theobald to die so that he can make Becket the archbishop. And then he'll need a new chancellor, won't he? Where do you think he's going to find one? From the chancellory, of course."

"Not necessarily," Gervaise said, though his eyes seemed to glow brighter at the prospect.

"He'll choose the man Becket recommends," Bartholomew said. "Perhaps you'd better let him win a game or two from you. The way I hear it, you presently stand very high with Becket."

"There are abler men than myself in the chancellory," Gervaise said. But Bartholomew, catching a glimpse of the pride and hunger in his eyes, knew that his friend was no less ambitious than himself. And the devil will probably beat me out, he thought. Of course, they must know Gervaise is mad. He'll do something crazy and they'll have to boot him out. And that, God knows, is my only chance!

The party of clerks was nearing the open gate, passing through the gardens and orchards that surrounded the city's walls. The trees were just coming into bud and green shoots had begun to break the loamy soil. Mist hung over the river, but through it came the soothing warmth of the April sun. Gervaise smelled the river. He felt the reawakening of those pagan gods who lived in the soil and in the sap of budding trees, in the gentle breezes and hazy sky of spring. O God, he prayed silently, hold me to my vows! And let me remember my sister not as she was in the days of Megin the witch and Carn the serpent, but as she was, please God, at Evesham on Thursday last. . . .

For it was on Holy Thursday that Gervaise had ridden away from Worcester and across the countryside to the small convent on the banks of the Severn, where, after an interview with the cautious prioress, he was allowed to see his sister in the cold and dusky garden near the river. Her pale face looked ghostly to him, the face of a being whose spirit had obliterated bodily needs and cravings.

"Good Geoffrey. Have you found peace at last?"

"No, my sister. None, or very little. But are you happy here?"

If she had told him she wasn't, he would have carried her away, and damned be the Church and all its laws. But he knew her answer before she spoke.

"Yes, brother. I am very happy now. And I pray for you every day."

"No doubt I shall need those prayers. As you see, Margarette, I am a priest now—but not a very worthy one, I fear."

"And does it still trouble you so much, what we did when we were young? You must not think of it. It is all behind us, and God has forgiven us."

"How can I forget it, Margarette, when I still love

92

you? And when I still hear Satan calling me like the wind off the moors?"

"You *must* forget it, Geoffrey! Megin was an evil woman to fill our heads with such fears—a witch who did the devil's work while mouthing corrupted pieties. I have learned much since coming here, and I know that Our Lord's love and forgiveness is unceasing. Have you no faith, Geoffrey?"

"Very little. And yet I think often of theological matters. Perhaps I have had too much education and seen too much of the world . . . but I still hope for my salvation."

"The Lord will help you. I will pray for you without ceasing! Do not despair, my brother. Perhaps God will send you a sign to strengthen your faith. And now I must leave you. I am expected in the chapel."

Gervaise took the hand she held out to him and raised it quickly to his lips. Its flesh was cold against his fevered face. With a sob of protest, Margarette tore away, turned and ran through the garden, her black cloak floating over the stones as if no body but only spirit moved beneath it.

A bride of Christ, Gervaise thought. And he, a jealous rival, having found his sister again after years of searching, guarded queries, false hopes—having found her at last, only to see how fully she belonged to another. But was he not pleased by his sister's peace? On the way back to Worcester, Gervaise saw only the familiar stars blossoming across the black meadow of night. There was no sign.

Nor had one yet appeared, though Gervaise believed that the prayers of a Margarette could scarcely go unanswered. Was the Lord perhaps as jealous of him as he . . . But no; that was blasphemy! Passing through London's northeastern gate, Gervaise saw the gray mass of the Tower rising above the rooftops, the cathedral spires of Saint Paul's still wrapped in wooden scaffolding. The streets were crowded with humanity, riotous with commerce. There were horse droppings in the mud, garbage and human excrement carelessly tossed from the windows of the narrow houses along

93

the way. Gervaise caught the scent of sawdust and fresh mortar, the yeasty odor of a brewery and the seaweed stench of fish from a merchant's cart. He remembered Paris. He remembered all the towns and villages he had seen since becoming a member of the king's traveling retinue. Where, in all this busy, thriving world, had he ever known peace? Nowhere, it seemed, but in old Eadmer's monastery. Perhaps he would return to that life someday, but not until he had learned to rule the demons which possessed him. At least here at court, all his resolutions notwithstanding, he could cut his temptations short by surrendering to them. He could barter desire for remorse, exchange the dagger of lust for a bludgeon of guilt. But was this a life worthy of a rational man?

The people along the streets greeted the procession with smiles, friendly gestures, a few shouts of welcome. Gervaise saw a young woman lurking in the doorway of a public house. She smiled up at the priest from beneath a tangle of dirty hair, then tugged down her blouse to reveal a full white breast and dark nipple. Gervaise tore his eyes away. Damn these women! Damn their filthy devilish cunts! And damn that fiend within his own breeches who would not give him a moment's peace.

I shall keep a vigil at the chapel tonight, Gervaise thought. I shall spend the entire night on my knees, praying for a sign.

"Nearly home," Bartholomew sighed, as the procession neared the west gate and the road to the palace. "I suppose we'll get another wretched supper. The cooks will barely have time to unpack their pots and pans. But at least the fish and meat should be fresh, and the wine good. Don't forget our game of chess this evening."

"I won't," Gervaise said, thinking how it was only at the chessboard that he experienced a temporary suspension of torment and doubt. The game had been for years his only taste of freedom.

The Lord, Gervaise thought, will not be served by slaves.

Nor by hypocrites like good Bartholomew.
Nor by madmen like me.

There were documents and supplies to see safely
stowed away in the chancellory, and Gervaise was busy
with these arrangements for the remainder of the afternoon. Near suppertime, a page with the crafty look of
an experienced pimp (one of Queen Eleanor's French
urchins, Gervaise thought) put a note into the priest's
hands and left without awaiting an answer. Gervaise
carried the scrap of parchment over to a window, away
from the flurry of clerks and servants still unpacking
supplies. He saw that the note was written in French:

Dear Priest—I am in great need of shriving and
cannot bare my soul to the queen's chaplain. As
you love God and hold dear your sacred office,
come to my chamber tonight when you see me
leave the hall. This I command in the name of her
royal highness, whose kinswoman I am. Yours in
faith,

Annjenette DeLorreaux

Gervaise crumpled the parchment in his large fist and
let his head rest against the stone casement. So! He
had forsworn the whores of the city only to fall prey to
the whores of the court!
He had seen Annjenette looking thoughtfully at him
when last he brought papers to the king's private
chambers and had wondered then if he was to be
chosen the next of her victims. Queen Eleanor's cousin,
just turned seventeen, with the face of an angel and the
body of a pagan goddess . . . how many knights had
she teased and taunted and finally taken to her chamber? How many had written their insipid verses to gain
her favor, had strutted and posed and sung mournful
ballads, challenging one another to battle in the tour-
neys over the dubious issue of her honor? Gervaise had
once overheard a conversation between Becket and the
king:
"Marry the slut off to some provincial baron, my

lord. You must get her out of the court before she destroys the moral fiber of your best knights."

"Thomas, my friend, that's easier said than done. The queen is fond of her company, and used to having her way in such matters. But why don't you marry her? Couldn't we keep her in court as your wife?"

"I would not have such a harlot to wife! Besides, I have not entirely forsaken the notion of one day taking holy orders."

"Perhaps it's just as well. I could use you, Thomas, in the Church—if only I could spare you at the chancellory."

I won't go, Gervaise thought. Better by far that he should mount the fat and stinking whores of the city. Such simple, honest sins, plainly branded and sincerely regretted in due course, were far less dangerous to one's soul than the pagan whimsies and heresies such a woman might put into the mind of a poor, lust-ridden priest.

But what if she did need a priest to hear her confession? Could he turn down an earnest plea for aid? Then why should she scorn the queen's own chaplain and turn to a lowly clerk?

That night, at the clerks' table along the side of the great hall, with the fire roaring in the open area between the tables and the hounds gnawing their bones beside its warmth, Gervaise watched Queen Eleanor and her maids of honor picking disdainfully over their humble English fare. Mother Venus and her nymphs, Gervaise thought. How they love to prey on men, and how they delight in their wickedness. How false and foolish it all is—and yet how damnably enchanting! A man of faith and reason should rise above such snares.

He saw the golden-haired Annjenette seated next to the queen, her fine complexion unpolluted by her reputed crimes. Had the girl been wronged? But how could she still be innocent, to have come of age at the infamous Court of Love? Annjenette's blue eyes turned, all innocent and childlike, in his direction.

Christ, I will not bear it!

"What say, Gervaise," asked a young clerk, slapping

him on the shoulder, "are we off to the city this evening?"

"Nay, nay," cried Bartholomew from across the table. "Haven't you heard? Gervaise has sworn to have no more of London whores. We are playing a quiet game of chess this evening, like good boys."

Gervaise said, "I'm sorry, Bartholomew. I cannot play chess with you tonight after all. I have business of a priestly nature."

Bartholomew's eyebrows rose. "Another of your long chats with Becket, perhaps, or some party of politicking monks from the abbey? Gervaise, you're after something."

"I have a duty to attend to. I can say no more about it."

"Then you can go to hell, for all of me," Bartholomew said.

"No doubt I shall, eventually," Gervaise sighed.

At the king's table, where Becket in his dandy's robes held forth as usual, amusing the Lord Highs with his wit and rhetoric, Henry had risen from his seat. It was difficult for the king to remain seated even long enough to partake of his simple meal, and, a joint of mutton in his fist, its grease dribbling down his sleeve and chin, he began to pace up and down the table, arguing with Becket above the heads of his counselors. Gervaise watched them with woeful envy. It was in Henry's nature to scheme and plot and fight for power, and then to govern wisely and efficiently, for he was an extraordinary man, chosen by God for a special role in the destiny of nations. But what of Becket? A commoner, and a product of the schools like Gervaise, how had Becket learned to assume such power?

Gervaise wondered if it was the power he envied or the way in which the exercise of that power protected such men from their human frailties. Did the king call for a concubine or seduce a serving maid? No matter; he might have gone hunting or dicing instead and returned to business with as keen and easy a mind. Such men were like unto gods who sometimes, as a brief respite from the chores of divinity, condescended to dally

with mortal women, then rose unsullied from their cop-
ulations, ready to rule again.

If I had such power, Gervaise thought, if I had mere
human enemies to contend with (be they as powerful
as the King of France)—then even I might retain some
semblance of sanity. But it seems my fate to contend
with those demons which infest the mind and pollute
the soul—those invisible foes who come upon us in the
night.

The most horrible thought of all, Gervaise knew,
was that there was no God.

Without God, the pursuit of reason and order was itself a madness. Prayer was a travesty, and the struggle
to achieve goodness an absurdity beyond equal. Better
to suffer damnation and everlasting torment than to exist for even a few paltry years in a godless world. And
what was faith, finally, but an act of the will—a freely
made decision not to live in a Godless universe? That
was a decision, Gervaise felt sure, he would always
make, even if it led to hell.

The lady Annjenette rose from the table, paid brief
homage to the queen and demurely left the hall. Would
she turn to cast one single beckoning gaze upon the
priest? No, she would not. She enjoys this game, Gervaise thought bitterly. Ah, but what a small, fine body
she has! How soft her skin must be, how smooth her
thighs, how fine her maiden's fluff. Quickly, Gervaise,
to your prayers!

The small chapel reserved for the lower clergy of the
court stood dark and deserted at this hour. Gervaise
knelt before the uncandled altar, in the damp and dark,
the musty scent of a winter of disuse. There were prayers which, by the rule, he should say at this hour. But
the Latin phrases, the formal supplications and well-
couched entreaties of legalistic minds, were neither
direct nor forceful enough for his impassioned mood. O
God, help me. Lord Jesus Christ, help me. Blessed
Virgin, pray for me. Saintly Margarette, my own betrayed and stricken sister, pray for me. I am a wicked

man and harbor wicked thoughts . . . yet still I do not, will not, cannot despair. O God, send me a sign!

In the gloom he could see the crucifix above the altar, the emaciated and brutalized body of the murdered Christ. How had this outrage come to pass? What was man that he could kill his God, and what was God Who would submit to an agonized death at the hands of His creatures? Whose God *are* You, Gervaise demanded, and why have You put us all upon the cross?

He could not pray now. It was wrong to have expected a sign; wrong of Margarette to promise one. Old Megin had produced signs. Megin was a witch, and Carn the spell she conjured to destroy his soul. His guilt would not be prayed away.

Gervaise rose and left the chapel. In the palace courtyard, away from the main gate where the watchmen sat by their fires, he could look up and see the stars. What were they? If one could rise high enough to grasp them, would they burn one's hand, or were they as cold and hard as they looked? Could a bird fly through them? Did angels hold them in place or were they attached to the black fabric of the sky? But dusk came not as a cloak, as the ancient poet had described it. Dusk was but a deepening of the blue, at first nearly imperceptible, then darker and darker, as a tomb might darken when a candle was withdrawn. An enormous tomb in which all men were buried alive to wait out the long night of their Savior's death, to watch in hope of His Resurrection.

The answers he'd been given were not satisfactory. His mind tested them and found them false. And yet, on occasion, the mysteries did define themselves in his mind, finding words which could clarify the terms of uncertainty. When the words came, Gervaise wrote them down. In a chest in his chamber, with him on all his journeys, there were many such words scratched hastily on scraps of parchment stolen from chancellory supplies. Of late, the words had begun to form themselves into lines of poetry, and sometimes the lines became stanzas. They were not Latin words nor French ones, but words in the language his mother, a peasant's

99

daughter, had used—the language of the monks at Wellesford and of old Eadmer himself. The ancient tongue, as fresh and vibrant and mysteriously potent to Gervaise as the stars themselves.

Yet for all its force and honesty, this language was too limited for all he now knew—the writings of the ancients, the heathens, the contemporary scholars of Paris. There were no models for the poem he wished to write. A sort of *Historia Calamitatum* in verse, his own personal trials ennobled and enlarged by allegory. Gervaise had never read such a poem as his. It was harder than playing chess, though in ways more satisfying. For chess was but a symbolic world, whereas this poem of his—should he ever complete it—might speak to the full mystery of things.

A vain pursuit, no doubt; but in those moments when faith failed him, a man might turn to art. Or to the ruling of kingdoms, like Henry and Becket. To magic, spells, heathen rituals . . . to the sweet, hot poison of a lady's lips and sopping loins.

O Lord, Gervaise thought, have I failed You once again? Or have You failed me? Perhaps we've failed one another, for I am tending, it seems, toward the bedchamber of the lady Annjenette.

It was perilous in the extreme for a lowly clerk to be caught skulking in this wing of the palace where the noblewomen slept. Yet peril was a pleasure in itself; damnation a most adventuresome vocation. Your audacity knows no bounds, Gervaise. And why is it that when you are being most despicable, your mind is at its sharpest? Do you cherish guilt, you awesome bastard, for the sake of wit?

One of the serving women appeared from the shadows and motioned for him to follow. The slut knew I'd come, Gervaise thought. All my agony for nothing; it's been preordained. The serving woman opened a door and quickly withdrew. The room was large, rich with draperies and sweet with perfume. The young woman sat waiting for him before the fire. Her hair was undone, a cascade of golden tresses down her slender back, and she wore only the thinnest of shifts.

"Good Gervaise," she said softly, "come hither and attend to my confession."

"My lady, this is not seemly. This is an outrage in the eyes of God."

"But I worship another god, kind sir. And he shall bless our sacrament . . . in his own way."

"Pagan! I've heard of your gods."

"They are kinder by far than yours. Why do you look so stern? Is it so painful for you to gaze upon a pretty face? And upon . . .?" Her eyes dropped to her own breasts rising sharply against the flimsy linen and to the shadow of her womanhood where her thighs shone whitely beneath the shift.

"And your confession?"

"Is a confession of love. I have seen the way your eyes burn with desire for me. That fire has lit a like contagion in my own breast. You have seduced me with those eyes, that great black beard, those snarling lips that even now would curse me if you dared. I long to unite my fire with your own, so that together we may blaze as hotly as the sun which warms my distant homeland."

Gervaise stood over her, conscious of the fire's warmth and of the small gold cross that reflected its light as it lay against his chest. "My lady, I cannot oblige you. I am a priest of the one true God."

Annjenette's blue eyes revealed a momentary anger, quickly hidden. "I have heard of your exploits. Your vows have oft been forsaken, I think."

"True, my lady, but I have vowed to forsake them no more."

"Not even," she asked, rising with the hem of her garment in hand and her legs already bared to the knee, "for me?"

Gervaise shut his eyes. A universe swarming with stars—vast, chaotic and godless—filled his mind. When he opened his eyes again the lady was naked.

"I have taken a horrid chill in this hideous climate, Gervaise. Will you not have pity on me and warm my poor cold body? Won't you bless me with the healing powers of your mighty staff? Why do you look at me in that mournful way? I am young, I am beautiful, I am passionately in love with you, and I beg your mercy."

Gervaise removed his cross. "You have no mercy on me, my lady," he said, and covered the small gold object with his clothes.

10

Abbotswold

ᘒ

On Sunday morning I boarded a nearly empty railroad car and rode a lonely two hours beneath watercolor skies across the glistening green plain of East Anglia. Of course I had brought along my notes on the Westchurch manuscripts and the pamphlet Archie had given me; once out of the station, I opened my briefcase and took out the little book. *Bromley House: A Short History.* by J. R. Wedgkins, M.A., D.Phil., Fellow of Duke's College, Cambridge. The first part contained profiles of Sir Maxwell Bromley and other irrelevant gentlemen who had owned the house prior to 1885. The second part was devoted to Bromley's most illustrious master, Sir Percy Wickham George.

A physician, psychologist and fellow of King's, Sir Percy had become interested in the scientific study of the occult at that curious moment of history when such matters also captured the attention of men like William James and F. W. H. Myers. Over the years Sir Percy conducted many experiments designed to render the supernatural a fit subject for scientific inquiry. None of these experiments, so far as I could tell, had proved in any way conclusive. Not sure whether he was involved with physics or metaphysics, psychology or demonology, Sir Percy traveled the globe, from Liverpool to Timbuktu, seeking out instances of ghostly phenomena and subjecting them to his frenetic and schizoid analysis.

In a section subtitled "Sir Percy and the Duke's Ghost," Dr. Wedgkins reported that upon hearing of several new manifestations in the College library (!), Sir Percy received permission from the Master to investigate the case and showed up one All Hallows Eve with (1) a learned delegation from the Society for Psychical Research, (2) a battery of technicians and a drayload of clumsy late-nineteenth-century ghost-hunting equipment, and (3) an Anglican priest armed with bell, book and candle. Even the press was in attendance, and the pamphlet included a portion of an article that subsequently appeared in one of the morning dailies:

Scarcely had the clock struck twelve than a light appeared behind the stained-glass windows of the College library, causing great consternation among all present. "There she is, sir," cried the College porter, "just as we've seen her these past six nights—but I'd swear an oath the library was locked up tighter than a bank vault at half-past six!"

Sir Percy immediately ordered out his men and, the porter unlocking the massive door, a party of six, including Sir Percy and the Reverend Hugh Goodblood, entered the horrid gloom. Your reporter was not far behind. The light having extinguished itself when the door was opened, the intrepid ghost hunters proceeded to prowl the labyrinthine interior with lanterns and lighted candles. Several minutes of the most severe and agonizing suspense had elapsed when suddenly, from the back of the library, near the iron gates which seal off the College's highly valuable Special Collections, the minister of God was heard to cry out in alarm. He was then seen by the search party backing across the room, ringing his bell and chanting the exorcist's rite. Sir Percy later reported seeing a shadowy figure behind the

103

iron bars, reaching out from between them like a prisoner begging release. The Rev. Goodblood himself described a tall man in a monk's robe and cowl, and also spoke of the "malodorous effluvience of evil" that seemed to emanate from the figure.

The apparition, if such it was, seemed to vanish as the members of the party approached the gate. Later, the entire room housing the Special Collections was diligently searched, dusted for fingerprints and subjected to other forms of scientific analysis. No evidence of an intruder was found. Nor was it determined that any human creature could have gained access to the room after the library doors had been locked for the night. "Confounded peculiar," was Sir Percy's comment to this reporter on this latest and most extraordinary episode in the long history of the haunted College.

In his later years, Sir Percy was obliged to curtail his psychic investigations because of a weakened heart. He spent these years at Bromley House compiling ponderous tomes on folklore and mythology in an attempt to vindicate in theory that branch of science he had been unable to establish via experimentation. He died in 1926, according to the College pamphleteer, "a weary and embittered man."

Serves the old bastard right, I thought, as I tossed the book aside and gazed at a landscape of windmills, canals and rustic hamlets.

On the flyleaf of Archie's pamphlet I jotted down a list of names and dates:

Geoffrey Gervaise, d. 1175 (burned at the stake)
Earl of Westchurch, d. 1649 (beheaded)
Gerald Brice, d. 1789? (disappeared in France)
Sir Percy Wickham George, d. 1926 (bad heart)
Throcknagle, 1930s ("repugnance")
Dilbey, 1940s ("oppression")
Jameson, 1950s (pyromania)

Dr. Greggs and Rev. Stemp, d. March 1962 (accidents?)
David Fairchild—two "visitations," March & April, '62

Scarcely a full account of everything those manuscripts had been up to over the centuries, I was sure, and yet there was logic and coherence enough in the whole affair to persuade me that what I'd stumbled onto—of all the preposterous perils of scholarship!—was a *haunted manuscript*. Burned at the stake for his reputed dealings with the devil and practice of the dark arts, Geoffrey Gervaise had somehow survived both fire and the grave—had survived for centuries, unknown and unsought save by a few eccentrics and devotees—and now here he was at last, an incredible anachronism in this age of atomic bombs and space satellites, showing himself to me!

I need not detail the reluctant frame of mind with which I regarded this proposition. That I had become nervous and irritable as a result of "overwork," and thus subject to hallucinations, was simply not the case; I had never lived a life as serene, as lucid, as free from anxiety and self-doubt, as I had lived these past seven months at Duke's. The intricate hieroglyphics of Gervaise's poem intrigued and fascinated me, but I could hardly believe they had led me to the brink of madness. If I could, therefore, doubt neither my senses nor my sanity, I had no choice but to conclude that the universe was other than I had formerly supposed, and that somewhere in its ambiguous immensity there was a place for spirits such as Geoffrey Gervaise.

What I found most difficult to understand, under the circumstances, was my remarkable steadiness of mind. Either I was a braver man and more dedicated scholar than I'd ever realized, or—and this was the more likely answer—it had somehow come to me that the ghost of Gervaise meant me no harm.

Perhaps I was just the one he had been waiting for—in preference to all those other dreary, earnest scholars, whom I wouldn't have cared for, either—in order to reveal the secrets of his magnificent poem. Yes,

I liked that idea. I could see how, as another outcast, another man misplaced in time, I might strike Gervaise as just the fellow for the job he had in mind. Not that I expected that the ghost would sit down to tea with me and cheerfully explain, like a writer being interviewed by the *Paris Review*, what he'd been thinking of when he wrote some of his most impenetrable lines. But mile by mile, I became increasingly convinced that if I could only be watchful and receptive enough, if I could continue to remain sympathetic and unafraid, Gervaise would find some way to put the whole of his genius before me in perfectly usable fashion.

Of course, I didn't really believe any of this. And yet events seemed to be carrying me into a world where the merely plausible was not a relevant factor; where I would have to let go of certain prejudices regarding "reality" and "proof" and "common sense" (those shibboleths of the dullard modern consciousness) and allow the currents of experience to determine my course. It wouldn't be the first time that I'd found myself intellectually adrift, and I'd not lost faith in my ability to swim ashore whenever the water became too treacherous.

Toward noon, the rain becoming a nasty squall, my train pulled into Wimsett-by-Sea, a dismal little resort town of closed shops, empty hotels and wet cobblestones. Professor Trevor-Finch, in Rex Harrison tweeds and floppy-brimmed hat, was waiting on the station platform. We shook hands like old friends, after which there was an awkward moment as we both remembered we were not.

We proceeded through the small station, put my suitcase in the trunk of the professor's Volkswagen, and set out through gusts of wind and rain. A narrow winding lane took us out of town and up to the hills that stretched south along the coast, where, nearly torn from the road by sudden blasts, the little car crept along a fairly spectacular series of cliffs. Silhouetted against the stormy sky I saw what looked like the ruins of an ancient castle.

106

"Curious things, those," said Trevor-Finch. "There are a good many of them along this coast. Old forts dating back to the Napoleonic Wars, most of them unusable now, but I have one on my land which is in better shape than most. I've had it fixed up as a sort of laboratory. You might find it of some historical interest, even if its scientific features don't intrigue you."

I told the professor I would be interested in anything he wanted to show me—that I'd come for the full tour.

"And a full tour you shall have," Trevor-Finch promised. "I'm fond of this spot of ground, and my roots here go back a long way. There was a Philip of Trevorre who came over with the Conqueror, and who was known as one of the harsher of the Norman warlords—though his sons were reported to be even worse."

"And the land has been in your family all this time?"

"One branch or another has had it, yes. My father commissioned the College of Heralds to authenticate our coat of arms and we dredged up a bit of family history in that way. Daddy was rather a snob, I fear. When he inherited the remains of the feudal domain— only the house and a few hundred acres—he exhausted his modest fortune in renovations and genealogical research. Wanted to set himself up as a proper country gentleman. But the land proved useless for farming or anything else—of no earthly value beyond family pride. Fortunately, Mama has a trust fund from her side of the family, or I should've been obliged to sell the place long ago. The taxes alone are catastrophic."

"Does your mother live out here all alone?" I asked.

"She has her nurse and companion, a most respectable old thing named Mrs. Archer. And we have a couple to care for the house. I come down for the vacs, do a bit of shooting and fishing when I can, and tinker in my laboratory. My daughter also comes up from London now and then with some of her friends. She'll be joining us, by the way. Clever girl; I think you'll like her. She could've gotten into Cambridge—Girton College—but she chose a more active life. A regular 'career girl,' as you'd say in the States. Doing quite well in the fashion industry."

"As a model?" I asked, for a man can always hope.

"Heavens, no; as a designer. Stephany's much too bright to function as a mere manikin. She's not that sort of a girl at all."

I anticipated one of those stocky, mannish women who would humiliate me at tennis and try to treat me as a great chum, but I told the professor I would look forward to making Stephany's acquaintance.

"She's anxious to meet you, too," Trevor-Finch said. "She's quite fond of Americans. Finds them refreshing, she says."

By this time the road had swung inland and we left it at the next ridge to follow a muddy lane that ran across a hillside meadow, where the sea seemed to hover above us like a single immense wave. I was glad when we reached the brick wall at the meadow's end and passed into the wooded grounds of the manor. I caught my first glimpse of the house itself waiting for us at the end of a long avenue lined with tall, mossy-trunked trees.

Abbotswold was larger than I'd expected, its compedium or architectural styles testifying to a long and confused history. The central core of the house, built of Norfolk stone and slate, was no doubt the oldest, rude and barbaric in appearance, with a medieval tower that rose above the tiled and many-planed rooftops. On either side there were newer wings—one of rosy Georgian stone, the other of Victorian brick which had weathered to a variety of mournful shades. The classical simplicity of one side vigorously contradicted the neo-Gothic extravagance of the other, so that the house seemed to suffer from a split personality, its opposing factions held forcibly together by the primitive dominance of the phallic tower.

As the professor's car pulled up before the massive though unadorned front door, a short, stocky, shabbily dressed old fellow came shuffling out to greet us with a pair of umbrellas.

"Giles Mortimor, my caretaker," Trevor-Finch said.

"He'll take your bag, Fairchild. Run along in while I put the car away."

I accepted the umbrella the old man pressed upon me, caught a glimpse of his red nose and grizzled chin, his dark and inhospitable eyes, and went on ahead to the house.

Beyond the large front door was an anteroom, unfurnished but for hall tree, umbrella stand and several pairs of muddy galoshes. Beyond that, and down several steps, I entered the great hall—dark, drafty, tainted with cellar dust and mold. The floors and walls were made of great blocks of stone, and there was a gargantuan stone fireplace against the inner wall. Heavy wooden beams spanned the shadowy ceiling and two long, narrow windows looked in from either end. The furnishings were few and austere, large clumsy pieces hand-hewn from oak and obviously very old. I felt as if there ought to have been display cases, a suit of armor or two along the walls, and a little old lady in ruffled lace to sell me a ticket and guidebook for a shilling. It was hard to believe that anyone could still live in such a house.

Trevor-Finch came up behind me. "Great gloomy old place, isn't it? This part goes back to the twelfth century and is still structurally sound. A few of the outbuildings and a portion of the cellar may be even older—remnants of the very first castle built on this site by Philip of Trevorre. The rest of the house isn't exceptionally old. The east wing, where we dine and entertain, was built around 1750. The west wing, where most of the bedrooms are located now, wasn't put up until rather late in the nineteenth century. It's a nuisance, actually, having a house this large on one's hands. I've often thought it should have been made into a school—perhaps even an orphanage or a lunatic asylum. But there's nothing I can do with it as long as Mama remains alive." At which point the professor glanced quickly up and to the left, as if somewhere in the house Mama might have been listening in.

"Let's get you settled in your room," he continued. "Then you can pay your respects to Mama, we'll have a bite of lunch and go out for a look at my laboratory. Giles here will show you the way."

Old Giles stood dripping in the entryway with my suitcase. "Right along here, sir," he rumbled, and started up the broad curving stairway.

In the darkness of the second-floor corridor something small and furry slipped in front of us and I broke my step, my neck prickling, before I realized it was just a cat. The cat curled along the wall and watched us pass with glowing eyes. I then realized that the faintly sour odor I'd noticed downstairs was the lingering aroma of cat-mess.

Giles seemed to be wondering which of the many rooms he should give me. He looked into a couple. "Huh—chimney smokes in that one, and the casement's a bit drafty in the one over there. Don't know which the missus has made up for you. . . . Ah, this should do. Got a nice lookout, too. Right in here, sir."

I followed him into a small but comfortably furnished room with double windows providing a view of the sea, tall oaks in the foreground, their barren branches supporting a colony of cawing rooks. The room was already occupied by a large gray cat, which observed our arrival with typical feline insolence from the center of the bed. "G'wan—get out of here!" the old man said to the cat, but it refused to budge until he took a swipe at it with his cap.

"Is the professor fond of cats?" I asked.

The old man squinted at me. "I don't know as he likes 'em very well at all, sir. It's the missus and me as raise these creatures. We've always had lots of cats."

"You're fortunate that the professor puts up with them," I said.

"Aye. We've got a bit to put up with ourselves, if it comes to that," he said, and left, taking the cat with him.

The room was cold, but a coal fire had been laid in the small hearth, so I put a match to it. Then I laid my suitcase on the bed and began to unpack. The first dresser drawer I tried was filled with lacy underthings. I checked the large wardrobe and it contained several dresses. Either Giles had made a mistake, or the professor's daughter used the room to store extra clothes. The dresses did not look particularly large and some of them gave off a most promising scent. I was debating whether or not I should try to find another room when a car rumbled up to the house. I went to the window in time to see a girl jump out and run through the rain to the front door. In mac and rain scarf, she passed too quickly out of view for me to guess what she looked like.

I sat on the bed and waited. Presently I heard high heels clicking smartly along the corridor. She opened the door and came right in.

"Oh—you've taken my room," she said.

"I'm sorry," I said, rising from the bed. "This is where they put me."

"That's all right. I didn't mean I actually wanted this room. You're here now, so I'll take another room. Well! You must be Daddy's young man from the College. I'm Stephany."

She extended her hand, taking off her rain scarf with the other and giving her head a vigorous shake to loosen her long light-brown hair. It's amazing what flowing locks and shining tresses will do for a woman; on the instant, she was beautiful.

"David Fairchild," I said, taking her hand. "I'm very pleased to meet you."

"Fairchild," she said flirtatiously. "What a wonderful name for an innocent abroad! Daddy says all Americans are innocents—but then he has all these horrid prejudices."

Though her handshake was firm, she was hardly the tweedy, mannish type. Her raincoat was partially unbuttoned and in the gap I could see her full breasts pushing out against a green sweater. No, she wasn't nearly thin enough to be the model I'd first hoped for, but I certainly wasn't going to hold that against her.

I had to say something to disguise the fact that I could scarcely keep my eyes off her breasts. "I think your father means to subvert me. He's very big on politics, isn't he?"

111

"Oh, God," she said, with an attempt at sophistication which wasn't quite convincing. "He can be quite a bore on the subject, I'm afraid. Do you have a cigarette? I ran out on the way up here and didn't want to stop in all this beastly rain."

I gave her one of my Senior Service and lit it with my all-American Zippo. I leaned against the dresser and watched her take off her raincoat, sit on the bed and cross her legs. Stephany's eyes were blue; her complexion was delicate; and if she had a bit too much of her father's brow and nose, she had a mouth so sensuously molded it must have come from her mother's side of the family. I liked the way she sat there smoking, as if she were being a very naughty girl to take such liberties in a gentleman's bedroom. It made me think that the world of the London fashion industry had yet to spoil the child in her—but then I was prone to romanticize every attractive woman I met.

"Will you be staying long?" she asked. "I hope so. It gets so dreary here with just Daddy and Grandmama. I wasn't going to come at all, until I heard about you."

"I guess I can stay several days," I said, "or until your father feels he's done all he can with me. I intend to resist his indoctrination, and I can be very stubborn."

"Drag it out for as long as you can. There'll be other things for us to do between debates."

She gave her head another toss to show me once again how fetchingly her hair could caress her cheeks and shoulders. "Are you interested in painting? I often go out with my watercolors when I'm down here. There are some lovely spots along the coast. We could make a day of it, when the weather improves."

"I'll pray for fair skies," I said.

She chuckled and ground out her cigarette. "Not if you listen to Father, you won't. Daddy's deadly on religion. Well, I must get out of these wet clothes. See you later, hum?"

"See you later," I said.

After she was gone, I walked over to the window and pressed my burning forehead to the cold glass.

Whoever would have thought, I mused, that a pompous old ass like the professor would have such an altogether charming daughter? Wait until Archie Cavendish hears about this!

I stood looking out at the sodden lawn, the black and shining trees, the bleak expanse of sea just a shade darker than the glowering sky. The rooks, perched among the tree branches like a convocation of demons, cawed imprecations down upon the dismal scene. Giles Mortimor, in his cap and mac, was just coming up the drive from the barnlike structure where he'd stowed Stephany's car. He paused and looked off into the woods. He put his hand to his mouth, and I thought he was calling to someone, but the sound of his voice was indistinguishable from the ceaseless squawking of the birds. Then I saw a large, dark, rain-soaked figure emerge from the woods and shuffle toward the old man along a muddy path. He was hatless, his fair hair plastered to his skull, and though he was huge and powerfully built, he stumbled along the path like a child who had just learned to walk. Old Giles gestured angrily, shaking one fist and pointing back into the woods with the other. Then I recognized the thing the large shuffling man held dangling by the tail. It was a dead cat.

11

Pennies from Heaven

The old woman watched us with a falcon's alert and predatory gaze. "I was wondering when you'd come up to see me, Kenneth," she said. "After so long an absence, you might have shown a greater eagerness to pay your respects."

Trevor-Finch gave me an embarrassed glance, then leaned quickly forward to kiss the old woman's polished brow. There was no love in the gesture, nor did it evoke an affectionate response from the mummy in the wheelchair who glared up at him—and at me—with undiminished distrust.

"You were sleeping when I arrived last night, Mother. At any rate, I'm here now. And I've brought a friend to visit you—Dr. David Fairchild, from America."

The old creature turned her dark eyes on me. She didn't offer the withered hand she held curled in her lap, so there was no need to touch her ancient and somehow repugnant person. I simply smiled and nodded, my most disarmingly boyish smile and nod.

The old woman was not disarmed. "An American, are you? How nice. You must feel terribly honored to have attracted the attention of my illustrious son."

"Mother, really!" Trevor-Finch said. "Fairchild is much too ignorant of modern physics to understand the slightest thing about my work. I asked him down so that he could meet you, among other things." He gave me an apologetic grin, as if acknowledging that he had meant all along to throw me to the family wolf.

"How generous of you," the old woman said. "Another way to avoid seeing very much of me yourself, I imagine. What is your field of study, Dr. Fairchild?"

"Medieval literature."

The professor and his mother exchanged not quite a glance, but a signal on a wavelength I could intercept but not interpret. "Now, that *is* interesting," she said. "You must tell me about your work. I have a considerable interest in the medieval period myself . . . but here's Archer with our tea. Sit down, please. Surely you can spend a few minutes with your mother, Kenneth, having neglected her so shamefully all winter."

Mrs. Archer, a hatchet-faced old nurse, who looked robust and blooming in comparison to her mistress, wheeled the tea cart to the old woman's side. Mrs. Trevor-Finch tried to pour, but her grasp was too weak, her hand too palsied. With an impatient nod, she let Mrs. Archer do the honors.

We were in the sitting room of a suite on the third

floor of the Victorian wing. There were windows on two sides of the room and the clouds had broken up since the downpour, so that the room passed through phases of sunshine and shadow, its antique furnishings alternately gleaming and fading, as if an electric torch were probing the darkness of a pharaoh's tomb. The fire in the tiled hearth was making it uncomfortably warm, but the old woman seemed to be repressing shivers in her tangle of blankets and afghans.

When we had our cups of tea to balance on our knees, the professor said, "Actually, Mother, Fairchild's present concern is with some papers in the College library, some manuscripts from—which century did you say it was, Fairchild?"

"They're usually dated in the late thirteenth to early fourteenth centuries," I said, "though I'm convinced there's one which is much older—a remarkable poem from the twelfth century."

"And it's this poem, I gather, which you've associated with our local legends—is that right?" the professor asked.

The old woman glared at me; the professor was inspecting the shine on his shoes. A scythe of sunlight swept the room and was gone.

"Yes. I've tentatively identified the author as one Geoffrey Gervaise, an obscure priest and scholar who lived for several years at Creypool Abbey, was captured there and burned at the stake."

The professor's mother looked as if I had just dropped something obscene in her blanketed lap. Trevor-Finch said, "Isn't that an amusing coincidence, Mama? I mean, those manuscripts in the College library having something to do with our own Creypool Abbey, not five miles from the house. I told Fairchild he ought to have a look at the place, and a chat with Parson Tompkins."

"Tompkins is a fool," Mrs. Trevor-Finch said. "He's been going about the country with that tape recorder of his, stirring up all sorts of ridiculous tales."

"It's all foolishness, to my way of thinking," the professor said, "but these literary chaps quite go in for that sort of thing. Fairchild's ears stood up when I told him the abbey is supposed to be haunted. Of course, everything's supposed to be haunted in England! There's money in it—from the tourists, you know."

I wondered if I was really picking up an urgent transmission between the professor and his mother, or if my own preoccupation made me too quick to interpret the discomfort of their reunion. I said, "Would that include, by any chance, this house?"

The old woman's eyes narrowed and hardened; her frown was majestic and I felt for the first time the full force of her great age. She was perhaps eighty, yet she gave the impression of having survived from an era of barbarian conquest and pagan sacrifice. She had been witness, I felt sure, to horrors.

"I think that you are not quite serious, Dr. Fairchild."

"Serious? I'm pretty serious about some things, Mrs. Trevor-Finch. Unfortunately, I may have to return to America before I've finished my research."

Mrs. Archer, who'd sat down with us and had been listening to our conversation without much interest, suddenly said, "Ah, America! I'd love to visit America. I have a niece who lives in California."

Mrs. Trevor-Finch turned slowly. "Shut up," she said, as if putting two calm, deliberate slaps across Mrs. Archer's ruddy cheeks. "Go on about your business. Why don't you start preparing my luncheon, for heaven's sake?" And then to me: "I never have more than a little soup, and seldom leave these rooms any more. I'm afraid my confinement here has made quite a horrid person of me, especially since my son and granddaughter so seldom visit me."

"Well, Mama, what can you expect?" Trevor-Finch said. "When we do come, all you do is grouse at us for not coming more often. And bully poor old Archer for our edification. I'm sure you've made a dreadful impression on Fairchild."

"I don't think I care what Dr. Fairchild thinks of me," the old woman said. "His opinions would no doubt shock us all, were he not clever enough to conceal them. But I am willing to talk to you again, young man. We may get on somewhat better when my son is not watching us like some deranged matchmaker. I don't know which one of us you expect to sit up and do tricks, Kenneth, but we're neither the sort for staged performances, I think."

"Certainly, Mother. Whatever you say." Trevor-Finch got quickly to his feet. I rose more reluctantly.

"I would like to talk to you again," I said. "I think you could be very helpful, if you wanted to."

"How could I possibly help *you?*" the old woman asked.

"By giving me some insight into the history of the region. One never knows just what one is going to find until one looks at all the possibilities."

"And sometimes," the old woman said, "one finds more than one bargained for. Have you never found that to be the case, young man?"

"Oh, I'm very fond of bargains," I said with a smile. "Try me out and you'll see."

"I'm sure you take whatever you can get," the old woman said, and waved us away, calling us back from the door only to ask the professor to send Stephany up—"at her convenience, if it isn't asking too much."

On the stairs, the professor, who had not smoked in his mother's presence, paused to light his pipe. He puffed furiously for a moment, then glanced sheepishly at me, as if to say, "Well, even distinguished physicists must have mothers," and led the way downstairs.

We crossed the great hall and entered a library in the Georgian wing, where Trevor-Finch looked a good deal more comfortable. He poured me a glass of sherry.

"Don't be too put off by Mama," he said. "She's had a wretched time of it these last few years. Her health is very bad, and I daresay it gets lonely, and monotonous. She was quite an admirable woman in her day, believe it or not."

I believed it, but I said, "She didn't seem to take to me very much, did she?"

"She's naturally suspicious of strangers," Trevor-Finch said. "Give her a chance to get used to the idea of having you here, and she'll come around."

A large, broad-bottomed woman of middle age, with frizzy gray-brown hair and a wonderfully homely mug, looked into the library and asked the professor if he was ready for lunch.

"Yes indeed, Mrs. Mortimor. Is my daughter joining us?"

"No, sir. She already had a bite and went off to see a friend in Wimsett. But she said she'd be here for dinner."

"Jolly good. I'm anxious for you to meet my daughter, Fairchild."

I explained the circumstances under which we had already met.

"Clumsy of Mortimor," the professor said, leading the way into an adjoining dining room. He pulled out a chair at the head of the long, lustrous table. There was a yellow cat curled up on the chair, and it blinked up at the professor.

"Scat!" he said, and gave the cat a whack across the flank with the rolled-up newspaper which had been waiting at his place. "Damned insolent beasts," he muttered as he plopped down.

The dining room could easily have accommodated a small banquet. There was a row of French doors looking out on the puddled terrace, several murky paintings on the walls, a few potted ferns, and a glorious cut-glass candelabrum as a centerpiece. Mrs. Mortimor arrived bearing steaming plates of steak and kidney pie. She uncapped two bottles of beer, then stood anxiously by to make sure everything was satisfactory.

The professor sent her off with a nod of approval. "Now tell me, Fairchild—what do you know about radio astronomy?"

"Not the slightest thing," I said around a mouthful of hot and excellent pie.

The professor explained that radio astronomy was born in the 1930s, when a young radio engineer—"a Yank, by the way"—first detected radio waves originating in outer space. As the technology developed, radio sources were discovered on the sun, on Jupiter, and in the constellations Sagittarius, Cygnus and Cassiopeia. "My own setup is quite modest," the professor said, "but by correlating the data from a number of widely spaced sites, we are sometimes able to pinpoint the exact origin of these signals. So far, we've located over two thousand of them."

"But what causes these radio waves?" I asked. "Is someone out there trying to reach us?"

"Hmm. Extraterrestrial life is a possibility no scientist would dispute," Trevor-Finch said, "but these radio waves do not indicate any calculated attempt at communication. The current theory is that they're caused by turbulent gases. The radio source on Jupiter, for instance, may be a gigantic electromagnetic storm on the surface of the planet. Other signals probably emanate from exploding stars or even the collision of entire galaxies. Some of these sources are extraordinarily distant—nine or ten billion light-years from earth—which means, of course, that these waves, which travel at the speed of light, originated some ten billion years ago, in the early development of the universe. What we're getting is in fact a kind of after-image or delayed report of the cosmic cataclysm which started the whole thing. . . . Am I going too fast for you?"

"It does boggle the mind," I said. "I'm afraid I've never studied astronomy."

"Of course, your education in serious matters has been shamefully neglected. I daresay that most of the people on this planet still live in what is essentially a medieval universe."

I was going to suggest that if a man could choose which universe he wanted to live in, a few things could be said for mine, but I let that go.

"Tell me, Professor—if all this happened so long ago and far away, does anyone know what's out there now?"

Trevor-Finch looked a little surprised. "That's a good question, Fairchild. The fact of the matter is, once one starts dealing with these sophisticated problems of time and space, there's no such thing as 'now.' Or rather, it's *all* 'now,' since the universe may exist, metaphorically speaking, in the blink of God's eyelash. It's only our limited and highly localized perspective which provides us with the concept of historical time."

"And would the stars have looked much different, do you suppose, to the astronomers of, say, the twelfth century?"

"Not noticeably. Of course, new stars do appear on occasion. We call them novae or supernovae, depending on their brilliance. There was one reported by Oriental astronomers in 1054, for example, which was probably an exploding star of great size, perhaps that which formed the Crab nebula. So you see, the ancients were wrong—in this as in most everything—to speak of the 'unchanging heavens.' It's quite a busy show up there, if one knows how to look at it. Have you finished your lunch?"

We left the house by a back door and crossed a cold though sunny garden. A few crocuses were blooming and the daffodils were swelling at their tips. We passed a shed where old Giles, surrounded by several of his mangy cats, worked at a bench stacked high with clay pots and bags of fertilizer. He glanced at us, but did not speak.

A path left the garden and entered the trees, and along this path we encountered the large person I'd observed from my window that morning. He was seated on a stone bench with another of the ubiquitous cats in his arms and he was gazing up at the barren treetops. He was younger than I expected—in his late teens or early twenties—with pale smudges of down on his chin and upper lip.

"Hullo, Jamie," the professor said. "Getting a bit wet, aren't you?" For the bench was glistening and situated beneath several dripping trees.

The boy stared at us with eyes as bland and vacant as the wintry sky. His lips moved in a vain attempt at greeting, then slipped into a lopsided dimwit's grin, behind which I saw broken and discolored teeth.

"That's Jamie, the Mortimors' son," the professor

said as we continued along the path. "Hopelessly re-tarded, poor chap. His parents can't bear to give him up, so I've got to keep him on, though he's not good for much. It's incredibly difficult to get servants these days, and Mrs. Mortimor is an excellent cook."

I glanced over my shoulder to see Jamie still staring after us. "He's harmless, I hope."

"Oh, quite. Just an innocent simpleton."

We had reached the end of the trees and a narrow strip of heather along the cliff edge. I could see an expanse of sandy beach and a very dark blue sea, running high, with thunderous explosions of surf along the concave shoreline. A quarter of a mile or so downshore, on a rocky promontory where the breakers flashed in the sun, stood a barrel-shaped tower. A large metallic saucer perched on the cliff just above it.

The professor led the way down to the beach. As we came out onto the sand dunes, he took my arm. "Now mind where you step—this entire coastline was heavily mined during the last war. Because of the tides and shifting sands, they haven't all been recovered. I take rather long strides, and the mathematical probability is that I've not yet tested every inch of surface between here and the tower."

He grinned at me and set off across the beach. I followed, matching my strides to his impressions in the sand, and we arrived at the tower unannihilated.

The professor unlocked a switch box and activated the current. Then he began removing the various padlocks, bolts and chains that secured the heavy door. It was dark and clammy cold inside, full of the smell of sea rot and brine. We went up a spiral stairway to the top of the tower, up through a hole in the floor to a large round room where patches of concrete marked the old gun emplacements. The professor's radio equipment stood shrouded in sheets of canvas. We removed the coverings to reveal a bewildering array of instruments. The professor gave me a broom and I dislodged a couple of spiders as he turned things on, adjusted dials, made notations on a clipboard, then put on a pair of earphones and sat down to listen.

After several minutes he broke into a smile and looked like a man who had just received a long-distance phone call from old and dear friends.

"Here, listen to this," he said, and gave me the earphones.

I clapped them over my ears, but all I heard was static, and said so.

"That, Fairchild, is the music of the spheres—the stars in their courses, the cosmic wheel of time."

I listened again, with the professor beaming at me from his panel of instruments, as if it were he himself who was making the universe go. I still could hear nothing but a belabored wheeze, as if the universe had caught a bad cold.

The professor took back the earphones, listened, adjusted certain dials, and had me try again. "Now surely you can hear that," he said. "Note the pulsations—they're quite distinct."

"I'm getting them," I said. "What is it?"

"It's 3C–213," the professor said, "or number 213 in the Third Cambridge Catalog of Radio Stars—to which I've contributed a few finds myself. This one is a cloud of turbulent expanding gas in the constellation Auriga, a quarter of a degree northeast of Capella. You can scarcely see it with the naked eye, but recent photographs from Palomar show the remnants of an explosion. We calculate that 3C–213 passed through its nova phase not too many hundreds of years ago—about the twelfth century, in fact."

"And was it visible in this part of England?"

"For a few months or years it was probably the brightest star in our sky. Strange that we have no record of it, but the English were not keen astronomers in those days. Once lord of the heavens, 3C–213 is just a cloud of dispersing gas now, its light about to go out. Rather touching, don't you think?"

We spent another hour in the laboratory, eavesdropping on the gossip and chatter of an amazingly hectic universe. The professor conjured up a collision of two galaxies, their millions of stars slipping through one another's web like intangible phantoms. We picked up distress signals from another galaxy just then exploding like a Fourth of July rocket, spewing sparks and gaseous plumes into the great black emptiness. All that celestial violence, that birthing and dying of worlds, reached us through the professor's radio apparatus as but the faint and timid scratching of a cat's paw on the door of time.

I was thoroughly numb by the time we finally put the laboratory to bed and started back to the house.

Sherry at six-thirty, dinner at seven. I wore a coat and tie. Stephany (her hair done in Wimsett, her face lovely and mysterious by candlelight) wore a dinner dress of her own creation and designed, I was sure, with her own endowments in mind. I talked a good deal about my research. Stephany asked intelligent questions; the professor gave an occasional grunt to indicate that such matters were beneath consideration by a man of science. It was settled that we would visit the abbey the next morning, and that later in the week we would have the village parson out to dinner.

"Perhaps I'll invite a few of my friends, as well," Trevor-Finch said. "Some chaps from the local scientific community I'd like you to meet."

"Oh, Daddy, not those dreary men again," Stephany said, with a wink in my direction.

"Dreary?" Trevor-Finch said. "Quite good company, I'd call them. Besides, if I'm going to humor Fairchild's regrettable preoccupation with our sordid past, I think he can submit to some civilized conversation on occasion."

"I'll submit to anything," I said, returning Stephany's wink. "Especially if it's good for me."

"Of course it will be good for you," the professor said. "Why, we'll drag you kicking and screaming into the twentieth century if we have to, won't we, Steph?"

"If he's going to kick and scream," Stephany said, "we'd better leave him where he is. The Middle Ages do seem to suit him, you know. He can be our knight in shining armor, come to rescue us from the evil spell that broods over this awful house."

Though her tone was light and mocking, her choice of imagery drew a sharp look from the professor. "Indeed! Well, shall we adjourn to the library? You say this poet of yours was a famous chess player, Fairchild. I take a mild interest in that game myself. Would you care to take me on? I believe there's a set somewhere about."

I had hoped that the professor would go off to bed early and give me a chance to become better acquainted with his daughter. No such luck. The professor was neither good enough to win quickly nor poor enough to allow me an easy victory. Stephany sat fetchingly on the davenport, her fine long legs on display, and watched us match oedipal hostilities. I took the professor's queen. He assassinated both my bishops. As the game dragged on, Stephany yawned, stretched, nodded sleepily. Finally, she went up to bed.

An hour later, the professor stared in astonishment at the board. It was, I thought—it always was—a little like murder.

"Well done, Fairchild. Will you give me a rematch?"

"I'm sorry. Not tonight. I'm pretty bushed myself and I'd like to turn in."

"Go along, then. I'll get you another time. Can you find your way up? I've a couple of new journals here I've been meaning to look over."

"I can manage. Good night."

We had drunk a quantity of wine with dinner and port in the library. My blood was running high with alcohol and with the heady sense of triumph at the chessboard, and I was convinced that all those looks and smiles Stephany had given me during dinner had to mean something. I was half persuaded that I would find her waiting for me upstairs, in her room or even in mine.

The stairway was dark and I searched for a light switch. Instead, I located a box of candles mounted on the wall, took one, lit it, and proceeded up the stairs amid looming shadows. I suppose the romance of the moment had me fairly giddy: young American scholar on the trail of the unknown, guest in an ancient manor house, out to seduce the master's daughter. Just what anyone would hope for during a year in England. I was perhaps halfway up the stairs when I realized someone was waiting for me at the top.

I paused and raised the candle, but it failed to dispel the darkness in which the figure stood. A woman in a long white nightgown, I could see that much, and I hurried up to meet her, my heart thundering with wicked joy. But before I'd reached the top step, the woman turned away and started down the corridor toward my room. I followed her through the shadows, my candle the only light, but my lust providing an auxiliary glow in which I noticed that the woman's yellow hair had been put into braids that trailed nearly all the way down her back. Stephany's hair wasn't that blond, or that long, and it did seem strange for a young lady of this day and age to braid her hair before bed—especially if she intended to share it with a new lover.

I held back and raised the candle higher. At the same instant the figure in white drew even with the corridor's single window, stopped, and began to turn toward me. A cold draft seemed to leap along the corridor and my candle went out.

There was light enough from the window, however—a blue-white glimmer of moonshine—to show me the woman's face. If in fact you could call it a face. Her features were blurred and indistinct, a white death mask with neither expression nor fleshly substance, an impression I was able to account for, after a moment's shock, by the discovery that the light from the window did not glow upon her face—it glowed *through* it. Her white gown was equally translucent. Indeed, she seemed to possess no physical being whatsoever, only a congealed and intensified essence which throbbed and crackled in the dark hallway like an electrical discharge—a violent displacement of the atmosphere in which she stood.

I gasped for breath; there was a pressure against my chest and another inside my skull. It wasn't simply terror. There was also that feeling I'd had before—that sense of something ancient and corrupt, putrid and defiled. Instinctively I fought to prevent its evil from rushing out to possess me.

The vision itself could have lasted but a few seconds. Yet even as she began to melt into the moonlight that flowed through the window, I became convinced that the creature—woman, demon, spirit, whatever she was—meant me no harm. Her soundless cry seemed to ring in the air even after her image vanished, and it was a cry, I was sure, for help.

I could not immediately move. I was not sure that I still possessed a body. Finally, I dug in my pocket and found a book of matches. Relighting the candle, I proceeded to my room, having no wish at the present to pursue my designs on the professor's daughter.

After I had chased out the cats, got into my pajamas and made one last nerve-racking trek down the hall to the bathroom, I was still too wrought up for sleep. I opened my briefcase and sat down on the bed with my notes. Before the Special Collections had been closed, I had translated several passages of the Westchurch poem into modern verse. They gave little indication of the poet's skill or power, but were fairly true to the content of the poem—and at present, all I had to work with. I sorted through my index cards until I found the one on which I'd rendered several lines from the last long section of the poem. As I suspected, they seemed very much to the purpose of the professor's astronomy lesson.

Oh damned star, oh fiendish light!
Where yesternight was but a well,
A blackish hole where hope could dwell—
Now the heavens blanch with fright,
And hope and faith have lost to hell.

12

The Pleasure of
Their Company

🙚

It was raining again by morning, but the professor, Stephany and I wedged ourselves into the Volkswagen and set out for Creypool, a bucolic hamlet several miles inland and sheltered by a range of low hills. The abbey stood on a bit of high ground between the village and the fens. Only the foundations, a few jagged pieces of wall and several precarious arches were left to claim the protection of the National Trust, but the surrounding gardens were well kept. Within a perfectly symmetrical confluence of grassy plots, graveled paths and freshly turned flower beds, we found an ancient sundial. Its eroded and moss-stained stone spoke eloquently of the passage of centuries.

Trevor-Finch turned up his collar against the drizzle and, pipe clenched between his teeth, looked upon the debris of a rival tradition. "The Puritans, good swine, tore the place down," he said. "Too bad; it might have done for a hospital or a school. Until the Trust took it over, it was nothing but a sheep pasture—though my father did some excavating and poking about here in his time."

We roamed the broken stonework with its occasional seams of concrete and patches of brick. I inspected the remnants of the abbey's chapel, library and dining hall. Farther on, we encountered a maze of individual cells, most no larger than a good-sized broom closet. They were open to the wind and rain, and weeds sprouted among their paving stones, but they would have been dark and secretive once. I reflected that it must have been in one of these tiny cells that Geoffrey Gervaise worked over the lines of his extraordinary poem. Good and evil, faith and despair, being and nothingness—the great cosmic drama, miniaturized and made to perform its ageless pantomime in a cell barely six feet long and four feet wide. It occurred to me that our modern philosophers had not been the first to discover the miracle of relativity.

Trevor-Finch wandered off to look at something and Stephany and I found ourselves alone. She took my hand and drew me back into the shadow of a precarious archway.

"Isn't this a romantic spot?" she asked. "It's like something out of Byron or Shelley—so melancholy, yet so serene and ageless."

We were agonizingly close in a well of cold, wet stones, with massive blocks poised directly above our heads. There were raindrops like tears on Stephany's lashes, a slight flush on her china-doll cheeks. A lock of hair clung wetly to her slender neck, and there was something touchingly submissive about the way she huddled close to me in the little niche we had found.

"Stephany, is there some mystery connected with Abbotswold? Something your father doesn't want me to know about?"

"Why do you ask that?"

"Last night at dinner, when you mentioned an 'evil spell,' your father seemed momentarily upset. And yesterday, when I talked to your grandmother—"

"Grandmama knows all the family stories," she said. "You'll have to ask her. They don't want me to know."

"Who doesn't want you to know what, Stephany?"

"Daddy and Grandmama. They don't want me to know about the ghost and all that rubbish. They're afraid it will put ideas into my head. It's so silly, really. I mean, at my age: What ideas haven't I already thought of, hmm?"

"So there *is* a ghost! Do you know anything about her, Stephany?"

"Her? What makes you think it's a 'her'? I'm afraid

I can't tell you a thing, David. I've always been dreadfully protected. Ever since my mother . . ."

"Yes, what happened to your mother?" I asked, when she paused. But she seemed confused and her large blue eyes pleaded with me not to ask any more question. I still held her small, warm hand in mine, and I thought I could probably kiss her if I tried, but as I lowered my lips to hers I heard footsteps crunching gravel behind us. Stephany slipped away with a teasing smile, and then Trevor-Finch rounded the corner.

"What have you two been up to? There's a rather interesting bit of business I want to show you."

We followed the professor across a courtyard lined with the stumps of thick pillars, then through the glistening rubble of the roofless chapel. Beyond the abbey's rear wall—an uneven row of impacted, rotting molars—we reached the verge of the slope that led down to the fens. As far as I could see to the south and west, the land was flat, green, wet and empty, but just to our left there was a small, brushy hillock.

"Over here," Trevor-Finch said, and led the way into the brush and up the muddy incline. We pushed through the branches, to come out on a stone platform. "Now, what do you think this was?" Trevor-Finch asked, with a smugness which indicated he was about to score a point.

I saw that the flat stone floor had once been walled and possibly roofed over. It was octagonal in shape and not more than eight feet across, suggesting one of those miniature temples one sees adorning the classical landscape in old paintings of nymphs and goddesses. "Some sort of a shrine?" I asked.

"Observe the curious markings on the floor," Trevor-Finch said. "Do you see? The four corners of the compass and, here, the signs of the zodiac along this circular track. It was an observatory, no doubt modeled on the stargazing facilities of the ancient Persians and introduced into this country through Islamic influence. You see how it works? The observer stands here, in the center of the room, orients himself by the markings on the floor, then looks up through a series of arches and apertures at various portions of the sky. A crude but effective way of keeping track of the stars for astrological purposes."

"It would be interesting to know who used this observatory," I said, "and what they were looking for."

"Signs and portents, I suppose," Trevor-Finch said.

He looked up and so did I, but all we saw were the low, dense clouds of an exceedingly dismal day.

"I should have thought," Stephany said, putting her arm through her father's but smiling at me, "that this would have been a charming spot for a tryst."

The professor frowned. "No doubt it's served that purpose as well, but nastier things than that go on here from time to time. There was a young woman found murdered in these ruins some years ago—raped, strangled and mutilated, according to the papers. A damned ugly spot of ground, if you ask me!"

The professor's face had turned so gray, and he released such a shuddering grunt of discomfort, that I thought Mrs. Mortimor's fried breakfast was causing him some serious distress. He sat down for a moment on a largish stone, got his pipe going and recovered his normal ebullience. "Well, shall we start back? Beastly weather for sightseeing, I must say."

We ambled back through the ruins, but found no new corpses moldering among the rubble—just a few crushed cigarette packs, beer bottles, wads of tissue and an occasional prophylactic. A large black bird came gliding in through the murky sky and settled, with extended wings, upon one of the higher fragments of the ancient wall. It sat there, glaring down at us like a proprietary ghoul, as we climbed into the car. Stephany and I took the back seat. The professor's anxious eyes searched for us in the rear-view mirror, but I was fairly sure he hadn't seen me take Stephany's hand.

We stopped at the gingerbread parsonage in the village, but Parson Tompkins was apparently not at home. Trevor-Finch left a note wedged into the door inviting the parson to dinner on Wednesday.

"I'm not so sure he'll want to come," Stephany said. "You always browbeat him so unmercifully about religion."

"He'll come," Trevor-Finch said. "My note mentions that you'll be there."

I wondered just how old the parson was. There had been no Mrs. Tompkins to answer our knock.

That afternoon Stephany paid her visit to Grandmama and the professor and I settled down before the fire in the library. The professor had decided it was time to talk about politics, so I resigned myself to a long afternoon. The rain beat against the windows and the wind whistled down the chimney. Trevor-Finch worked his way through the ideological arsenal of the British liberal: nuclear disarmament, the curtailment of American imperialism, the disbanding of NATO, the socialization of the Western world and the coming of the Marxist millennium—when, it began to appear, the clouds would part and the author of *Das Kapital* would be seen descending upon the earth amid angelic choirs, attended by an elite guard of Cambridge dons. Trevor-Finch was enraptured by his vision of a mankind redeemed through the application of scientific principles, liberated at long last from ignorance, poverty and superstition. He refused to acknowledge that it is in the nature of the beast to exist in darkness, in a labyrinth of self-deception and false hopes.

I pretended to give the professor's proposals my earnest attention, but my mind was busy with quite different problems. Abbotswold had a ghost of its own, and I had seen it. Could there be some connection between this apparition and the one which haunted the College? And what of the spirit that was said to dwell at the abbey? Could Gervaise haunt both the College and the abbey—and if so, who was Abbotswold's lady in white? The more I thought about it, the more convinced I became that Professor Trevor-Finch knew more about Geoffrey Gervaise and his posthumous career than he was willing to admit. He had not brought me to Abbotswold simply to badger me with

131

political clichés. He wanted something else from me, but I was damned if I knew what.

The rooks kept up their mournful chorus in the tall trees and the day grew progressively darker. Old Giles came in to refill the woodbox and Mrs. Mortimor served tea. Stephany's description of me as a knight came to mind, and I imagined that this was some trial by tedium which I had to undergo in order to obtain my holy grail. It was not so different, really, from the game I had been playing all my life—that solipsistic pastime of the academic mercenary who knows all the questions yet lacks the faith to come up with any of the answers, so that ultimately his life becomes a grandiose but trivial game. Our pieces are the stars and planets, our board the great black emptiness in which we live. We gamble recklessly with galaxies, wager worlds on the roll of cosmic dice, rake in our winnings when we can and shrug off our losses when we must, for there is really nothing to win, and nothing to lose, except time.

It was going on five when the professor finally bored even himself with his secondhand opinions. "Well, Fairchild, I expect you've had about enough for one day. Care for a nap or a bath before dinner?"

I noticed that the rain had abated. "Actually, I'd like a little fresh air. I think I'll take a stroll."

"Good idea; I've given you plenty of things to mull over. Dinner at seven, as usual."

It was good to get out of the house. Leery of venturing too far with darkness and another storm coming on, I sought the rear gardens, where, passing the Mortimors' cottage, I saw the three of them seated around the kitchen table. Mrs. Mortimor was peeling potatoes with a brisk, experienced knife. Old Giles was puffing on his pipe and sipping a pint of beer. Jamie sat sullenly across from them, stroking a cat, his idiot's eyes fixed on nothing in particular.

I veered wide of the window and continued on toward the garage. Its doors were open and I made out the professor's Volkswagen, Stephany's sports car, and another small vehicle, which I hadn't seen before. I stepped into the garage for a closer look. Green cat eyes peered at me from the darkness. Outside, the wind was picking up and the old structure creaked and rattled. I struck a match and confirmed my impression that the car was gray, but layered with grime and rust. The cat watched me from the hood as I came to the front to search for the manufacturer's insignia. It was an Anglia—a battered, dirty, rust-spotted gray Anglia.

I heard footsteps approaching the stable and crouched by the Anglia's front bumper. It was Jamie's heavy, shuffling stomp, and soon his great bulk filled the rectangle of gray light at the front of the garage. He stood there for a moment, then, in a surprisingly soft and high-pitched voice, said, "Here, kitty—here, kitty-kitty-kitty."

The cat gave a properly suspicious and reluctant mew from the hood.

"Nice kitty," Jamie said. He was coming toward me between the vehicles. I tensed and got ready to run for it around the other side of the Anglia. It would have been a tight squeeze, but I couldn't stay where I was. Jamie was within three feet of me when the cat cried out and tried to leap from the Anglia to the adjacent sports car. Jamie caught it in midflight. The cat hissed and clawed at him; he grunted in pain and anger. Then I heard a sickening snap of bone and cartilage. The cat gave a last gasp.

"Nice kitty," Jamie said, and left the stable with a limp hunk of fur in his arms.

I waited until he was well away, then hurried back to the house. The wind was blowing hard again and the night seemed filled with demons.

"Are you a music fancier, Fairchild?" the professor asked at dinner. "I seem to remember you at our last musical evening at Bromley House. My daughter is quite an accomplished pianist—and I've brought along my violin."

"We're not going to make David suffer through one of our duets," Stephany said. "There are limits, you know."

"I'd love to hear you play something," I said, much to Trevor-Finch's satisfaction, so after dinner we went upstairs to what the professor called the music room, though in size and splendor it rivaled the Cambridge dance hall. There were sheets and layers of dust on everything, the chandelier encased in a bag like a giant cocoon. We uncovered the piano and the professor and Stephany debated their first number, finally settling on something by Mozart.

I sat back with my port and cigar and closed my eyes. Stephany played very nicely, and the professor sawed with passion, if without great virtuosity. Before long Mozart began to have his way with me, for I've always found his music relaxing and slightly erotic, and my recent association with things Viennese only enriched the effect. Augustan nymphs with overflowing décolletages wafted across a refurbished ballroom. Some of them looked like my lost Yvetta, some like Stephany, and one, with long golden braids . . .

Even before I opened my eyes I had heard the discordant element in the room, strident and shrill, as if a third instrument had entered the serenade and was contending with piano and violin for the lead. I looked around for the source of that jarring note, but there was nothing in the shadows, nothing in the filmy mirrors or at the rain-streaked windows. Yet I could feel *her* presence in the room—a violent intrusion which set the very molecules to scampering about us like frightened mice.

And then I noticed something else. The professor's brow was gleaming with sweat. His eyes had become fixed and desperate. He hit a sour note, then another. He lost the beat and struggled to regain it as Stephany, apparently having heard nothing untoward but sensing her father's distress, tried to adjust to a new rhythm. But Trevor-Finch was by now utterly distraught. His violin uttered one last screech and slipped from beneath his chin. His bow dropped to the floor, and those nervous, shifty eyes of his were revealed to me at last as the terrified and half-mad eyes of a haunted man.

134

"Daddy—what's wrong? You're as white as a sheet!"

Trevor-Finch shook off the spell and smiled weakly. "Nothing, dear. Just my stomach. That Yorkshire pudding of Mrs. Mortimor's really is a bit rich."

"Can I get you anything?" Stephany asked. "Perhaps you'd better lie down for a while."

"No, no—I'm all right. It will pass in a minute."

The presence had departed, but Trevor-Finch was so devastated that he finally had to admit that he could not continue the duet. Stephany said she would see him off to bed. "You will excuse us, won't you, David?"

The professor looked at me like a man caught exposing himself in public, and a wordless recognition passed between us.

Stephany turned back from the door. "By the way, the weather forecast for tomorrow is quite promising. Clear skies and warming temperatures. Perhaps you'd like to turn in early yourself. I have a full day planned for us."

"Good idea," I said, and smiled them out of the room.

I poured myself another glass of port and relit my cigar. I had several things to think over, including the fact that on both occasions back at Cambridge, when the apparition I now believed was Gervaise had appeared to me, the professor had been near. Had Gervaise been waiting for me that night beneath the archway, or for the professor? Was my own haunting then but a by-product of his, or was there some other reason why we two had been singled out for such visions?

Suppose Gervaise and this other ghost had something they wanted to tell us, or something they wanted to ask of us . . . would that not account for the impression I'd had on each occasion of an attempt to violate—or perhaps only to penetrate—my mortal shell? So far the effort had been all on their side, but what if it were reciprocated? This line of thought smacked of self-willed hysteria, and there was an embarrassing absurdity in the experiment I was tempted to try. Yet what other way was there to get to the bottom of this thing, and could Gervaise help me if I was not prepared, at least a little bit, to help him?

I sank back in my chair and closed my eyes, summoning echoes of Mozart and trying to recreate the moment at which the ghost had made its presence felt. *All right*, I thought, *I'm ready for you. Let me know what it is you want.*

I gave it several minutes of intense effort, but nothing happened. Feeling silly, disappointed and not a little relieved, I rose from my chair and turned out the lights.

Back in my own room, I dislodged a cat from beneath my dresser with a shoe, got out my notes and sat down at the desk to reread those passages from the poem which I'd translated.

Gervaise had some bitter opinions regarding the female sex, an antipathy extreme even for a medieval ascetic. I had translated only one of his antifemale outbursts, and it offered no clue to the identity of Abbotswold's lady spook:

> Lustful cauldron of the ages!
> All our nights are spent in cages,
> As the fire in us rages,
> As we rot and die by stages.
> In that foul swamp I'll dig no deeper.
> If God made woman, let the devil keep her!

Scarcely had my eyes skimmed these lines than a draft blew through the room and my blood jumped in alarm. *Who is it?* I nearly cried aloud, and then saw that the door was open. I must have left it ajar when I put out the cat. I went to shut it and, returning to the desk, noticed that one of the index cards had fallen to the floor. It was lying face up beneath the desk and its lines immediately caught my eye.

> Upon this parched and barren ground
> Three lonely roses may be found.
> One red as blood, the scholar's whore,

136

Whose deadly kiss shuts heaven's door;
One white and pure, the wise man's dove,
Which leads the saint to God's own love;
And yet another, both red and white—
The boy's first love, the man's delight.
If thou shouldst wander this arid land
Take but the last rose in thy hand.
For though its thorns may prick and wound . . .

But I had been unable to find a modern word to rhyme
with "wound" and had left the last line untranslated.

Three roses, I thought, each one symbolic of the
poet's loves. Yet none of the three necessarily referred
to specific women. I had already deduced that the
"scholar's whore" was probably chess—a game Gervaise both loved and loathed. The "wise man's dove"
might have been theology or prayerful contemplation, a
pursuit for which, in his later years, Gervaise felt himself increasingly unworthy. But what was the third,
"both red and white," a boy's "first love" and a man's
"delight"? I felt I had been given an important clue—a
nudge, as it were, from beyond the pale—yet until I
could return to the manuscript and compare my clumsy
translation to the original, there seemed little I could
do with it.

"Well, thanks, anyway," I told the ghost, for I
wanted to make sure I remained on her good side.

And then I did the bravest thing I'd yet had to do in
my brief career as a seeker of ghostly secrets. I got
ready for bed, turned off the light and, with barely a
trepidation, crawled between the cold sheets and went
to sleep.

13

A Village Tragedy

Einstein has told us that our universe is shaped and defined by light. We live in a visual cage, and what we call time is simply the ever-moving shadow of the bars which confine us. But suppose that by some miracle of technology not allowed for in Einstein's metaphysic we were able to outrun the waves of light which undulate across the universe. As we leap seven hundred and eighty light-years across the galaxy we overtake and leave behind us the light which left the surface of the earth nearly eight centuries previous. The image of a certain Geoffrey Gervaise has proceeded no farther than this on its heavenly pilgrimage. It will travel forever in this everlasting night, seeking its home among the stars, reaching ever outward toward some hypothetical destination at the universe's problematic end. Is light then the stuff our souls are made of? And do our smallest and most secretive acts hang forever on display in the celestial gallery, awaiting the verdict of a Cosmic Critic?

Let us pause now somewhere in the Milky Way to allow poor Geoffrey's laggard light to catch up with us. We are looking back upon the earth of 1165 A.D. It is springtime in Wendlebury. In the fields men plod behind teams of oxen, guiding their wooden plows through loamy soil. In the village the women have swept out their cottages and planted their gardens. Pigs forage in the narrow lanes and cattle graze just beyond the low stone walls which separate, in theory, the life of the men from the life of the beasts. As evening nears, the peasants head home from the fields and the sun dips behind the tall trees across the river. Cooking odors seep from the cottages and black smoke issues from the crude holes in their thatch. The village priest—a tall, thin, black-bearded man in a coarse gray cassock—leaves his cottage and sets out to meet his penitent parishioners at the church. Let's get a closer look at that priest.

Gervaise (for it is he!), what are you doing here? Fugitive though you are, you need not have come to this primitive backwater to wait out Becket's exile. Couldn't you have returned to your Yorkshire monastery, followed Becket to France, pursued your career as legal scholar in Rome or at one of Europe's great universities? But no, I see now that it's simply your old madness which has led you to assume the life of a humble country priest. Still trying to save your soul, aren't you, Gervaise? Still seeking ways to confront the devils that torment you? But what makes you think you will find a less formidable foe here, among these peasants whose ancient servitude to loathsome gods is given testimony in the hoarse, urgent whisperings of the confessional?

"Bless me, Father, for I have sinned. My last confession were just last week, Father, and I've been receiving the sacrament regular now for forty year, Father, ever since I were a girl of ten."

"Yes, daughter. And what sins . . . ?"

"Ah, Father, it's the very same ones. Satan has come to me again in the night, makin' me want to run naked through the village. Someone's put a curse on me, Father."

"Now, now—these are only idle thoughts and not sins. The Lord will protect you for your faithfulness, and no curse can harm you if you cleave to the sacraments."

"Bless me, Father. I killed a chicken and put his entrails in the woodpile to keep away the fairies. . . ."

"I used a charm to cure my daughter's warts. . . ."

"I wanted him to touch me. . . ."

"I have these wicked dreams. . . ."

"And I hit—"

"I struck—"

"I swore—"

Gervaise sighs inwardly as the penitents proceed through the confessional. What a scavenger Satan is! What trivial sins he cultivates among the simple; to what lengths he will go to trouble innocent hearts. It is all very sad, and though Gervaise pities these souls, he envies their comfortable mixture of faith and superstition in which the old gods and the new have found a grotesque reconciliation. Surely none of his flock has ever sinned as he himself has sinned, and none of them carries his burden of eminent damnation.

Ah, Annjenette, Gervaise thinks as the penitents come and go. What have you done to me? I am an outrage to the God I meant to serve, a pollution in His holy Church. You bitch, you whore, you sweet morsel of damnation! How I rode you, a Bellerophon astride his Pegasus. How high we soared, and how far we fell. Who humps you now, you bitch?

"Bless me, Father, for I have sinned."

"Yes, my child. And your last confession . . . ?"

" 'Twas at Christmastime, Father."

Gervaise thinks he recognizes the husky female voice which comes to him through the grille. He fights against that image of her dark eyes and rosy cheeks, full breasts and sleek young animal's body, which the devil promptly provides.

"And your sins, my child?"

"Father, I have committed a most terrible sin, though I didn't want to. My heart was set against it—I prayed to the Virgin—I begged God for mercy—"

Another peasant seduction. Lust along the Wendle. Gervaise has learned much about rural rutting since taking up the duties of a village priest. Yet how do they differ, these lecherous rustics, from the bawds and whoremongers he knew at court—except in being more frequently sorry for their sins?

"My child, if the deed was done against your will, there was no sin. If you resisted, you are innocent in the eyes of God."

"Yes, Father. I heard what you said in last Sunday's sermon—how the Lord will not condemn those who do evil against their will. And before God I am innocent, but my own father will not think so."

If this is the girl Gervaise thinks she is, her father is an ignorant brute, a violent, obstinate freeman who confidently calls God's curse down upon all those who offend his pagan pride.

"You need not tell your father, then," Gervaise assures the girl. "This matter need never leave the confessional."

"But, Father, I think I am with child."

Of course. The innocent ones always nurture the seed. Only whores are barren. Is fertility itself a crime? Increase, multiply, and be damned!

"If you will tell me the boy's name, I will speak to him. He must accept responsibility—"

"But, Father, he can't. He won't. He is . . . much above me in station. He never would. . . ."

At last Gervaise understands. There's only one nobleman in the parish, and Lord William Fitzjames has debauched peasant maids before. Gervaise's own father had done the same. The barons sire bastards as they breed dogs and horses—for sport, for sheer idleness, and perhaps even for policy. In some villages, the lord's bastards are a highly respected class of their own. But in this village, and with this poor girl's father . . .

"My child, you must give me his name, and your own. If I try to help you, I must be sure."

The girl whispers the names; the priest's suspicions are confirmed.

"Daughter, you have been most cruelly used by one who has never understood the Christian duties of his station. There's little hope, I fear, but I shall talk to him. Perhaps, having brought this trouble upon you, he will be good enough to provide you and your child with his protection, as servants at the manor."

"Oh, Father, if only he would! I shall have nowhere else to go. It's been four months now, and soon my father will suspect—"

"Yes, child. I will come to your father's cottage as soon as I have Lord William's answer. And now, though you are guiltless of any sin in this, say your act of contrition and I shall give you absolution."

"But, Father, my other sins—"

"Yes, yes, I can imagine what they are. Do not trouble yourself with trifles. Put your trust in God, my child. He is merciful and forgiving."

As he says the Latin words of absolution—"May God forgive you and by His power I forgive you"—Gervaise wonders if that mercy can extend even to so wretched a sinner as himself. For he knows that his own worst sin is simply his inability to believe in the mercy and love which he preaches to his flock. If I could disbelieve in Satan as I disbelieve in God, Gervaise thinks, I could find peace in indifference. Yet how can one deny the evil which one sees every day, and which one feels within oneself? Though God may or may not be, the devil most certainly *is*.

Supper is now in progress at Fitzjames Hall. There is no philosophic discourse here, no ingenious argument over the rights of kings or the intricacies of law. There is no music, no troubador to sing of Arthurian exploits, though the food is somewhat better than the Spartan fare at Henry's court, and there is wine and mead in great abundance. The lord and his family sit at the high table. The lord's retainers and soldiers (for Lord William keeps a small army with which to tyrannize the peasants, harass the neighboring barons and bargain with the king) are gathered at another. At a third table, closest the door and farthest the fire, sit the servants, the field workers attached to the manor, the vagabonds and travelers who have sought a night's refuge—including, Gervaise sees as he enters the hall, two monks in the brown robes of Cistercians. There is a Cistercian monastery not far away, where the priest has friends.

He sits with the monks and partakes of the meal. These two are new to the order and do not know Gervaise. They ask questions concerning the village, the spring planting, the fish in the river. Gervaise keeps his eye on the lord, who has surely seen his parish priest enter the hall, though he does not beckon to him. Lord William has in general no time for priests, and it was only the abbot's wealth and influence which persuaded him to give the village church and its meager living to this fugitive. Lord William rather enjoys sheltering an enemy of the upstart king, but he has had reason over the past twelve months to regret his charity. A troublemaker, with a zealot's righteous fervor . . . Such priests are more than a nuisance. Let the bastard tend his flock and leave the ruling of this fiefdom to its rightful master, the lord thinks, as he continues to avoid the priest's gaze.

After the meat and bread, after the ale and puddings and cakes, the tables are cleared by the lord's servants. The lord's women—a shrewish wife and three shrewish daughters—depart for another chamber. The knights amuse themselves with more drinking, with dice and chess, storytelling and arm wrestling and an occasional outburst of cudgels. The monks leave for whatever humble accommodations the lord has given them, and Gervaise resolutely approaches the high table.

"What is it this time?" Lord William snaps. "You've come on some bitter business, I can see that by the hellish glint in your eyes. Which peasant has come whining to you this time?"

"There is a girl, my lord, a peasant's daughter whom I think you know. Her father is Richard the Red—not a serf, but a freeman in the village."

"Richard the Red. A pity my father ever gave the rogue his freedom. He's a villainous fool, and too damned proud of his standing in the village. He still owes me his obedient service and his rent, by God."

"Yes, my lord. Hasn't he paid you?"

"He has, but only with great resentment and ill will. I'd like to set my dogs on him, the insolent beggar."

"You have done worse, I think. This daughter, who has just turned fifteen, and of whose virtue he is so watchful—she is now three or four months with child."

"Ha! It serves the old fool right. He hates it when his neighbors get a chance to laugh at him."

Gervaise grips the back of the lady's empty chair

and leans forward to press his gaze and his words upon the nobleman. "I am not concerned for Richard the Red, my lord. It is the girl who needs your help. She is young and innocent and was taken against her will by a man in station far above her. There is no hope of marriage, so her only recourse is her father's mercy—which she will not receive."

"So? What is that to me? These peasant brutes must manage their own affairs. You're not suggesting that one of my knights . . ."

"No, my lord, not one of your knights. I have married and baptized and buried a good many of your peasants in the past year, and I know the conditions under which they live. I also know who most delights in the defilement of simple maids in this parish."

Lord William slams his cup down on the table and glares drunkenly at Gervaise. "Christ's blood! You have the gall to accuse me of siring this wench's bastard?"

Gervaise finds a certain cruel pleasure in meeting and mastering the gaze of his lord. "I do."

Lord William reaches for a jug of wine and overturns it. Apoplectic, he shakes a bone in Gervaise's face, then tosses it to his dogs. "You mind your tongue, priest, or I'll have it sent to the Angevin as a proof of my loyalty. I've taken considerable risk for your sake. A man lacking my boldness wouldn't have done it. But I won't have you meddling in my affairs. Your business is with souls, is it not?"

"At the moment it is the girl's body, and the use you have made of it, which endangers her soul. Cast out in her condition, she shall have no choice but to leave her home and become a whore. Her child shall grow up a beggar and thief, and then the fate of two souls shall be laid to your door, William Fitzjames."

"And what would you have me do, marry the slut? Has the Church then turned in favor of harems such as the heathens keep?"

"I don't commend her to you as a concubine, my lord. You must take the girl into your household as a servant and put her child under your protection."

"What? Bring up a peasant bastard? The wench lies, Gervaise. I won't have her in my house. Good God, man, you'd have every peasant within a day's ride bringing me his daughter in the hope I'd enlarge her belly and then make her one of my servants. No, no; it's out of the question."

For a moment Lord William regards Gervaise with outrage; then a crafty smile appears. "Perhaps, good Father Geoffrey, you could use a wife yourself—someone to cook your meals, care for your cottage, warm your bed...."

"I am forbidden by Church law to take a wife."

"Nonsense. All our village priests have had wives in the past and were much the better for it. Besides, you needn't marry her. Take her as your servant; I'm sure she'd repay your kindness, as only a woman can."

Gervaise sees the fiend in Lord William's eyes, urging remedies he dare not consider. "You refuse, then, to do anything for the girl? This is your final answer to the voice of your conscience and the authority of the Church?"

"Don't parade your churchly authority in front of me, zealot. I can send you packing anytime I like. The damned country is crawling with clergy, and an ignorant village lad would suit our needs much better than a scholar like yourself. Go back to the village, where you belong, and let the pretty maidens stroke your pious balls. God's blood, I hate priests!"

Gervaise turns to go, then swings suddenly back upon the drunken nobleman. "I shall leave your house, Fitzjames, but I shall not abandon my flock. Nor shall I abandon the poor girl who bears your bastard. I shall tell the villagers from the pulpit whose child she carries. And every man in the village shall curse you as a tyrant, fiend, and enemy of Christ!"

Outside the manor house, Gervaise sees the stars brilliant and cold above him. He walks back to the village, his eyes turned up to the stars and to us who watch him from the other side of time. But there is no sign from heaven—after all these years, still no sign!—and the priest's mind turns as ever to that poem

145

over which he labors by candlelight, night after night, seeking not the answers he knows he will never find, but the pleasure of a more artful question. How is it that the just can live by faith whereas the doubters must make poems? To make a world of words is not to rival but surely to mock the Creator. Hell must be full of poets, and chess players too.

Gervaise is already crossing the pasture outside the village when he hears the sound of horses and armor. He is slow to turn, and already the horsemen loom above him, black shapes like centaurs against the stars. He jumps from the road, but can't evade the flat of a sword, which topples him senseless into the ditch.

The riders draw in their horses, dismount and gather around the fallen priest. Though their faces are hidden behind iron masks, Gervaise knows who his assailants are, and who has sent them. He expects the rush of steel through his innards, the explosion of gore; he is almost glad life will come so abruptly to an end.

But the knights have not come to murder Gervaise. They beat him with mailed fists, armor-sheathed arms and legs; they kick at him with heavy boots. Sparing only the shell which encloses his madman's brain, they leave him battered and senseless in the blood-smeared mud of the ditch.

Gervaise lies moaning in delirium a long time beneath the silent stars. Spirits and demons, the imps of ancient Celtic legend, peep out at him from the nearby grove of trees, the hedgerow, the dew-drenched grass of the meadow. The stars shine upon his agony with cold indifference. The priest's blood seeps into the earth and the dampness of the soil permeates his body.

Toward dawn the two monks set forth from the manor and find Gervaise in the ditch. Knowing better than to seek help at the manor, they go into the village, where a peasant offers his ox and cart. The journey to the monastery takes the better part of the day, and the peasant's wife holds Gervaise's head upon her lap while her husband shields the priest's eyes from the sun. Gervaise cries out in agony as the cart bounces along the rutted track. By evening he is back within the shelter of monastery walls, once more a refugee.

Learning of the source of his friend's injuries, the abbot sends his servants to the village to fetch Gervaise's few belongings. As a scholar and disciple of the archbishop, the priest is welcome at Blackstone for as long as he cares to stay.

The servants return bearing word of a recent tragedy in the village. Richard the Red has murdered his daughter. Her bruised body was found lying in the church, in a pool of blood from her aborted fetus, and just beneath the body of her father, who had hanged himself from the wooden angel which adorns the confessional.

14

The Rites of Spring

By Tuesday morning the clouds were gone, and Stephany informed her father at breakfast that she was taking me up the coast past Wimsett to scout seascapes. Trevor-Finch seemed pleased and blessed the excursion by saying he had some calculations to test in his tower laboratory which would keep him busy all day.

I was in my room lacing up a pair of hiking shoes when Mrs. Mortimor appeared in the doorway.

"Sorry, sir. I thought you'd gone off. I was just going to do up your room."

"Go right ahead," I said. "I'll be off in a minute."

She emptied ashtrays and ran a dust rag across the dresser top. "Lovely day, ain't it, sir?"

"Indeed it is. I was beginning to wonder if spring ever does come to the British Isles."

She chuckled, glad to take a break for a little conversation. "It does seem ever so late this year. Of course, the spring is always late up here. I do miss them lovely springs we used to have in the south."

"You're from the south of England?"

"Dorset. Mr. Mortimor and me, we had a nice little bed-and-breakfast establishment in a little town called Wopping. Don't suppose you've ever heard of Wopping, but it's right on a lovely little river and ever so nice."

"The Wendle, by any chance?"

"Why, yessir. Do you know that part of England? We were just a few miles from Paxton-Brindley, where all the tourists go to see Westchurch Hall. It's been restored right back to what it was in the old days, and they have a lovely little museum, too."

"I haven't been there, but I'd like to see it before I leave England."

"It's well worth the trip. Mr. Mortimor used to have a good many friends in Paxton-Brindley. He belonged to an outing society of sorts, though it did seem they spent most of their time in the pubs. They was good chaps, for the most part. It's a pity we had to leave—and just when our little place was doing so well, too."

"Why did you leave?" I asked.

Her plug-ugly face clouded over. "Them were troubled times for us. Our poor boy, Jamie, got himself into a bit of trouble, you see, and. . . . But I shouldn't be telling you all this, now, should I? There's Miss Trevor-Finch, waiting for you out in the hall."

Stephany gave me a disapproving look as I left the room. "Really, David," she said as we went down the stairs. "If you want to become a proper English gentleman, you must learn not to get on so well with the servants."

"How do you know that's what I want?" I asked her.

"It's fairly obvious," she said. "If it weren't for your accent, and that habit you have of leaving your collar unbuttoned so that your tie comes loose all the time, you'd be scarcely distinguishable from the real thing.

Not that there's any great merit in making yourself like us, for heaven's sake."

"I admire the English," I said. "And English girls are totally charming. I dote upon English girls."

"I'm sure you've known a good many," she said with a smile, and led me out of the house.

"By the way," I said, as we settled ourselves in the bucket seats of her sports car. "Did your grandmother have anything to say about me yesterday?"

Stephany revved up the engine. "Only that I shouldn't trust you." She laughed, and pulled away from the house with a squeal of tires.

I said no more until we were well on our way to Wimsett and I had accustomed myself to Stephany's passionate performance at the wheel. She was leaving a good deal of rubber on the turns and I had several dizzying glimpses of the surf foaming over rocks below us.

"Do you trust me, Stephany?" I finally asked.

She took her eyes off an approaching curve and barely got them back in time to corner the sports car smartly. "I don't really know you yet, do I? Why don't you ask me that on the way home?"

"You started to tell me yesterday about your mother."

"There isn't much to tell. She left us when I was quite young. During the war. I was brought up by Grandmama, and in a series of perfectly awful boarding schools, where I was dutifully taught how to charm young Americans."

"And you were never told why your mother deserted you?"

" 'Deserted' me? That sounds so harsh. I'm not sure she did, really. A lot of people simply disappeared over here during the war. Some died in the air raids, and some just couldn't put up with it all and ran for cover. My own theory is that Mother fell madly in love with some dashing Yank from the local air base, and that they're living happily ever after somewhere in your splendid country. . . . I'd like to think, you see, that *somebody* I know has found happiness."

Stephany's face set itself in hard lines, and her foot

came down on the accelerator, putting an end to my questions. We drove through Wimsett and continued along the coast. Finally, Stephany braked sharply, pulled off the road and onto a lane that twisted down through the heather to a deserted beach. The white dunes stretched for miles beneath a placid sky. Stephany gave me a blanket and picnic basket from the trunk and we started off across the dunes.

"Uh—what about the mines?" I asked her.

"Mines? Has Daddy been worrying you with that old fairy tale? Three years ago a couple of schoolboys managed to blow themselves up on a beach near Lowestoft and he's never gotten over it. I suppose there's a chance in a million that we could both be blasted sky-high with the next step, but what the hell? It's too nice a day to worry about that."

And so it was. The wind did magical things with Stephany's hair and billowed her skirt. After a while she took off her shoes, leaning against me, and wet her toes in the shining wash of booming waves. She ran on ahead and shore birds scattered before her. She was a lovely girl, and our escape from Abbotswold made us both buoyant and blissful. I knew it was going to be one of my lucky days.

After a mile or so we came to a sheltered cove where the heather encroached on the beach and the sea crashed on some fairly picturesque rocks. Stephany picked out a hummock of sand and sat down with her box of paints and sketch pad. I was a little surprised that she really intended to paint.

"Would you like to try?" she asked me. "You can use my paints."

"I'll watch," I said.

She quickly dabbed colors onto the pebble-grained paper. The scene took shape with a few deft strokes— an entirely conventional seascape, but not without its nice touches. Stephany hummed softly as she worked. The wind ruffled her hair and rouged her cheeks. I grew restive and put my arm around her. She ignored it. I tried kissing her ear, but she brushed the kiss away with a sharp toss of her head. I was beginning to wonder if I had drastically misread certain early signals, when she finished her painting and put the sketchbook aside.

"There. Daddy doesn't know the first thing about watercolors. He'll think it took me all day to finish that."

And she turned to me, her eyes shining, her hair full of sunlight, her mouth parted for a kiss. When, a few moments later, I put my hand to her breast, I found that she was already freeing the buttons of her marvelously burdened blouse.

It was late afternoon when, gritty with sand and salt, pink from sun and wind, but full of the friendly familiarity of lovers, we stopped for tea at a small, stupefyingly sedate hotel along Wimsett's pastel sea front.

"Isn't this a lovely little place?" Stephany asked. "It would make the perfect setting for an illicit weekend. So refined, you know; so teddibly, teddibly British!"

"Perhaps we can arrange one after I've gone back to Cambridge," I suggested.

"Oh, no. In order to have a proper illicit weekend, we'd both have to be married to other people. That's how it's done, you see. One suffers in silence for as long as one can bear, and then one finds a fellow sufferer—male or female, it scarcely matters which these days—and escapes for a discreet and cruelly poignant two or three days of bliss."

"You seem to know a good deal about it," I said.

"I've been to the cinnie," she said, "and read all the novels."

"And your own life?"

"Oh, my own life is quite satisfactory, thank you. I have my *scintillating* career in London and my set of *fascinating* friends. I'm really quite an advanced, liberated sort of woman, or hadn't you noticed?"

She sounded bitter, so I said, "I think you're a nice girl, Stephany. I like you a lot."

She laughed and offered me the plate of pastries. "Said with true Yank simplicity! I can see why Father likes you, and why he brought you down here."

"Then maybe you can fill me in," I said.

"Isn't it obvious? Daddy thinks I should have married a long time ago. He doesn't approve of the life I lead in London. If he knew more about it, I'm sure he'd be properly horrified."

I reflected upon the advantages of becoming the professor's son-in-law. Once he knew me, however, Trevor-Finch would no doubt regret his choice.

"Of course, it's all nonsense," Stephany said brightly. "I'm perfectly happy as I am."

"Stephany," I said, "have you decided whether or not you can trust me yet?"

She sipped at her tea and avoided my eyes. "I'm not sure it matters, pet. I rather like having an affair with a man I don't quite trust."

I wanted to break through the glaze of London sophistication and self-mockery she relied upon to keep me off balance. "You mentioned yesterday that Abbotswold has a ghost. Last night your father looked as if he saw one."

"Do you think so? He often has such spells. . . ." She drummed her fingers on the table, looking out at the old people on the promenade and at the gulls soaring above a bile-colored sea. "Poor Daddy! He's had a difficult life. But then, all the Trevor-Finches have been miserable wretches. There's a kind of bad luck—almost a curse—which hangs over our family." She turned suddenly and took my hand. "David, if I do decide to trust you—if I tell you something about my father—will you try to help him?"

"What makes you think I could help your father? He seems quite pleased with himself just the way he is."

"It's all a pose," she said. "I know he had a nervous breakdown some years ago and that he's been seeing a psychiatrist ever since. Whenever he visits me in London he claims to have come on scientific business, but I found out he's actually there to see his shrink. It's all got something to do with Mother's leaving him, and the way his father died."

"How did his father die?"

"I'm not sure, actually. There was an accident. At the abbey, I think, where Grandfather was conducting an experiment of some sort. . . . I really know so little about this, and it's all so muddled. You must talk to Grandmama. She knows"—Stephany paused to give the next word emphasis—"everything!"

I was not surprised to hear that the old lady might be omniscient, at least where family history was concerned. "Will you give her a good report on me?" I asked. "Tell her I'm worthy of her confidence?"

Stephany squeezed my hand. "Yes, if you promise to help us."

I lit a cigarette and gazed at the elderly couples at the little tables around us, each with white linen and a single red rose in a china vase. "I really don't understand yet what I could possibly do to help anybody. If it involves my research and something I may learn about your family in the process—yes, I will try to help, but your father will have to ask me first."

Stephany's face fell. "He's much too proud. He has nine hundred years of family tradition to uphold."

"That's an interesting situation for a radical," I said. "What makes him so proud of his family name?"

"It isn't just the name. It's the sorrow and suffering behind the name. Madness, suicide, broken marriages—God knows everything we've had to endure in nine hundred years. Daddy feels it all quite keenly. We all do, David. That's what it is"—she stopped to consider—"to be one of us."

And with that we seemed to reach an impasse, our friendly intimacy abruptly broken. I had an impression of growing suddenly older. Stephany seemed older, as well, the two of us fit company for the weary, life-worn couples who surrounded us in that abysmal tearoom, men and women still unsure of one another after years of marriage, still hiding from one another through long and terrifying silences.

We drove back to Abbotswold in the dusk. As we were putting the car away in the garage, I asked Stephany who the gray Anglia belonged to.

"The Mortimors," she said. "They hardly ever drive it; it's about ready to fall apart."

And so it was, but I had a hunch that little car had made it to London and back not long ago.

I did not know what to make of Stephany, so bright and carefree one moment, so solemn and troubled the next. It was as if several personalities contended within her, each of which I sometimes glimpsed but could not fully grasp. I knew one thing, however. Our outing had affected me in ways I hadn't expected, and which made me distinctly uneasy. For I seemed to have become a member of Stephany's peculiar family and a party to their fears and sorrows—not quite a son-in-law, mind you, but a shirttail relative from America who nurtured some slim hope of gaining a permanent place within the clan.

That night Stephany came to me in my room. She wore a long white nightgown, her hair scented and shining, a candle in her hand—the shyly amorous heroine of a schoolgirl's Gothic romance.

"Stephany, it is you, isn't it?" I asked, as I admitted her to my bed.

"Of course, darling. Who did you expect? Mrs. Mortimor?"

Hardly, but there was a female on the premises whose presence I could not quite forget, though Stephany and I made sweet, sensual, insatiable love while just down the hall the professor lay snoring and dreaming his dreams of social justice.

Toward dawn I woke to hear her sobbing softly beside me.

"Stephany, what's wrong?"

"Nothing, sweet. Just a dream. It always upsets me."

"What sort of dream?"

"I don't know if I can explain it . . . it gets all mixed up when I try to remember. I'm locked in a room somewhere in the house—in the tower, perhaps. I hear my mother calling and I want to go to her but I can't get out. Then sometimes it seems as if it's my mother locked in the room and she wants me to free her, but I can't unlock the door. And then all of a sud-

154

den it's me again who's locked in, but I'm no longer myself. I don't know who I am—and I wake up crying."

I put my arm around her chilled shoulders and before long found ways to make her forget her unhappy dream.

The next morning, when Trevor-Finch went off to consult with the stars once more, Stephany took me on a complete tour of the house—up to the twelfth-century tower and down to the murky, moldly cellar, into rooms which had been locked up for generations, through secret passageways and abandoned pantries—showing me all the haunts and hiding places of her curious childhood. There was always a cat or two to peer insolently at us from some regal perch, always gloom and mildew and the dust of centuries—and always, to my mind at least, a sense of someone or something watching over us as we pondered the secrets of the past.

We were just leaving the garret room where some nineteenth-century Trevor-Finch was said to have made a mess of the place by applying a fowling piece to his already addled brains, when Stephany turned suddenly and put herself into my arms, clinging to me with such ferocity that I glanced uneasily down the shadowy staircase.

"Oh, David—don't you feel the evil that infests this house? The way it's preyed upon everyone who's ever lived here? My God, I've never realized until just this moment how much I despise this place!"

I said, "Stephany, if it's the house which has been the cause of everybody's problems, there's a simple solution. One can always leave a house behind."

"Or a country?" she asked me. "Is that why you left America, David—because you're in the habit of running away from things you don't like?"

I didn't attempt to answer her until we were strolling the sunny veranda of the Georgian wing, the sea glinting at the end of a green sweep of lawn on which, since morning, the daffodils had bloomed.

"When I came to England, Stephany, I *was* running

away—from the utter inconsequence of my life back in the States. Now that I've found something that really matters to me, I don't think I'll run away again."

"And what is it you've found?"

I was going to say the Westchurch manuscripts, of course, but something in her quick smile made me hesitate. A gentle breeze touched her hair; her eyes were the color not of that bland April sky but of the darker, more sinister blue that looked down at us from the upper windows of the ancient house.

"Come with me," she said, before I'd found an answer to her question. "There's another place I want to show you."

And tugging on my arm, she led me out across the lawn, through the daffodils, into the grove of budding trees and up the muddy slope where wild flowers peeped through last year's soggy leaves, over the crest of the hill to a secluded glen where a tiny stream trickled among the rocks and the ground was carpeted with new green moss.

"This is the place I love," she said, drawing me down beside her on the moss. "Here, where everything is fresh and clean, where we can *breathe*."

I glimpsed a small stone building back among the trees. The building had no windows, and there were slabs of stone protruding from the mossy ground all around it. Good God, I thought. It's the family crypt and burial ground!

"I used to come here all the time as a child," Stephany said. "I came to hide from Grandmama, and to look for my mother. I could always feel her near me here—and over there, among the stones. And her voice would sing to me in the music of the brook. But—but what was I thinking of? My mother isn't dead. She didn't die, David. She ran off to America. . . ."

I took Stephany in my arms and let the moment pass. We didn't make love that afternoon, though perhaps what we did make was closer to it than anything I'd known for many years. It was a peaceful spot, and as long as the sun penetrated the higher branches of the surrounding trees we talked comfortably, Stephany's head on my lap or mine on hers. There were many things I had to tell her about myself; only a few, it seemed, that she had yet to tell me. Finally, when the shadows made us shiver, she turned over my wrist to look at my watch. "I suppose we ought to be getting back, darling. We have guests coming for dinner."

We came down from the hill along an old and deeply rutted road. The woods were dense on either side and we heard footsteps coming toward us before we caught sight of the Mortimors, father and son, laboring up the slope with their heads down. Stephany pulled me off the roadway and into a thicket.

"I'd rather not meet up with those two," she whispered. "Jamie curdles my blood, and the old man is almost as bad."

We hid in the thicket until the lumbering oaf and his wheezing, muttering father had gone by and turned off into the woods. Through the trees I saw another building—a small stone cottage with an earthen roof.

"Where do you think they're going?" I asked.

"After firewood, I suppose. That's an old woodcutter's cottage, where the axes and things are kept."

We heard one of those axes ring through the woods before we reached the house. "Why does your father keep them on?"

"English gentlemen have always been intimidated by their servants," Stephany said. "It's all part of that dreadful class thing Daddy wants to do away with."

I could see that it was, but I recalled that Trevor-Finch had never allowed himself to be intimidated by the servants back at the College.

I came down at six to find the professor's guests already gathered for sherry in the library. The three scientific gentlemen were about what I'd expected—intense, humorless men who asked a few polite questions about my line of work and then engaged the professor in a ramble through higher mathematics. Parson Tompkins was something else again. A young, robust clergyman with ruddy cheeks, curly blond hair and a look of priestly mischief in his eyes, he gave me a fierce Rotarian handshake and seemed to size me up for some vital parish committee.

"So you're the young chap who's interested in our local legends. I take quite an interest in that sort of thing myself. Read folklore when I was up at Oxford, so naturally I began collecting tales of the region when I was assigned to this parish. Quite a suspicious lot, these Norfolkmen; it took me years to gain their confidence. But now I've got some really extraordinary stuff on tape. I daresay it will make my reputation as a folklorist when it's finally published."

"I'd like to hear those tapes," I said, "or borrow the transcripts for a while."

"I can't let go of the transcripts yet," the parson said. "There was a bloke up from London not long ago who wanted to buy them, but I wouldn't sell. I'd be glad to play the tapes for you, though, if you'd care to stop by the parsonage."

Giles Mortimor appeared with a new bottle of sherry, and he and the parson exchanged looks—puzzled and wary on the parson's part, fiercely hostile on the old man's. I wanted to ask a question while Giles was still near enough to hear it.

"That man from London who was after your transcripts—was that by any chance the Reverend Samuel Stemp?"

"Oh, no. I know Stemp," the parson said. "He was up here several times a few years ago. I played all my tapes for him—everything I'd collected up to that point. How's Stemp getting on with his work? Do you know?"

"Not very well," I said. "He was killed by a truck on Hampstead Lane just a few weeks ago."

"Oh, dear—sorry to hear it. Poor Stemp! Now, that must've been just about the time this other chap inquired as to the purchase of my tapes. What was his name again?"

Giles lingered at the table with his back to us, stretching out some trivial task.

"A Mr. Simon Regis, perhaps?" I asked the parson.

"Regis," the parson said. "That was it. Simon Regis.

Said he was a dealer in rare books. Do you know him?"

"Not as well as I'd like to," I said. "I've been trying to get in touch with him about the papers he purchased from Stemp's widow. They could have a bearing on my own work."

"The fellow seems to have an interest in all our fields," the parson observed. "Not a very likable chap, I must say."

I was going to follow that up, but Giles had already started for the door. He was met by Stephany, who made her entrance in one of her own exotic and highly flattering creations. The parson was rendered momentarily speechless by the sight of so much black chiffon, with so much Stephany snugly fitted inside.

"Good evening, Miss Trevor-Finch," the parson said with enthusiasm. "It's so good to see you again."

"How nice to see you, Mr. Tompkins," Stephany said. "You've been comparing notes with our visiting medievalist, I see. David's been anxious to meet you."

"Yes," I said, trying to get the parson's mind back on the track. "I was just going to ask him about the legend of Creypool Abbey. You have some material on the abbey, I trust?"

"Indeed," the parson said. "And on the Black Monk, as he's called around these parts, who was executed for witchcraft back in the twelfth century. Quite a juicy tale, that one!"

"I've seen a document at the British Museum," I said, "which suggests the Black Monk may have been Geoffrey Gervaise, once a clerk in the chancellory of Thomas à Becket."

"That's who Stemp thought he was, too," the parson said. "I recall there was some connection between Gervaise and this Earl of Westchurch Stemp was studying."

"The earl owned one of Gervaise's manuscripts, which now belongs to Duke's College. At least, that's what I'm trying to establish. But can you tell me, Reverend, just exactly what the Black Monk did to get himself burned at the stake?"

"Oh, dreadful things," the parson said. "Used to hold regular parlances with the devil at the abbey, so the legends say. The devil gave him all sorts of evil powers over the people of the village—especially the women. He was supposed to have sired a horde of demonic offspring upon poor peasant girls—perhaps even upon a lady or two—and a cult grew up around him in the years following his death. The abbey became a hellish place, the scene of Satanic rituals and orgies. I have evidence on tape which suggests that even after all these centuries, the cult may still exist. In fact, I've heard it said that the Black Monk's ghost returns to the abbey on special occasions to sire new monsters. It's a terribly cruel and wretched superstition, because when any child in the village is found to be a little different—malformed in some way, or dimwitted—there are those who say the poor creature is one of the Black Monk's children."

"That *is* dreadful," Stephany said. "The poor things! What happens to them?"

"That varies," the parson said. "In the old days—as late as the seventeenth century, in fact—they were burned or hanged as witches. At other times they've been simply tolerated or even given a position of honor and privilege. These things go in cycles. It all depends upon how active the cult is at the time, and who's in it—which is always kept a secret, as you can well imagine."

"And at the present time?" I asked.

"I believe the cult is sleeping quite peacefully at the moment, thank heavens. But these ancient superstitions are extremely difficult to uproot. There was an outburst of devil worship around the turn of the century, another as late as the 1940s, when most of the village men were off at war. Of course, I find the survival of such ugly superstitions a scandal to the Christian community, and I've petitioned the Church for the power to conduct a thorough investigation. The bishop has advised me to let sleeping cults lie; he's afraid of the adverse publicity if the Church starts witch hunting in this day and age. But it seems clear to me we really

160

must do something to squash this evil before it surfaces again."

"The manuscript I've been studying," I said, "was not the work of an evil man—though certainly a troubled and perhaps insane one."

"I wonder if we aren't too quick to rationalize away the power of evil in our century, Dr. Fairchild. I fancy myself an enlightened clergyman. Ghosts, witches, demons—I don't really believe in all that. But there's something out at those ruins—something which infests this entire region. A psychic contagion, if you will, which lies dormant for generations and then strikes the entire population like a plague. In my opinion, we need a general inoculation before it strikes again."

"Ah, Tompkins," exclaimed Trevor-Finch, who had joined us during the parson's speech. "Your scientific metaphor is most encouraging. But if you wish to inoculate the populace, there's only one serum that will do the job. Plain, honest, scientific truth! The sooner we bury all religion, the sooner we'll lay all these bloody ghosts and hobgoblins to rest!"

The parson was starting to protest, when Mrs. Mortimor opened the door to the dining room and we saw that dinner was about to be served.

Parson Tompkins was determined to sit next to Stephany. I wound up between the science master at the local school and another amateur astronomer. The dinner progressed smoothly, with a good deal of expert knife-and-fork work and a few bits of easy conversation, until the parson asked the professor if he didn't find the principle of indeterminacy a most persuasive argument for the existence of God.

The professor found it hard to believe that the parson would so willingly put his head on the block. "I am not aware of any scientific theory," he said, exchanging a glance with his colleagues in atheism, "which in any way supports even the most tentative assertion of a Supreme Being."

"What I mean," the parson said, "is that the principle, if I understand it correctly, demonstrates the ultimate incomprehensibility of the universe to the purely rational intellect."

"Incomprehensible, my dear parson? Perhaps; but irrational, no. Extremely difficult to predict, but by no means incapable of analysis. You really must allow that your layman's understanding of the term—"

"But isn't incomprehensibility one of the attributes of God—in fact, what the very name of the Deity signifies to philosophers and mystics alike?"

They were off, and I saw I had to take the parson's side, not only to stay in character, but to give the poor man a chance to escape with his head. We each made several attempts to justify, or at least retreat gracefully from, his rash position. Our plates were removed by the silent Mortimors. A decanter of port and a box of cigars made the rounds. Stephany rose from the table, returned my questioning gaze with a nod to the terrace, and exited via the French doors. The parson was drifting into waters where no one could save him, and after a few minutes I followed her.

It was a mild evening, stars twinkling through the haze, a scent of blossoms in the air. Stephany was waiting for me in the shadows. As we kissed, I could hear Trevor-Finch making one of his favorite points: "The riddle of the universe, my dear parson, points not to the mystery of God, who very likely does not exist, but to the mystery of man, who does."

"But what," the parson persisted, "if the mystery of man *is* God?"

"But what if it's not? I say, where has Fairchild gone to? He really ought to hear this—it's right down his alley."

But Stephany and I had already left the terrace and were walking across the garden, and the professor's voice grew fainter and fainter, and at last faded out.

15

Quaint Customs of
the Country

Stephany and I were having a late breakfast when Trevor-Finch burst into the dining room with Armageddon in his face. My first thought was that America had just bombed Moscow, or maybe even London; my second was that the professor had guessed where Stephany had spent the better part of the night.

"Daddy, what's wrong?" Stephany asked, as the dumbstruck man dropped into his chair and stared at the glossy tabletop.

"The—the parson," Trevor-Finch managed to say after a minute. "Good Lord, it's incredible! I admit I badgered the man, but I always said he was a good chap."

"What's happened to the parson?" I asked.

"I just heard about it from old Giles as I was coming back from my walk," the professor said. "He'd been into Creypool for groceries and they were talking about it all over the village. Stephany, we must go into Creypool straightaway and see if there's anything we can do."

"But, Daddy—what's happened?"

Trevor-Finch took a comfortless puff on his cold pipe, then probed the ashes with a finger. "Last night, on the way home . . . his car lost the road and plummeted down the cliff."

"That's horrible!" Stephany said. "Is he . . . ?"

Trevor-Finch nodded. "I should have driven him home. I thought he looked a bit flushed as he bade us good night. Too much theology and port, the poor devil, and that *is* a treacherous road at night."

"Was there any evidence that the car had been tampered with?" I asked.

Trevor-Finch gave me a horrified stare. "Who would have tampered with the parson's car? And why should anyone want to kill an innocuous chap like the parson?"

I didn't attempt to answer that, but the parson was the third "innocuous" scholar to have his career cut short since I'd reached a crucial point in my research. There'd be scant chance of getting hold of the parson's tapes now: his murderers would surely have seen to that.

The professor and his daughter left for Creypool. I poured myself another cup of coffee and paged through the professor's *Guardian*. Presently Mrs. Mortimor came in to remove the breakfast dishes.

"Wasn't that a dreadful thing about poor Parson Tompkins?" she asked me, and I was surprised to see her eyes were red and moist.

"Very sad," I said. "Were you one of the parson's admirers too?"

She sniffled over a clatter of cups and saucers. "I only knew him from his visits here, sir, but he was such a fine gentleman I'm sure he gave lovely sermons. I always wanted to attend services at Creypool, but Mr. Mortimor wouldn't hear of it."

I watched her wipe the crumbs from table to apron. "I guess most people don't pay too much attention to religion any more," I said.

"A person don't have to go to church every Sunday to have a sustaining faith in the Lord. I don't know how I'd have managed all these years if I hadn't had my faith, and that's a fact."

"You've had quite a lot to put up with, then?"

"If you only knew! But you don't want to hear about my troubles."

"I can tell by looking at you, Mrs. Mortimor, that your difficulties have only enriched your character. I believe you mentioned some problem with your son which caused you to leave Wopping?"

"Them's family matters, sir, and family matters is

164

best left in the family, Mr. Mortimor says. But I can tell you I've suffered a good deal for that boy. And for his father too." She wound her large red hands in her apron and bit her thick lower lip. "It ain't been no holiday, lookin' after the likes of them two."

"I guess it's fortunate that you've been able to keep Jamie with you at Abbotswold," I ventured.

She sighed. "You don't know the half of it. They've tried to take him away from us any number of times. Wanted to put him in hospital, they did, or in one of them horrid schools for them as are a bit slow. But Mr. Mortimor wouldn't hear of it. He was always determined the boy would stay with us. I give him credit for that."

"Commendable, I'm sure—though you know that such places often can help a person with Jamie's problem. Was he always . . . different, even as a child?"

"He weren't so far behind the other boys his age when he was a little one. Not till he were eight or nine, and then we began to notice something strange about him. Almost uncanny, it were, as if he could hear things and see things we couldn't—and somehow they scrambled his poor brain so that he couldn't do what other boys his age could do."

"And did you have him looked at by a doctor?"

"Mr. Mortimor was against it, but I snuck the lad to a doctor in Salisbury. He said our boy had been 'traumatized,' whatever that means. I knew it was bad when he wouldn't say it straight out in plain English."

"Psychiatrists use the term to describe a severe emotional shock, Mrs. Mortimor—one which may have lasting effects on the personality. Do you recall anything like that in your son's background?"

"Well, it did seem the whole thing may have started with that trip the boy took to Brixton Barrow with his father."

"Brixton Barrow? That's an ancient Celtic burial ground, isn't it? With some prehistoric megaliths?"

"Great big stones, sir, up on this funny little hill. It was an outing of the club Mr. Mortimor belonged to in Paxton-Brindley, the one I told you about. I said the

165

boy was too young to go on an overnight trip, but Mr. Mortimor insisted. And then, when they got back, I saw right away—"

But at this moment we heard footsteps in the pantry and Mrs. Mortimor shut her lips and looked at the door with a most revealing expression. The door opened and Giles Mortimor looked in on us.

"What you be doin', gossipin' with the professor's young guest when you should be attending to your chores?"

"It's all right, Mr. Mortimor," I said. "I was just asking your wife if she could tell me where I might go for a walk this morning."

The old man glared at me, his pipe clenched between broken teeth. "A smart lot she'd know about that," he said. "My wife scarce sets foot outside this house. Now, Jamie and me, we get around the countryside a good deal, and we could tell you where to go, if you'd come to us."

"That's what I'll have to do, then," I said, returning his hostile squint with a bland and cheerful smile.

The old man seemed to consider the possibilities, then motioned his wife into the pantry, where I heard something that sounded very much like a blow. I finished my coffee, left the dining room and crossed the hall to the stairs. To the best of my knowledge, I had never looked a killer in the eye before, and it left me feeling a bit giddy, as if I'd bet on filling an inside straight and won. But did I have the courage to cash in my chips?

On my way to my room, I noticed that the professor's door, which I'd seen him unlock before entering, was ajar. He would be gone for another hour at least, and such an opportunity seemed too good to pass up. I went to the door and debated. Of course, it was distasteful to snoop on one's host; it was equally distasteful to bring a guest into one's home for reasons one refused to reveal. The hall was empty, the house silent. I knocked once, just to make sure there was no one within, and the door swung open another foot. I quickly stepped in and shut the door behind me.

The room was large and sunny, with bed and dresser at one end, desk and chairs arranged around a fireplace at the other. The professor's pipe and slippers and a collection of scientific journals waited at an easy chair beside the hearth. A game of chess was in progress at a small table. The arrangement of the pieces looked familiar. Beside the chessboard there was a pad of paper on which the professor had worked out the consequences of several moves, all of which led to white's mate.

Two photographs on the desk: Stephany and Grandmama Trevor-Finch (or so I guessed) as a stunning young woman. On the dresser I saw a thirtyish Trevor-Finch in uniform, holding the hand of a pretty child of seven or eight. The photograph had been cropped to delete a third person, whose fingers still clung to the child's other hand, as if attempting to draw her away from her father and into the void of those whose images are no longer cherished.

I tried a couple of desk drawers, found the usual chaos of paper clips, pencil stubs, defunct fountain pens, and a few pages of rough draft from one of the professor's articles on quantum physics—or so I supposed, for it was somewhat less intelligible than Greek to me.

I listened at the door and checked the hall to make sure the Mortimors were still downstairs, then went back to the chessboard. White was in serious trouble, all right, but there seemed obvious remedies to his dilemma. Why couldn't he save his queen by moving it two or more spaces, out of the black knight's reach? Or why couldn't the white bishop move down from his position across the board to take the knight and put the black king in check?

Of course! It struck me with the force of inspiration that the game was being played by medieval rules, in which neither queen nor bishop was allowed to move more than one square at a time. *Now* I knew where I'd seen this game before. In fact, I'd seen it twice: once in the study of the Reverend Samuel Stemp, and once in my own notes to the Westchurch poem.

The professor had had a chessboard set up in his room at Bromley House on the night those notes were stolen.

It took ten minutes of searching to locate the sliding panel in the professor's closet, another five to find the key in a dish of pins on the dresser. I unlocked the panel and then held my breath, sure I had heard a footstep in the hall. For several minutes I cowered in the closet, then crept across the room to check the door once more. The hall was empty.

Back in the closet, I slid open the panel, to find a small compartment filled with what seemed at first merely a collection of books. Was the professor a closet pornophile? But no; these were books on medieval history, astrology, witchcraft and the occult—shameful possessions for a man of the professor's persuasion, nonetheless. I glanced through them and found that a certain Robert Trevor-Finch had put his signature on the inside cover of each. The dates of copyright were old enough to support the thesis that Robert was the professor's father.

Wedged into one of the books—*Witchcraft Then and Now,* by Sir Aubrey Rice Poulter—was a narrow strip of photograph, clearly the cropped portion of the family portrait on the dresser. The young, attractive woman who had been holding the child's hand certainly had Stephany's sensuous mouth and crystalline complexion, and in her anxious, apologetic smile I saw a restless and unhappy spirit already contemplating the desertion of her family. A portion of Sir Aubrey's text had been underlined on the page marked by the photo, and ran as follows.

The most common drugs employed by witches of the middle ages, and still in use today, are the mandrake root, henbane, monkshood and thorn-apple, the last of these commonly applied as an ointment in preparation for the witches' sabbath. Among its effects are extraordinarily vivid sexual hallucinations, the illusion of extrasensory perception, and the sensation of flying. Visions of a most unsavory sort (frequently involving intercourse with Satan or his representative) were followed by great guilt and a compulsion to confess. One can only wonder at the sado-masochistic impulse which could lead young women of excellent families to engage in such debasing and self-destructive practices. . . .

One could only wonder, indeed, and I put the book away with the sense of having probed deeper than I wished into the professor's private sorrows.

The last item I found in the closet hiding place greatly eased my conscience. It consisted of several of my very own six-by-nine index cards—my missing notes on the Westchurch poem's game of chess. It *was* the game recreated on the professor's board—a game in which the white queen falls to the black knight while the white bishop is left futilely stranded across the board. At which point black has only to advance another pawn and the game is over. Occurring near the end of the poem, the passage marked a climax and ended with those mysterious lines concerning the appearance of a new star in the sky.

It was more than I could put together at present, and the professor and Stephany would be returning soon from the village. I copied down the material on my cards before returning them to the closet cabinet. Then I drew a diagram of the game on the professor's board. I made sure the room was just as I'd found it, and slipped out. Only one of the Mortimors' cats, perched lazily on the window ledge where I had seen Abbotswold ghost, observed my departure.

Trevor-Finch was gloomy and distracted at luncheon, unable to muster a single cliché with which to delight and instruct us. Over coffee he announced that he was leaving immediately for London. There were some calculations he wanted to make which would require a special computer.

"Another visit to his shrink," Stephany said after the

169

professor had gone off. "Poor Daddy. He's taking the parson's death awfully hard."

"The bad luck of the Trevor-Finches seems to be catching," I remarked. "Your father has had young men from the College down before, I gather. Have they all made it back alive?"

"Our misfortunes are no laughing matter."

"So who's laughing? Stephany, I've really got to talk to your grandmother, preferably before your father gets back tomorrow afternoon. Will you see what you can do?"

"I owe Grandmama another visit, anyway. I'll spend the afternoon with her—she likes that. If you can exist that long without me."

"I'm going out for a ramble. If I'm not back by sundown, send out the Saint Bernards."

The Mortimors, father and son, were working in a flower bed at the other end of the long lawn. The old man turned the soil while Jamie stood by, a two-hundred-pound bag of fertilizer held effortlessly in his massive arms. I didn't think they saw me round the house.

I went up the old road which Stephany and I had used the day before. Well beyond the woodcutter's cottage it left the woods for an open pasture. I followed it to a high point about a mile from the house and saw that it eventually joined the highway. If I had my geography straight, Creypool wasn't more than three miles to the southwest, the abbey somewhat closer. The road was decrepit, but still passable. All of which meant that the abbey was more convenient to Abbotswold than I'd realized.

A few sheep gazed sluggishly at me as I headed back; a billy goat brayed a warning but, seeing that I could outrun his horns, returned to his feast of spring grass. It was a gorgeous day, and I found it sad and not a little silly that, with all this lovely countryside at their disposal, the Trevor-Finches had never succeeded in being anything but miserable. What would it take, I wondered, to lay old ghosts to rest and give this land back to the living?

There were fresh tire tracks in the mud. They turned off the road and followed an overgrown lane to the woodcutter's cottage. Cautiously, I proceeded to the verge of the clearing. Cords of wood were stacked in the yard. The cottage had a heavy padlock on the door. I went up to one of the small, dirty windows and cupped my hand at the glass to peer in, but the darkness was impenetrable. I was becoming quite a hand at snooping into people's private affairs, and I felt sure the Mortimors' would prove more interesting than most.

Around in back I found a lean-to shed, the door of which was unlocked. The shed was full of axes, saws, sledges, scythes—but there was also a box of candles and a door into the cottage proper where a broken lock might not be noticed for quite some time. I lit one of the candles and went to work with a crowbar, prying out the iron plate that held the lock. The door opened on creaking hinges and I stepped into a vile-smelling darkness and raised the candle.

What I saw was hard to believe; it might have come straight out of Sir Aubrey Rice Poulter's account of the eccentric pastimes of witches and assorted ghouls. At the hearth was a cauldron and in the cauldron some tarry substance which explained the offensive odor of the place. The beams and rafters were adorned with spider webs. Laid out on several tables were the dried corpses of snakes, bats, toads and lizards, along with several cages which hissed and squeaked at me as I passed the candle before beady rodent eyes. On a set of shelves I saw bunches of herbs and weeds, jars filled with powders and pastes. Farther along these shelves I found bones, scraps of fur and skin, jars of internal and sexual organs from what must have been a great variety of beasts. In the first cabinet I tried there were horns and masks, black robes, whips and straps and several large phallic objects. It was almost laughable, this grotesque collection of lunatic treasures, but what I discovered in the next cabinet gave me an ugly jolt. Weren't those *human* teeth, fingernails, locks of hair? Then—I couldn't side-step recognition now—those other things the cabinet contained—bones, skin, shriveled organs, jars of blood and what appeared to be semen—were also likely human, and a large bottle of pickled eyeballs stared back at me like the condensed essence of some fiendish massacre. I shut the cabinet in a hurry, and turning away, encountered a leering, ruddy, blank-eyed Satan, the mask hung just above an upside-down crucifix.

I was already heading for the exit when the sound of an approaching engine came dimly through the stone walls. I shut the door and fit the iron plate and lock back in place. The broken lock would no longer catch and a breeze would have blown the door open. I held it shut with my shoulder as footsteps approached the cottage. A car pulled into the yard; its door opened and closed.

"Well, Giles, right on time, I see," said a pleasant and cultivated voice.

"Aye, sir. Did you have a good trip?" I was surprised at the note of cordiality, even servility, in the old man's voice.

"All but the last few miles. I'll be glad when your employer leaves and I can come up the main drive."

"He's gone off to London to see our friend the doctor, but Miss Trevor-Finch and the Yank are still here."

There was a sound of a key in the front padlock. They entered the cottage and I could hear their voices quite well by putting my ear to the door. By the sound of those heavy footsteps, Jamie was with them.

"Well now, Giles," the gentleman said, "the business with the parson—it was successfully handled, I take it?"

"It was, sir. The parson's out of our hair for good."

"And the tapes?"

"We've got them with us. Jamie, give Mr. Regis the bag like a good boy."

"Hmm. Should make interesting listening," the gentleman said. "Now we'll know if we have any tattletales in the coven—right, Giles?"

"Just you tell me who they are. I'll take care of 'em; you can count on that."

"I've always been able to count on you, Giles. You and the boy have proved invaluable. It was a brilliant stroke, getting you this position. Has the professor given you any trouble?"

"Not since we let on how much we knew about him. 'Course, we keep him in the dark as much as possible, and he's a cowardly soul in any case—would rather not know about the likes o' us. But if I might make one suggestion, your honor?"

"Yes, Giles?"

"It's the Yank. He's been talkin' to my missus, tryin' to pry things out of her. There's little enough she knows—we needna worry on that score—but the Yank's got his suspicions. He knows too bloody much already, and it's time we went to the root o' the problem, as you might say. 'Twould be easy enough to put a little pinch o' this or that into his food, and—"

"I think not. I've discussed Fairchild with the elders. We can kill him later, if we have to, but I have a slightly different strategy in mind. It's time that Dr. Fairchild and I got to know one another. I'll set something up and let you know the outcome. Now, do you have the items I asked you to prepare for me?"

"Aye; here they be. Nice and fresh, too."

"Lovely. Have Jamie load it all into the car. We have another Sabbat scheduled for Winston-Orley later this month. I'll need more of everything then."

"And when shall we be having the honor of a Sabbat at Creypool, might I ask?"

"Not until this messy business is settled. Your coven is welcome at Winston-Orley, you know."

"Aye; but Creypool is special. There's none can match the high times we have at Creypool! Even the old days at Brixton Barrow was naught compared to what we have here."

"And that's just why we must be especially careful, Giles. The sacred rites of Creypool must survive at all cost. . . . Well, Jamie, all loaded? I must be off, then."

The door was shut and locked. Footsteps crossed the yard; the car door opened and the man called Regis said, "I'll be in touch, Giles. Not to worry; the Yank won't trouble us for long."

I waited in the shed until I was sure they had gone their separate ways, then peeked out at the brightness of midafternoon. It had been a most foul and disgusting warehouse of horrors, and to cleanse my mind of what I'd seen and heard, I made my way through the woods to the brook Stephany had shown me, where I washed my hands and splashed cold water on my face. Then I lay down on the carpet of moss and gazed up at the vast, indifferent blue of a sky which would never look quite the same to me.

Quite unintentionally, I had set up the poor parson for murder; in a sense, I was also responsible for the death of Greggs and Stemp. That alone seemed to require that I go to the police with what I knew. The contents of the woodcutter's cottage would be enough to ensure a thorough investigation, but I had no way of knowing what that investigation might mean for the professor and Stephany, or whether it would impede my own efforts to redeem Geoffrey Gervaise from literary obscurity. Was a poem, no matter how great, more important than human life? A few weeks earlier I would have said, "Show me the life first." Now I didn't know what to think. But this was no ordinary poem, and its mysteries had assumed a human—and even ghostly—importance I felt duty bound to understand. The police, then, would have to wait their turn. The first crack at solving these mysteries went to me.

The sun was going down, the shadows long across the lawn, when I finally made for the house. The rooks cawed down at me from the tall trees. A cat glared at me from beneath the shrubbery. If Giles or Jamie had come suddenly around the corner, I might have fainted dead away.

16

The Magician

~~

A winter dusk in the mountains of nothern Wales. Wind and rain verging on sleet. Dense, clotted clouds cluster along the ridges and mountaintops, blot out the valleys. A lone traveler, wrapped in a cloak of ragged furs, urges his horse up the steep and icy path. As he ascends a shallow U-shaped valley, strung like a hammock between two craggy peaks, the rider encounters large boulders fallen ages ago from above, piled on top of one another like crude monuments. Nearly indistinguishable from the boulders is a primitive hut of earth and stone built into the mountainside. The rider dismounts and ties his horse to a stunted bush in the lee of the hut. Its door of rough-hewn logs is adorned by a pair of massive ram's horns, to which are attached sprigs of mistletoe. A bell of weathered bronze hangs beside the door. Its harsh clang is carried off by the shrieking wind. The rider waits, huddled in his cloak, then beats on the door with his fist. At last a light appears through the chinks in the logs. A bolt slides back, the door opens a foot and the light of a lantern falls upon the muffled face of the rider, revealing two intensely eager eyes.

"Who is it?" a voice asks. "What do you want with me?"

"Are you the one they call Gwynneddon?" the rider shouts over the wind.

"Why seek you old Gwynneddon on such a foul night?"

"I have come to test your wisdom and beseech your help. My name is Gervaise."

"I thought you might be. Come in, man—come in out of the cold."

The hut is small and low-ceilinged, crudely furnished with stools, a table, a pallet of straw piled with filthy blankets and furs. Gwynneddon, an old hunchback with long white hair and beard, his dwarflike figure crouched beneath its hump as if beneath a peddler's sack, leads Gervaise to an inner door which opens upon a flight of stairs.

Down, down, into the rocky core of the mountain they descend. A huge subterranean chamber appears—a natural cavern filled with the paraphernalia of the alchemist's art. In the center of the chamber there is a large kiln in which a fire roars. Around the kiln there are tables and shelves stacked with the necromancer's supplies—vials, urns, pestles and mortars; bins filled with powders, crumbled minerals, strange chunks of ore; vats of grease and bad-smelling pastes; other jars filled with herbs, roots, acorns, berries, cones. There are also ancient books and parchments, various implements for weighing, measuring, dissecting, distilling. The light from the kiln plays over this cluttered laboratory and reveals stalactites like giant daggers suspended from a roof hidden in darkness. Other chambers open off this one, dark sockets in the porous, glistening wall. From the shadows peer the yellow eyes of several watchful, wary cats.

Gervaise removes his cloak and throws back his cowl. He looks uneasily around the chamber as Gwynneddon fetches a jug and two cups from one of his cabinets.

"A drink to take off the chill of this ferocious night. A hard journey you've had of it, by the look of you. Sit down."

Gervaise samples the brew with but a sip; then, finding it palatable, he drains the cup and extends it for more.

"You know who I am?"

"I've heard of you from the spirits, Gervaise. So few come to seek the counsel of old Gwynneddon in these days, I am glad to see you. Here at last!"

"And what have your spirits told you about me?"

176

"All that is needful. You are a priest and scholar, a philosopher like myself, though of a different faith. You currently dwell in a monastery in West Saxony called Blackstone. Men say you are learned in the ways of the ancients, but your wisdom has not satisfied you. Thus you have sought out me, whom all the world seems to have forgotten. Yet the spirits have not told me why."

"I am surprised your spirits know me so well, old one. There is a monk at the monastery who hails from these mountains. He was once your apprentice before he embraced the true faith and escaped the powers of darkness that dwell here. He says you are a wondrous magician, adept at casting spells and reading omens, and that your power has been given you by the devil—"

"He whom *you* call the devil, Gervaise. You and your kind, who have driven his followers into exile. I know the lad of whom you speak. I could put a curse on him even now as he cowers behind your monastery's walls. I could snuff out his traitorous life within the hour. But I have spared him out of pity and my old regard, and perhaps—who knows?—because the spirits knew that eventually he would lead you to me."

"These spirits you speak of—they are demons?"

"They are the ancient spirits who ruled this land and lived in peace with its inhabitants before the invaders came. They still live in our trees and rocks and running water, and they shall haunt your people for generations to come. I have looked into your Bible and heard your priests; I know the lies your Church has spread across this island, and across all Europe. But there are many gods, and many powers in the unseen world which no man can comprehend. Can your God withstand all of them? The hour of reckoning will come. The banished gods will claim their due."

"I know something of these other gods. I have learned to read many languages, and I have studied the Cabala, the writings of the Gnostics, the Islamic philosophers, the Pythagoreans, Platonists, Manicheans, and all the great astrologers and alchemists. . . ."

"And you have learned?"

"Nothing I might not have known before, through the exercise of reason and native wit. I have learned that we are creatures of the earth—fashioned from dust, conceived in animal frenzy, born in agony and wretchedness and fear, to die in ignorance and despair."

"That is the legacy of your religion, Gervaise. It is not so for those of us who cling to the old beliefs."

"What is true for some must be true for all. All men must die, and all men live their lives in the shadow of the grave. Yet our souls know of another world. It is the resurrection of Our Lord Jesus Christ which has freed us—"

"You are not free. You would not have come to me if you were."

Gervaise replies thoughtfully. "I have never been free, as a Christian should be free in heart and mind. My—my slavery has driven me close to madness. You are said to converse with demons, to cast mighty spells, to raise the dead and foretell the future—"

"No doubt my powers have been exaggerated. The spirits work through me to do what they will and to claim what dominion may be left to them. I am a scholar like yourself, and a seeker after truth. What is it, priest of the Christus, that you seek? Are you willing to renounce that jealous God of yours in order to attain wisdom, power, riches, immortality?"

"I shall never renounce my God," Gervaise says with passion, "and I seek only the freedom to follow Christ, as the saints have followed Him, to everlasting glory."

"That you cannot get from me! I deal in herbs, potions, spells. I can teach you how to bind others, but not, alas, to free yourself. You may, of course, choose the terms of your bondage, but no man is free."

"So I have often thought myself. Since my childhood, old one, I have been possessed by evil spirits. They have made me unworthy; they have denied me the blessings of grace, my birthright as the child of God. I can bear my deprivation no longer."

The old man peers closely at Gervaise, then breaks into hoarse laughter. "A strange dementia, this! So you have sought your God and been rebuffed. And now you seek commerce with His enemies. . . ."

Gervaise rises. "Only to confront them. I have come here to challenge Satan. Let him meet me, face to face, so that I may look upon him and engage him in battle. I am determined to overcome this evil or perish in the attempt!"

"Aye; but to perish may not be the worst of it. Are you willing to wager the fate of your immortal soul?"

Gervaise drops back into his chair. "My soul seems lost in any case. Do I suffer damnation for a life of sin, or for a lost wager? What I seek is the chance to win—or at least to fight my enemy on equal terms."

"Your strength is surely but that of a mortal man. Your weapons are of human making. How can you stand against such a foe? Think clearly. There is much at stake."

"There is a way in which I may put Satan to the test, and he may test me. Place him here before me and I will present my challenge."

The old man looks admiringly at Gervaise. "I respect your courage and warrior's spirit, but you are a fool. Your enemy—for you have made him that; he would gladly be your friend—could squash you beneath his thumb."

"Then let him try!" Gervaise cries.

The old man rises and, stooped beneath his hump, a symbol of all the burdens men must bear, paces the chamber. "I must commune with my spirits on this matter," he says at last. "I must know their will."

"Do you wish me to withdraw?" the priest asks.

"It is not necessary. The spirits may come and take counsel with me in your presence. Remain in your chair but do not speak or move. Let nothing frighten you. You shall see things, perhaps, which one of your faith has never seen before."

Gwynneddon goes to a cabinet in the shadowy reaches of the chamber. Over his hermit's skins he puts on the long white robe of the Druid, and over his shoulders a shawl embroidered with mysterious figures and symbols. To the table he brings a large jagged

179

stone marked with bright encrustations and embedded veins of precious metals. He lights two candles, placing them on either side of the stone. Beneath their flickering light, the strange elements in the rock twinkle and shimmer; they seem to move across its jagged surface, to leap out from its recesses like distant stars. The old man fixes his gaze upon the stone and places both his hands upon it. He begins to mumble in an ancient tongue, using words and phrases which Gervaise believes he may have heard, long ago, from the lips of the old woman who first taught him to fear the devil. The stone begins to glow with an inner light. Gwynneddon's eyes become glassy. He falls into a trance.

After a while, Gwynneddon stirs, moans. His arms shake as he holds to the stone; his eyelids flicker beneath quivering brows. The mysterious light of the stone seems to fade. Gervaise pours more brew from the jug and waits for Gwynneddon to throw off the lingering stupor of his trance. The man must be a hundred years old, Gervaise thinks, perhaps two hundred. The sad light of centuries is in his eyes.

"Well? And what have the spirits said to my challenge?"

"Return to your monastery, Gervaise, and dwell there yet another fortnight, till the nights be dark and moonless, the stars at their brightest. You shall recognize the night by the brilliance of the stars. Tell no man your purpose, but go alone to the top of the hill you can see from the window of your cell. Do you know the one?"

"Brixton Barrow?"

"It is an ancient burial ground of my people, a spot sacred to our gods. Once a temple stood upon that hill. Before the invaders came to this island we worshipped there. The ground has been consecrated by blood."

"And Satan will come to me?"

"Enter the ring of large stones that remain upon the hilltop. Find the innermost stone and lie down beside it. I shall give you a potion brewed on instruction from the spirits, made of herbs that grow on these moun-

180

tains. You must drink the potion and lie down to rest beneath the stars. You shall fall into a deep sleep and in this sleep you shall see visions. The one you seek shall come to you in your dream."

"Only in a dream? But I have had many dreams. This is not the meeting I have asked for."

"There shall be other meetings. You shall see the world transformed before your waking eyes. The heavens themselves will show signs and wonders. This first night is but the beginning. Our gods have accepted your challenge. May your own God have mercy on your soul!"

"I am not afraid. If the Lord will not help me, my own wit shall."

"I have never seen a man so curiously intent upon his own destruction—and all in the name of faith! So be it. Yet one word of advice I would give. . . . Some success you may have at first. Do not be misled, nor duped by your own pride. If you are given the chance to quit your strange contest as the winner, do not let it pass you by. The gods always win in the end."

"I shall remember your advice, and I thank you for it. One of the gods must win, and I pray it shall be He whom I wish to champion. Now, can you give me the potion of which you spoke? I am anxious to begin my journey home."

"It is a pity that you are so intent upon this odd business. We might have compared our philosophies and delved deeply into the mysteries we have studied. I could have taught you much, Gervaise."

The old man shrugs and turns away. Gervaise watches him prepare the potion from the jars and vats of his workshop. Gwynneddon measures, mixes, stirs. He heats the mixture over a small fire and a curious odor wafts across the chamber—vaguely sexual, like the reek of a whore's bedchamber, or the fertile smell of spring fields. Gwynneddon pours the mixture into a vial, which he seals with stopper and wax and gives Gervaise. Then he takes up the lantern and leads the way from the chamber. As they ascend the stairs, and as the light from his lantern diminishes, the blazing hell mouth of the kiln casts its red glow over the cavern, and in its shadows reappear the gleaming eyes of several cats.

17

The Matriarch's Story

The letter was waiting at my place when I came down for breakfast Friday morning—a plain white envelope with "David Fairchild, Esquire" written neatly across the face in black ink. Mrs. Mortimor was just bringing in our breakfast. "A lad brought that round to the kitchen this morning," she said. "A gentleman stopped him on his way to school and gave him sixpence to run it up to the house."

I tore open the envelope and extracted a card displaying the same fastidious though archaic penmanship:

> Dear Dr. Fairchild,
> It has come to my attention that you would like to speak with me. I also understand that we have certain interests in common and may be able to help one another vis-à-vis a certain manuscript. If you will meet me at 4 P.M. this afternoon, at the Royal Mariner Inn, Wimsett, we can discuss these matters.
>
> Cordially yours,
> Simon Regis

I read the letter again as Mrs. Mortimor puttered about and left for the kitchen. At first Simon Regis had been only a name, then a voice behind a door. Now he had become an elegant pen which put a fanciful flourish to his signature. I felt sure that the more of himself he revealed to me, the less I'd like having made his acquaintance.

"What's that you have?" Stephany asked, coming bright-eyed and beaming into the dining room.

"Nothing," I said, and slipped the envelope into my pocket. "Did you sleep well?"

"You should know!" She laughed, and bent over to put a kiss on my cheek, just as she customarily kissed her father before sitting down to breakfast. It seemed so natural and right by now to receive her kisses (and Stephany was a very kissing young lady) that I couldn't help wishing we could greet the professor on his return from London with the news that in future, Miss Trevor-Finch would regularly render that service at my breakfast table.

An hour was coming, I thought, when we would all have to speak and deal plainly with one another, and then we would see just how many of these tender sentiments had survived.

Stephany set to work on her eggs, bacon, fried bread and tomatoes, beans and toast—one of Mrs. Mortimor's lighter breakfasts. "Well, darling, are you up to facing Grandmama this morning?"

"She's ready to see me?"

Stephany nodded, her mouth full, then swallowed and said, "Mrs. Archer caught me as I was leaving my room. Grandmama has thought it all over and wants to talk to you."

I emptied the coffeepot and saw Stephany off with her sketch pad and box of paints before I climbed the stairs to Mrs. Trevor-Finch's suite. Mrs. Archer opened the door to my timid knock.

"She's just having her tea on the sun porch, sir. But I feel as if I ought to warn you: she had a difficult night and is not quite herself this morning."

I thought that could only be an improvement, so I said, "Lead the way. I'll take my chances."

Mrs. Trevor-Finch, looking not a day over several centuries, was waiting for me in her wheelchair on a bright, glass-enclosed porch. Though it was airless and warm, the old woman was wrapped in blankets and shawl; her bright eyes stabbed me as I crossed the threshold.

"Well, young man? And what is it you think we have to say to one another?"

I sat down across from her; Mrs. Archer brought another cup and poured my tea. "I suppose you've heard," I said, "that Parson Tompkins was killed in an automobile accident the night before last."

"I'm not sure—be off about your business, Archer, and allow Dr. Fairchild and myself to discuss these matters in private—I'm not sure why I should find the death of that foolish, prying clergyman a matter of particular concern."

"Perhaps," I said, "because it's the third death in the past several weeks, all somehow connected with my work on the Westchurch manuscripts. I may be the next to go. If I had any sense, I'd catch the next flight back to the States."

"You mustn't do that," she said quickly. "Please—don't give up your work now."

"And why shouldn't I? How can my work matter to you, or to your son? It's time you leveled with me. I want to know everything you can tell me about the ghost which haunts Abbotswold, and about this village cult the parson was investigating, and how they're both related to my work on the Westchurch manuscripts."

My direct approach had succeeded in surprising the old girl, at any rate. Her knotty fingers moved nervously in her lap and her bright eyes darted momentarily about her glass cage. "It seems to me as if you've already discovered quite a bit on your own. The parson told you about the cult, but who's been talking to you of our ghost?"

"No one had to talk to me about her," I said. "I've seen her for myself, the first night I was here. I've been waiting for a return engagement, but there hasn't been one. However, I think your son has seen her."

"Kenneth has seen it too?"

"I think so, though he won't admit it. And there's something else I ought to mention. Your servants, the Mortimors, are clearly implicated in at least two mur-

184

ders. The old man is running a witch's supermarket at the woodcutter's cottage, and both he and his son are members of the cult. Eventually all this will have to come before the police, and I'd like to do what I can for all of you before that happens. I can't help you if you won't help me."

The old woman thought it over. "I am a good judge of character. You are an opportunist. You are selfish, conceited, totally unprincipled—and yet you seem to be the one who has been sent for our deliverance. Tell me, do you love my granddaughter?"

The question took me by surprise. "I'm very fond of Stephany."

"You're lying," the old woman said. "She means nothing to you. What, then, do you hope to get out of all this for yourself? There must be something. Do you mean to blackmail us?"

"Of course not," I said, genuinely appalled at the extent of her suspicions. "My intentions are perfectly honorable. I simply want to do the work I came to England to do—and to know the truth."

"The truth!" she said. "The truth is seldom relished by those who mean to use it for personal gain. Yet, if you have a heart in your breast, and if you have learned to care for my granddaughter at all . . ."

She closed her eyes for a moment, and pressed her withered fingertips to her temples, where I saw blue veins like the tendrils of death beneath her papery skin. Then, with a deep breath, she began her story:

"My husband was a man of spirit and character. When he inherited this house a few months after our marriage, from an uncle who had died childless, he told me about the legends which had come down through the generations in his family. It had long been said, you see, that no good could come to those who dwelt in this house, and that Abbotswold was haunted by a malevolent spirit. Of those previous owners whose stories were known to us, two had gone mad, one had committed suicide, and one had resigned his inheritance after only a few months in the house."

"Yet you were not afraid to live here?" I asked.

"We were enlightened young people of an age which did not believe in ghosts. We thought of our new life in this old house as a glorious adventure, and we were determined to purge our legacy of its morbid associations by uncovering the ancient source of these legends. My husband commissioned the College of Heralds to research his genealogy and undertook a study of his own in the county archives. He also obtained permission to begin certain excavations at Creypool Abbey, which was said to harbor an evil spirit of its own—for we had guessed that the legends might have a common origin."

"Excuse me," I said. "This would have been about . . . ?"

"We came here in 1910. I was not yet thirty, my husband somewhat older. He had spent his youth in the idle fashion of young gentlemen of his day and had been waiting for some great goal to seize his imagination. The solution of these ancient mysteries became his goal, and so it became mine. We threw ourselves into the project with youthful enthusiasm. There were weeks, months, when we seldom thought or talked of anything else. We were happy then. We were very innocent and foolish. My husband expended a considerable portion of his fortune in the effort to reconstruct the past."

"And what did you find out?" I asked.

"Our search took us back to the very beginning of the family line, to a certain Philip of Trevorre, who was given the land called Abbotswold (after the existing monastery at Creypool) as a fiefdom under William the Conqueror. For several generations the Trevorre barons were among the most powerful and independent of the Norman war lords and a frequent source of irritation to the crown. Finally, in order to undermine their independence and forestall future rebellions, Henry II arranged a marriage between a high-ranking lady of the court—a cousin of Queen Eleanor—and the reigning lord of Abbotswold, Michael Trevorre.

"The marriage was not a success. The lady was a child of Aquitaine and its courts of love; she longed for the chivalrous customs and amorous license of her homeland—at least, so we reconstructed her unseemly behavior. She so outraged her proud and jealous husband that he imprisoned her in the tower and allowed her leave only to visit the abbey, where the monks were instructed to soften her resistance to her husband's will. This was the situation in the year 1175, when England was visited with plague and famine. The suffering was particularly acute in this part of the realm, and the people believed that the pestilence had been visited upon them because of a renegade priest and sorcerer who had been given refuge at the abbey in defiance of both prelates and king. This sorcerer's name, as I'm sure you've already deduced, was Geoffrey Gervaise."

"Of course," I said. "Gervaise must have come here in 1171, shortly after the murder of his great patron, Thomas à Becket. But was he a sorcerer?"

"The common people believed he was. According to the legend, he was betrayed by one of the monks and lured from the abbey for an assignation with a peasant girl. He was captured by the villagers, summarily tried and burned at the stake. The judge who condemned him to death was Michael Trevorre. Upon hearing of the execution, the Lady Trevorre took her own life in the tower."

"Then she and Gervaise . . ."

"Were lovers. We could only conclude that she had known Gervaise at court and had been his mistress before her marriage, and that she had been using her 'devotions' at the abbey to continue their affair. It was not simply for witchcraft that Gervaise was executed, but for offending the jealous pride of the Trevorres."

"Then he may not have been a devil-worshipper."

"I am not so sure of that. There was evidence against him. . . . But you may be interested to learn what we discovered during our excavation of the abbey. A crew of men had been hired from the village. My husband and I rolled up our sleeves and joined in the work. For months we dug away at the ancient foundations with little to show for our labor, and then one day I arrived on the site to find my husband in a state of great excitement. He led me to the foundation of what had once been a small structure outside the abbey walls, an ancient observatory—"

"I know the place," I said. "Go on."

"—and showed me a rust-eaten iron box he'd just uncovered beneath the paving stones. We opened the box together. It contained an astrolabe—a device for measuring the heights and charting the positions of the stars and planets. There was also a set of chessmen carved from ivory and ebony, clearly of medieval origin, and a curious iron grate or grille, about two feet square, the purpose of which we could never guess. The grille contained sixty-four individual squares, the number of spaces on a chessboard. There was also evidence that the box had once contained a number of sheets of parchment or vellum, but these had crumbled to dust."

"And are these things still in your possession?"

"Unfortunately, they were stolen shortly after they were found. We suspected that one of the workmen from the village made off with them, but of course we had no proof. Soon after their disappearance, my husband found it impossible to get anyone from the village to continue the work. We were obliged to import laborers from Norwich—but then, when one of the men was killed in an accident, and strange stories began to circulate in the village—"

"What kind of stories?"

"We never knew, exactly—although of course we knew that the abbey had been the site of Satanic rituals in ages past, and that a ghostly monk was said to haunt the ruins. The village parson begged us to discontinue our work, saying that his parishioners had become terribly agitated and that he feared another outbreak of the mania which had afflicted the village at various times in the past."

"And so you abandoned the project?"

"We did more than that. Shortly thereafter, we left Abbotswold, intending never to return. Our life here had begun to have an adverse effect upon our marriage. My husband had become subject to sudden fits of depression; he had terrible nightmares and was frequently afraid of a 'presence' he felt in the house. He fell into long periods of anxiety and morbid watchfulness. Our . . . marital relations were suspended. I was a young and passionate woman and I loved my husband deeply, yet as his depression increased, my own desires seemed to become all the more acute. For months I struggled with unprecedented temptations. I seemed to become another person altogether, as if some alien being had taken possession of my soul. It was a horrid time, a time of suspicions and hostility, of accusations and countercharges, and finally . . . finally, there was a disgusting interlude with one of our stable-hands. Excuse me—"

She broke off and I saw her shoulders shake as she hid her face behind skeletal hands. When she removed her hands, her eyes were clear and proud once more, two droplets of glistening black oil. "I need not burden you with our domestic crisis. It will suffice to say that we lived for several years abroad, where the symptoms of our mysterious affliction seemed to abate. Kenneth was born. We recovered confidence in ourselves and faith in one another. Had we sold Abbotswold, as we intended, and remained abroad, we might have escaped altogether the insidious influence of this accursed house. But the war forced us to return to England, and it was on the ship from Venice that we met Sir Percy Wickham George."

"Sir Percy—the Cambridge ghost hunter!" I said, thinking how amazing it was that I kept running across that old diehard's trail.

"Sir Percy was returning from some expedition to the Orient which had received considerable attention in the papers. My husband thought that if he heard our story, he might offer his assistance, and so he did. Sir Percy persuaded us—much against my own better judgment, I might add—to return to Abbotswold so that he could conduct certain experiments."

"And what were these experiments?" I asked.

The old woman then told me how Sir Percy and his

colleagues from the Society for Psychical Research spent several nights at Abbotswold and at the abbey, endeavoring to make contact with the supernatural agency or agencies which had persecuted the family for centuries. It was at last determined that a séance should be held, and Sir Percy produced a famous medium—a certain Madame Sokoleyev, who had contacted the spirits of many a great family and whose reputation for honesty was unimpeachable. Sir Percy took great pains to ensure the veracity of the experiment. The ritual was carefully followed. A party of seven, including Mrs. Trevor-Finch and her husband, gathered in the great hall. The medium fell into her trance and began to moan and to utter strange primitive cries. A cold wind seemed to blow down from the tower; the candles were extinguished, but an eerie luminosity enveloped the medium.

"Who are you," Sir Percy asked, "and why do you haunt this place?" Many times he repeated these questions, and then, in a voice not her own, the medium cried out: Annjenette—I am Annjenette DeLorreaux."

"And who," I asked, "was Annjenette DeLorreaux?"

"The wife of Michael Trevorre—the lady from Aquitaine and the mistress of the sorcerer Gervaise. We knew her name and her story; we had often wondered if she might be the ghost of Abbotswold. To hear her voice addressing us from the world beyond the grave—it was an experience I shall never forget. Even now my flesh crawls as I remember it."

"And did the spirit tell you anything else?"

The old woman nodded; she closed her eyes and frowned in the effort to recall the precise words. A web of shadow from the budding branches of a tree near the porch moved over her shrunken figure with the play of an unfelt breeze, and for a moment it seemed as if she herself were the medium by which I heard the words of the dead.

When asked again why she haunted Abbotswold and persecuted the family, Annjenette replied, "I wish you no harm. It is the Father of Evil who has placed me here to share my lover's torment. I must abide with you until the spell be broken and my lover freed from Satan's bondage." And then she began to cry out in a most pitiful voice, "Release me! Release me!" And at last the old medium fell into a swoon and the presence departed.

There were subsequent attempts to reach the spirit of Annjenette's imprisoned lover. Gervaise himself never answered the call, but Annjenette returned on two occasions. On the first, Sir Percy asked her what Gervaise had done to become the devil's slave, and why the family had to suffer along with two such unhappy spirits. Anjenette replied, "It was you who unjustly accused him, and you who put him to the stake. It was you—villain, brute, murderer—who drove me to my death. The game was not yet done, the wager not yet lost, when you lit the fires which still consume us. You have made our punishment your own and are condemned to suffer with us until you repent your sins and set us free."

"Game?" I asked the old woman. "What was she speaking of?"

"We could only conjecture that Gervaise had wagered his soul in some contest with the devil, and that it was my husband's ancestor who cut the game short by ordering his execution. When she accused my poor husband of causing their deaths, she was of course speaking to him as a descendant of Michael Trevorre."

"So the sins of the father have returned to haunt his line. And the sins of the mother . . .?"

"Have come down to us as well. Annjenette has been, in a way, mother to all the women in this accursed family—if not by blood, then by the influence of her ghostly presence. I am convinced that when I betrayed my husband it was her adulterous and defiant spirit which possessed me."

"But how," I asked, "could you be expected to free them? If Gervaise risked his soul in a wager with the devil, he would seem to have damned himself. He ought to be beyond anyone's help—unless . . ."

It was a tantalizing thought, and the old woman saw

at once that it was her own. "Yes—unless the game might still be won. Which is precisely why your work is so important to us. If there is a way to free Gervaise, it will likewise free all those who have been condemned to suffer with him. And this is what I have wanted all along to ask you, yet could not until I had told you our story. This poem you attribute to Gervaise—does it concern a game?"

"Of course," I said. "The game of chess! The answer to the riddle, the way to free Gervaise, is hidden somewhere in that poem. Which is why certain people are so determined that I shan't get any further with my work. And why Gervaise and Annjenette—at least, so I construe it—have been trying to help me. They want us to win the game for them. But did Annjenette ever tell you any more about all this?"

"On her third and last visit she said that a rose, both red and white, would provide the key to her lover's freedom. 'Look for the rose,' she said. 'My lover's words conceal the prize. It is Satan's guile to have placed it where none shall ever find it.' "

"None but a competent medievalist, perhaps," I said, with a nearly dizzying sense of what I might have the power to do. For Annjenette had brought a rose to my attention, as well, and now I knew that the devil himself couldn't keep me from getting back to that poem.

But Mrs. Trevor-Finch had not quite finished her story. Madame Sokoleyev, she told me, died that year of a stroke and subsequent mediums proved unable to raise Annjenette's spirit. However, in the spring of 1923, Sir Percy returned to Abbotswold in great excitement. He said he had lately uncovered new information on Gervaise in the library of Duke's College, and he was anxious to conduct one final experiment at the abbey, where he believed the ghost of Gervaise himself might be raised.

"He prevailed upon us to accompany him, though my husband had degenerated to a mere shadow of his former self and was unfit for any strenuous activity.

"As soon as we entered the abbey grounds and saw

the ruins faintly visible in the starlight, I was gripped by a strange compulsion to flee from the others and seek out something that seemed to be waiting for me in the darkness. I was seized with what I can only describe as a longing to be ravished by the thing I knew was waiting for me. My will was not my own. I slipped away from the party and hid in the ruined chapel. My heart was pounding with excitement, anticipation, loathing. I could hear Sir Percy and my husband calling for me in another part of the abbey as from across a void. I watched as a figure emerged from the shadows and drew slowly nearer. I was paralyzed with fear, yet also with a fierce longing. The figure approached my hiding place, as if it could smell my lust rising in the warm spring air, and then I saw . . . I saw . . ."

"Gervaise?" I asked, when the old woman seemed unable to continue. "Was it Gervaise?"

"I don't know. It was a monk, very tall and gaunt in his black robes, with a black beard and two gleaming eyes that seemed to express both desire and hatred as he reached out to wrap his black cloak around my body. Just then my husband entered the chapel with a light. He cried out and ran toward us. The apparition instantly fled. But my husband stumbled on some bit of rubble, fell forward and struck his head on the stones of the chapel floor. I ran to him and swore that it was not I, but some demon which possessed me, that sought that evil creature he'd seen me with, but my husband . . . my husband, Dr. Fairchild, was dead."

She shut her eyes tightly against the memory and hid her wrinkled, ravaged face in her hands. Then her own fiery eyes were upon me again and she said, "Under no circumstances shall you repeat this account to my son. He knows only that his father died in an accident while conducting an experiment related to the abbey ghost—which is one of the reasons, I'm sure, that he has always pretended to scorn the old legends. You see, some time before his death my husband wrote a long account of all our investigations, which he left as a letter for Kenneth to open on his twenty-first birthday. I am certain Kenneth has read that letter, but he has always attempted to defeat the powers that confound us by refusing to believe in them. My husband and I did not believe in such things, either, until it was too late."

"Perhaps your son believes more than he's willing to admit," I said. "He brought me here, after all, and he seemed anxious that we talk to one another."

"Yes; he must know by now, despite all his mockery and scorn, that the evil we face is real enough. He has himself known much sorrow."

"His wife?"

She nodded. "After his marriage, Kenneth wisely chose not to live at Abbotswold. But during the war, when he knew he was to be sent on a dangerous mission, he brought his wife and daughter here and asked me to look after them. There was nowhere else for them to go, but I saw at once that his wife might fall prey to the same sickness which had afflicted me in my youth. I tried to warn her, but she thought I was a meddling old fool and laughed at my 'superstitious tales.' She was a flighty, vivacious woman and became quickly bored by her life here. She made friends in the village and somehow became involved in horrid rituals at the abbey. Shortly before Kenneth returned from the war, she was found murdered, her body mutilated."

"My God!" I said, remembering how ill the professor had become when he mentioned a murder at the abbey. "And this is what you've been keeping from Stephany?"

"From everyone," the old woman said. "The shock quite destroyed Kenneth. He was hospitalized for over a year. Afterwards, he was adamant that the dreadful affair be buried along with all our family's secrets. But the evils which plague us have not gone away. And even now I can see how Stephany is surrendering to the same evil which, in its time, has worked its will upon all the women who have lived here."

"Stephany?" I asked in dismay.

"You do care for her!" the old woman said triumphantly. "Perhaps, then, I have not told you my story for nothing. Annjenette's wicked passion for her doomed lover has lived on in this house and it shall never die and leave us in peace until those wretched creatures are freed from their unnatural existence."

"But if Stephany were to leave Abbotswold . . . ?"

"Do you think evil is so easily escaped? We tried in our time, and vain hope brought us back. The Trevorres have always clung to their doom, and will cling, hopelessly, until an outsider, a man like yourself, with nothing to win and nothing to lose, intervenes."

It occurred to me that this was a task I could still decline. I had not come to England to rescue worldly maidens in distress, or to cope with their pompous and overbearing fathers.

The old woman must have guessed some of these thoughts, for after a moment's silence she said, "I have thought much on the meaning of my life, and on the sorry history of this family. It has occurred to me, many times, that the evil which has lived on in this house over the centuries could not have survived had it not been fed, nourished, fattened, by the sins of many generations—by the accumulated weight of human pride, folly and despair. Somehow, someday, all this misery must come to an end, and one who is noble and pure in spirit must end it."

I could have said that, in that case, I was clearly not the man for the job—yet I did wonder if, underneath all my cynicism and cultivated detachment, I might not be a better man than I'd ever realized. It would be interesting, for once, to find out.

Mrs. Trevor-Finch had sunk down into her wheelchair and blankets, exhausted by her long tale and the emotions it had aroused in her. I got to my feet and saw the watchful Mrs. Archer waiting at the door to show me out. "I'll do what I can," I told the old woman. "I won't betray you—you have my word on that."

She held out her hand, and this time I did not hesitate to touch her withered flesh. I was surprised at the warmth and strength of her grip. She was not, after all, a mummified corpse from another era, but a living human being who had earnestly requested my aid. I still felt the pressure of those bony fingers on my hand as Mrs. Archer escorted me to the door.

At the turn of the stairs, I paused and looked down into its shadowy well. Gervaise, I thought, if you're *not* out there, old man, and if you haven't been leading me on for some good purpose—well, then I've been dreadfully sold!

18

A Devilish Proposition

The professor returned from London in high spirits. "Some perfectly amazing statistics came out of the computer," he said at luncheon on the terrace. "I shall probably get a paper out of it. By the way, I ran into an old chum—a chap I was quite close to during the war. Colonel Lionel Buzby. He's retired now and has gone in for ghost hunting."

"Ghost hunting?" Stephany asked. "Not one of your friends, surely?"

"He's not much of a scientist, I grant you that, but he's devised some rather ingenious pieces of equipment and travels about the country investigating one sort of supernatural tomfoolery or another. When I told him about the abbey, he was keen to have a go at the place with his instruments. So I invited him down for the weekend. I thought you might find it amusing, Fairchild."

"I'm sure I shall," I said, "but are you eager to find out what's behind these old legends, Professor?"

Trevor-Finch gave me a sharp look. "I don't see how it could matter to me in the slightest. It's only meant as an evening's diversion. Now, if you two will excuse me, I've got a few things I want to do at the lab."

As soon as he was out of earshot, Stephany said, "I've been dying to ask you, David: did Grandmama come clean this morning and tell you all our dreadful family secrets?"

"She did."

Stephany waited a moment and then said, "But you're not going to share them with me, I gather."

"Not for the time being. Your grandmother swore me to silence."

Stephany sighed. "I'm scarcely a child, now, am I?"

I felt an urge to test her in some fashion. "Would you be willing to leave this house for good, Stephany? Would you leave England and return to America with me?"

She looked both pleased and confused by my proposal. I myself was a bit surprised to hear it come out sounding so much like an offer of something permanent.

"I don't know," she said at last. "I'm very fond of you, but I do have my career. And there is such a thing as family feeling and one's sense of responsibility. I don't know what Grandmama may have told you, but if your proposal—it *was* a proposal, wasn't it?—was meant simply to 'save' me from the nefarious power of this old pile of stones, I can assure you that I scarcely ever think of Abbotswold when I'm in London."

"Then perhaps you ought to stay there," I said. "I don't want to frighten you, but there are dangers here—for you in particular. That's why I asked if you could put your family and this house permanently behind you."

"So it wasn't a proposal!"

"It was whatever it sounded like, and I'll stick by it, if you ever want to take me up on it. Can I borrow your car for the afternoon? I have some business in Wimsett."

"My, we've become mysterious all of a sudden, haven't we? I'll ask Giles to bring it around for you."

"Don't do that. I'll get it myself when I'm ready to go."

At precisely five minutes to four, I eased Stephany's sports car into a parking space beside the Royal Mariner Inn. It was an old stone building with its back to the harbor in a part of town dominated by the reek of fish. The few people on the street were fishermen or sailors swaggering from one pub to another.

A few old salts were playing cards at a rickety table in the lobby and a few more dozed before the "telly." There was a desk, and a desk clerk reading one of those English tabloids devoted to the latest in rape and murder.

"Is there a Mr. Simon Regis staying here?" I asked him.

"You'll find him in the tearoom, guv," the clerk said with a jerk of his head. "He's waitin' for you."

The tearoom was at the back of the building, with a row of windows overlooking the harbor. All the tables were empty save one, where a middle-aged man in a dove-gray suit promptly stood up at my entrance. He was tall and slender, his gray hair neatly barbered and his mustache waxed at the tips. His nose was long and thin, his brow high, his chin and cheekbones sharply defined beneath smooth, well-cared-for skin. There was an aroma of after-shave lotion and pomade about him, and he looked very much like a successful, respectable and rather vain businessman who knew how to pursue his trade on the most amiable of terms.

"Dr. Fairchild, I presume." He extended his soft hand, on which I glimpsed a large, ornate ring. "I've taken the liberty of ordering tea. The pastries here are rather better than you might expect. It's been one of my great finds in Norfolk. Won't you sit down?"

His voice was familiar, but lacked the tone of authority I'd heard in the woodcutter's cottage. His eyes were a pale gray, with something of an ironist's twinkle. I sat down.

"I appreciate your promptitude," he said. "I can see

you are a man with whom I shall enjoy doing business."

"Are we going to do business?" I asked him.

"Perhaps. But won't you have a spot of tea? Never talk business over an empty cup—that's my motto!"

The table had been supplied with a teapot and a tray of frosted pastries. On the wharves outside the window, a row of gulls watched hungrily as I helped myself.

"Cigarette?" Regis asked, extending a gold-plated case. I declined and he lit one for himself, which gave me another chance to observe his ring. The emblem on its broad band seemed a stylized representation of a goat's head. There was a similar emblem on the stickpin in his black silk tie, and another, even tinier version on his cuff links. He inhaled smoke greedily and expelled two streams through his flared nostrils.

"I believe you've been trying to get in touch with me," he said.

"I have one of your cards," I said. "It was given to me by the widow of the Reverend Samuel Stemp, but when I went to your stated address, I found only an empty warehouse."

"A printer's error," Regis said. "Would you believe I gave out dozens of those cards before I noticed the mistake? You can imagine the business it's cost me."

"And what is your business, Mr. Regis?"

"I deal in rare books, as it says on the card. Lately I've taken an interest in scholarly papers of various sorts—the Reverend Stemp's, for example. One never knows what might turn out to prove extremely valuable, so one buys whatever one can."

"And you are also interested in medieval manuscripts?"

"They bring a very good price these days, if one can find them. In fact, I have a buyer just now who is anxious to obtain the very manuscripts on which you've been working in the Duke's College library."

"The Westchurch manuscripts? I don't think the College would ever sell those."

"Indeed not. However, it has occurred to me—won't you have another of these excellent sweets?—it has occurred to me that in lieu of doing business with the College itself, you—how shall I put it?—might accept a commission to obtain them for us."

"Me? But I have no authority . . ."

"Of course not. You do, however, have access to the manuscripts."

"Not at the moment. The Special Collections have been closed. The manuscripts will be kept under lock and key until the College gets a new head librarian."

"Still, I shouldn't think that a man in your position—familiar with the library, and known to the College porters—would find it difficult to get hold of a key."

"Are you suggesting that I steal them for you?"

Though we were alone in the tearoom, Regis made a gesture imploring me to lower my voice. He poured more tea into his cup, then emptied the pot into mine. A gull landed on the window ledge and looked in at us with a beady, ravenous eye.

"Let us look at the situation objectively," Regis said. "You received a rather meager grant, I believe, from an American foundation and came to England for one year to work on said manuscripts. Duke's took you in, accorded you temporary privileges as a fellow of the College and set you to work in their own vineyard, so to speak. When you leave England, your work completed, you shall leave behind a set of manuscripts which are surely more valuable, for your efforts to restore our understanding of them, than anything you yourself may have gotten for your troubles. I am not unfamiliar with the academic world and the way in which it operates. Your research will be rewarded in time—provided that you are able to publish your discoveries—by an American institution. But those rewards will be paltry, compared to what I am able to offer you. The group of buyers I represent are prepared to name a very attractive price. In short, I am offering to make you an entrepreneur."

"You put it very nicely," I said, "but it's still robbery. Duke's has done well enough by me."

"I daresay they've humored you a bit, but American

scholars are not respected in England. Those Cambridge dons are frightful snobs. In the end they'll decide you just aren't their sort, and send you packing."

That might well have been the truth, but I said, "Just who are your buyers, Regis, and why are they so eager to get hold of these manuscripts?"

"They wish to remain anonymous, and their reasons are their own. One must not inquire too directly into 'reasons,' Dr. Fairchild. You will be amply paid for whatever risk may be involved."

"It's not just the risk," I said. "I have every intention of making those manuscripts my life's work."

Regis's eyes grew colder and harder, and his face seemed to change into something ugly and sinister. "In that case, Dr. Fairchild, it would prove a very short life, I fear. The people I represent are not only anxious to obtain the Westchurch manuscripts; they are also determined to ensure that their secrets remain inviolate. I have no idea of the lengths to which they might go to prevent an indiscriminate exposure of the contents of those papers."

I sat back with something on my face which I hoped resembled a smile. "I think you've just threatened me, Mr. Regis."

He gave me an injured look. "My dear fellow, I am simply urging that you not ask too many questions about these people, their activities or their motives. The less you know, the easier it shall be to arrange our transaction. What would you say to one hundred thousand pounds?"

"One hundred thousand pounds? You've got to be kidding!"

Regis's elegant hands urged me once again to lower my voice. "I assure you I'm quite serious. My buyers are members of a very wealthy and influential organization—what you might call a fraternal order. I should accept their offer if I were you, no questions asked. There are places in the world where you could live a princely life on one hundred thousand pounds. Believe me, Dr. Fairchild, it's the chance of a lifetime."

And so it was. I looked out through salt-glazed windows at the small harbor. Rusty freighters, squat fishing vessels, a few sloops and dinghies, gulls perched along the wharf. The brackish water glinted oil, floated bits of debris. The low sun glowed orangy-gold off derricks, smokestacks, masts and rigging. Some of those boats would be leaving with the evening tide, heading for far-off places. It was really amazing, I thought, the way I wasn't tempted.

"Your offer," I said, "is certainly very generous, but I can't help wondering what makes these manuscripts so valuable. After all, they've lain neglected and forgotten in the College library for a couple of hundred years. Now, all of a sudden, this fraternal order of yours is willing to pay a small fortune to get them out. I don't understand."

"It's just as well you don't," Regis said. "However, as long as the manuscripts were 'neglected and forgotten,' my buyers were quite content to leave them alone. It was your arrival in England, and your unprecedented energy and success in coping with the difficulties they present, which demonstrated the need to make other arrangements."

"I don't think I like your 'arrangements,'" I said. "In at least three instances I know of, they look a lot like murder."

"I really hope I have not misjudged you, Dr. Fairchild. I thought you were a man we could do business with. Of course, this offer must be kept in strictest confidence. Any attempt to report our conversation to the College authorities or to the police would be exceedingly futile. You are not in a position to bargain with us, nor do you have a shred of evidence to use against us. It would be—and *this* you may construe as a threat—dangerous in the extreme for you to pursue your studies in defiance of our wishes. Should you do so, I doubt that even America would be large enough to hide you."

"That's a pretty big claim," I said, "for a pipsqueak cult of cockeyed devil-worshippers."

Regis had been about to leave the table, but this last remark had the desired effect of setting him back in his chair. He glared at me, attempting to master his anger. His slender fingers gripped the table. The waxed tips of his mustache quivered. I had never seen a man lose his good humor and urbanity so quickly.

"You are speaking of things," he said, "of which you are abysmally ignorant. What if I were to tell you that the order I represent is older than Christianity; that some of the world's greatest men have belonged to it in times past; that even today it attracts men of great power, wealth and influence? You would be surprised at the vast numbers which have embraced this ancient and honorable faith."

"I'm sure Satan's always had his following," I said, "but so far I haven't exactly been impressed by the quality of the congregation. You're the first one I've seen, Regis, who wasn't close to a gibbering idiot."

"You have perhaps seen more of us than you realize. The term 'Satan' means 'enemy' in Hebrew. The Bible identifies this enemy with Lucifer, a mere exiled minion of the Hebraic God. Our order cherishes a different tradition. The Christians fear and hate us, for we dare to challenge their simplistic notion of the world, their allegiance to an absurd and enfeebling faith. They know that the god we worship is real, whereas this God of theirs—who has ever seen Him? Who can rely upon Him? Indeed, the entire history of the world might well be seen as the unfolding struggle between their God and ours."

"And was one of your eminent disciples by any chance a poet named Geoffrey Gervaise?" I asked.

In the waning light from the harbor, the eyes of Simon Regis had taken on a reptilian opacity. His skin had turned yellow and scaly. His cultured voice had become a kind of hiss. "You have asked far too many questions and received, I'm afraid, too many answers. But I will tell you this. In the battle of which we're speaking, hostages are sometimes taken. The author of the Westchurch manuscript was a vain and foolish man who challenged our god and relied too greatly upon his own ingenuity. He is now paying the price for his arrogance and doing much good for our cause. His text is precious to us as a token of his submission. For nearly two centuries that text lay safely in the College library, where one of ours, in his wisdom, had placed it. Now it is no longer safe and we have made you an offer for its return. You have forty-eight hours in which to make your decision."

"And where shall I find you?" I asked, as Regis rose from the table, a dark figure looming over me in the dim light.

"We shall find you, Dr. Fairchild. You must make up your mind before we do." And with that he turned and walked swiftly from the tearoom.

His departure seemed to clear the air of some unpleasant odor I had scarcely been aware of, or had taken for the rotting fish smell of the harbor.

I found that I had no interest in drinking the rest of my cold tea. A smutty young waitress came to clear the table and give me the bill, which I had no choice but to pay. A nice touch, I thought. One might have known the devil would employ a cheapskate.

There was a pay phone in the lobby and I put through a call to Abbotswold. Mrs. Mortimor answered and I asked for Stephany.

"David, what's wrong? Has anything happened to my car?"

"It's fine—but something's come up and I'm going to have to keep it for a while longer. I've got to drive back to Cambridge tonight."

"Cambridge? Whatever for?"

I didn't expect her to believe me, so I said, "To steal the Westchurch manuscript."

Ten minutes later I was driving across the twilit fens toward Cambridge.

19

A Letter to
the Archbishop

His Excellency the Archbishop
Thomas à Becket
At the Court of King Louis VII, Paris

My Lord:

In obedience to your will, I have made discreet inquiries concerning your onetime friend and protégé, the infamous Geoffrey Gervaise. I am most grieved to inform Your Excellency that what you have heard rumored of Gervaise does indeed seem the truth, and that Your Eminence has no recourse in this matter but speedy excommunication, pronouncing both the man and his heathen works anathema to all faithful and right-minded Christians.

I feel these measures are necessary because there are many here in England still faithful to your primacy (and who long for your return to your rightful place as head of the Church in England) who remember that Gervaise was once your friend and will deny him sanctuary only when the archbishop himself has spoken. When you have heard the facts in the case, you will not, I am sure, suffer this wretched creature to trade upon the esteem your countrymen and fellow religious hold for you.

I have been able to reconstruct Gervaise's history from numerous sources. Forced to flee the court when Your Excellency chose exile to capitulation to the king, Gervaise prevailed upon the good abbot of Blackstone to speak for him and thus found refuge as a humble country priest in the village of Wendlebury, under the patronage of Lord William Fitzjames. There were many who warned Gervaise that he was unfit for the life and duties of a village pastor, but the headstrong man was not to be dissuaded. There followed a series of altercations with Fitzjames, culminating in some angry words over a peasant girl whom Gervaise accused Lord William of abusing in the manner of country gentlemen. He was soundly beaten for his pains and was obliged to seek a new shelter at the monastery at Blackstone. It was at this time that the king, anxious to keep peace with Fitzjames and willing enough to persecute one of your supporters, issued a warrant for Gervaise's arrest on the grounds that he had made off with chancellory supplies and funds—one crime, I am fairly sure, the fellow did not commit.

The good abbot of Blackstone, ignorant of Gervaise's wicked propensities and ever faithful to you, provided the man sanctuary for well over a year. During this period Gervaise seems to have developed his interest in the forbidden arts and to have undertaken forms of study which were clearly perilous to his immortal soul. He absented himself from the monastery for nearly a month in order to seek out a certain sorcerer called Gwynneddon, who had hidden himself away in the mountains of Wales. Some say he learned the secrets of the ancients from Gwynneddon and became himself a sorcerer of great powers. Others say the old pagan introduced Gervaise to the devil and that an unholy pact was sealed between them. And still others—those who have fallen under the spell this man seems to cast, or count themselves among his friends—have tried to claim that Gervaise met Satan only to defy him, and did defy him successfully, so that he alone among all men can count himself free from Satan's power.

In any case, Gervaise left Blackstone to travel the highways and byways of England, frequently but a few hours ahead of the king's soldiers. He found refuge and sanctuary wherever he went, and many miracles and good works were attributed to him by the common folk, though the evidence for such prodigies, I hasten to add, is slight. Nevertheless, shrines were established at places where he had been, and there were many, including a sizable number from among the lower rank of the clergy, who became his disciples. If Gervaise had confined himself to an evangelical crusade, few would condemn him, whatever the audacity of his personal claims. But wherever he went he also sowed dissension and unrest, preaching against the powers of the aristocracy, attacking the wealth of monasteries and bishoprics, railing against all those whom God has placed upon this earth to govern and to save souls. In village after village, his presence led to ill will, conspiracy and open revolt. In some instances, manor houses were looted and burned by the peasants, shops and warehouses sacked, churches defiled. The very monks of Wiltonham Priory broke into the prior's treasury and distributed gold and jewels to the poor. Is it any wonder, then, that the king doubled, tripled and quadrupled the reward for Gervaise's capture, and dispatched an entire company of his best soldiers to hunt the villain down?

Still Gervaise eluded capture. He was by now too famous for his good works and too beloved by peasant and priest alike. The nadir of this horrid affair came when Lord William Fitzjames, Gervaise's old protector and now his chief foe, was actually drawn and quartered by the peasants of Wendlebury, pieces of his corpse impaled at every crossroads for miles around. Gervaise let it be known that he had had no hand in this outrage and repudiated all acts of violence, yet it was clear to all whose inflammatory preaching and wretched example should be held accountable.

These troubled times continued in England for nearly three years, from the spring of 1166 to the winter of 1168. Then, mysteriously, Gervaise disappeared from view. Some said that his demons had carried him off to hell; others believed that the king's soldiers had dispatched the villain without a public trial. And still others claim to this day that Gervaise has only gone into hiding—some even say with you, my lord—and that he will soon return to resume his crusade. In which case, it is believed, nothing can stop Gervaise until he has made himself the lord and ruler of England. I suspect it is this last rumor which most troubles our king, for he is known to be anxious to crown his eldest son as his successor while he is still alive, and to this end, it is rumored, he has even made secret overtures to Your Eminence concerning your safe return to England—since even Henry acknowledges that only the Archbishop of Canterbury may lawfully crown an English king. . . .

My lord, it is now several hours since I wrote the above lines, and I take my quill in hand once again to describe for you the extraordinary event which interrupted my account.

I have seen the very devil himself, Geoffrey Gervaise!

Our interview came about in this wise. My secretary, the faithful Botolph, of whom you've often heard me speak, came to my chamber to inform me that a hermit had appeared in the cathedral close and begged leave to speak with me. I have long made it a practice to turn away no weary pilgrim in search of the bishop's blessing. I therefore instructed Botolph to send the fellow to the small reception room I have reserved for such occasions.

No sooner had I entered the chamber than the hermit leapt from behind the door, slammed it and threw the bolt, thus trapping me alone with him. I cried out for my guards, but the hermit took me by the throat and put a dagger to my jugular. "Send away your guards," he cried. "An hour's audience I beg of you, or by the devil, I'll slit your throat!"

I had no choice but to grant Gervaise this audience, for I realized by now into whose hands I had fallen. I had not seen the man for many years, and I can hardly describe for you the way in which he has changed. Tall and thin he is as ever, but exceedingly gaunt, as if he has been fasting. His hair and beard are still black and thick but much longer, filthy and unkempt. His clothes too were ragged and filthy, as if the man had just crawled out of his own grave. A hellish fire burned in his eyes, and I recognized that, with no hope of rescue or escape, I would be wise to humor his dementia.

The rogue informed me that he had heard of my inquiry into his case and that I was to write for Your Excellency an account of what I'd learned. He had also heard—I don't know how; perhaps through his demons—that the king has asked you to return to England and that you are but waiting for some further sign of Henry's good faith. He demanded that I include in my letter a message from himself, urging Your Eminence to grant the wretch an audience immediately upon your return to England.

His message I will place before you; but I can in no way advise Your Grace to subject yourself to the contamination, peril and misery of such an audience. The fiend wishes me to tell Your Grace that he has engaged the devil . . . *in a game of chess!* He says that the magician Gwynneddon, whom he visited in Wales, gave him a certain drug which he was fool enough to take, and that he was visited by Satan himself, while so drugged, at a pagan burial site called Brixton Barrow. He promptly challenged the devil to a game at the board, and to an accompanying wager—his soul against the devil's promise to grant Gervaise immunity to all temptations and supernatural affliction. If you needed further proof that Gervaise has gone quite mad, you have it now in his very own words!

At this point Gervaise's account, or my understanding of it, grows confused. A game there was, perhaps two games. I gather Gervaise emerged victorious, and that Satan pretended to honor his side of the wager. Thus we have an explanation—if we could but take it seriously!—for the miraculous powers Gervaise exhibited when he began his wanderings across England. Believing himself a victor over Satan, the fool set out to make himself a second savior of the race. Oh, he acknowledges Christ as the first Savior—he does Our Lord that justice! But Gervaise believes it is up to him, and others like him, to shoulder crosses of their own. As you can see, Gervaise is no theologian, but a mystic, and you know how mystics are wont to trample reason and authority underfoot. When I asked him how this blasphemous wager could serve any justifiable Christian end, he replied that his damnation—should it come to that, as I think it shall—will clearly prove the existence of a God whose power exceeds that of Satan. I should have explained earlier, my lord, that a third contest between Gervaise and Satan is apparently now in progress, and has been in progress since Gervaise disappeared nearly two years ago. On this point he was exceedingly obscure, but I gather that Satan has introduced certain variations and refinements into the rules of the game. There was some mad business about the stars, and about a move each night, or once a fortnight, or whenever Satan demands it; I don't know. I am still quite upset and my wits don't seem to function. I keep seeing those wild eyes, that dagger which he held to my throat. . . . I gave him my promise that I would deliver his message, and with that he left me. I sent the guard after him at once and dispatched a messenger to the castle, but I have no doubt the wary brute has escaped once again.

My lord, please listen to one who loves you and do not suffer this man to come near you! In fact, I must urge that you do not return to England at all until Gervaise is dead and the king has regained a somewhat calmer mind. The king has not been himself, they say, for many months. The queen imprisoned, his sons fighting among themselves and daily giving him new cause for concern—and now this lunatic Gervaise once more aprowl across the land . . . I should not count upon Henry's rationality under such circumstances, nor would I trust his promises.

But I can go no farther. The memory of that man's burning eyes haunts me still. It will take much prayer and penance, and perhaps a long vacation at my country estate, before I am myself again. And so I close, with all reverence and love and admiration, your most humble and obedient servant, who has served you in this matter as faithfully as he could, and who begs your

210

indulgence for any flaws or inadequacies in this most trying account,

Written this evening of November 7,
the year of Our Lord 1170.

Robert Hastings
Bishop of Ely

20

Larceny

$\sim$

"Steal the Westchurch manuscripts? Have you gone crazy?"

"It could be I have, Archie," I said, sinking down into one of his chairs before the gas fire, "but I'm going to steal them, and I'd like you to help me."

Archie sat on the arm of the chair opposite and looked at his suitcases near the door, awaiting the porter's call the next morning. I could see he was intrigued by the notion of a last prank on the dons who had dictated his exile, yet reluctant to commit himself to anything quite so criminal. I'd been counting on his penchant for reckless escapades and felt sure I could talk him around.

"Now see here," he began, trying very hard to be firm with me—then caught himself playing the role of my British nanny. "Have a glass of whisky, lad, and tell me just what's been going on down at Trevor-Finch's place."

I gratefully took the glass of liquor he handed me and began my explanation. "There *is* a cult of Satanists connected with those manuscripts, Archie. Not only did they murder Dr. Greggs, but they've murdered two other men besides, and offered me one hundred thousand pounds to steal the manuscripts for them—with the suggestion that my death will be next if I refuse."

"One hundred thousand pounds! They've actually made you such an offer, and you've accepted? So what's my cut, if I lend a hand?"

"Archie, I'm not stealing the manuscripts for the cult. I have to learn what makes them so important to these people—and incidentally, to our friend Trevor-Finch. I've got just forty-eight hours to come up with some answers, and I could use your support back at Abbotswold, if things get rough."

"I'm sure you could." Archie savored his whisky and cast another glance at his waiting suitcases. "I think you'd better start from the beginning. How in the world did Finchie ever get mixed up with a cult of Satanists?"

I took Archie through it step by step, telling him as much as I could without betraying too many family secrets. It was a relief to share my recent experiences with someone of Archie's temper and sympathies, even though I could see he found parts of my tale hard to swallow. When I'd finished, he thought for a while and then said, "But what makes you so sure the solution to all these mysteries is embedded in your precious manuscripts?"

"If it isn't, three men have been murdered for nothing. This isn't some little group of crackpot rustics we're dealing with. Regis indicated that the coven at Creypool is part of an international brotherhood, with a good many wealthy and powerful constituents."

"Then surely it's nothing for us to tangle with. Why can't you simply go to the police with what you know?"

"The police will have to be informed, of course, but not until I've learned the secret of those manuscripts and kept my promise to the professor's mother. It may surprise you, Archie, but I've learned to care for these people, and I seem to be the only one who can help them."

Archie obviously found my expression of commitment in bad taste. "That's all very well, Fairchild, but how do we keep from getting killed?"

"I've been thinking about that. Do you still have access to your laboratory?"

"I'm turning in the key tomorrow."

"Could you cook up something that would give us some fire power—something we could scare them with, perhaps? A lot of smoke and noise should do."

"Yes, I could arrange that all right, but don't think I've decided to throw in with you just yet. Finchie would hardly welcome me at his 'ancestral manor,' you know."

"We can risk his displeasure. When it's all over, he might be very appreciative of what we've done for him—enough to get us both permanent places in the College, don't you think?"

Archie grinned. "By God, do you suppose we could pull it off? You'd have Abbotswold and the professor's daughter, and I'd still have Cambridge. A coup d'état!"

I knew he was nearly won over, so I said, "Our first job is to get hold of those manuscripts."

Archie cocked an eyebrow. "You have a plan, I suppose?"

I did, and when I'd described it for him, he said, "I can see you've taken my natural propensities into account. Of course I can make a drunken fool of myself, but my performance is bound to be improved by a bit more of the real thing. Bottoms up, lad."

We had another drink. It was just after eleven, and the sparsely populated College had already settled down for the night. The gates would close at twelve, so we had less than an hour to wait. Archie looked at me with great amusement.

"You're a prodigy, Fairchild, you really are. Here I am risking my neck and a hefty prison term, and I'm damned if I'm not looking forward to it. Eight centuries with a ghost in the family, hey? No wonder Trevor-Finch has always been such a beastly bore! All things considered, it's a wonder you didn't take that one hundred thousand pounds. I would have. This whole affair has turned your wits."

"I don't know quite how to explain it myself," I said, "but I seem to have developed a conscience."

"Ah," Archie said, and rolled his eyes. "It can happen to the best of us."

"Try to imagine what it's like, to realize you've actually seen a ghost," I said. "There's a moral shock involved, a sudden awakening to the fact that, if Gervaise's soul is immortal, then mine is too. And if mine is—"

"Then everyone must possess such a soul? And if we're not all just molecules scrambling around in this bloody stew of a universe, then there may be more to the ideals people used to live by than we've recognized? I've thought of that already, and it's why I'd like to believe in your story. But what if . . ." Archie pulled at his collar and looked flushed from the liquor he'd consumed. "Well, damn it all, lad, what if . . ."

"I've simply been seeing things? That's a possibility, I know, but there's a curious logic to the whole affair that I find irresistible. I'm not just out to save poor old Gervaise and the Trevor-Finches, you know. I have a theory to prove."

"A scholar to the death," Archie said, and we drank to it.

At ten past midnight I was waiting outside the porter's lodge with a briefcase I'd borrowed from Archie's room. At a quarter past, Archie (who'd gone out the back way at eleven forty-five) began hammering on the gate. I could hear him singing some bawdy working-class ballad at the top of his voice as the porter's man unlocked the gate. Archie stumbled across the threshold, then collapsed in the porter's arms.

"Here, here, sir. You've had a heavy night of it," the porter said, struggling to keep Archie upright.

"It's the rich what gets the pleasure," Archie sang, *"and the poor what gets the blame. . . ."*

I slipped into the lodge and found the keys on the big pegboard behind the porter's desk. I grabbed the

214

two I needed, ducked out and set off across the New Court for the library, Archie's song wailing through the night: *"It's the same the whole world over—ain't it all a bloody shame?"*

A few lights had gone on around the court, but I knew the aroused sleepers would be looking to the commotion at the front gate and not to the library. I unlocked the main door and let myself into air stale with the scent of paper and aged bindings, the dust and mold and stifled aspirations of scholars long since dead and buried. I had brought along a flashlight from Stephany's car and I kept its beam on the floor, guiding myself down the long aisle toward the Special Collections.

At the iron gates, I paused to fit the second key in its lock. I could hear none of the ruckus Archie was raising. The silence of centuries lay over the library. I wasn't frightened—just mildly excited, a little drunk, and very determined to do the job I'd come for. I felt sure that Gervaise was somewhere close by, perhaps even visible in the shadows if I took the time to look for him. His encouragement spurred me on.

I turned the key and the lock slipped back with an echoing clang. My flashlight illuminated the shelves, cabinets and drawers which housed the College's most prized and precious holdings. The Westchurch manuscripts were kept in a special airtight vault with a combination lock. I knew the combination; old Greggs had given it to me last fall and I'd used it dozens of times, yet I hesitated, suddenly unsure. The wrong combination would set off an alarm.

I reached out to touch the dial. With the first turn my confidence returned. The numbers were there when I needed them, as if another hand guided my own. Right twice around to 16 . . . left to 32 . . . right to 0 . . . left again all the way around to 2. The latch snapped and the vault swung open. The Westchurch manuscripts, in seven labeled boxes, sat waiting. I needed only the box which contained Gervaise's poem. I put it into Archie's briefcase and shut the vault. Heading back up the aisle, I paused for a second beneath the concordance to Shakespeare. Steady, big fellow—give my regards to Hamlet's father.

A great sense of elation was waiting for me as I stepped out into the chill night air and locked the library behind me. I went back to the porter's lodge, returned the keys to the pegboard and proceeded to the main gate; its little night door had been shut but not locked. I stepped out into the artificial glare of the Cambridge street. Stephany's car was parked just around the corner.

Colin Douglas had gone to Spain for the vac but had left me the key to his flat. By the time Archie called for me at nine the next morning, I was on my twelfth cup of instant coffee and the last few lines of the poem.

"You look perfectly dreadful," Archie said as I let him in. "No sleep last night for a guilty conscience?"

"My conscience never felt better, Archie. I've been up all night reading. It's amazing what sense it all makes now that I know what to look for. And what a magnificent poem it is. There's not a line that isn't alive, that doesn't bristle with genius."

"And has it told you how its author may be freed?"

"I think so. But I almost hope I'm wrong. We'll have a chance to test my theory tonight. The professor has a ghost hunter coming up from London, and there'll be an expedition to the abbey. What did you get for me at the lab?"

Archie put a briefcase, nearly identical to the one I'd borrowed for the manuscript, on the desk and opened it up. He took out a metal container the size of an American beer can. "I've brought you six of these," he said. "It's that new explosive I told you about—similar to nitroglycerin, but much safer and easier to use. If you twist this little tab on the top of the can, the chemicals now held separately inside are allowed to mix. It's perfectly harmless until you twist the tab, and then, within seconds, you have yourself a veritable hand grenade. Makes a lovely flash and bang when it goes off, too."

"How powerful is the explosion?"

"Hmm. One of these canisters should knock a man down at twenty yards; could give him a nasty burn if he were any closer. Of course, if you set off all six at once you'd augment the explosive force by something like thirty-six times—there's a complicated formula to account for that."

"I'm not sure I want to play with anything that lethal."

"It was the best I could come up with on such short notice. And besides, it's perfectly safe until you twist these tabs. Even then, it would take quite a jolt to set off an explosion. You'd have to give the can a good toss, or hit it with something. . . . Well, shall we be on our way?"

I had one stop to make before we left Cambridge, a small junk shop I'd noticed on my bike rides around the town. The proprietor looked on as I rummaged through his wares in search of the thing I wanted. In a back shed, where he kept those items he no longer hoped to sell, I at last found something close to what I was looking for.

"What the devil is that?" Archie asked as I held it up to count the squares.

"An old grate, most likely off someone's cellar window. Only forty-eight squares, but it will have to do. How much do you want for this?" I asked the proprietor.

"That's a rare old piece, guv," the junkman said. "That'll cost you thruppence."

"A steal at half the price," Archie said.

I paid for the grate and a pair of used binoculars I'd picked up during the search. We put both in the trunk of Stephany's car, along with the two briefcases, and set out for Abbotswold. Neither Archie nor I attempted to say goodbye to Cambridge and it struck me as a small act of faith on both our parts to assume that we'd ever see the town again.

21

An Experiment
in Nonsense

❧

There were a few tourists roaming the ruins when we
stopped at Creypool Abbey, but we attracted no attention as we carried the grate and the binoculars to the
back wall and left them hidden in a clump of bushes
near the remains of the little observatory.

We pulled up the drive at Abbotswold shortly before
one. A large green van, unmarked, with an oddly
designed antenna on its roof, was parked near the front
door. A portly man of late middle age climbed down
from the rear of the van and came to greet us. He was
dressed in the tweed cap and jacket, jodhpurs and
boots, of the British sportsman.

"You must be the major's young Yank from the
College," he said. "I'm Colonel Lionel Buzby, RAF,
retired. Trevor-Finch and I took on the Krauts together. Met in a German prison camp, as a matter of
fact. You're something of an authority on this abbey
ghost, I hear."

The colonel had a military mustache, jowls and pale,
shrewd, sleepy eyes. His handshake was vigorous.
"Scarcely an authority," I said, "but I have an interest
in the place. This is my friend Archie Cavendish, also
from Duke's."

The colonel sized Archie up with a commanding of-
ficer's interest in a recruit. "We can use an extra
hand," he said. "You never know what you're going to
run into on one of these expeditions, do you?"

"I'm new to the field," Archie said. "Have you actually scared up a few ghosts, Colonel?"

"I can't actually say they were ghosts," the colonel

replied. "'Psychic phenomena' is what we call them these days. Things which defy a purely natural explanation. It's a hobby of mine, and I've rigged up a few gadgets using ideas from my former career in electronic surveillance. Care for a look? I've just been testing the instruments."

We climbed into the van. It was filled with the sort of equipment a mobile TV unit might use to cover a soccer match—banks of dials, switches, meters, view screens and tape decks.

"The function of all this portable hardware," Colonel Buzby said, "is to provide us with some reliable data on these otherwise inexplicable manifestations. Say a chap sees a ghost and it can't be explained as a mere hallucination. Many such sightings can't. Well, if there's something out there which goes against the known laws of nature, it ought to create some sort of disruption in its immediate physical surroundings, right? So we have these various scanners—heat sensors, Geiger counter, x-ray and infrared cameras, radarscope, microphones and so on—enough to give us a rather complete reading on the material consequences of one of these psychic disruptions.

"Over here we've got a new device I've just designed and I'm anxious to try out. I call it my portable molecular analyzer—'the Mole,' for short. I press this button, and the Mole emits a wave of charged particles. The particles will pass through ordinary matter without a trace, but if they enter the magnetic field of particles with different properties—what we commonly call an 'antiparticle'—we get a reaction in the form of ultrasonic signals, which the Mole picks up, 'reads' and feeds back to the recording devices in the van. With the Mole, I should be able to track a ghost, or whatever phenomenon it is that's causing the disruption, over terrain the van couldn't manage. Later, we can run the data through a computer to see if it makes any sense. No matter what my good friend the major says, science is one day going to get around to the whole question of psychic physics, and then my data will prove invaluable—"

"Psychic physics, indeed!" said Trevor-Finch, appearing at the open door of the van. "You're an ingenious technician, Buzby, but an incurable romantic. You'll find nothing to impress science at the abbey, I can assure you of that. . . . Glad you made it back, Fairchild. I was beginning to fear that Stephany and I had been boring you, but this little experiment in nonsense ought to catch your fancy."

Archie came up from the front of the van and the professor started at the sight of him. "I say, is that you, Cavendish? What are you doing here?"

"I brought him along, Professor," I said. "I hope you don't mind. He'd like to get in on our ghost hunt."

"Nothing better to occupy your time, Cavendish? Well, as long as you're here, I suppose I can put you up for a night or two. Mrs. Mortimor is serving sandwiches on the terrace. Won't you all come along?"

After lunch, Trevor-Finch took Archie and the colonel down to the beach to inspect his tower laboratory. One glance from Stephany and I knew how she wanted to spend the afternoon, but I pleaded lack of sleep and a sick headache (both true), got the briefcases from the car and went up to my room alone. I was too tired even to chase out the cat sunning itself on my window ledge, but collapsed on the bed and fell into a deep sleep.

I awoke late in the afternoon from a trying dream, my brain still reeling with rhymed couplets and sonorous medieval vowels. A rose "both red and white . . . The boy's first love, the man's delight." In my dream I had seen the rose, not variegated or striped, but a magical rose which changed its color as I gazed upon it—first a throbbing. blazing red, then a pure and dazzling white. People came to me in the dream and pleaded with me not to pluck the rose, but I grasped the stem, whereupon one of its thorns stung me to the quick.

I lay on the rumpled bedspread in the dusky room and listened to the birds chattering outside the house. Then I heard a footstep in the hall. I lay very still with my back to the door and presently I heard the knob turning. I waited another few seconds, then groaned and rolled over like a man just waking up, and caught Giles trying to slip back out through the door.

"Beg pardon, sir. I just came up to see—that is, the professor wanted me to tell you they're having sherry in the library." I could see his eyes flick quickly at the desk, where I'd left one of the briefcases in plain view; the other was behind the bed.

"Thank you, Giles," I said. "I'll be down after I've had a wash."

"Very good, sir. Sorry to disturb you."

The old bastard knows I've got the manuscript, I thought. It was possible that Regis had had me followed to Cambridge. If so, he might not wait the entire forty-eight hours to collect his prize.

I took both briefcases—the one containing Archie's bombs somewhat lighter than the other—made sure the old man was no longer in the hall, went softly down the stairs and let myself out of the house. The last rays of sunlight departed from the treetops as I cut across the lawn and picked up the path to the beach. I wanted a hiding place well away from the house, yet one I could get to quickly if the need arose. The professor's tower had seemed the logical spot, but the door was locked. There was no time to scout another locale; I would have to hide my booty on the beach. Looking up at the cliffs, I saw the professor's dish antenna silhouetted against the purple sky, the evening star already winking through its beams and struts. The cliff was about thirty feet high at that point and slightly overhung. Its side of clay and loose rock was steep but looked climbable just off to the right, along a small gully. I took the briefcases up one at a time and found a place, where the clay had washed away from the concrete footing of the structure, that would accommodate the two of them very nicely. I lowered the heavier briefcase into the hole, then opened the second briefcase and twisted the tabs on each of the six canisters. I gently lowered the armed bomb until it rested firmly atop the other briefcase, an effective booby trap. I concealed the hole with several large rocks, then worked my way back to the path without returning to the beach and came across the lawn in the dark.

Back in my room, I'd just changed clothes and was knotting my tie when Stephany knocked once and came in.

"Are you all right? We're waiting dinner for you."

"Sorry. I couldn't get myself out of the tub."

"Poor love," she said, coming over to put a hand on my brow. "Does your head still ache? What were you doing in Cambridge that kept you up all night?"

I put my arms around her and kissed her forehead. "Dearest Stephany, whatever I've done—and whatever I may do in the next few hours—I've had your best interests at heart. I hope you'll remember that."

"Of course I will. Don't look so glum. This wretched old house is starting to affect even you."

"I wish you wouldn't go with us to the abbey tonight."

"I want to come. You don't think we're actually going to find a ghost there, do you?"

"I'd just feel better if you stayed home."

She looked curiously at me for a moment, then removed herself from my arms. "Honestly! I never should have sent you up to see Grandmama. I intend to come along, and that's all there is to that!"

I might have known the professor would have a headstrong daughter, and that there was more drawing Stephany to the abbey than she realized.

Trevor-Finch, Archie and the colonel had been getting on famously all afternoon. Intoxicated by the stars, they'd gone heavy on the before-dinner sherry and then consumed an enormous quantity of wine at the table, the professor twice sending Giles to the cellar for another bottle. He accepted Archie's presence at his table with good grace, humored the colonel, and joked affectionately with his daughter. Only to me was he as rude as usual, several times mentioning that I had not proved as apt a pupil as he had expected. "Fairchild's bright enough, I daresay," he told the others as if I weren't even there, "but he insists upon clinging to ob-

222

solete notions on everything from politics to religion. That's what comes from the study of poetry."

"I hope to show you before the evening's over," I said, "that the study of poetry can be of practical value."

"By finding us a ghost at the abbey?" Trevor-Finch's derisive laughter verged, I thought, on hysteria. "Come, come—we are not children frightened by ghost stories in the dark. Even the colonel here knows better than to be afraid of ghosts!"

"I wouldn't say that," the colonel said. "I respect the supernatural, same as I would a live bomb. You never know what's going to happen when you start messing about with psychic phenomena. For one thing, there's usually some purely human disturbance behind a good many of these ghostly episodes."

"Yes, such as insanity, ignorance, mass hysteria, congenital imbecility, charlatanism and fraud," the professor said.

"The origin of the human fear of the supernatural," I said, "has been traced to the individual's sexual anxiety and guilt—usually the consequence of an imaginative and narcissistic adolescence. If we weren't frightened, we wouldn't be human. On the other hand"—for once I managed to make my point before the professor could overwhelm me with objections—"one can only wonder at the sadomasochistic impulse which could lead otherwise rational individuals to engage in such a debasing and self-destructive pursuit of occult experiences as, for example, witchcraft."

The professor looked at me so sharply that I was sure those phrases from Sir Aubrey Rice Poulter's book had rung a bell. He fell into an uncharacteristic silence, his long, agile fingers flicking nervously at the crumbs on the table, as if seeking an arrangement that would satisfy his scientist's craving for symmetry.

"Well," Stephany said at last, "are we going to the abbey tonight or aren't we? Another glass of port, Daddy, and you'll be too drunk to remember whether you've seen a ghost or not."

"I've a good mind to call this farce off," Trevor-

Finch said, "but I suppose the rest of you are determined to make fools of yourselves, so I'd better come along."

Trevor-Finch had some difficulty in rising from the table, and his intoxication made his eyes look shiftier than ever, as if he were a pickpocket in a train station full of bulging purses and fat wallets.

Stephany, Archie and I rode in the back of the van with the electronic equipment, while Colonel Buzby and Trevor-Finch took the front. We could hear them bawling out their favorite marching and drinking songs as the ghostmobile rolled across the dark and quiet countryside, beneath the brilliant stars.

I was filled with the glum sense that my effort to solve the mystery of the Westchurch manuscripts had come down at last to this silly escapade by a group of inebriated thrill-seekers.

We pulled into the empty parking lot outside the ruins. Colonel Buzby came back to warm up his instruments and to issue arms—flashlights for Stephany and me, a portable tape recorder for Archie, an infrared camera and (just in case the ghost should turn nasty) a double-barreled shotgun for the professor. "I'd like the chance to shoot a ghost," Trevor-Finch exclaimed. "I'd have it mounted and hung in the senior common room, where all you bloody humanists could puzzle over him."

It struck me then that the professor and the colonel, despite their differences, were indeed members of an army of intrepid scientists steadily advancing upon the world with their computers and instruments, methodically disproving the existence of everything the human heart had ever invented to people this lonely universe. They would not stop, these zealous crusaders, until there was nothing left but them and their instruments, and then the universe would be that nearly perfect vacuum they desired.

The colonel took up his portable molecular analyzer. He flipped a switch and the Mole began to emit a series of beeps. "As long as the beeps are steady," he said, "we know the particles have encountered nothing extraordinary. If they speed up, it means we're onto something."

The doors of the van slammed shut behind us. We approached the abbey in a closely gathered group. There was no moon yet. The stars, bright and numerous, shimmered in the moist, mild air of the spring night. Mist rising from the fens sent milky tendrils toward the abbey walls. Stephany moved closer to me and took my arm. Archie released a short, nervous laugh. "My God, it *is* a spooky old place!"

"Quiet, please," Colonel Buzby said. "I think we're getting a reaction."

The Mole had begun to beep at an accelerated rate with our first step beyond the gate. Now it was ticking rapidly and insistently, and I felt my own heartbeat racing to match its pace. The colonel swung the box in an arc, so that its stream of charged particles probed the dark recesses of the abbey. The ticking tapered off, then picked up again as he brought the Mole back toward the central core of the ruins.

"Could it be there's someone else here tonight?" I asked.

"If we were picking up human body temperatures from off in that direction—even a large animal or any warm-blooded creature—this little green light would go on. Besides, the particles wouldn't respond to a human presence."

"This is absurd," Trevor-Finch said angrily. "You've never even tested this contraption of yours."

"I couldn't very well test it, Major, until I had something to test it on. We're getting a reading, all right. A very definite gap or break in the physical structure of our immediate surroundings. It could be caused by some energy source—or possibly by a bit of antimatter."

"Why, the presence of antimatter would blow this place apart," the professor said.

"Under ordinary conditions, yes, but these are clearly not ordinary conditions. Let's proceed a bit farther. This is going to give us some magnificent data."

We continued on into the ruins and the ticking from

the colonel's box continued to accelerate. Stephany and I shone our lights across the broken walls and down dark passageways, but all we saw was the pale mist that had begun to penetrate the skeletal structure. By now I didn't need the Mole to tell me that we were closing in on something. I recognized those symptoms I had felt before—that shrill alarm within my skull, that pressure inside my chest—which indicated that we were in the presence of a mysterious and unnatural being.

As peculiar as it may seem to one who has not tramped about a haunted monastery in the dead of night, it came to me that there were certain rules of propriety which one would do well to observe in any form of ghostly intercourse. Did one do violence to a ghost's integrity by attempting to analyze its molecules? I suppose it was not until this very moment that I realized how much I believed, and how much I wanted to believe, in the apparition named Geoffrey Gervaise. The ticking of the Mole began to taper off. The colonel swung the box in an arc and abruptly the ticking became more rapid.

"Ahh," the colonel said triumphantly. "Whatever it is, it can move."

Trevor-Finch flew into a rage. "This asininity has gone far enough. I'm going back to the van. Come along, Stephany."

"If you turn back now," Stephany said, "won't you be admitting that you're afraid there really is something here?"

The professor drew himself up. "That remark is in very bad taste. Of course I'm not afraid. It's simply an insult to a rational creature to play these absurd games . . . but very well. Show me that damned ghost, Colonel, if you can!"

I was sorry that the professor had regained his nerve, and I saw I had slim chance of reaching Gervaise if I remained with the others. They had set off in a new direction, guided by the ticking of the Mole and huddled close together like children crossing a graveyard. I hung back. In a moment they were dim shapes moving through the mist. In another moment they were gone. I slipped behind a portion of wall and set off in the opposite direction, propelled by a wild sense of freedom.

Gervaise, I'm here! I'm alone!

I felt sure he would know who I was, that long ago he had recognized me as the one who could help him and had marked me for his own. His ghostly influence had been at work in my life, drawing me toward this moment of revelation. All that was necessary now was that I break the shackles of my own disbelief.

I cut through the desecrated chapel and stepped over the abbey's outer wall. The promontory with its thorny shrubs was just ahead. The sky was swarming and alive with stars, but on the horizon I saw a pale glow and knew the moon was about to rise. If I wanted to test my theory under optimum conditions, I had to move swiftly.

I found the grate and the binoculars where Archie and I had hidden them in the bushes. I pushed my way through the thicket, twigs snapping at my face, and came out onto the paving stones of the old observatory. With the aid of the flashlight, I oriented myself according to the markings on the stones. I stood in the center of the platform facing due east, toward the sign of Aries, then shifted my gaze approximately ten degrees to the north to adjust for the precession of the equinoxes. Into my field of vision came the familiar constellations—the Big Dipper, Draco, Leo, Virgo. It was the proper season, give or take a few days, and the right time of night. Here on this very spot, a little less than eight centuries ago, Geoffrey Gervaise had read his fate in the stars.

Using the references in the poem as my guide, I worked my way from star to star northward until I was facing the sign of Capricornus. Then I raised the heavy metal grate to arm's length above my head and saw the brighter stars shining within its squares like pieces on a chessboard. Gervaise must have had a way of fastening the grate to one of the openings in the roof that once bridged the platform. Lowering the grate to give my arms a rest, I recognized Perseus and the Pleiades, Auriga, the Charioteer, with Capella, the goat star, shining brightly on his northern shoulder. I raised the grate again and saw Capella dominating the square which corresponded to king's bishop three. The next phase of the experiment was the most awkward. I had to hold the grate steady above my head with one hand, then raise the binoculars and train them as well as I could at the adjacent square, king's knight three. My hand shook. The slightly brighter and more well-defined stars jumped and swam in the circular field like frenzied fireflies. It took several attempts to focus on the square, and then I caught just a glimpse of the star I wanted before my arm gave out and let the grate drop. But now I knew just where to look and I aimed the binoculars at the very faint star just a quarter of a degree northeast of Capella. Had it been shining as brightly tonight as it shone for those several weeks or months back in 1175, when it first blossomed in the heavens, it would have proclaimed itself a commanding presence on the board—a "fiendish light," as Gervaise's poem had it, "where yesternight was but a well/A blackish hole where hope could dwell."

I lowered the binoculars and stood for a time looking up at the sky, the devil's trap for the overconfident Gervaise. It should have been an exhilarating moment of triumph, yet it rang false and hollow. Where was Gervaise? Why hadn't he come to me? I understood now, at least in principle if not in all its details, the fantastic game he had played. I knew further how he had been beaten, and I knew the consequences of his loss. I also knew how he might at last be saved, and it was this certainty which undercut any elation I might have felt. There was only one way to deprive the devil of his prize, and it was going to require a sacrifice I wasn't sure I could make.

The moon broke above the horizon and flooded the fens with its white light. Overhead, the stars lost a good deal of their brilliance; the fainter ones disappeared altogether. With their passing faded whatever hope I had left of a visit from the poet whose cause I'd meant to serve. Feeling bitter and betrayed, I left the observatory and made my way back to the abbey wall.

I was about to step over the row of stones that marked the chapel nave when I heard the professor's voice from somewhere in the abbey. I heard my name called several times. Then I heard Stephany's name. Wasn't she with the party? My God, how could I have let her out of my sight?

Suddenly, as if granted a reprieve when I least expected it, my heart jumped as from an electric shock. My scalp, my back, even my fingertips tingled with the knowledge that Gervaise was close by—perhaps even here in the shadows of the chapel.

"Fairchild! Stephany!" the professor called. "Where are you?"

His voice seemed to come from the courtyard just beyond the chapel. Frantically, I searched the moonlit rubble, the creeping mists, the black shadows. *Gervaise, show yourself. It's our last chance.*

Now I could hear the insidious ticking of the colonel's black box, footsteps on the paving stones outside. Having sniffed out Gervaise's presence in the chapel, the Mole was in a frenzy. I looked toward the sanctuary—at the barren altar, several broken columns and a headless, armless statue. It struck me that this was a moment I would look back upon, in years to come, with embarrassment and utter disbelief.

Something caught my eye in the shadows behind the altar. Had the darkness moved? The Mole had gone berserk. A beam of light glanced off a column to my left.

Run for it, Gervaise! Don't let them see you!

A beam of light slid across the mossy stone wall, along a row of broken columns, into the recessed sanctuary. Shadows leapt away from its rapid flight, and within those shadows, another shadow leapt as well.

"There it goes," cried Colonel Buzby.

My ears were stopped by the roar of the shotgun; the side of my face was scorched by the blast. The shot echoed and reechoed off the stones, banging away into the night like a chain reaction of exploding galaxies.

"I say—you almost shot young Fairchild," said Colonel Buzby.

I swung around on the professor, grabbed the hot barrels of the gun and tore it from his grasp. "You crazy old bastard," I snarled, and threw the gun down on the pavement. The professor was astonished. His face, in the light of his own flash, showed that he recognized the contempt he saw in mine. We stared at one another, each seeing the other for the first time.

I heard a grating, grinding noise from overhead. Trevor-Finch glanced up. I followed his gaze . . . and beheld a universe in motion. As if the stars had broken free of their moorings and were about to swing dizzily away on celestial currents, an entire slab of sky had begun to move.

But then I realized it was not the stars themselves but a large black object between us which had been set in motion—part of an ancient arch, hanging just above our heads and prodded from its niche by the blast of the professor's gun. Very slowly did it seem to ease itself forward. The dry powder of its mortar sprinkled down on us; then the huge stone broke free and came rushing down at my upturned face.

I had an instant during which to resent the absurdity of such a death, but I did not have time to set myself in motion. Archie Cavendish snatched me from beneath the stone and fell with me onto the damp pavement, where we felt the simultaneous impact of the murderous block.

Trevor-Finch looked stupidly at the stone which had nearly deprived him of both his feet, then sat down upon it.

"That was a near one," Archie said, helping me up.

The Mole had reverted to a sober, stately beep. The colonel swung it around the chapel and told us what we already knew: "Whatever it was, it's gone now."

However, the Mole's green light had winked as it passed the sanctuary. The colonel took the flashlight and played it upon the altar. Stephany rose from behind it, one hand shielding her eyes from the glare.

The professor jumped to his feet and ran toward her. "Stephany! Are you all right?"

She seemed dazed. Her hair was mussed, her blouse torn partly open, but she put herself submissively in her father's arms and said, "Yes, I'm all right."

"But I don't understand," Colonel Buzby said. "The Mole clearly indicated the presence of—"

"Damn your foolish gadgets," Trevor-Finch said. "This is what comes of humoring amateurs."

"I beg your pardon," the colonel said, but Trevor-Finch had already turned his wrath upon me.

"Just what were you doing with my daughter, Fairchild? How dare you try such an outrageous—such a villainous, two-faced—and after I took you into my home, you damned pup!"

I waited to see if Stephany would defend me, but she stood quietly in her father's arms, her eyes downcast. In the dim light I couldn't tell if her cheeks were bruised, or merely reddened by a fierce shame.

"We've all learned quite a bit tonight, haven't we?" the professor said. "Not about these foolish ghosts of yours, Buzby, but about each other. Come along, Stephany. As for you, Fairchild, I'll thank you and your friend to leave my home first thing in the morning."

"I'll be glad to, Professor, but not until you've heard what I have to tell you. It's important that you listen to me."

"I'll be damned if I will," the professor said, and led his daughter away.

22

Fool's Mate

❧

Can you see him? Can you see how he watches at the window, alone in his cell at dusk? The evening star glimmers above the fens like a light upon a tower, only to be extinguished by the rising mist. The cell is small and damp. There is a pallet of straw, a heavy wooden stool, a crudely fashioned table on which sit scraps of vellum, writing implements and a chessboard. The tall, gaunt man paces back and forth before the table. He scarcely glances at the chessboard. It has been weeks since the last move, yet he ponders still the complexities of power laid out on the pale squares. There are no moves he has not considered. He has memorized the distribution of pieces, the intricate combinations, the spheres and corridors of his enemy's strength. He could shut his fierce eyes, red from their nights of watching, and see the game imprinted on the underside of his lids, just as he saw it diagramed in the stars. He knows it is hopeless, yet still sometimes pauses to study the board again, almost believing that by some fantastic oversight he has missed the move which can save his soul.

Twice he had won! Twice!

The slap of sandals in the corridor. Gervaise straightens, turns his face to the door. It is Brother Anselm, with a candle whose flickering light turns his sanctimonious smile to an evil leer. Gervaise imagines hell as an assembly of such grotesque faces, goading him with Brother Anselm's smirk as the ages of torment slowly pass.

"You have no light," Brother Anselm says.

Gervaise has learned to see in the dark. He had not noticed, "My light, Brother, has gone out long ago."

"Christ's blood, can't you damned mystics ever speak plain English?"

Brother Anselm puts the candle down on the table, glances disinterestedly at the chessboard, then squats on the low stool. Gervaise goes to the window.

"Watching for that wench from the village, Brother Geoffrey? Or your old comrade the devil?"

Gervaise turns upon his tormentor. "Do you still take the sacraments?"

"Of course. I eat my Savior's body each sunup, regular as the cock crows. A tasty morsel, though rather meager for a man of my appetites. It's a pity Our Lord didn't institute the sacrament with a hunk of rich red meat."

"It's a wonder the Host doesn't burn your blasphemous tongue," Gervaise says. "How can you receive Him, when you don't believe?"

"How could I if I did?" Anselm laughs.

"The hypocrisy of this monastery," Gervaise says, turning back to the window. "I've traveled the length of England and seen nothing like it!"

"We know all about your travels. We know how you scattered miracles about this island like the Second Coming. But you must admit it's a bit hard for us to take you seriously as a saint when you spend your afternoons mounting the mistress of the manor."

"That has ended," Gervaise says. "I have not seen her—"

"—since her husband began to suspect it was something more than piety that made the lady's eyes shine and her hands tremble whenever she set out for her devotions. They say you knew the slut at court. Is that true?"

Gervaise considers a lie to spare the lady's honor, but sees no point to it. Annjenette has never cared for honor.

"Yes; I knew her there."

"And you knew Becket, and John of Salisbury, and

233

Peter of Blois? And the king? You even supped with the king?"

"I dined in the great hall. The king's table manners are no better than yours, Brother Anselm. Though his conversation is more civilized."

"So I've heard. What I wouldn't give to visit the court! To travel with His Majesty to foreign lands, to lord it over the peasants, to sample the sweets of Normandy and Anjou and even glorious Aquitaine."

"You would be happy at the court, Anselm. You have the character for it, being a born schemer, intriguer, hypocrite and kisser of royal behinds."

Anselm's eyes flare up. "Watch yourself, Gervaise! Remember whose guest you are. If it weren't for us, you'd have burned to please the bishop a long time ago. Ely considers you a monster of villainy and a scandal to the Church. And the peasants in the village tell the wildest tales about you. That you converse with the devil and raise the dead—that you fly through the skies at night on a demon horse and ride the waves in a ghostly boat. Now they're dying by the score all over East Anglia, and some superstitious fools say it's God's wrath visited on this part of the realm because we have given you shelter."

"I can't believe that God would punish others for my sins," Gervaise says. "There was a time, Brother, when I could have cured those people, when a touch of my hand would have quelled the disease and brought them back from the brink of death."

"What miracles have you performed lately?"

"The power was taken away from me," Gervaise says quietly.

"I wonder why. Could it be that God likes your pompous zealotry no more than I do?"

Gervaise whirls from the window. "Leave me, fiend!"

Brother Anselm rises quickly and retreats toward the door. "Your piety does grow tiresome, Brother Geoffrey. I'll try you again tomorrow. . . . Oh, by the way, I nearly forgot. There was a peasant girl here this afternoon to buy some prayers for her dead grandmother. She asked after you. I told the wench you were at your devotions and couldn't be disturbed. She said she'd wait for you tonight out on the fens—at a certain shed you know of, by the big windmill. I told her you'd sworn off that sort of thing, but I pass on the message."

"Tempter," Gervaise says. "Serpent!"

"A pleasant night, Brother Geoffrey. Don't let the moonlight fall upon your pallet. I hear that makes a fellow mad."

And laughing, he exits from the cell, taking the candle with him.

Gervaise stands brooding at the window. The moon rises above the mist, a naked goddess pale and dripping from her bath. Within the depths of the abbey, the nocturnal ritual has begun and Gervaise is reminded of the voices heard once, long ago, in the courtyard at Wellesford, that memorable night when he became old Eadmer's charge. I was happy there, Gervaise thinks—as happy as I've ever been.

But no; there were times when he was happier. In sweet Margarette's arms, clinging to her small body as they listened to Satan's eerie call . . . and in the fierce embrace of Annjenette, when all gods and demons seemed but the fancies of the monkish mind. Yes, and at the chessboard those first two times, when, fairly beaten by a skill greater than his own, Satan acknowledged his defeat and acceded grudgingly to the victor's demands. . . .

He lies upon his straw mat and promises himself that he will remain safe within his cell, yet all the time knows that he is only delaying that inevitable foray to the cowherd's shed where warm and ample flesh awaits him. Sins which are simple and honest and human—for which a man might easily be forgiven. Gervaise takes consolation in them now. A lustful man may always repent. Only pride and hardness of heart can damn a soul. Gervaise's heart is petrified; on the rock of his heart's mad pride, he shall hang for an eternity.

Perhaps another shall hang with him. "I'll never let

235

you go," Annjenette had said at their last parting. "Not even death shall take you away from me."

"Why do you speak so foolishly?" Gervaise asked her. "You don't love me. You have never loved anything but pleasure."

Her teeth pressed hard against his lips; her nails dug into his flesh. She pulled back from the kiss to gaze at him with eyes which have always betokened for Gervaise the triumph, even the deification, of carnality. "Do you call this pleasure—this agony we've shared since we were young?"

"You were never young, bitch. *I* was young once, but you have made an old man of me."

"And was it I alone who did this to you? Your faith has brought old age upon you—this jealous God of yours who will not let you give yourself to me, fully and truly, as lovers should."

"No doubt He has had a hand in it. I defy Him even now by holding your soft white hand."

"And yet your hatred has only made me love you more. You think me vain and foolish—you think me corrupt—and yet I have suffered much for you Geoffrey. I shall never let you go."

She wrapped her arms around him and forced upon him once again her frantic kiss, in which Gervaise felt his soul devoured. "I'll come for your kiss," she promised him, "from the grave."

Oh God, Gervaise thinks, stretched out upon his pallet, the moon's white light on the stones just above his head. What might my life have been, if I could have made that woman's god my own?

He rises from the pallet, sweeps the chessmen from the board in a burst of anger and leaves his cell. As he proceeds along dark corridors, the Latin chant grows louder, then softer. He is crossing the courtyard when a monk steps quickly from the shadows.

"Father Geoffrey!"

It is Brother Terrence. His youthful, beardless face appears pale and saintly in the moonlight. He puts a soft hand on Gervaise's arm.

"And why are you not at your devotions, my little friend?"

"Please, Father, I must speak with you. I have heard rumors. The villagers are angry because we have given you refuge, and the lord of Abbotswold has sworn to kill you. Yesterday one of his knights came to speak with Brother Anselm—"

"And does Anselm mean to betray me? I suppose he would."

"Do not leave these walls, Father. Your life may depend upon it."

"My life ended some weeks ago. Look. Do you see that one bright star shining to the north—there, hard by the constellation of Auriga?"

Brother Terrence looks up. "The one that appeared a few weeks ago? Some have taken it as a sign."

"A sign it was—a sign of my defeat. Had that star not blazed forth—and who could have predicted it?—the devil would bow down before me and put his head beneath my heel."

"Then it's true that you have made a blasphemous wager with Satan. How could you have done such a thing?"

Gervaise puts his hand on the boy's shoulders. "You are young and innocent, Terrence, and fortunate in that evil has never touched you as it did me when I was a boy even younger than you. For some of us—for those whom Satan has defiled—blasphemy becomes a kind of worship. I loved God and longed to serve Him, but—"

"Surely your love will save you. God would not damn a faithful servant!"

"In this case, Terrence, I'm afraid He must, and will. God cannot save me if I reject His forgiveness."

"Then repent," the boy cries, "and accept what He freely gives you."

"Satan owes me one more move. He has promised a way by which my bondage may be broken. While that possibility exists, I cannot admit defeat. I will not be driven from the field by"—Gervaise's eyes fasten on the brilliant star—"a trick played upon me in the heavens."

"But how can you win if you fall into Lord Michael's hands?"

Gervaise thinks for a moment. "Do you know those manuscripts I keep in the chest in the corner of my cell? Here is the key. Take it. If I do not return from the fens tonight, you must transport the chest to the monastery at Blackstone. I have friends there who will understand what I have written. Tell them they must study each line carefully. 'Your own words,' Satan told me when he last appeared, 'conceal the prize.' And now I must go. God be with you, Terrence—if you can accept the blessing of the damned."

"Father Geoffrey, wait!"

But the tall, gaunt man is already striding across the courtyard toward the abbey gate. The bar slides back, the heavy gate swings open. Brother Terrence watches as Gervaise passes beneath the arch and steps across the threshold into a ghostly world.

Brother Terrence can no longer see Gervaise, but we can. We see him hurry across the fens, down soggy paths, beneath the twisted branches of stunted trees. All around, the land is flat and marshy, its empty distances veiled by moon-bright mists. A riverbank, a sluggish current, a crude wooden bridge. Low stone walls and hedgerows, no barrier to Gervaise's growing lust. A windmill stands dim and formless, its great arms suspended like the wings of a monstrous bird. Behind the windmill there is a shed, a place where hay is stored and animals fed. The door stands open. Gervaise enters its darkness and senses rafters just above his head. He smells the sour density of rotting hay, domestic animals, and another scent which tells him the woman is already there. The goat-keeper's daughter, heavy-breasted, with broad and fleshy bottom, a peasant's sturdy thighs. He gropes for her, pulls her to him. His mouth fastens savagely on hers. She is pliant, submissive to this violent union. He pushes her down into straw, tearing at her clothes. He hoists his own robes up to his waist and tears apart her thighs. She cries out once at the ferocity of his entry, but moments later she responds, thrusting hips upward to meet his onslaught. Oh, yes, Gervaise thinks. Oh, yes. After all these years, after faith, madness and despair—nothing but this. A knot of madness gathers and swells within him and he hurls himself toward the fire, the release, the cold clear light of perfect sanity as the wave recedes.

Lost in his ecstasy, Gervaise doesn't see the sudden brightening of the shed, the torches at the open doorway, the men crowding in with swords and clubs and a heavy chain. Rough hands grasp his shoulders. He clings to the woman, on the verge of release, but they yank him away and his loins burst at the moment of separation. As he falls back in their grasp, his seed spurts futilely across the woman and the hay and the coarse woolens of his captors. It is, Gervaise thinks, a last gratuitous victory for Satan.

"The filthy beast—he's got his dirty stuff all over me," the woman exclaims.

"Don't worry, slut," cackles one of the men. "We'll burn your clothes and the shed too. Be thankful you haven't got this devil's spawn inside you."

And we see Gervaise in chains, bits of straw still clinging to his robe and to his tangled hair, as he is pushed out of the shed and led away across the fens. We wish to see no more. There is nothing but horror to come.

23

Scholar's Mate

The lights of Abbotswold greeted us as we came up the drive; in fact, there was light blazing at every window, as if an all-night party raged within. No cars were parked before the house, however, and the front door stood open.

We followed the professor into the anteroom, from which we could see the great hall filled with light, its old pieces of furniture pushed helter-skelter, as if abandoned in the midst of a general housecleaning.

"Mortimor!" the professor shouted. "What's been going on here?"

Mrs. Archer appeared in the library doorway. "In here, sir. Your mother wants to see you."

The old woman sat waiting for us in her wheelchair. The library furniture had been similarly shoved about, leather sofa cushions on the floor, books tumbled from the bookcases, papers strewn around the desk, so that the matriarch looked like the miraculously unscathed survivor of a hurricane.

"Mama! How did you get downstairs, and where are the Mortimors?"

The professor's mother glared at him with a determination to answer none of his questions until he'd answered hers. "You've been to the abbey? Where is Stephany? Is she unharmed?"

"Here I am," Stephany said.

The old woman extended a pair of scarecrow's arms. "Come to me, child. Thank God you've not been injured!"

Stephany knelt beside the wheelchair. At the touch of the old woman's hands, she broke into tears and hid her face in her grandmother's blanketed lap. It was the first emotion she'd shown since coming out from behind the chapel altar.

"You are a great fool, Kenneth," Mrs. Trevor-Finch said. "Whatever possessed you to expose this child to those horrors?"

"Mother, please! It wasn't what you think. I had . . . something to prove. Now, for heaven's sake, tell me what's happened."

"Your servants have ransacked the house and fled," the old woman said. "Just after you left, the old man and the boy began tearing the place apart. They even

240

forced their way into my apartment and turned it upside down."

"But what on earth . . .? Did they take anything?"

"I know what they were after," I said. "When did they leave?"

"Not more than half an hour ago. I overheard the old brute say you were all at the abbey, so I prevailed upon Archer to help me down the stairs. I tried to call the police, but the phones are dead. You see what your stubborn disbelief has led to, Kenneth. You knew what the Mortimors were, yet you refused to fire them. You knew the danger to Stephany, yet you deliberately took her to the abbey. Will you not be satisfied until you've destroyed this family?"

"Mother, not in front of the others, I beg of you. I've made mistakes, I admit, but my worst mistake was in bringing this charlatan"—he pointed at me—"into my home."

"Well, young man?" the old woman said. "Have you forgotten your promise?"

"No, I haven't. And if the professor will listen to me—"

"I will not listen to an arrogant scoundrel who has abused my hospitality—"

"He may be that," the old woman said, "but he's also the only one who can help us. I've told him everything, Kenneth. Things even you don't know. Now I insist that you listen to him and do what he tells you to do."

"I'll see us all in hell first," the professor said, but there was already a whine of futility in his voice which told me his mother would eventually prevail. I went to the door, where Archie and the colonel stood waiting in embarrassment.

"The Mortimors know I've got the manuscript, Archie. They've gone to look for us at the abbey, but they'll probably be back before long with the rest of their coven. I don't know if there's time to get help, and the professor and I have something to settle which can't wait. You and the colonel had better guard the house."

241

"Did you say a coven?" the colonel asked.

"Archie will explain it to you outside. One of you guard the front. There's another road that comes in from the back; the other had better watch that. If anyone tries to approach the house, let us know at once."

"The canisters, Fairchild?"

"I'm afraid I've hidden them and there isn't time to go after them. Get the shotgun from the van. Do you have a weapon, Colonel?"

"A service revolver, but see here—"

"Archie will explain. Go on now. The professor and I have to talk."

I turned back to the others. The professor's mother was giving instructions to Mrs. Archer, who apparently couldn't drive, but was to set out on foot in search of the nearest phone. Stephany sat pale and frightened on the sofa; she still couldn't look at me. Trevor-Finch had found an unbroken bottle of whisky in the mess behind the bar and poured himself a glass. I went over, took the bottle from him, and poured one for myself.

"I've had about all I can stand from you," the professor said. "As soon as the police get here, you can pack up and get out."

"What I have to say won't take long, Professor. If you remember the contents of your father's letter, and what you have hidden in your room, you already know most of what I'm going to tell you."

"By God, you've even burgled my room?"

"I simply returned the visit you paid to my room, back at the College, when you stole my notes to the Westchurch poem. With them, you were able to reconstruct the checkmate which cost Geoffrey Gervaise his soul, and has haunted your family ever since. You know that story, don't you, Professor?"

"Yes, I know it, but you don't expect me to take it seriously."

"The cult at Creypool does. For centuries they've been able to conjure up Gervaise's image—that much at least. Then they make drugged and tortured young women believe that they've had intercourse with the 'Black Monk.' Sometimes they even make them think

242

they've conceived his children, and sometimes—as in the case of Jamie Mortimor—they make the children believe the Monk is their father. For all I know, he may be the Monk's child."

The professor snorted contemptuously and drained his glass. Whisky dribbled down his chin and spotted his already soiled shirt. He looked quite crazed, and ready to fly at my throat.

"Gervaise isn't the only ghost," I said. "Don't you think it's time you told your daughter about the one here at Abbotswold—and about what really happened to her mother?"

Trevor-Finch had been about to refill his glass. The bottle slipped from his hands. "Stephany—go upstairs! I forbid you to listen to this insanity."

"No, Kenneth," his mother said. "Dr. Fairchild is right. We were wrong to keep these things from her. If she saw what I think she saw at the abbey tonight, she must be told the truth."

I crossed the cluttered room and sat beside Stephany on the sofa. I tried to take her hand, but she shied away from me, sitting very stiff and straight, her eyes on the door. "What happened to you tonight, Stephany—what we think may have happened—was what happened to your mother before you, and to your grandmother. There's a spirit in this house—not your mother, but a distant ancestor of yours named Annjenette—who is trying to use you—"

"I don't want to hear about it," Stephany said, with that toss of her head I'd found so charming when we first met. Tonight, however, I saw a darker meaning in the gesture—a marionette's feeble attempt to free herself from an unseen power intent upon manipulating her life.

"Stephany," I said, "Annjenette had a lover. It's a tragic story. His death was arranged by her jealous husband and she killed herself in order to be with him. But the only way she can reach him is through the possession of someone in this house—"

Stephany swung around to glare at me with eyes I scarcely recognized. "You're making this up," she said fiercely. "You're angry with me and you're trying to frighten me!"

"No, child," the old woman said. "Dr. Fairchild knows these things because I told him—because I too, in my time, had dealings with Annjenette."

"Oh!" the professor burst out in exasperation. "This madness has persisted in our family for much too long."

"You're right," I said, "to call it madness, but I don't think it's one your psychiatrist can cure."

Trevor-Finch did a double take. "My personal difficulties have no connection with—"

"I'm afraid they do, Professor. Your psychiatrist is either a member of the cult or a paid informer. How else would the Mortimors have gotten the information they used to blackmail you, after you discovered their connection with the cult? They forced you to keep them on and to overlook their little business enterprise at the woodcutter's cottage. They even forced you to conspire with them, didn't they, Professor? There was too much in your family, and in your own private life, which you couldn't bear to have known. Didn't you wonder where they got all that information?"

Trevor-Finch couldn't answer. He went to the windows and looked out at the darkness and his own pale image.

"You gave the Mortimors a key to the College library—though you probably didn't know they intended to kill Dr. Greggs. You also passed along information about my work—information you could have picked up easily enough in the senior common room or from Greggs himself. They've been using you, Professor, rubbing your nose in the very horrors you were afraid to face, and all because of your damned pride."

Trevor-Finch collapsed into a leather armchair and stared at the carpet. "No doubt you think me a great hypocrite. But it wasn't just pride—nor even shame at the things I've sometimes been driven to. I've never known how to deal with the irrational. It frightens me—quite paralyzes me. It's so utterly dehumanizing! And then there was Stephany. I wanted her to have a chance at a life free from the past and all its madness. If we dredge up all these old scandals and horrors now—"

"We don't have to dredge them up; what we have to do is lay them to rest, once and for all, before the cult shows up and demands the manuscript."

"Manuscript?" he said, looking up.

"Last night Archie and I stole one of the Westchurch manuscripts from the College library. I had to have it, in order to learn how Gervaise might at last be freed—and now I need your permission in order to—"

I stopped, aware that I was going too fast and that to obtain the professor's consent I would have to build my case. I checked my watch and went to the windows. The Mortimors had been gone not quite an hour. It shouldn't take them long to round up the members of their coven, yet the grounds were still silent, Archie and the colonel on guard.

"This is outrageous," Trevor-Finch was saying. "That manuscript belongs in the College."

"You may feel differently when I'm through," I said. "You've got to understand that the Westchurch poem is a record of Geoffrey Gervaise's obsession with evil and his struggle with his personal demons. He was a master at the game of chess; it represented the one element of sanity in his twisted, tormented life. I won't go into the events which led up to it, but somehow, whether drugged, dreaming or hallucinating, Gervaise arranged to meet Satan across a chessboard. There were three games. Gervaise won the first two, but became in the process so addicted to the risk, the excitement of the game, that he granted Satan's request for a third match—winner take all, Gervaise's soul against the devil's dominion over the human heart—and this time Satan devised the rules. They're described in the poem, but only if one knows how to interpret certain cryptic lines."

"Do you expect me to believe that all this actually happened, just as it's described in the poem?" Trevor-Finch asked.

245

"It doesn't really matter," I said, "just how it happened. We know what Gervaise himself believed, and we know the consequences of his belief. If you'll be honest with yourself, Professor, you'll see those consequences in your own life."

"Please, Kenneth," said the professor's mother, "try not to interrupt, and don't look so pained. We know you're an eminent physicist and can't take such things seriously. You will please believe them nevertheless."

"This time," I said, "what Satan proposed was a game of celestial chess—a contest waged among the stars, played out night by night against the panorama of the heavens. Such a game must have had an overwhelming appeal to Gervaise's imagination—even though he knew the rules had been designed to ensure his defeat. The way I reconstruct it, Satan must have given Gervaise a list of fifteen stars—his sixteen pieces, less one—each identified according to its chess value. Polaris might be the king, Venus the queen, Alpha Centauri the *feu*, or bishop, and so forth. Gervaise was then allowed to choose sixteen stars as his own pieces. The night of the match was not specified in advance, but could occur whenever Satan demanded a move. Thus Gervaise had to know, by computation, where each one of those thirty-one heavenly bodies would appear on each night of the year, and how they would relate to one another if a certain portion of the sky— the coordinates are given in the poem—were divided into the sixty-four squares of a chessboard. That's where the iron grate your father found at the abbey comes in, and the astrolabe. No doubt there were many observatories like the one at Creypool, where Gervaise could mount the grate in such a way that the stars shone through its squares like pieces on a chessboard. Now, if he could keep track of every star throughout the year, he could anticipate all the devil's possible moves—all but one, since there was always one star, representing one piece, which the devil would not reveal ahead of time.

"When Satan appeared, each player had one move. If a piece was taken, it could no longer figure in the

246

game. New lists were drawn up, minus whatever pieces had been lost, and Gervaise would go back to his study and his calculations for the next encounter. Each night a new chess problem was diagramed in the stars, and Gervaise never knew when he might be called upon for another move. Only a genius, and a madman, could have kept it up."

"And are all these moves described in the poem?" the professor asked.

"Not all of them. The game lasted nearly eight years. Gervaise was a fugitive from the king's soldiers, and after Becket's murder in December of 1170, he must have chosen Creypool Abbey as his last place of refuge. He would have known that his old mistress was now Lord Michael Trevorre's wife and therefore a patroness of the abbey. He counted on her protection, at least, but her husband found out about their meetings at the abbey. He arranged to have Gervaise captured, tried for witchcraft and burned at the stake. But by this time the devil had sprung his trap, and Gervaise knew his soul belonged to Satan."

"My God," the professor said, sitting up. "3C-213!"

"And what," Mrs. Trevor-Finch asked, "is 3C-213?"

"A stellar radio source," I said, "which supernovaed in March of 1175. It's dimly visible even now, and I saw it tonight. If you transpose the stars in that portion of the sky, as Gervaise saw them in March of 1175, to a chessboard, you will find an exact replica of the devil's mate. As it happens, 3C-213 was just a pawn, but a pawn where Gervaise never expected to find one. It was the unnamed piece, you see—the star whose position Gervaise couldn't calculate ahead of time, the bullet in the sixth chamber. 'Two lowly pawns have the king undone,' as Gervaise says in the poem. 'Two pawns where I'd have sworn could be but one.' "

Trevor-Finch simply stared at me, at last impressed by something I had done. Mrs. Trevor-Finch realized, however, that I'd not yet disposed of the central problem. "You've told us how Gervaise was ensnared. Now will you tell us how he can be freed?"

"The game is not quite over," I said. "The devil

owes Gervaise one more move—one last chance to save his soul. Everyone who's ever tried to save the man—and there have been many over the centuries, including the monks of Blackstone and the Earl of Westchurch, not to mention your old friend Sir Percy Wickham George—everyone has naturally sought that winning move on the chessboard, or in the stars. But the solution isn't there. It's in the poem itself—the record Gervaise kept of spiritual torment."

I took an index card from my coat pocket. "What I have here is a translation of several lines near the end of the poem. It's not clearly indicated in the text, but the passage makes sense only if we assume these are Satan's own words, addressed to Gervaise and taken down by him as the game drew to a close:

> First thy flesh shall taste the flame;
> Then thy soul shall know the same.
> Much evil will thy own words do,
> A poet's feast and devil's brew.
> The stars shall never free thee, man—
> But look to them, for fire can.
> When thy first love has turned to smoke
> 'Twill mark the end of Satan's joke.

"Please tell us what the lines mean," Mrs. Trevor-Finch said.

"The key," I said, "is in the phrase 'first love.' In a much earlier passage, Gervaise described three roses, each one symbolic of one of his loves. A red rose stands for chess, 'the scholar's whore, whose deadly kiss shuts heaven's door.' The white rose represents theology, 'which leads the saint to God's own love.' The third rose, both red and white, he calls 'the boy's first love, the man's delight.' I asked myself what other love could have equaled Gervaise's lifelong fascination with chess, and then I realized that the combination of red and white, chess and theology, sacred and profane, is perfectly represented by the poem itself. 'If thou shouldst wander this arid land,' Gervaise says, 'take but the last rose in thy hand. For though its thorns

248

may make you bleed, my soul is here—a soul in need.'"

"Then"—Trevor-Finch frowned as he tried to put it all together—"then the manuscript must be *destroyed?*"

"'Turned to smoke,' Professor, as it says in the poem. There is a curious legend that the Earl of Westchurch ordered his own library burned before his execution. More recently there was a research student named Jameson who worked on the poem and who subsequently tried to burn down the College library. Now we know why. And we also know why the cult is so determined to reclaim the manuscript. It was given to Duke's in the eighteenth century by a member of the cult, one Gerald Brice, who hoped to ensure its survival by setting up the Special Collections. It's possible the cult put a spell of some sort on the manuscript; in any case, it has discouraged its few readers and defied scholarly analysis for nearly two hundred years. We have a chance now—perhaps the last chance anyone will ever have—to end this chain of horrors. Burn the manuscript, Professor, and you free Gervaise; you free Annjenette; you free yourself and all your family."

"That manuscript is College property," Trevor-Finch protested.

"You're a senior member of the College—some people say you'll be the next Master. I'd say you have the authority to dispose of College property, in an emergency, as you see fit. I'll burn it only at your command."

Trevor-Finch's confused eyes recaptured some of their shrewdness. "And you will expect my protection, I suppose?"

"Of course. Both Archie and I will expect you to shield us from any criminal charges."

"And are there other conditions?"

I had intended to point out that I was sacrificing a text which had come to mean a great deal to me, which could have made my reputation as a scholar, which might even have got me a fellow's place at Duke's. Yet now that I finally had the professor over a barrel, I'd lost my taste for bargains.

"I suppose you will want to remain at Duke's," Trevor-Finch said. "You can forget that right now. You're not the sort we want, Fairchild—not the sort at all. The next thing you'll demand is that I accept you as a son-in-law—"

"Daddy, that's uncalled for!"

"You've always been a bore, Kenneth. Can't you leave that to Stephany and the young man?"

I had one last move to put the professor in check. It was a move that would almost surely mean the loss of someone I had learned to care for, but it was precisely because I cared for Stephany that I made it.

"I'm not the one who threatens to take your daughter away from you, Professor. You must realize by now she wasn't with me in the chapel tonight. Like her mother, like her grandmother, Stephany had gone to the chapel to meet—"

"Oh, no!" Stephany cried, and looked at me with such a painful accusation of betrayal that I almost believed I had made a mistake.

The old woman reached out to embrace her granddaughter, but Stephany recoiled from her and fell sobbing to the sofa. "It's not true," she cried. "You're all crazy! You've worked this up between you and you're trying to drive me mad."

Her small fists beat against the sofa cushions; her body shook with sobs. As if on cue, one of the Mortimors' mangy cats came out from behind a chair and leapt up beside her, where it looked around at us with a victor's smug contempt.

"Well, Professor?"

Trevor-Finch was still staring at his daughter when I sensed someone at the door. It was Archie. I didn't know how much he'd seen and heard, but from the expression on his face, he must have seen the worst. "Three cars just entered the drive and stopped at the far end. They're still down there, but I'm quite sure I saw figures moving across the lawn."

"Professor, I need your answer *now*."

Trevor-Finch fell back into his chair and hid his face in his hands. "Yes, yes—burn it!" he said.

"Thank God," the old woman said, and the last dregs of life seemed to go out of her. It was as if, in breaking the professor's resistance to my will, I'd given her permission to die.

"Archie," I said, "get the others upstairs! Find a room you can secure and stay with them."

"Won't you be needing me down here?"

"I think I've got a better chance alone. If you hear an explosion, you'd better come looking for me on the beach."

Archie didn't like it, but did as he was told. He carried the old woman, while the professor took his daughter. They were joined in the hall by Colonel Buzby. "There are a couple of blokes skulking in the bushes out back."

"Come with us, Colonel," Archie said. "Fairchild has some heroics to attend to."

The colonel gave me his revolver. "I'd stay with you, but I'm getting a bit old for this sort of thing."

"Never mind, Buzby," Trevor-Finch said. He paused on the stairs and tried to find something fitting to say to me. Nothing appropriate occurred to either of us.

As soon as they were upstairs, I turned off the lights in the library and went to the French doors. There was moonlight on the lawn and glinting along the sea's horizon. Around each tree and shrub lay a pool of blackness. I knew they were out there, waiting to see what I would do, hoping I'd lead them to the manuscript. They wouldn't kill me until they had it, and that gave me a chance to use the canisters. What I had to gamble on was that I could lead them all to the beach—that none would stay behind to watch the house. If I made a run for it, created some sort of confusion, they'd be more likely to come after me without waiting for instructions.

I grabbed some books from the floor and tore out pages by the handful. These I stuffed into the metal wastepaper basket and ignited with my lighter. As soon as the flames licked over the rim, I kicked open the

French doors and threw the blazing basket across the terrace. It sailed out into the yard like a small comet, struck the lawn and rolled, scraps of burning paper spilling in its wake. At once I heard a kind of communal shriek from the darkness. Human shapes leapt from the shadows and converged on the burning basket. Feet stamped the burning leaves, and one man plunged his hands into the basket to extract the flaming bundle. I came through the door, firing the revolver.

The large gun jumped and lurched in my hands. The noise was terrible. I sprayed bullets across the lawn and at the treetops until the gun clicked empty. I tossed it aside, vaulted the hedge and ran across the lawn. There were confused shouts as the cult regrouped behind me, and over the other voices I heard the sharp command of Simon Regis: "It's a trick! Don't let him get away!"

I raced toward the heavy shadows of the trees and the path to the beach. I flew by instinct, shards of moonlight only a barrier to vision. Behind me men crashed into the underbrush as they lost the path, got in one another's way with shouts and curses, blundered through the darkness with the single purpose of running me down. By the time I reached the cliff, they were getting very close. The easiest route to the professor's antenna was the most circuitous—down to the beach and up again. The trail was steep and treacherous, but I didn't break stride until my ankle buckled and sent me sprawling another ten feet down the hillside. From there I rolled to the bottom. I staggered out across the sand with raw knees and an ankle that felt badly sprained. I still had a quarter mile of bright white beach to cover, with my pursuers coming down the path behind me.

The next several minutes took on the slow motion of nightmare. The best I could manage was a cripple's lopsided lope that frequently spilled me onto the sand. By the second fall, I realized the cult was no longer trying to overtake me. They had guessed that I was leading them to the manuscript and they were content to follow me along the beach like a pack of sullen, wary dogs. I saw their silhouettes appear for a moment at the crest of a dune, near a shrub or a clump of rocks. I spit sand from my mouth and slowed my pace, saving strength for the run back up the cliffs. There was a gentle surf on an outgoing tide and the moon's white fire was on the water. I could smell the ancient rot and regeneration of the sea—the sea which had strewn its wastes, its death, its ladles of cellular soup upon this shore long before the Normans, the Danes, the Saxons, the Romans and all the other would-be conquerors had driven their boats upon the sand and come ashore to tangle with the dark gods who ruled these isles. I felt myself awash upon the tide of history—another missionary rousted by the savages, another emissary put to flight.

I paused in the shadow of the tower and looked back up the beach, where I made out Simon Regis's tall, sleek outline, the stooped figure of old Giles, the brutish bulk of Jamie. I counted thirteen figures in all—a full coven. Regis motioned several of them to move around behind me.

"Dr. Fairchild," he called. "You have disappointed us, but there's still time to be reasonable. Give us the manuscript and we shall not harm you."

I measured the distance to the base of the cliff, sucked in a breath of ripe, salty air, and made a break for it.

Even as I took my leap for a first hold on the steep clay side, I could see that one of the dark figures was much too close. He was a big man and an awkward runner, but he got his start up the cliff just a few strides behind me. I dug my toes and fingers into loose, crumbling clay, heard it slithering down on my pursuer. I lost my grip and slid down on my belly, twisted onto my back and kicked the man away—but not before I had recognized Jamie's furiously determined face. I made another ten feet before his hand closed around my throbbing ankle. I clawed futilely at the clay as he hauled me in. Then a portion of the cliff gave way beneath us and I scrambled free, found a gully where the rocky bottom gave me a bit of traction, and made it up the last ten feet. I pulled myself over the outjutting rim and looked down to see some of the cult clinging to the cliff, the others fanned out around its base, with Jamie just an arm's length from the top.

The concrete footing of the professor's antenna was right behind me. I crawled along it, searching for the hole. Jamie's huge shadow fell across the rocks I'd left as a marker. I pushed them away, reached in and extracted the first briefcase as one of his big hands took me by the neck. "Here!" I shouted, holding up the briefcase so he could see it before he crushed several vertebrae. "Here it is, Jamie. You can have it!"

He released me to grab for the briefcase with both hands. I still had the handle and Jamie began dragging me toward the cliff edge. I was afraid the thing would go off in my hands, but I hung on until we had reached the very edge. Jamie set his feet and reared back with all his strength. I let go and his own momentum sent him hurtling backward off the cliff.

For a moment I had a glimpse of his body dropping lazily through the moonlight, the briefcase clutched to his breast, as foreshortened bodies scurried out from under. I threw myself back from the edge, sprawled face down and hid my head in my arms.

There was a flash like the blossoming of a star, a noise like the collision of comets. The earth shook and the professor's antenna hummed like a tuning fork. By the time the echo had come rolling back along the beach, it was raining sand.

When the shower subsided, I crawled back to the cliff edge and looked down. The moon shone serenely on the water. There was a great deal of smoke and the crumbling cliff and raining sand had already partially filled in the small crater. The chemicals had left a peculiar odor, in which I detected the reek of charred flesh. I could see a few dark objects scattered around the hole which, moments ago, might have been human. But there was no sign of life. Not even a twitch.

I went back to the concrete slab and dug out the second briefcase. The manuscript was still there, and I added my own index cards as a last tribute. I took the briefcase down to the beach, going wide around the mess I'd made, and set about gathering driftwood for a fire. It would have to be a very big fire—big enough to burn both the briefcase and its contents, since I didn't want to lose any pages to the wind. Not one word must survive. Not one precious, damning word.

There wasn't much wood to be had. I tried closer to the tower and then noticed several fuel tanks—oil to heat the professor's laboratory—at the tower's base. I carried the briefcase over to the tanks and set it down beneath a valve. It suddenly struck me that I was about to destroy a work of art, a testament to human genius, faith, suffering. My career was in that briefcase—everything I'd hoped to accomplish, everything I'd come to believe in and revere. I was tempted to open the briefcase and look through the poem again to confirm my belief in its greatness. But I removed only one of the leaves and crumpled it to a ball.

I needed a wrench to remove the pipe beneath the valve so that the oil could drain upon the briefcase. The threads were rusted fast and my hands so badly scraped I couldn't get a grip. I took a rock and banged at the pipe and valve. When they were loosened, I used a discarded length of pipe to pry them away from one another. I grabbed the valve with both hands and forced it to turn one inch, then two. . . . A trickle of oil began to fall upon the briefcase. Then there was a gush and its thick odor rose up from the sand. I stepped back to let the oil accumulate around the briefcase. I'd already taken out my lighter, when I realized I was not alone.

"Sorry to sneak up on you," Archie said. "I came looking for you when we heard the explosion. What happened to the cult?"

"They're over by the cliff, Archie—what's left of them. How's everything back at the house?"

"Good enough. I slipped out the back as the police were arriving. The old woman seems to have had an attack of some sort, but the others are holding together. So the bomb worked, did it?" He took a few steps toward the cliff, then turned suddenly back. I could see him grimace in the moonlight. "My God, it's ugly, isn't it? Did you have to?"

"It seemed like it at the time," I said.

"And how do you propose to explain those charred corpses to the bobbies?"

"I'll tell them the truth, Archie. At least, most of it. We shouldn't have too much difficulty, once we've shown them the woodcutter's cottage. The parson's tapes might be recovered now, as well. It ought to make quite a story."

"If anyone believes it—or if the professor and the College don't manage to hush it up. Say, is that my good briefcase getting soaked with oil? I'd appreciate it if you'd get it out, Fairchild."

I'd noticed that he was carrying the colonel's shotgun. "Sorry, Archie—the briefcase goes too. I'll buy you another."

"Yes, but it's not just the briefcase. I've no wish to threaten you, mind, but this gun is loaded and I do think you owe it to yourself—and to me, for that matter—to reconsider. We've gone to a bloody lot of trouble for Trevor-Finch and his kin, and a fine lot of thanks we're going to get for it. He hates you with a passion, and so does his daughter, and I'm not convinced we won't be prosecuted for our part in this little fiasco. We've got something here that's worth a bit of money, if we play our cards correctly."

"You're not suggesting we sell the manuscript back to the cult?"

"It's a thought. Better yet, we might find a collector somewhere who would meet their price. Or get in touch with some enterprising publisher—bring out a modern translation and facsimile text? You can always burn the original later, if it would make you feel better."

"Then you still don't believe . . .?"

"Fairchild, be reasonable. I can't be expected to believe in ghosts, for heaven's sake. You've been carried away by your own ingenuity. Years from now you'll regret having burned that manuscript on which you worked so hard; I'm merely trying to spare you that bitter awakening."

"No, Archie. I think I've gotten what I really wanted."

"Yes, I know how this whole business has restored your faith in the human spirit and all that. But faith won't pay the rent, and it won't save me from Yorkshire. Now before the bobbies get down here and start treating us like thieves and murderers, let's get that manuscript out of that dirty oil and—oh, my God!"

I followed the direction of his bulging eyes to a dark jumble of rocks beyond the tower, where a shadowy figure had taken shape. It glided toward us—tall, gaunt and hooded—through the strip of moonlight that lay between the tower and the rocks.

"Dear sweet Jesus," Archie breathed, and raised the shotgun. He seemed, however, unable to fire, and after a moment lowered the gun. The black, nebulous figure had entered the shadow of the tower and was drawing near the oil tanks. "Do something, Fairchild! Light your bloody fire!"

I bent down quickly and ignited the crumpled paper, then dropped it into the pool of oil. The fire leapt up with a roar, and in its sudden brilliance we saw the darkly fluid shape hurl itself at the flames. Was it simply the heat of the burning oil, or did I feel his demonic fury as he swept past me? The intense heat drove us back; the oil tank burst and then the other tanks ignited. We could see nothing at the base of the tower but a blinding core of light, as if the fiery furnace of the sun itself had come to nest at the foot of the professor's laboratory.

"Fairchild," Archie said sadly, "I feel like such a damned ass. Seeing isn't believing, you know—not unless you believe in what you see."

"You believed for a moment," I said. "Sometimes that's as much as one ever gets."

Great clouds of black smoke rose up from the burning oil and blew across the beach. The stars were obscured by its reeking billows, but the cold, quiet moon rode safely out to sea and put its ghostly kiss upon the water.

"Cheer up, pal," I said, slapping Archie on the shoulder. "There's still that beautiful, loving, warm-hearted female Yorkshirite."

Archie smiled ruefully in the light of the settling flames. "And that's another fairy tale I can't believe in," he said, and turned back up the beach.

24

At the Master's Table

The bells of Saint Catherine's were chiming the hour as I returned from my farewell stroll and crossed the busy street before the College. Colin Douglas was just locking his bicycle in the little bike yard and joined me on the sidewalk.

"Your last evening, is it? I'm glad you've decided to put in a final appearance at High Table."

"Actually," I said, "I'm dining in the Master's lodge this evening."

"So the old boy came across with an invitation in time for you to take him up on it. You'll carry that honor home with you, at any rate. . . . By the way, I've got the address you wanted, though I don't really advise that you take up with that little baggage again."

I took the slip of paper he handed me and put it in my shirt pocket. "Yvetta and I have some unfinished business. Besides, I've always wanted to visit Vienna and she'll be the perfect guide."

"Yes, well—the opera, the wine cellars, the coffee-houses—it's a splendid city. But be careful, David. This time she might not let you get away."

I looked up at the long, plain façade of the College, rather like a prison from the outside. One had to penetrate the interior to experience its charm, just as one had to live the life it offered in order to understand its appeal. Colin Douglas belonged inside those walls. They suited and sustained his personality, nourished his conviction that he already knew everything about life that was of any importance.

"This time," I told Colin, "I might not let *her* get away. I think I've gotten the best of what Cambridge had to give me. I'm ready for the next step."

Colin obviously thought it a step in the wrong direction, but he said, "Just so you see your way as you go, old man. A few of us are getting together for drinks at my place after Hall. There'll be a few birds up from London. Care to join us?"

"I may stop by," I said, with no intention of doing so. It spared us the necessity of saying goodbye.

We entered beneath the thirteenth-century gate. Colin went off to the buttery for his pint and I stopped at the porter's lodge for my mail. There was one slender envelope, addressed in a feminine hand and postmarked Saint-Tropez. I stepped out into the evening shadows of the court, opened the letter and read:

Dearest David,

It is still difficult to write to you after all that's happened, but I want to be sure you hear from us before you leave Duke's. We have rented a charming little villa with a view of the sea and Daddy is beginning to seem more like himself . . . or perhaps even better than himself, since he's taken quite an interest in the very respectable widow who has the villa next to ours. They spend a great deal of time together on the beach and this evening he has taken her into town for—of all things!—an "intimate dinner."

We were both greatly saddened by Grandmother's abrupt passing, but have come to realize that the ties which bound us to the past are finally broken and that our lives are now our own. Daddy wants to sell Abbotswold, but I'm not sure he will find a buyer (some rich American, per-

haps?). He was quite scandalized when I suggested that we might make enough money to keep the place by opening it to the public for tours and possibly even overnight stays. Don't you think the American tourists would leap at the chance to spend a night in a "haunted manor"? Daddy won't hear of it, but we'll see.

He says to tell you that he has written to the Master and taken full responsibility for the loss of the manuscript. Since the police bought our story that it was destroyed by the cult (and so it was, in a way), there is no reason why the College should not. In any case, you should have no worries on that score. Of course, Daddy adds, rather adamantly, I fear, that he wishes never to see you again and he insists that you leave Duke's before we return to England. He does thank you for all you've done for us, but knowing Daddy, you can be sure it was said with great reluctance and many "harumphs" and "ahems."

As for myself, I deeply appreciate the way in which you risked your life for us and all that you gave up in order to help us—if it really was us you went to so much trouble for, on which point I'll never be entirely sure. In any case, I know you were our champion and savior and I can never thank you enough for your noble and heroic service. That needs to be said first, before I tell you that I've found it impossible to forget all that was said on that dreadful night, and that I can take no pleasure in the prospect of seeing you again and of being reminded of how much you know about me—us—the whole wretched family.

And so, fairest Childe David, it is slim thanks you get for your hero's work, and it's only the thought that you desire no other that prevents me from being even more ashamed of my own attitude. Perhaps in years to come . . . But we shall never meet again, I'm sure of that. Fare thee well, my little "innocent abroad," and may only benev-

olent spirits accompany you on your journey to your homeland.

Love,
Stephany

I took the letter up to my room and tucked it away in my suitcase, along with such memorabilia as train schedules, ticket stubs, guidebooks and British coins. Then I got into my sleeveless sleazy black gown (the last time, I thought—but not with as much sadness as I'd anticipated) and set out for the Master's lodge.

The Master's guests that evening, besides myself, consisted of a young Russian engineer (let out of the Soviet Union to study British-American computers), a Japanese botanist whose English required great leaps of imagination on the part of his interlocutor, and two English dons—a historian and a mathematician. The Master greeted me cordially and provided introductions. Then he took me aside and said:

"Odd business, that, with the Westchurch manuscript. Why do you suppose Trevor-Finch removed it from the library?"

"That was partly my doing, Sir Henry," I said. "I thought it might substantiate certain legends in the professor's family."

"Damned high-handed of Trevor-Finch, I must say. Still, we won't make an issue of it. The College appreciates the way in which you've cooperated with the police in this matter—and the way in which you've resisted blandishments from the press. Are you still greatly bothered by reporters?"

"No. They've lost interest in me by now. I think Scotland Yard is continuing its investigation, in secret."

"Much the better way, I'm sure. And Duke's has avoided a messy scandal, which surely would have damaged our current fund-raising campaign. The only loser in the whole affair, then, was yourself."

"I can live with it," I said, and we dropped the matter.

We dined in comparative splendor, served by the Master's personal valet in the oak-paneled dining room with a view of the Master's private garden. The long, dark table glowed with exquisite silver and china, a large silver candelabrum as the centerpiece. It was growing dusky and the valet deftly applied a match to each of the long candles before pouring our wine.

I was seated next to the mathematician, who turned and said, "Sorry about your research having gone to smash. That's the trouble with a field like yours. I mean, if it's not written down in a book someplace, you have nothing to work with, do you? It's all so pathetically transient. Now, the laws of mathematics, on the other hand, are incorruptible. If every human record were wiped out tomorrow, the truths of mathematical science would still be there for us to rediscover."

He was baiting the historian, an old enemy, just across from us. "Now, see here, Maxley," the historian said. "You damned mathematicians would be in a pretty fix if the humanists hadn't preserved the discoveries of the past. Do you really mean to say you could recreate the work of centuries . . .?"

"Give me a computer," Maxley said, "and—"

"Yes, but what if I blew up your computer? That's a record too, isn't it?"

The Japanese botanist gazed with incomprehension at the heated Englishmen, and I thought I saw the young Russian smirking behind his wineglass. The valet served roast chicken and bread sauce.

"It's the whole 'two cultures' thing again, isn't it?" Sir Henry said. "We pride ourselves on being a community of scholars, but when you get right down to it, we're quite isolated in our separate fields. I wonder if we can ever bridge the gap that's opened up between us."

I noticed that dusk had fallen over the Master's garden and that the dining room was also growing darker. The candelabrum glimmered with concentrated brightness and the silver, china and glassware reflected its light, but the men around the table had suddenly become dark shapes without faces, voices without substance.

262

"Perhaps what you need," I heard myself say, barely able to distinguish my own hands upon the table, "is the kind of seminar we sometimes have in America, where men from various fields take up broad intellectual topics—a sort of forum where papers are read and debated."

"Yes, that's a possibility," the Master said. "But do we want anything quite so formal as all that? Couldn't we perhaps . . ."

But I had ceased listening now that I had said what was expected of me. I gazed at the silvery glow of the candelabrum and, as my vision went slightly out of focus, I saw its light expand and shimmer like an unearthly flame, like a nebula blazing light as it spread out across the darkness, its glowing gases cooling and solidifying to form myriads of new stars which would twinkle alone in the universal night. If I stared long enough, I hoped and almost believed, I would see those stars come together once again, coalescing with one another to banish darkness in a blaze of cleansing light.

No one who buys it,
survives it.

THE HOUSE NEXT DOOR

A terrifying novel
by
Anne Rivers Siddons

28172 $2.75

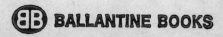

BB **BALLANTINE BOOKS**

G-1e